Covenant of Honor

By

William R. Kennedy

To Gina -
With best regards,
Bill

William Kennedy

This book is a work of fiction. Places, events, and situations in this story are purely fictional. Any resemblance to actual persons, living or dead, is coincidental.

ISBN: 1-4107-1341-5 (e-book)
ISBN: 1-4107-1342-3 (Paperback)

This book is printed on acid free paper.

1stBooks - rev. 03/10/03

Acknowledgements

I guess early on I had somewhat of a guilt complex about what was keeping me busy in retirement. People would ask me what I was doing with myself and immediately answer their own question with, "Playing a lot of golf, I'll bet." My response was invariably, "No, I don't play golf."

"What in the world do you do with yourself?" I found myself mumbling things like, "Oh, we travel" – or – "we go to Florida for about four months every year" – or – "trying to stay out of trouble."

Ever since I wrote my first novel *Diamond of Greed* which was published last year, and now *Covenant of Honor,* I am now able to defend myself with the comment, "I write."

I have to thank my family and friends for their continued encouragement and support. Special thanks to Pam who proved to be a fine editor with her helpful suggestions. My son Douglas, who has a great sense of what reads well – and in my case – not so well at times, was a welcome barometer of my work.

Thanks to Donald Sweet, a talented author, historian and friend who originally put the idea in my head that I might be able to write and then continually encouraging me to do so.

Bill Kennedy
Wyckoff, New Jersey

I married a girl who is my best friend.
This book is for Pam on our 50th Anniversary.

"There is no passion in the human heart that promises so much and pays so little as revenge."

Josh Billings

"Politics are too serious a matter to be left to the politicians."

Charles DeGaulle

CHAPTER 1

Doug Cromwell awoke early every morning and started his day jogging three-miles around the neighborhood. He had laid out the course for himself when he first moved into his new condominium on Colonial Road in Old Town, N. J. six months before. Old Town was an affluent bedroom community with a population of 29,000 located about thirty six miles northwest of New York City. It had a commuter rail running through the middle of town making it an ideal and comfortable daily commute to the city for many of the residents.

Like many of the surrounding towns, it was a diverse family-oriented community. In it's almost seven square miles, Old Town boasted of a highly-rated school system which attracted many of the young families to the town. Its residents enjoyed fifteen houses of worship, a two branch 200,000 volume library, many civic and social organizations and an unwavering spirit of camaraderie among people who gave generously of their time to help their neighbors. A full-time thirty-five person police force and forty-two fire fighters protected the town day and night.

Doug enjoyed his daily jog. The hour it took him to traverse the sometimes irregular sidewalk route gave him the time he needed to get his thoughts together in planning his day. A portable cassette player worn about his waist and a pair of earphones were his only companion during this routine run. He preferred instrumental music to the vocal variety as he wanted a clear mind for personal reflection. Someone else's words were a distraction.

Admiring eyes would invariably follow his six foot one inch 175-pound muscular frame as he made his rounds. Men would glance at him when they were sure he wasn't looking and tell themselves that they had better start getting back to the gym. Women looked at him openly with their own personal thoughts. After all, he was a thirty-nine year old successful bachelor - which was the rumor - making him fair game as a marriage prospect or, as some ladies would playfully suggest, for an adventurous fling.

His daily jog normally began at 6:00 a. m. but today he decided to give himself a break and sleep a little longer. Besides there was a pressing matter he had to handle later in the morning that took preference over any other personal considerations on this day. He had taken the day off from his duties as Senior Vice-President in Charge of Operations for Lucas Industries and decided that the several hours of extra sleep would be a welcomed change. After taking care of his personal needs and fortifying himself with a glass of orange juice, he was on his way. He harbored a suspicion when he started his jog that he could possibly be responsible for the death of another human being before the morning was over. He hoped that this would not be the case.

The Franklin Pierce Grammar School was the halfway point in Doug's jog. The school was one of six beginner schools in the town that also boasted of four middle schools and a high school that celebrated a state championship football victory the year before. A number of day care facilities throughout the town were also unofficially recognized as part of Old Town's educational system. Pierce serviced almost five hundred students from the west side of the town and, as it was Friday, the students looked forward to the coming weekend with anticipation. It showed in their spirited behavior.

As Doug approached the grammar school, he noticed a short burly man making his way towards the rear of the building. He thought at first it was Herman Axel, the maintenance man who was a familiar sight at the school. On closer inspection, he saw that the man was a stranger - someone he had never met before - but whom he knew would be at the school that morning. It was a person who was to be his unknown accomplice in a prearranged scheme that involved a family's honor.

The man kept glancing furtively about as if he didn't belong and was wary that someone might see him. Equally suspicious was the oversized bag that he was carrying. The stranger was not aware of Doug's presence nor that he had stopped jogging and was moving in the direction of the school. When Doug reached the rear of the building, he no longer saw the trespasser. He entered the building and began looking around. He knew that the stranger would be on the lower level of the school where he had less of a chance of being observed by unwelcome eyes.

Doug descended the stairway quietly. He noticed a two-foot length of pipe that workers had left in a pile of debris in the stairwell.

The pipe would come in handy as a weapon should there be a confrontation with the stranger. He was assured that this was highly unlikely, but because the man had a checkered history of mental problems, he was warned to be on his guard. Doug never did understand the decision to engage someone with a background of deranged behavior to handle such a sensitive assignment. He was actually a substitute for the original contracted accomplice who had taken ill. The replacement's specialty at physically handling explosives was therefore given priority over his sometimes wayward behavior. He was given the assignment.

Doug quietly and slowly made his way to the partially glassed partitioned doorway of the first classroom. He crouched and peered into the darkened room making sure that he was not visible to anyone who might be inside. Satisfied that no one was in the room he preceded to the next classroom. Same result. Empty. The third classroom, which was in the center of the building, was not empty.

Doug saw the stranger bent over the oversized bag from which he had taken an odd looking box which he was meticulously fingering. The man had propped a flashlight against the wall which provided light for him to see what he was doing. It was only after several minutes that Doug realized that the box was actually the homemade explosive device that he was told would be used in the assignment. "Be very cautious," he was warned. "It will be a homemade bomb and it will be armed."

The stranger had apparently completed his work. He was now backing away from the device and was preparing to leave. As planned, it was set on a timer as a safeguard to allow the man to leave the building before it exploded. More importantly, the timing device assured Doug's safety as he was expected to transport the bomb from the classroom to the deserted athletic field three hundred yards from the rear of the school. When it actually exploded, Doug would be safely out of the blast's deadly range.

It was only as the man was leaving that Doug saw that the bomber had chained and locked the explosive box to the radiator in the room. A sickening sensation engulfed him. He tensed as a coiled spring. "That fool. Why did he do that? He's jeopardized the mission." He pulled himself together and knew that he had to disarm that thing quickly or get it out of the building and let it do it's damage on the outside. His mind was racing. A confrontation with the bomber was out of the question. Too time consuming.

The stranger exited the room unaware that Doug was poised to strike him with the pipe. The blow was devastating when it struck the man solidly on the left side of his head. He went down without a word. He lay motionless. Doug knew by the lifeless staring eyes that the blow had been fatal.

No time for regrets. Doug moved quickly. He grabbed the flashlight and brought it to bear on the device that was emitting a near-silent ticking sound. He carefully removed the cover and was about to disengage the two multi-colored wires attached to six sticks of dynamite when he realized that he could set off the device with an inappropriate move. There was no room for error and the bomb was undoubtedly capable of inflicting serious damage to anyone in it's path.

Common sense prevailed. Doug wisely decided that the bomb could go off if he tried to disengage it and it would certainly go off if he left it where it was. A frightening thought suddenly engulfed him. "The children. The children. I've got to get those kids out of the building." Doug rushed out of the room into the darkened hallway, climbed the flight of stairs to the first floor and ran through the hall crying out, "Bomb. Bomb. There's a bomb in the building. Get the children out of the building."

Classroom doors opened and teachers spilled out into the hallway. Doug kept repeating his cry. "Get the children out of the building now. There's a bomb on the lower level that's about to go off. Hurry. Don't wait. Get the children out."

Principal Mark Stoddard and several of his staff came running down the hall. "What's going on here, sir?" Do you realize you're disturbing our classes? What's this about a bomb? There's no bomb in our school. I'll..."

Doug wouldn't let him continue. "There is no time. You must trust me. A man placed a bomb in a classroom on the lower level. I saw it. It's chained to a radiator. I'm afraid to try and defuse it. It might go off. There is no time. You must get the children clear of the building now. *Now!* Do it or a lot of kids will die here this morning. And somebody get me something to cut that lock."

Stoddard began sweating profusely. He looked around, confused. "Sir, this better not be a prank." He turned to his assistant and issued an order. "Mrs. Travis, sound the alarm. We must get the children into the park across the street immediately." Stoddard knew that the alarm would automatically signal the monitoring systems at the police, fire and emergency medical stations. Fifteen seconds later the alarm sounded. Children quickly formed orderly lines in the hallways on both floors of the school. It was evident that the school's fire drill procedure had been well-rehearsed.

All of the children had exited the school within fifteen minutes. Doug breathed a brief sigh of relief when he saw them safely gathered in the heavily foliaged park across from the school. Teachers quickly counted heads to make sure that everyone was accounted for. Terror gripped the faculty when they realized that one child was missing. Lisa James' class of nine year olds was on the second floor. "Oh, my God. I forgot about Jason. Jason Blair went to the bathroom just before the alarm went off. Oh, my God. He' still in the building." She immediately ran back to the school and tried to reenter the school. Doug intercepted her. "One of my boys is still in the building," she cried.

"Go back. I'll get him. What room is it?"

"Room 210. He was in the bathroom right next door when the alarm went off. His name is Jason Blair."

Doug turned and hurried into the building. Herman Axel magically appeared with a pair of cutters. "Good man. Now get out of here. That thing could blow at any minute," Doug said as he hurried on. He was on the second floor in seconds. Room 210 was empty as was the adjoining bathroom. He wondered where the boy was. No time. I can't go looking for him. Doug had planned to find the boy and get as far away from the building with him as fast as his three-mile-a-day jogger legs could carry him. "Damn," he said aloud, "that kid's somewhere in the building. I can't leave him. I'm going to have to get that bomb out of here."

Doug knew his time was running out. He was back in the bomb room two minutes later. The lock securing the bomb to the radiator was cut with some difficulty. The chain fell away. He carefully lifted the device and made his way to the rear door on the first floor. Adjacent to the school was a huge field that the town had converted into a cluster of athletic fields. Doug was confident that there would be no chance of anybody being hurt if he could get the bomb to the far end of the most distant field.

He didn't dare run with the bomb so he walked as cautiously as his anxiety would allow him. He felt as if he were walking through a field of mud. When he reached the spot he had singled out, he gently placed the bomb on the ground. He then took a deep breath and issued himself a command. "Run feet, run." The bomb detonated twenty seconds later. The full force of the explosion caught Doug as he was racing to safety. It threw him twenty feet in the air leaving him bloody and immobile when he hit the ground.

The police and medical unit had arrived on the scene shortly after receiving the alarm. They were being informed of the situation by Principal Stoddard when the explosion rocked the earth beneath them. Police Chief Tom Howard instinctively called the Fire Department on his cell phone. All of the front and back windows in the school were blown out. Automobiles were thrown in all directions when the full force of the explosion reached the staff parking lot. The playground equipment behind the school was obliterated. Fire engulfed the basement classrooms on the lower level which seemed to have taken the brunt of the blast.

The Fire Department arrived and expertly began extinguishing the multiple fires that had erupted throughout the school. The police were quick to cordon off the entire area surrounding the school not knowing whether another explosion or other threat was imminent. After a suitable time, Chief Bob Larson led a group of his fire fighters to the rear of the building to investigate the origin of the explosion. "If that fellow who carried the bomb out of the building was anywhere near it when it went off... well, we can forget about finding him." One of his men who was sent ahead to scout the situation cried out, "Hey chief. There's a body about a hundred yards from the point of impact. You'd better get a medic over here fast. I don't think he's alive, though."

The emergency medical crew was running across the field before the fire fighter had completed his sentence. An ambulance was close behind. They arrived to see a badly burned smoldering body lying in a pool of blood and debris without any visible signs of life. The lead medic issued a terse order. "Clean him off so I can check his vitals." Not another word was said until the same voice said, "I don't believe it. I've got a heartbeat and some blood pressure. We've got to get him to the hospital. Let's move guys and gals. I don't know how much time he's got." The hospital was ten blocks from the school.

Chief Howard reacted immediately. He turned to one of his officers and said, "I want to shut down all cross traffic up to the hospital. Let's make sure that ambulance has a free passage. You know the drill. Let's do it."

Four patrol cars dropped officers at each of the intersecting streets leading to the hospital. Traffic came to a standstill as the strident siren of the ambulance forewarned of its approach. Doug was in the emergency department less than a minute after arrival. The Chief Surgeon of the hospital Dr. John Powers was in attendance along with several specialists who happened to be in the hospital at the time.

Powers had a tear in his eye as he examined the injuries. He was heard to say almost to himself, "My grandson was at the school this morning. This young man saved his life along with everybody else in that building." Powers and his staff then went to work. Doug's pulse and blood pressure were dangerously low.

CHAPTER 2

Word filtered down rapidly through the town of the near-disaster at the Franklin Pierce. The explosion itself left a telltale smoke cloud that was ominously alarming. Persistent sirens confirmed that something was seriously wrong. Parents hurried to the school. When they found that the roads to the school were blocked off, they deserted their cars and made their way afoot. Principal Stoddard had anticipated this natural parent reaction. He called an emergency meeting with Superintendent of Schools Miles Ashley who had arrived minutes after the alarm had sounded. They agreed that an immediate announcement detailing the day's events was critical to calming the uncertainties and fears of everyone. Stoddard wanted to be sure that all the children were safe before making the announcement.

Lisa James assured him that Jason Blair was safe. She had run into the building to look for the boy when the Fire Marshall announced that the first and second floors were secure. She found him in the boy's lavatory on the first floor. While she was furious with him she couldn't help but hug him. "Jason, you're supposed to use the bathroom on our floor - not the first floor."

Jason was indifferent to what was happening around him. "I went there first but I couldn't go. I had to go but I couldn't go so I thought I'd be able to go in another bathroom. It worked. I was able to go here." All Lisa could do was to break into a tension-releasing giggle.

Principle Stoddard was able to immediately soothe the crowd with his first statement. "All of the children are here safe and sound. They'll be exiting the park by class so please wait until they are outside before you join them. That way we'll avoid any confusion and unnecessary delays." He quickly explained that a man unknown to them at this time had been seriously hurt while removing an explosive device from the school and that the man was rushed to Old Town Hospital. The teachers proceeded in an orderly fashion to dismiss their classes outside of the park. A half hour later the school area was deserted except for the police and fire personnel along with the curiosity seekers.

An NBC-New York television mobile unit appeared on the scene minutes after the ambulance left for the hospital. They were joined shortly by other broadcast and print media representatives anxious for the facts of the incident. The Police Chief held an impromptu press conference recounting the little information they had been able to gather. He ended by saying, "Look folks, your story isn't here. It's at Old Town Hospital. That's where they took the man who was responsible for diverting that bomb from the school to a safe area. He's your story."

Each of the television crews left a cameraman and reporter at the school to get background information and video footage of the damaged building and the bomb area. The rest of them rushed to the hospital. What greeted them was a complete surprise. Surrounding the entrance to the hospital was a crowd of several hundred people - mostly women with children - just waiting quietly and expectedly for news of Doug's condition. The news people set up their cameras in the most advantageous positions they could find and began documenting the scene. Senior reporter Pamela St. Pierre of the NBC-TV Network selected several women to be interviewed.

"Can you tell our viewers why you are here this morning?" Was her setup question.

A mother holding two frightened children by the hands stepped forward. "Our children are students at the Pierce where the bomb exploded. Thank God they were able to get out in time. God bless the man who found the bomb and took it out of the school."

Another equally distraught mother cried, "My kids were there, too. We're here to find out how that brave man is doing. We couldn't go home without knowing. We don't even know his name."

At that moment a hospital official exited the hospital and held up his hands for attention. "Ladies and gentlemen, may I have your attention, please." The crowd became quiet. "We have nothing to report at this time. A team of medical specialists are working to stabilize the patient. We won't know anything for awhile. May I suggest that you all go to your homes. The media folks are here. I'm sure they'll keep you updated during the day."

Nobody moved. A voice from the rear of the crowd asked, "Who is the man who saved our children. Do you know?"

The hospital official withdrew a piece of paper from his pocket and said, "Yes. According to identification he had with him, his name is Douglas Cromwell and he lives here in town at 437 Colonial Road in one of those new condominiums. We really don't have much more than that so if anyone knows anything about Mr. Cromwell, we'd very much like to hear from you."

Everyone looked at their neighbor to see if anyone had any knowledge of Douglas Cromwell. There was no response from the crowd. The hospital official again suggested that they disperse. No one left. He then returned to the hospital.

The press became impatient for news and began investigating the identity of Cromwell on their own. Reporter St. Pierre learned the location of Colonial Road from one of the policeman. "It's about two blocks south of here. You can't miss..." St. Pierre and her camera crew were gone before the officer could complete his sentence. They didn't bother trying to maneuver their van through the crowd. She knew it was hopeless. They all double-timed to Colonial Road. They entered the condominium complex and found the listing of residents in the vestibule directory. Doug lived in apartment 301. Pam and her crew were on the third floor in minutes. The plaque on the door opposite Doug's apartment read JAMES & MARY BENNETT. Pam ranged the bell. Seconds later a white-haired woman answered the door. "Yes, may I help you?"

"Good morning, Mrs. Bennett, I'm Pamela St. Pierre from the NBC-Television Network. We're doing a story on your neighbor Douglas Cromwell. We're trying to gather some background information about him and we wondered if you could help us?"

"I recognize you from the television, Miss St. Pierre. What's this all about?" Asked the anxious woman.

"I guess you haven't heard about the near-disaster at the Franklin Pierce School this morning. Someone placed a bomb in the school. Doug discovered it and was hurt while carrying it from the school. He's being treated at Old Town Hospital."

"My goodness. A bomb. Who in the world would do a thing like that? Is Doug all right?"

Pam knew that she only had minutes to get a scoop on her competition that would be close behind. She tried to set the woman at ease. "The hospital has no concrete news as yet but they're optimistic about his condition. Do you mind answering a few questions on camera? This is going to be a big story and we want to make sure we are as factual as possible about Doug. He's a hero who people will want to know about. He saved many lives today."

"I don't know. I guess so. My name is Mary Bennett. My husband and I are retired and we..."

"Let me first introduce you to our viewing audience, Helen. Then I'll just ask some questions. Okay?"

"Yes, of course. It's early. Do I look all right?"

"You look just fine." Pam motioned to her cameraman, "Roll camera, Hank."

Pam introduced Mary Bennett and then asked a series of questions meant to quickly establish the identity of Douglas Cromwell. A sketchy profile of Cromwell began to emerge as they talked. "Doug just moved in next door about six months ago. We've had him over for dinner several times so we got to know a little about him. Let's see... well, he's in his late thirties and a bachelor. He has very nice ladies visiting him from time to time. We see them in the hallway sometimes when they're visiting Doug. They're all very pretty and smart looking. All very proper, mind you."

Mary asked, "Did he mention what he does for a living?"

"Yes, he said that he was a Vice President of Lucas Industries. It's a very big company. They're located about twenty or so miles from here and my husband said that they're one of the largest manufacturers in New Jersey, or the country for that matter, of products that we all use everyday – things like Theracin Cold Tablets, Softee Baby Diapers, Fluffy Laundry Detergent, Lucas Water Softener, Safe Always Deodorant – you know, products like that. They employ a lot of people from Old Town. He must have an important job because he leaves for work early in the morning after his daily jog around the neighborhood and doesn't get home until very late."

While Mrs. Bennett was speaking, St. Pierre quietly told her assistant to call their office and get somebody to research Lucas Industries and Douglas Cromwell. NBC's researchers were adept at quickly weeding out biographical data for fast breaking news stories.

Without skipping a beat, Pam continued her interview, "Did he make many friends in town during the six months he's been here?"

"I don't know about that, Miss St. Pierre. He did mention that he got involved with coaching one of the town's Little League teams when he first got here. Seems he's a big baseball fan and he likes working with children. Bob Chester can tell you more about that. Bob's in charge of the town's sports' programs. He owns the hardware store on Chestnut Street. He's probably there right now if you want to talk to him."

"Yes, I would. Is there anything else you can tell us about Doug that you think our viewers might be interested in hearing?" Pam sensed that she wasn't going to get much more from this interview.

"Like I said, we really never got to know Doug that well. Oh yes, he did say that he was interested in politics. Said he majored in political science at college." Mrs. Bennett laughed and added, "Matter of fact, he said that one day he was going to become President of the United States. Doug is always kidding like that."

Nice anecdotal touch, thought Pam. We'll leave that in the final edit. She thanked Mrs. Bennett for her help and motioned for her crew to follow her. The NBC-Remote Unit had maneuvered their van through the crowd at the hospital and were waiting for Mary and the crew when they exited the building. Mary gave a terse order, "Hardware store on Chestnut Street. Let's get there quickly."

The small downtown area of Old Town was a beehive of activity on this day. Pockets of people were gathered throughout the town discussing the explosion at the Pierce School. Bob Chester's hardware store was centrally located in the heart of town. It was a traditional gathering point for folks wanting to gossip about everything and anything that touched their lives. The verbal exchanges were particularly active on this day. The NBC-TV network logo caught everyone's attention as it cruised through the town looking for the town's only hardware store. It had attracted a large crowd by the time it finally stopped in front of Bob Chester's storefront. Pam was out of the passenger seat of the van as soon as it came to a halt. Her support group was immediately behind her as she entered the store.

Bob Chester was easy to recognize. He looked like he owned a hardware store. He recognized Pam immediately and stepped forward to introduce himself. Pam told him that they had just left Doug Cromwell's condo after speaking with his neighbor. "She thought that maybe you could fill us in on Doug's background. Do you mind if I ask you some questions on-camera, Mr. Chester?"

"Mr. Chester is my father's name," said an effusive Chester. "Call me Bob. Everybody does. And sure, make me a TV star."

Pam cued her cameraman to start shooting. "We were given to understand that Mr. Cromwell has lived in town for about six months and that he coached a Little League team for you. Can you tell us anything about him that would help us in knowing him?"

It was obvious that Chester was going to enjoy his few minutes of national fame. "Well, sure. Doug and I were pretty good friends considering we only knew each other for a short time. He's really a good coach and the kids like him, that's for sure. Friendly as all get out. Why people have told me that..."

Mary interrupted Chester before he could get into a reminiscent rhythm. "Did he ever tell you anything about his early years. You know, where he was born, his parents, where he went to school - things like that?"

Chester thought for a moment and said, "Sure. He enjoyed talking about his early years. He was born in a small town in the suburbs of Chicago. It apparently was an up-scale area because he said his father owned a large advertising agency and he said - always modestly, mind you - that he lived kind of a privileged life growing up. He went to private schools right up to the age of seventeen. He graduated from Columbia University where he majored in political science. He really liked his politics. Used to talk about it all the time."

Pam saw an opening. "Did he follow up with a political career when he graduated."

"No, he went on to a graduate business school. Got himself a Master's Degree in Business Administration at Columbia. Said he wanted to go into politics but he had to make some money to support himself first. He was an independent kind of guy even though his folks apparently had some money. I think he still dreams about a political career one day, though." Chester then smiled sheepishly and asked, "You'll never guess what he said he was going to be one day."

"President of the United States," Pam answered, matter of factly.

"How did you know that?" Asked a surprised Chester.

Without answering, Pam continued, "We heard that he's employed by Lucas Industries."

"He sure is and he's done real well for himself with them. Doug's one of their Senior-Vice-Presidents. As I understand it, he's their operational guy. You know, in charge of making sure that everything goes smoothly. Quite an achievement for a young man to be one of the top people in such a big company. A lot of people in town work at

Lucas. The talk at the company is that he's destined for even bigger things with them."

Pam knew that the executive offices of Lucas Industries would be their next port of call. She thanked Bob Chester for his help and signed off. When they were back in the van she announced, "Down the Garden State Parkway. Next stop Lucas Industries."

CHAPTER 3

En route to Lucas Industries, St. Pierre made a telephone call to News Chief Les Sherrill at the NBC owned and operated affiliate WMAQ-TV in Chicago. She got through right away. "Les, this is urgent. You've undoubtedly heard about the bomb in the school at Old Town, New Jersey. We're on the story right now. Can you locate Mr. and Mrs. David Cromwell. They live in..."

"Pam, no need to go any further. David called me a little while ago to see if we had anything on what's happened out east there. Someone called him with the news. He's a personal friend. Very important guy in this neck of the woods. Cromwell Advertising. Big time operator. I have Joel Baer on the way to his office as we speak. Joel knows what's needed. We'll have it all wrapped up and to you in time for the 6:30 news this evening."

So much for a scoop, thought Pam. Let's hope we're the first ones talking to the Lucas people. "Thanks, Les. We'll keep in touch," she said, ending the call.

The NBC crew were greeted cordially when they were announced by the receptionist at Lucas Industries. It was almost as if they were expected. Pam breathed easily when she saw that there were no other news organizations in sight. They were immediately escorted into the office of the company's Chief Executive Officer Lawrence Kepler who came from behind his desk to welcome them. He introduced himself and his Human Relations Vice-President James Alston. They talked for a few minutes about the tragedy at Old Town. Kepler reassured them that he had talked to the hospital ten minutes before they arrived and Doug's condition seemed to be stabilizing. "Too early to tell of course, but the prognosis is optimistic."

Lawrence Kepler's time was money so he got right to the point. "We have anticipated that the press would want biographical information on Mr. Cromwell so Mr. Alston has put together a comprehensive dossier on him." Kepler motioned for Alston to continue.

Alston was equally economical with his words. "I will leave you with this package which we feel sure will be helpful in preparing your story. There is probably more information here than you'll need but we didn't want to leave any stones unturned."

Pam glanced through the packet she was handed and saw that it was just what she was looking for - and then some. They had even included photographs of Doug Cromwell in various personal and business settings. "This is perfect, gentlemen. Thank you," she said, somewhat caught off guard by the completeness of the package.

Alston suggested that perhaps NBC would like a formal on-camera interview with Mr. Kepler who would welcome the opportunity of expressing Lucas Industry's admiration for a highly regarded and respected member of their organizational family.

My God, Pam thought. These guys have thought of everything. It was almost as if they were aware of what had happened before it happened. Talk about corporate efficiency. "That is very generous of you, Mr. Kepler." The crew quickly set up their camera and sound equipment.

The interview was succinct and professional. Kepler's sentiments let the television viewing public know that Doug Cromwell was an outstanding young man who was a key executive with great promise. Kepler characterized him as a loyal and responsible associate - a selfless individual who cared deeply for the well-being of his fellow workers. He stated that no one was surprised that Doug put his life on the line to safeguard the lives of helpless children. Kepler asked all Americans to join him and his colleagues in offering a prayer for Douglas Cromwell's full recovery. The interview was concluded on this appropriately somber note. Pam thanked the two executives. The crew then departed.

Back in the van, Pam faxed copies of the printed dossier to the News Department in New York. She was always amazed at the speed in which news writers and editors could condense reams of facts into relatively short and cohesive stories. This was particularly true when the facts were coming in from assorted sources. She knew that the story would be ready for the 6:30 network evening news segment by the time they drove back to the city. When she finally had a moment to reflect on the days' events, Pam said to no one in particular. "Lucas Industries. They're good."

Lucas Industries *was* good. More than that they were a consistently profitable Fortune 500 company with an enviable record of growth in an industry where innovative product marketing was a prerequisite for corporate survival. The company was Sierra Enterprises' largest holding specializing in the manufacture and distribution of a broad line of family and home care products. They enjoyed brand leadership in many of the product categories that Americans relied on for their daily personal and household needs. Annual sales of the thirty-five different brands marketed by Lucas were $25 billion and accounted for sixty percent of Sierra's overall sales. It contributed substantially to providing the parent company with a *Triple A* credit rating and an enviable record of pleasing Wall Street by consistently showing favorable earnings – usually at least ten percent higher than the year before. They had to be good, Pam reflected, to put up those kinds of numbers.

The crowd that gathered at the hospital increased in numbers as the day progressed. It wasn't until late in the afternoon that the hospital official reappeared and announced, "Mr. Cromwell's condition appears to have been stabilized. While he is still listed as critical, let me just say that the attending medical team is extremely pleased by his miraculous turnaround in the past eight hours. We should know by morning the full measure of his recovery."

A spontaneous applause from the crowd was the official's reward for the welcome news. The crowd began to disperse knowing that Cromwell had survived the morning ordeal. Many remained and were joined by others during the evening hours in a candlelight vigil for the man who had saved the lives of their children and friends. News organizations from far and wide converged on the hospital. Regular programming of network and local television and radio stations were interrupted during the evening and daylight hours with a recap of the near disaster and the latest reports of Cromwell's condition. Newspapers were organizing stories for their early morning editions.

Morning came and the crowd had multiplied so that a meaningful police presence was needed to control the traffic. All eyes were on the entrance to the hospital anxiously waiting for news. The familiar hospital official emerged at 8:00 a. m. carrying a microphone. "Good morning, ladies and gentlemen. Let me get right to it. At this moment, Mr. Cromwell is awake, lucid and hungry. He passed the critical point in his recovery at 3:00 a. m this morning. Yesterday there were serious doubts that he would recover from the injuries he sustained from the explosion. This morning, we are announcing that a full recovery is expected. There will be a somewhat lengthy recuperative period but there is no doubt that he will weather that with flying colors. The doctors attribute his fast rebound to his being in superb physical conditioning and a strong will to survive. May I suggest that there's nothing more you can do here. Mr. Cromwell is in good hands. The press will let you know his progress as it's announced. Good morning." He was back in the building before the media could bombard him with questions.

In the days that followed, the hospital reports became more encouraging. The latest report signaled that he would be out of the hospital in about a month. His therapy was expected to continue on an out-patient basis. A hospital statement said that Doug would be back at his duties at Lucas Industries in about two months if his progress proceeded at its present pace.

Spearheaded by the families of the Franklin Pierce children, plans were underway for a special Douglas Cromwell Day to recognize and celebrate his courageous act of heroism. Mayor Robert Cole joined forces with the parents to assure that it would be a professionally managed day. The Mayor confided to several loyal associates that this tribute would blend in nicely with his reelection plans. After all, he said, Election Day is only six months away.

Doug's release from the hospital was to be June 15th. The Town Council proposed that, because the day was only two weeks prior to the town's Annual Independence Day Celebration, it would be a fitting tribute to have a double celebration on that day. In that way, the full resources of the annual celebration could be brought to bear on honoring their local hero. Everyone concurred.

Several weeks after Doug's release from the hospital, Principal Stoddard requested that Doug stop by his office at 10:00 a. m. as he had something important to discuss with him. When they met, they conversed for about five minutes which allowed the entire teaching staff to assemble in a double file outside of Stoddard's office. Stoddard put his arm around Doug and led him into the hallway. The forty faculty members and the school's administrative staff joined in an enthusiastic applause. Stoddard led him through their ranks. The two men stopped at the end of the double row and did an about face along with the staff members. They all then proceeded walking slowly towards the auditorium.

"This is your honor guard, Doug," Stoddard said. "Now, let's go meet the rest of the family."

When the doors of the auditorium opened, Doug was bombarded by a sound that gave him a paralyzing chill that shocked and exhilarated him. The auditorium was packed to capacity. Everyone was on their feet cheering and applauding as Doug was led up the center aisle to the stage. Every inch of space in the room was occupied. It was obvious that the building's fire code was being ignored on this day. When the two men reached center stage, Stoddard took three backward steps to allow Doug to languish in the unbridled praise of a grateful community. The enthusiastic response of the crowd continued for ten minutes.

Mayor Cole and the Town Council along with school officials joined the two men on stage. Principal Stoddard smilingly held up his hands in a silent plea for order. The crowd reluctantly took their seats. Stoddard then stepped to the podium and spent the next twenty minutes recounting the near-disastrous event at the school and Doug's heroic deed that followed. Stoddard concluded by saying with genuine emotion, "We will all be eternally grateful to Doug Cromwell for his brave and selfless act of sacrifice." The audience murmured their agreement in unison.

The Mayor followed with words of admiration but no one was more forceful in expressing the mood of the occasion than fifth grader Chris Williams. "Thanks for saving my life, Mr. Cromwell." This innocent comment brought tears to everyone's eyes. Doug Cromwell was no exception.

When Doug was asked to say a few words, he did so with characteristic modesty. "I consider myself to be a very lucky fellow to have been in the vicinity of the Franklin Pierce School that morning. I thank the good Lord for allowing me to be there. I know that if any one of you had been chosen instead of me, you would have done exactly what had to be done to save our kids." With that statement, Doug captured the hearts of the audience - and a nation. The media had been invited to document the morning event and had come out in large numbers. Mayor Cole made sure of that. Election Day was never far from his thoughts.

Stoddard saw that the emotional morning was beginning to take it's toll on Doug's strength so he concluded the meeting on a upbeat note. "We'll all be seeing Doug again on the Fourth of July. It'll be a time for everybody in town to show our love and appreciation for him. See you then."

CHAPTER 4

The Fourth of July was a day of remembrance and celebration in every city and town in the United States. This national holiday, which held a special meaning for all Americans, was traditionally celebrated across the nation with parades and pageants, eloquent speeches, organized firework displays and a feeling of unabashed patriotism among its millions of celebrants.

Such was certainly the case for the 29,000 residents of Old Town, N. J. and the many thousands of out-of-town spectators who joined the celebration. Not only were they celebrating the birthday of their country but, on this special day, they were all honoring the young man who had become a national hero overnight.

One of the members of the Celebration Committee had jokingly suggested that an invitation be sent to President of the United States Dewitt Marshall with the suggestion that he might like to be a part of their local celebration. "Why, we might even let him ride in the same car with Doug," said another of the group. Everyone smiled at the playful banter - except Councilman Lloyd Corrigan. Corrigan and Mayor Cole had been friendly enemies ever since high school. Now, years later, there was nothing friendly about their feelings for each other. They disagreed on just about any proposal brought before the City Council. If Cole supported an issue, Corrigan opposed it. And if Corrigan championed a suggestion, it was most assuredly challenged by the Mayor. Corrigan's fondest dream was to unseat Cole from his mayoral office and replace him with someone from his own party.

"Now, that's not a bad idea," said Corrigan. "Why not? The President is going to have to be some place on the Fourth. Why not here in Old Town? We can offer him something he can't get any place else."

Cole interrupted him. "What? What can we offer him? A ride up Main Street? Those network TV cameras are going to be honed in on the Capital on the Fourth. That's where he'll want to be."

Corrigan smirked and replied, "What we have to offer is a bona fide national hero who has been dominating the headlines ever since that bomb went off. Think about it. The President and Doug in an open top limo leading the parade right down Main. Maybe we can even get one of those armed forces bands marching in front of the limo playing some of those Sousa marches. Seeing the President and Doug and hearing that spine chilling martial music will do wonders for a Chief Executive who will be looking for a leg up in his next reelection campaign."

Mayor Cole saw that the idea of having the President "campaigning" in the state at this early date would be frowned on by the Democratic Party of which he was a conspicuous member. Marshall was a first term Republican president. Cole was a life long Democrat who had aspirations of moving up in the political arena of his party. Promoting a political adversary would do little for furthering that career. He immediately attacked the proposal. "Let's not lose sight of what we're trying to do here. The idea is to honor the heroic deed of one of our own. Our friend. Our neighbor. The presence of the President would only detract from the significance of that brave sacrifice."

Corrigan smiled inwardly and said to himself. Bullshit. I've got you old bastard. Just look at the faces of the Committee. They sure as hell like the idea. You're going to lose this one, my friend. He spoke up, "Nothing or no one can overshadow what Doug did at the Pierce. That deed is etched in the minds of every American." He then addressed the Committee members. "Think what this kind of positive scenario can do for the town. The publicity alone will have a telling effect on our local businesses. Besides, it will give our towns' folks a sense of pride that they can live with for the rest of their lives. And think what memories it will leave with Doug Cromwell." Cole was about to respond but knew that there was no countering that kind of argument. Corrigan continued, "Have we any friends in high places that can make this happen?"

Lester Choate who had been an active member of the New Jersey Republican Party for over thirty years spoke up. "Tom Enright can help us on that score. He's been in the Senate more years than I can remember and he's very tight with the President. Tom has been one of his strongest advocates for years besides being a close personal friend. If anybody can help, it's Tom."

Corrigan became enthused. "Lester, why don't you call Enright. Besides being a savvy Senator, he's a helluva politician. He'll see the merit of this thing. Tell him we'd like him and his wife to ride in a car right behind the President and Doug."

Everybody got excited at once. "What a coup if we can really get him," was heard.

"Old Town will become a celebrity overnight," another chimed in.

"The President of the United States right here in Old Town. Wouldn't that take the cake?" still another enthused.

Corrigan turned to Choate. "Lester, why don't you go into the other room right now and see if you can get the Senator on the phone. Let see if we can wrap this up right now?"

Choate said, "I'll be right back." Fifteen minutes later he returned smiling. "He loved the idea. He's calling the President right now. Said he'd call us back as soon as they've talked."

True to his word, Senator Enright called back an hour later. "Lester, it's a go. I don't have to tell you there's much to be done in preparing for his visit. One of the President's assistants will coordinate things with the Secret Service and the State Police. He'll be in touch with you to iron out the details. And, Lester, tell whoever came up with that idea that he or she did good." Cole sulked the rest of the evening when Choate repeated the Senator's complimentary comment to Corrigan.

The President arrived in Old Town by helicopter from Newark Airport on a picturesque July 4th morning that promised ideal weather for the big day. The copter landed at the municipal field in the center of town and, after a few words of greeting to the gathered crowd, he was whisked away to a waiting limousine. Doug Cromwell was seated in the rear seat of the limo with a calm that belied the anxiety he was feeling towards being singled out for this honor. He was not accustomed to this kind of public attention and, most assuredly, could not pretend to be comfortable sharing the spotlight with the President of the United States. His uneasiness was quickly allayed when the President said to him, "You know, Doug, I never could be completely at ease with this kind of attention. I guess it's the farm boy in me."

Doug immediately relaxed. He and the President Marshall exchanged pleasantries as they rode across town where the parade would begin. They continued talking when an early morning shower delayed the parade for ten minutes. The President encouraged Doug to talk about his background and seemed genuinely interested in Doug's rapid rise to his present position with Lucas Industries. Doug casually mentioned that he had majored in political science in college and that he had always harbored a secret ambition of getting into politics himself.

"It's a tough road, Doug. Fighting your way through that political jungle can deter even the bravest of hearts. You start at the bottom of the heap. You work very hard day in and day out - nights, too - until one day you see that your efforts produced something that had meaning - something that you knew would help a great number of people. That's when you'll be hooked. From that day on, you'll become a politician in every good sense of the word. Fortitude, Doug. Fortitude, dedication and just plain guts are what are needed. But, then again, you've proven you have the stuff. That's for sure."

"Maybe someday I'll get the chance, Mr. President."

Marshall became pensive for a moment. He suddenly turned to Cromwell and said, "You know, Doug, I wouldn't want to go on record as having said this but my people tell me I'm a shoo-in to win reelection next time around. I have to deliver a State of the Union speech to the Congress and the American people soon after I'm reelected and I want you to be a part of it. You won't have to say anything. I want you to sit with the First Lady while I tell America what they already know you did at the school. All you have to do is stand and be recognized. At the very least, Doug, you deserve that kind of recognition. What do you say?"

Doug was rendered speechless for a moment. "Mr. President, I'm... I'm flattered that you would want to do that. I don't know what to say."

Marshall was a past master at the one-line closer. "I'll tell you Doug, it couldn't hurt any aspirations you might have for a political career."

Doug's eyes widened at that suggestion. "Of course, Mr. President. I'd be honored and grateful."

The President closed out the conversation with a staged undertone, "Now, all I have to do is win that election." They both laughed and directed their attention to the Marine Corp band as they struck up the introductory chords of *Hail to the Chief*.

The parade and the ceremony that followed were a gigantic success and thrust Douglas Cromwell further into the public eye.

Oratory flourished in an overabundance of one upmanship among the gathered dignitaries. Brief mention was made of the country's birthday. All of the rhetoric was bestowed upon Old Town's local hero. The media coverage made sure of that. Time Magazine had selected him the week before as a candidate for their venerable Man of the Year Award. A prestigious publishing house offered him a lucrative book deal which he modestly declined with the comment, "Thank you very much but I've done nothing to warrant a book about my life."

As the President was boarding the helicopter for his return flight to Newark Airport, he took Senator Enright aside and confided in him his plans for having Cromwell present during his State of the Union message. "Tom, he's interested in a political career. We could certainly use someone like that in the party. You might want to have a talk with him to see the depth of his interest. I understand that you're having a mayoral election in Old Town this year. Could be a nice beginning for him. From what I've seen here today, all he has to do is throw his hat in the ring and he's in. He could be very useful down the road. He's got a lot going for him."

That evening Enright called Lloyd Corrigan and asked him to have a heart to heart talk with Cromwell. Corrigan was elated that the town hero would be going up against his longtime adversary. It was a decided no-lose situation for the young man. It was still early, so he called Cromwell and asked if he could stop by and see him. He had something very important to talk to him about. When they met, Cromwell made it immediately obvious that he was completely amenable to running against Mayor Robert Cole in the November election. It was on this day that politics seemed to become an all-consuming aphrodisiac for the young executive.

Douglas Cromwell's emergence into New Jersey politics was not the providential turn of events that it appeared to be. Corrigan knew that Cromwell had been trained most of his adult life for a political career that was conceived and charted by some very serious people. It was actually part of a carefully designed plan to assure that he would eventually become an influential policy maker at the highest level of the national government. It was an ambitious plan - one that would appear to have been conceived by a group of fanciful Hollywood screenwriters had it not been that it had the backing of some very committed and sometimes ruthless people. This group was accustomed to taking seemingly impossible challenges and making them a reality. They were patient men. Their plan had been painstakingly mapped out. They now felt that is was ready to be made operational.

The first phase of the plan was for Cromwell to gain credibility as a successful business executive with one of the largest industrial companies in the United States. He had taken a position with Lucas Industries immediately after obtaining his Masters Degree in Business Administration from Columbia University. Two years earlier he had received a degree in Political Science from Columbia. He advanced rapidly at Lucas when he was found to be an intelligent and resourceful executive. The fact that Lucas Industries was an integral part of the Sierra Industries' empire was an influencing factor in his fast ascendancy in the company.

The incident at the Franklin Pierce School was carefully planned to establish Cromwell as a hero to the town. It was to provide the basis for his being elected Mayor of Old Town in the next election. The bomber was a paid accomplice with a long record of mental problems who was supposed to plant the bomb in the classroom and disappear. His history of mental disorder was to be the reason for his planting the bomb if he were to be investigated. Cromwell was to discover the bomb and sound the alarm but when he saw that the man had decided to be creatively stupid and had chained the bomb to the radiator, he followed the orders he had been given. "If anything goes wrong and there is a chance that the bomber could be interrogated – or threatens the assignment in any way, he must be dealt with!" The deadly finality of that statement was implicit.

His assurance of winning the Old Town Mayoral election in November was to be the beginning of a political career that was expected to include the Governorship of New Jersey after serving a suitable period of time as Lieutenant Governor. A short internship as Vice-President of the United States would be his stepping stone for assuming the office of President when the then sitting chief executive would be unable to fulfill his present four-year commitment. In no instance, other than the Mayoral position, would he be elected to public office. Managed circumstances would control his appointments to the other offices.

Doug Cromwell, through the guidance of the elder Cromwell, the influential Sierra family and one of the nation's most astute and ruthless political *consultants,* Gino Cruz, were to play significant roles in Cuba's eventual progress towards a democratic rule and free market economy. Doug was ready for the challenge. He had made a lifetime commitment of helping to depose the Castro regime from his native land and to finally satisfy the family's debt of honor for the murder of his father and his friends.

CHAPTER 5

The lives and fortunes of many Cubans changed following the country's 1959 Revolution when Fidel Castro and his army of rebel guerilla fighters emerged from the Sierra Maestro Mountains and changed the country from a one-man dictatorship to a Communist satellite. While his forces numbered only several thousand, they were a well-trained and committed group of revolutionaries dedicated to overthrowing the existing government.

Prior to Castro's takeover, Cuba was governed by the strong hand of Fulgencio Batista who gained power first as President in the early 1930's and then as Dictator from 1952 until Castro came upon the scene. Batista's Cuba had been a police state where intimidation and bribery were the order of the day.

Corrupt government officials enjoyed limitless ways of satisfying an insatiable appetite for easy money. They demanded bribes from fellow Cubans for public services and took broad liberties with raids on the public treasury. Payoffs from American gamblers who owned casinos provided a ready access to the always attractive American dollar. In the end, the large, well-equipped army of Batista could not put down the popular revolt. He fled the country in January 1959 leaving behind a political vacuum that was quickly and ruthlessly filled by the Castro forces.

Wealthy landowners and influential Batista supporters who were judged to be "enemies of the people" were treated severely. To the dismay of his many supporters, Castro soon assumed dictatorial powers, imposed martial law and imprisoned and executed real or suspected enemies following trials before hastily convened military tribunals. Large estates and haciendas were confiscated by decree of the new government. The regime began to create a series of nationally-owned companies by systematically seizing foreign-owned properties and enterprises.

The world was shocked by the extreme measures. Many Cubans felt betrayed by the new government when Castro declared the country a Communist state. The rush by many Cubans to find a more compatible place to live became an embarrassment to a nation in turmoil. Some 700,000 Cubans emigrated from the island during the first year after the takeover. Many attempted to depart the island and enter the U. S. using homemade rafts, falsified visas and even resorted to contracting with alien smugglers to relocate them to friendlier shores. Miami, Florida became a logical and safe haven for these displaced refugees given its close proximity to Cuba.

One of the principal targets of the new regime was the powerful Sierra family whose influence on the island was significant. They were no strangers to the government-by-graft policies practiced by the local politicians - and, they were only too happy to oblige the ubiquitous demands of the Batista opportunists. The rewards to the family were substantial. The downside was that Alberto Sierra, the patriarch of the family, became Castro's number one political target.

Sierra had long known that the Batista government was doomed. His intelligence sources had alerted him early that Castro was mounting an offensive in the mountains on the southern part of the island. Alberto knew that his family business Sierra Enterprises would be ripe pickings for a nationalization program if the revolution were successful and he had no doubts that Castro would persevere. The new government would simply confiscate all of the family holdings in Cuba leaving him helpless to do anything about it. The family's influence on the political and economic life of Cuba would be at an end.

Alberto Sierra had been an astute businessman. He had recognized early that Cuba would eventually become less than an ideal environment for the family business. Not only were their various enterprises outgrowing the limited scope of the local economy, but he saw that the country itself was becoming a political risk. The disquieting talk that Fidel Castro was mounting an aggressive revolutionary movement was a rumor that could not be ignored. He began to limit the family's business presence on the island. He made sure that his production and distribution facilities for all his enterprises were securely based in the United States and friendly Central and South American countries to avoid the imminent threat of these physical assets being nationalized.

The senior Sierra's pride would not let him abandon his native land when many of the enemies of the new regime were leaving the country. Instead he stayed but wisely insisted that his immediate family be taken out of harm's way to their family estate in south

Florida. His wife, their three sons and two daughters secretly left the country several weeks before Castro's forces entered Havana. Other family members followed including the families of his two brothers. Sierra's decision to remain proved to be his death warrant. He was found murdered in his home three days after Castro's forces took control of the country. Official reports said his death was the result of "a failed robbery attempt by unknown perpetrators" but the family knew the truth of who was responsible for his death. It was one of Castro's death squads who had murdered Alberto.

With the death of Alberto, Castro became a lifelong enemy of the Sierras. The elder son Juan immediately took over the reigns and directed the destiny of the family. Juan had been well-versed in the family business by his father ever since he was a young lad. He grew into a handsome six-footer who favored the Brooks Brothers look to flatter his trim figure and button-down manner. He was bright and an enthusiastic learner having received a Bachelor of Business Administration degree in 1952 from New York's Columbia University. He completed a graduate course in finance at Columbia two years later. His Phi Beta Kappa identified him as an academic scholar.

Shortly thereafter, Juan took on ever-increasing management responsibilities and was eventually recognized as the guiding force behind Sierra Enterprises. Alberto had held back nothing in assuring that his eldest son was made completely familiar with every facet of the family business. He became president of the conglomerate at the age of twenty seven. Juan was an executive who led by example rather than by strong-arm, one-sided decisions. He mixed easily with his staff and always discussed all administrative and operational decisions with his associates before asking them to carry out an assignment with which they may not agree.

Having lost their holdings in Cuba was not as critical as it may have appeared. The family losses in Cuba were damaging but not life threatening. The losses were actually viewed by the family as insignificant frustrations; however, the assault on the family's self-esteem and wounded pride was considerable. It was viewed with contempt and fostered an unwavering commitment by the family for revenge against Fidel Castro and his political cohorts. The overthrow of the new government became an obsession with Juan Sierra.

Juan understood that it would not be an easy task to unseat the new government once it was in place, but he was convinced that Cuba's freedom from the communist menace would eventually become a reality. And, he vowed that he would do everything within his power to make it happen no matter how long it took. *A debt of honor had to be repaid.* He was also a realist. He knew that the family's only hope for an independent homeland - and for the eventual elimination of Castro - was for the United States to take a strong and uncompromising position against the newly defined Cuba.

From the beginning, the United States had become more and more disillusioned by the ruthlessness of the would-be liberator and the country's move into the Soviet orbit. Relations between the two countries became seriously strained. It was reasonable to assume that the U. S. would never let a communist state coexist just ninety miles from its shores without a responsive action. The threat to the democratic stability of the region was too great for there not to be strong counter measures taken either economically or, perhaps, even militarily - or both.

In the 1960 presidential campaign, John F. Kennedy vowed to expunge communism from Cuba. The U. S. showed its initial determination by declaring a trade embargo on all goods into the country with the exception of food and medicine. A U. S.-backed invasion of Cuban exiles at the Bay of Pigs in April of 1961 was further evidence of America's resolve in this matter. A brigade of some 1,400 Cuban exiles, trained and backed by the U. S. Central Intelligence Agency, unsuccessfully tried to invade and overthrow the regime. They might have succeeded had the U. S. provided the agreed-upon air cover in support of the invasion. President John F. Kennedy and his brain trust had belatedly decided to withdraw this all-important backup that was essential for a successful invasion. Without it, the expedition was a failure. Cuba's revolutionary army and militia were able to kill or capture almost all of the brigade invaders. It was an embarrassing foreign policy disaster for the U. S. and the Kennedy administration and provided Castro with a major issue in which to rally the people of Cuba.

Relations between the two countries became severely crippled when, in the fall of 1962, the United States learned that the USSR had brought nuclear missiles to Cuba. Reconnaissance aircraft photography detected construction of intermediate-range missile sights on the island. After a threatening warning by Kennedy, a Cuban blockade was put in force. U. S. warships patrolled the Caribbean to intercept ships destined for the island. A force of 140,000 troops in Florida prepared for an assault against Cuba. The world waited breathlessly for several days not knowing if this confrontation with the Soviets might lead to nuclear war but the Russians finally backed down. Both Cuba and the USSR were humiliated by this brave and uncompromising stand by the young American president who emerged from this conflict as an able crisis manager and a courageous leader.

And even though four decades had passed since the Bay of Pigs debacle and the missile crisis, tensions between the U. S. and Cuba remained strained. The Sierra family was committed to perpetuating that discord.

One of the Sierra's hidden secrets, known only to the widowed Alberto and his oldest son Juan, was that Alberto had fathered an illegitimate son who was two years of age at the time of the Revolution. Kathleen Cummings was an American journalist who had come to Cuba for Time Magazine on a special story assignment on the island's thriving gambling casinos. She and Alberto met and became romantically involved. They were together in Cuba and the United States during the next two years. Their love affair resulted in the birth of a healthy son but the delivery proved fatal to the young mother. She died in childbirth. Alberto was shattered. He had very much loved Kathleen and while he knew that he couldn't bring the boy into the family, he wanted to care for him as he would one of his own. He arranged for the boy to be legally adopted by David Cromwell, one of Chicago's leading citizens and advertising entrepreneurs, with strong loyalty ties to the Sierra family. He was also Alberto Sierra's son-in-law and had become a close confidante of the family.

David Cromwell was the Chairman of the Board and sole owner of a Chicago-based advertising agency bearing his name. Cromwell Advertising, the leading agency in the third largest populated city in the country, enjoyed a list of clients that included some of the most prestigious consumer product companies in the U. S. Lucas Industries, one of the many successful businesses of Sierra

Enterprises, was the account that gave Cromwell his start in the advertising business. The account billings were modest at the beginning but, over the years, Lucas grew to be the agency's top spender and one of the country's leading consumer product advertisers. David Cromwell's *hard sell* business philosophy and his innovative creative approach to advertising were viewed by the business community as a refreshing breath of fresh air for the uninspiring advertising that seemed to be the accepted norm of the times. Cromwell's success with Lucas Industries brought him to the attention of other aggressive marketers who wanted to benefit from his highly successful methods. His business thrived from the beginning.

Cromwell had first met Alberto Sierra while serving as a junior naval officer at the U. S. Naval base, Guantanamo, Cuba in the early 1950's. In his capacity as naval attaché, he found himself acting as an intermediary between the military and the always demanding political leaders of the country. The United States clearly understood the need for maintaining a favorable relationship with the ruling class of Cuba being that the island's strategic location was a natural fortification to the underbelly of the U. S. In private life, he would have been thought of as a public relations specialist. Unofficially, he was considered by his superiors as a "helluva buffer between those nut cases and us".

The initial meeting between Alberto Sierra and Lt. David Cromwell happened one evening quite accidentally when they both were attending a testimonial dinner for President Batista at the Nacional Hotel in Havana. Cromwell had just valet parked his car when Sierra's limousine, carrying his family to the affair, pulled in behind his car. Almost before the limo came to a complete stop, Alberto's youngest daughter had opened the rear passenger door adjacent to the oncoming traffic and was about to step into the traffic flow. David saw her predicament and quickly protected her with his body. In doing so, the fender of a passing car grazed him - knocking him to the ground. Several of the family members quickly rushed to his aid. To show that he was not hurt, he flashed a smile at Alberto who was the first to reach him and said, "No harm done. I hope the young lady wasn't hurt."

Alberto and the other family members were profusely grateful to the young officer for jeopardizing his own safety and saving their 16-

year old Maria from a critical injury. Alberto was not satisfied with a perfunctory thank you. Instead, he insisted that the young hero visit the family at their shore home the following weekend. David modestly accepted the invitation. The shore home turned out to be a palatial estate on the southern tier of the island. It was here that Cromwell met and became friends with the Sierra family. The friendship that developed between the eldest son Juan and Cromwell was particularly close. They would meet many times in the months ahead and would spend endless hours together talking about many subjects of interest. American and Cuban politics always sparked a lively discussion. Juan's reservations about the long term future of the Batista regime and David's particular fascination with the business of marketing and advertising were favorite whipping boys. They became fast and lifelong friends.

It was during one of these discussion sessions that Juan confided in David of the family's plans for introducing a new line of pharmaceutical products into the American market. He proudly stated that product development for a list of thoroughly researched cold remedy products had already been placed on a fast track to assure that production would be ready in two to three years.

"You could play a big part in our plans for getting these products launched?" Juan enthused. "We'll need someone we can trust stateside. Who better than you to be that person. We all trust you implicitly. You've become like part of the family." Juan encouraged him to think about it. "It's a great opportunity."

David thought about the offer that evening and accepted enthusiastically. He felt confident that he was qualified to make a meaningful contribution to the family's ambitions in the U. S. He had earned a graduate degree in Marketing from the University of Chicago in the late 1940's. Advertising had always intrigued him. He had worked several summers at the Leo Burnett Advertising Agency in Chicago and learned that he not only enjoyed the creative challenges the business offered but he was quite competent at coming up with ideas that more experienced copywriters and art directors were able to transform into effective television and radio commercials and print ads. He gained the reputation of being able to develop practical creative points of view for sometimes difficult marketing problems.

David became serious about learning as much as he could about the impending Lucas product line launch. While still in the service, he spent the next several years learning how best to introduce an over-the-counter pharmaceutical product into the U. S. market. He schooled himself thoroughly in every aspect of the marketing process for this product category. When he was satisfied that he had thoroughly done his homework, he then put together a carefully conceived marketing plan outlining the specifics of his diligent planning. He presented it to Juan who was impressed with the imagination and innovative thinking expressed in the professionally documented plan.

When Juan had finished reading the plan he said, solemnly. “This is remarkably good - just what we’ve been looking for. There are some things, though, about our plans that still have to be finalized. Tell you what. Let’s you and I revise your plan to incorporate these other unresolved issues when we get a handle on them. We’ll then present it to dad.”

Several months later, Alberto reviewed the revised plan very carefully and he, too, was duly impressed. He was particularly intrigued with the advertising section that featured an exciting concept for promoting the family of products coupled with consumer copy that focused on the distinctive benefits of the individual products in the line. The elder Sierra immediately put David on-the-payroll in spite of his still serving his tour of duty in the military. He saw the young man as a talented innovator who could be a decided asset to the family’s future plans. Besides, as time went on, he began thinking of David Cromwell more and more as a member of the family.

When he was discharged from the service, David came back to Chicago to begin a career for which he had prepared himself during his tour of duty in the military service. One of his first assignments was to find an advertising agency to handle the introductory launch of the Lucas product line. He interviewed ten advertising agencies - both large and small - and after reviewing presentations from each of the contenders, he decided that none of them were right for the assignment. Shortly thereafter, Cromwell Advertising was born. He had decided to open his own advertising agency and do it himself.

Six months later, Lucas Pharmaceuticals successfully introduced their Theracin line of cold remedy products in ten test markets in the U. S. One year later, the brands were introduced nationally and enjoyed an immediate success. At the forefront of this marketing triumph was David Cromwell's unique and innovative creative presence. He was to become one of the guiding forces behind the development of other Sierra Enterprise companies. The success of these companies would eventually identify the giant conglomerate as one of the most prestigious Fortune 500 companies in America.

David Cromwell did, in fact, become a member of the Sierra family. The chance meeting between Maria Sierra and David developed into a strong friendship - and later a serious love affair - after he had saved her from being struck by an automobile three years before. Maria had grown into a beautiful and vivacious young woman. She and David were married when she reached her nineteenth birthday. Having lost his own parents at an early age, David grew to think of Alberto as his father and the younger Sierras as his siblings. His close association gave him a strong prejudice towards their points of view regarding most important family matters. Juan was to test that commitment shortly after Alberto was murdered.

CHAPTER 6

Gino Cruz was a staunch anti-Castro crusader who had left Cuba a year before Castro took power. He and Alberto Sierra were close friends since boyhood and became close business associates later in life. Cruz handled all of Sierra Enterprises legal undertakings which at times included backroom style political exploitation. His son Pedro had graduated from Georgetown University in 1967 and was quite familiar with the U. S. way of doing business - particularly the business of politics. As Alberto Sierra had taught his son Juan all there was to know about the family's affairs, Gino Cruz was as diligent in the education of Pedro in his family's business enterprises. Father and son now lived in McLean, Virginia and practiced law and *political consulting* at their law office in nearby Washington, D. C. Gino was a widower and lived alone. Pedro lived with his family.

Now in his late sixties, the senior Cruz was considered one of the shrewdest political power brokers in the nation's capital. He was closely connected to just about every influential politician who could make a difference in the Washington power structure. Some of his detractors said he was an opportunist who had perfected the art of reading public opinion on major issues and then finding ways to insert himself and his clients into any situation that offered a favorable climate for political exploitation.

But, the defining strength in Cruz's portfolio of political assets was the extensive files he had locked away in a securely guarded location in the nation's capital. There was a file on every politician of consequence in the country. He diligently made sure that these files were kept current and confidential. He had a professional staff of investigators who made it their business to unearth incriminating wrongdoings about anyone whose past could be used for political advantage. It was a business that provided the Cruz interests with powerful political leverage and financial gain.

He was responsible for the making and breaking of many careers within the legislative halls of the U. S. Congress. Veteran and aspiring politicians found it unwise to have Gino Cruz as an enemy. A U. S. Senator, who learned this lesson the hard way, advised his colleagues that "if you're masochistic enough to lock horns with Cruz, my advice to you is to get yourself a 1,000 pound gorilla instead and challenge it to a fight. You'll do better against the anthropoid than going up against Gino."

Gino Cruz could never be described as a friendly man. His muscular body in a short frame and deep-set angry eyes suggested to strangers that he was a man to be dealt with at arms length. His appearance somehow gave the impression that he was always looking for a fight despite his advanced years. Many found him forbiddingly solemn with a controlling personality. Contrary to appearances though, he *was* a friendly man who could be very charming and even witty when the occasion called for tact and political expediency. He had a high IQ but a low boiling point. He had never completely come to terms with a prodigious temper that was easily provoked.

His uncompromising singularity was that, in a competitive situation, he liked to win – every time – even though the odds were not always in his favor. *Standard operating procedure*s were words that never determined his way of doing things. He used his own playbook in politics and his personal life. Gino made decisions first and looked for the necessary support for them afterward. He had few personal friends as bad things seem to happen to people who became too inquisitive about the dark side of Gino's political dealings.

Except for physical differences, Pedro Cruz was very much his father's son. At times, it seemed that they were both painted with the same brushstroke. While Gino was reminiscent of a pugnacious bulldog, Pedro was tall, angular and Latin handsome with a pleasant demeanor and an equally warm and engaging smile. He never seemed to lose his composure. His blue eyes were in sharp contrast to Gino's dark penetrating eyes that always seemed to be in motion. The son was an intense and hardworking attorney with a highly developed self-confidence. He always acted decisively so there was never any question about his position on matters of importance. Words used to describe him were sharp, incisive, steady and reasonable.

Pedro had been well-schooled in his father's Machiavellian ways for getting things done in difficult political and business situations in which the family had interests. Their methods were not always governed by Marquis of Queensbury rules but, as his opponents rarely played by the rules, their motives and actions were considered acceptable norms in the political arena in which Cruz and Cruz, Attorneys-at-Law, operated. "If the other side was consistently contemptuous of the rules, you were absolved from observing those rules yourself," was the Cruz credo for finding comfort in their actions.

After graduation from law school, Pedro joined his father's firm. He was put through a rigorous training at Gino's side and quickly learned the good and the bad of political realities which included the legal and not so legal ways of doing things. He discovered early that politicians were highly motivated and, at the same time, easily manipulated. He also learned that blackmail could be a strong ally in separating winners and losers in the world of political mischief.

Pedro Cruz and Juan Sierra had many things in common - most notably, a steadfast loathing for Fidel Castro and what he was doing to their native Cuba. They had been close friends for many years. Juan's contempt for the present leadership of Cuba was compounded by the fact that they had murdered his father. Both families were outspoken in their commitment to rid Cuba of the tyrannical leader and his perverted government. It became a serious game with them to devise ways in which they could achieve this goal.

"It would have to be an ingenious plan," Pedro had said. "You couldn't just kill him. "There would always be someone standing in the wings ready to take his place. Just killing him would be quite unproductive."

Juan agreed. "And, then you'd have to kill his successor and then *his* successor and everyone else who came along to fill the void. No, that's not the way. Their government must be made to disappear. Depose the government and Castro will follow." They were quick to conclude that it would be necessary to use America's powerful arsenal of intimidation to effect any major change to Cuba's political structure. They needed the United States as an accomplice. It was the only way.

Pedro reflected on what his father had taught him about the expediency of buying people. "You can buy all the politicians in the world to try and get something like that done, but that would be fraught with all kinds of problems. Think of the administrative complexities of trying to manage massive payoffs to politicians who, even under normal circumstances, find it difficult to keep their mouths shut. There'd be too many risks for leaks. The public would soon know what you were doing. What you would really need is a top official in the administration who could exert political leadership to disrupt the system they've set up down there. He'd, of course, have to have some real influence with the president. You'd need the president on your side to make anything of consequence happen."

"So, we'd have to buy the president," Pedro suggested, mischievously. "It wouldn't be the first time."

Juan became serious. "That's true but that would also be too risky. It would be impossible to control someone in that position with the only reward being money. Money wouldn't be enough. But, you're right, Pedro, it would have to be someone with the power and political muscle to move legislators to make tough decisions. You'd almost have to *create* a president to your own specifications to make something like that work."

Pedro smiled while reflecting on that thought. "A manufactured chief executive officer - now, there's an idea. Trouble is that it would take years to get a handpicked confidante in place." The two men were becoming fascinated with the game they were playing. What started as whimsical byplay was beginning to take on an identifiable form as they spoke.

"Think about it," Pedro continued. "Think of the power someone could wield if they could educate and train someone for the expressed purpose of he or she becoming President of the United States."

Juan challenged the practicality of the idea, "That sounds like a tall order. Even if you were successful, who's to say that he'd remain loyal to the real purpose of his being there in the first place? And how do you instill in someone - who would probably be a stranger to you to start with - with a dedication to do whatever is necessary to make Cuba a non-communist country again. Every minute of that person's life would have to be controlled both before and after he reaches that Oval Office.

Pedro responded, "It goes without saying that our man or woman would have to be completely sold on the basic reason he's there in the first place. He would have to be a patriot to our cause and it would help if he could be instilled with an unrelenting hatred for what Castro did to the Sierra family. Revenge would have to be a strong ally in the person's makeup."

Juan seemed skeptical. "Where could we find someone who could have that kind of fervor - or even be manipulated to have passion for that point of view?"

Pedro was quick to respond. "Actually, controlling a person's future is quite common in everyday life. Young people are constantly being manipulated to live up to the expectations of parents or other people."

"How so?"

"Okay, take me for example. Gino's a lawyer." Pedro always referred to his father by his given name. "From birth, my parents wanted me to follow in his footsteps. Ever since I can remember, the conversation at home centered on the wonders of the law and how successful my father was at the profession he loved. As I got older, they kept reminding me that it was a very satisfying and rewarding way to make a living. Look at Gino – my mother used to say - he's very happy with his success. Look at how well we live. They were relentless in instilling me with the desire to become an attorney. It became an all-consuming passion for me to become a lawyer as I was growing up. They backed it up with all the right schools and the assurance of a promising career with my father's law firm. It took over twenty years, but they were rewarded for their diligence with a *manufactured* attorney-at-law. Like I say, Juan, it's done all the time."

"I see your point, Pedro, but we're not just talking about a lawyer, we're talking about creating a President of the United States. And, we're not talking about raising someone as a child to be our subject. We can't wait forty or fifty years to see results. We would need someone within our lifetime."

They ended their conversation that afternoon with Pedro saying, "It can be done. With a little imagination and some of that political clout that Gino has made an art form, it can be done."

The two friends parted. Juan had a haunting feeling about their conversation. Could it really be done, he would ask himself many times in the next several weeks. He wanted to pursue the subject with Pedro and vowed that the next time they met he would ask Gino to join them. He's good at analyzing impractical situations and, more times than not, coming up with practical solutions. He'll know if the idea has any merit or not. Besides, he always enjoys these kinds of talks in spite of his busy schedule.

Pedro was already formulizing a scenario in his mind as they parted. It *was* a game to him and he loved the thrill of a challenge - however theoretical. After all, he told himself; theoretical was a first step in arriving at some very logical and exciting realities.

Juan and Pedro were having lunch with Gino at the Jackson Room of the Regency Hotel on a muggy Washington summer afternoon. The topic of conversation was a much-discussed topic among the three when they got together - U. S.-Cuban policy. Juan titillated Gino with his first comment. He asked him what he thought of the idea of grooming someone to become President of the U. S. for the expressed purpose of masterminding political reform in Cuba. Gina was amused at the absurdity of the question but sensed that Juan was serious. Juan then briefly outlined what Pedro had said about it being a very doable proposition with the proper diligence and a heavy dose of political manipulation."

A questioning expression came over Gino's face. He had no sense of humor when he was discussing anything that smacked of political maneuvering. He was quiet for several moments. He finally said, "Any idea that advances a vision to rid our beloved homeland of the system that continually betrays the people of Cuba is of vital interest to me. Tell me, what's on your mind."

The three men talked for most of the afternoon. They were so absorbed in their conversation that they had forgotten about the food that had gotten cold as they talked. Juan could see why Gino was recognized as the standout political guru among his Washington peers. Even his severest critics thought of him as having a sense of political shrewdness second to none. Many of the most influential sitting politicians in the nation's capital owed their congressional and senate seats in no small measure to the wily efforts of Gino Cruz. If a friendly congressman needed votes to get a troublesome bill through committee, Gino was there with the appropriate leverage. Problem-solving was his forte.

That afternoon he was able to take Juan and Pedro's idea and give it a practical spin that encouraged the two younger men that their flight of fancy had a chance of becoming a reality. By the end of the luncheon Gino had set forth in very concise terms how he thought the *project* should be handled. His parting words were, "Let us think some more about what we've discussed and meet again this Friday at my office. Juan, would you ask David Cromwell if he would join us. He's in Washington this week. I think he could be of help here."

When the four did meet in Gino's office several days later, Cromwell saw that the usually taciturn Cruz was in a congenial mood and anxious for a lively discussion. The elder Cruz had asked his son to provide the introductory comments so he could concentrate on Cromwell's reaction to the idea. Cromwell listened attentively. His first comment was, "I have to admit that the idea is provocative but to put something like that in motion would take a very serious commitment by a great number of people. I frankly wouldn't know where to begin."

Gino was quick to respond. "You start at the beginning. The beginning is finding a subject - the person who would eventually become the President of the United States."

Cromwell asked, "And where do we find this subject - this person to be trained to be president?"

Gino smiled and said, "You have the lad living with you in Chicago."

Cromwell was speechless for a moment. "You mean Douglas? Why...why, he has no training or background whatsoever for what you're suggesting. He's, ah..."

Gino quickly added, "I don't think we could find a better candidate for the project. Think of it. Alberto Sierra's youngest son now living in the United States and being raised by one of his dearest and most-trusted friends who, along with Alberto's family, share the need to avenge Alberto's murder."

Juan and Pedro looked at each other and shook their heads in agreement. They then returned their attention to Gino who continued, "I believe that the four of us could develop a plan that would be a productive way for Douglas to be of service to his family and to himself. What better way for him to pay tribute to someone he loved and admired? And what better way for all of us to pay tribute to him than by devising a clever and cunning way of ridding Cuba of this lunatic government?"

Cromwell continued to marvel that they were speaking so calmly and seriously about something that appeared to him to be improbable. It's an exciting idea, he told himself, and it must have merit if Gino is endorsing it. Gino interrupted his thought with added argument,

"Remember David, as president, Douglas would have many other broad-reaching responsibilities and challenges. His focus would not only be on restoring Cuba to a democratic rule. He would also be responsible for all of the presidential actions required to maintain and nurture the needs of a great nation. What a fulfilling career he could have."

Pedro joined in, "Certainly, his journey to the presidency would not be easy. He'd have much to learn in a relatively short time but he's extremely bright and ambitious. We're convinced he can make it. With his intelligence and some politically sound management running interference for him, he can make it."

"Douglas already understands the injustice that was served up to his family," said Gino. "The evil that Castro perpetrated on the Sierra family must be in the forefront of his consciousness at all times so that he maintains an unwavering determination to satisfy the family's debt of honor."

Juan continued, "His first office will be as mayor of a small suburban town close to a large metropolitan city. We have New York in mind. To gain instant recognition, we will have him do something heroic that will endear him to the voting constituency of the town. These heroics will be arranged by us and be convincingly inspiring and motivating to assure a one-sided victory on Election Day. At the same time, he will gain national recognition for his selfless act through national press coverage. We'll place one of our operatives in the town to organize and fine-tune Doug's mayoral role. He'll also act as his confidante in all future political matters. The man we have in mind has had major responsibilities in the election of several former Republican presidents. During Doug's term as mayor, he will be recognized as a strong administrator who is a staunch advocate for the people who elected him. He will champion many programs that benefit the town. His time in office will be conspicuously heralded through favorable and widespread professionally-planned publicity."

Gino saw that Cromwell was beginning to get caught up in the enthusiasm of the others. He continued, "The next step will be as lieutenant governor of the state. We'll make every effort to assure that the present holder of that office is amenable to stepping down either by attractive political inducements or, if need be, by uncovering damaging facts about his misdeeds in office or his personal life. There is always a damaging morsel or two in one of these sides of a politician's life which can prove fatal to a promising career if used judiciously. The governor will be convinced that Douglas's mayoral time in office plus his statewide popularity will bode well for his selecting the young man as his new lieutenant governor. This second highest office in the state will allow Doug to distinguish himself so that he becomes a visible and viable alternative to the then sitting governor."

"It is in this office that he will gradually develop a strong national presence. Promises of higher office - or other extenuating circumstances - for the governor will open the door for Doug being logically discussed as the next head of state by the party politicos. His choice for the high office will further enhance his reputation as someone to be reckoned with in the national arena. However; Doug will never serve as governor. Instead, the office of vice-president of the United States will suddenly become available and Doug will be appointed to that office by the president with an assist from influential party chieftains. Doug's selection will be a widely accepted and a popular choice. Polls will tell a convincing story of the positive reaction of the American people to the news of Doug becoming vice-president."

Gino then motioned for Juan to continue. "The next giant step in our scenario will be to the office of the President of the United States. How that will be achieved is a question only future circumstances will answer. Let it be said, though, that without the benefit of a national election, young Cromwell will become President of the United States. And, that's when the Sierra family's revenge against Communist Cuba will begin in earnest.

Cromwell smiled inwardly and thought - what a masterful job they did in triple-teaming me. The strong positive vibes that Cromwell was feeling as the three spoke had turned into a silent commitment by him to pursue what he now felt was a conceivable scenario. But then, Cromwell didn't need much convincing. He was as dedicated as the others in wanting to bring honor back to the sullied Sierra name.

CHAPTER 7

Election Day came and went in Old Town, N. J. leaving in its wake a newly elected mayor. Predictably, Douglas Cromwell was elected in a landslide. Ninety three percent of the voting electorate chose him in a record setting voter turnout. He confronted his new position as he had approached every new challenge that confronted him in his life - head on and with a determination to succeed. His campaign promises were given top-priority on his agenda. Fulfilling these promised commitments was essential to building a trusting relationship between the citizens of Old Town and himself. His approach to the office was tempered by having been elected - not for his political prowess - but rather because of his selfless act of heroism that was contrived to get him elected mayor of the town and to establish him as a viable candidate for future and loftier political offices.

Every four years, two months after his election to the nation's highest office, the President of the U. S. speaks to the American people in a State of the Union Address and shares with them his administration's visions and plans for the coming four years. The much heralded speech delivered before both Houses of Congress by recently reelected President Dewitt Marshall was a reaffirmation of the programs that had been initiated in his first term of office.

The predictable partisan responses to the Republican President's words echoed throughout the chamber. His speech was interrupted seventy five different times by applause in acknowledgement of everything said that spoke favorably of his party's views and accomplishments. In contrast, the Democratic senators and congressmen appeared impassive towards the President's rhetoric. They were careful not to be too conspicuous in their resistance to the President's words as the television cameras were quick to record their reactions for the world to see.

True to his word, President Marshall sent a formal invitation to Douglas Campbell to be his guest of honor at his State of the Union Address. While the American people looked forward to seeing the newly elected President, they were particularly anxious on this occasion to see, for the first time in person, the hero of the near-disaster at the Franklin Pierce Grammar School in Old Town, N. J. Hundreds of children owed their lives to the selfless act of this modest and unassuming young man who had stolen the hearts of all Americans.

President Marshall had a photographic memory and was a past master at memorizing an entire address and making it sound like it was spoken off-the-cuff. On this occasion, he was at his oratorical best. Near the end of his speech, President Marshall spoke of the bravery and heroism of the U. S. Armed Forces who were presently waging a struggle with all those who were a threat to the peace and freedom of everyone in the world. "And, at home here in America, we see the sacrifices that its citizens are willing to make to protect each other from harm. We saw a striking example of that type of concern for others a short time ago in a small New Jersey town." With those words, the television cameras focused on the young man seated next to the President's wife in the balcony of the chamber.

The President continued, "On that day, Douglas Cromwell, without concern for his own safety, put himself in harms way and saved the lives of over four hundred children. We all know the story of his self-sacrifice and his willingness to make the supreme sacrifice without consideration for his own well-being to save the lives of those children. Douglas Cromwell represents all that's good about America. Let us all take this opportunity to thank Douglas for showing us how we Americans care for each other. Fellow Americans, join me in saying - a job well done, Douglas Cromwell."

With that comment, the President applauded the young man who stood at the First Lady's urging to receive a tumultuous greeting that lasted for several minutes. When everyone had taken their seats, the President concluded his remarks by saying, "As you undoubtedly know, Doug was recently elected Mayor of Old Town in my home state of New Jersey. I'm sure we'll be hearing a great deal more from Douglas in the years to come." He then quipped, "Whatever the future holds for him, he'll get my vote." This light hearted comment was to be the harbinger of Cromwell's political career. It gave Gino Cruz confidence that they were on the cusp of fulfilling Douglas Cromwell's destiny.

It seemed that every member of the Congress wanted to shake Doug's hand and express their admiration for him at the President's reception following the formal proceedings. The President and Gino Cruz were at his side introducing him and chatting with members of Washington's political leadership. Cruz and Marshall had been political friends for many years. Cruz was instrumental in helping to direct the campaign that brought Marshall into the Oval Office for his first term. He had done the President many favors over the years which were duly reciprocated. When the President needed political leverage, Gino was always there with his political weapons. He had a leg up when discussing Doug's future with the President. Marshall had taken a distinct liking for the young man when he first met him. He saw the potential that Cruz was unabashedly praising and he agreed that the party could use this attractive youth in the future. What the President didn't realize was that this young man's future included replacing Dewitt Marshall as President of the United States.

Cruz hosted a luncheon the following day at his private dining club to which he had invited a group of congressional leaders whom he characterized as the shakers and movers of Capital Hill. These were the men and women whom Cruz had targeted to support Cromwell's journey to higher offices. There was no formal agenda as Cruz merely wanted it known that Douglas Cromwell was a potentially valuable and marketable political asset. He made sure that each of the guests was photographed individually and as a group with Doug and that prints of the photos were sent to their local newspapers. It seemed that every politician wanted to be associated with the top news attraction of the hour.

Back in Old Town, Cromwell's popularity seemed to take on even greater significance as he proceeded to fulfill his campaign promises. These were not empty promises to be forgotten after Election Day. These were assurances that would help establish the trustworthiness of a man committed to public service in the eyes of not just Old Town but all America. A carefully planned public relations campaign, handled by Cromwell Advertising, would assure that Americans everywhere were kept abreast of this new political personality's achievements.

Old Town had always been a sleepy upscale community that was a haven of tranquility for the harried New York commuter and folks that worked in the surrounding areas. When the family providers went to work in the morning, they knew that they had left their families in a safe and socially friendly environment. There were shopping malls, restaurants, motion picture theaters and other recreational attractions in the surrounding areas so their social needs were adequately satisfied. The problem was that the town's proverbial sidewalks were pulled in at night and the downtown area became a virtual ghost town. The daytime activity of the town was also almost non-existent. *The Group* saw this as an opportunity for exploiting their plan to promote the new mayor's managerial skills. Mayor Cromwell's challenge was that he had to convince the complacent townspeople that their lives could be better served and more fulfilling with radical changes in their perceptions and ambitions for their town. He had first to persuade the Town Council of the merits of his plan which - with the convincing support of Lloyd Corrigan - was accomplished almost immediately. A planning committee was appointed and the work began in earnest.

A meeting was held at the Franklin Pierce Grammar School in which the residents of the town were invited. The school, the site of Mayor Cromwell's heroic victory, was deliberately chosen for the occasion. When Cromwell took center stage to explain the plan, he was greeted enthusiastically. He had a good feeling that his plan would pass unimpeded by this emotional greeting. He began with a huge smile, "Welcome one and all and particularly the children from Franklin Pierce. It is so good to see you all so happy and healthy." He then walked over to the group and gave several of them a hug. He then continued, "First, let me begin by thanking everyone for honoring me by selecting me to be your mayor. I am flattered and humbled by your generosity and promise that I will do everything within my power to serve you well during my term of office."

He then hesitated and surveyed the sea of faces before him. They all looked back approvingly. "It was obvious to me when I first came to Old Town that there was a sense of pride in the community that bound everyone together. I found out later that it was more than just that. There was a spirit and a willingness to do whatever was necessary to preserve the qualities that make our town very special. And Old Town *is a very special town*." Spontaneous applause followed. "It is for that reason that your Town Council has unanimously approved a plan that will make our town the envy of the state." A smile crept on to his face, "I daresay, if you agree with the plan, I wouldn't be surprised if we become known as the Garden Town of the Garden State." Laughter and applause followed.

Cromwell became serious. "Here is the plan." He then proceeded to describe the four basic elements of the program. "Our first thought was to upgrade our education system which was almost immediately rejected. There is nothing wrong with our educational system. The curriculums are sound, our teaching staffs are, without a doubt, the best in the state and our administrators and support teams are simply superb." Again, there was spontaneous applause. "The major emphasis of our plan has been placed on a Revitalization Program of Old Town's downtown area. Let me hold off speaking to this point until I've covered the other three."

He hesitated for effect, "Our children are our greatest asset. We will..." He was abruptly interrupted by loud cheering from the children. Laughingly and bowing to the group surrounding him, he continued, "Yes, you are. And, we want to make sure that your future is secure and happy. So, here's what we're planning to do. We're going to build a recreation center right on Oak Street. It will be a three story building equipped with everything from state of the art fitness centers for the varying ages including one for the adults. There'll be several basketball courts and even a hockey rink. We'll have dressing areas and showers and they'll be a reception area with a snack bar for our young people to socialize with one another. We've even planned for a ten lane bowling alley. There will be more but what we'd like everyone to do is make suggestions as to how you feel the space in the building can be utilized. It's your facility so you should have a word in what goes in there."

Someone in the audience yelled out, "And, we'll name it the Douglas Cromwell Recreation Center" - a comment that was followed by a loud burst of applause.

Doug said, "Well, I think we can find a better name than that."

Everyone chimed in, "No, no, that's what we'll call it."

Doug modestly continued, "Along the same line, we feel that the athletic fields in town could be upgraded. Our Recreation Department folks do a splendid job of maintaining our properties. With their guidance, we believe that they can really do justice to making our athletic fields even friendlier for our kids." The dads in the audience were particularly enthused with the idea as expressed by their cries of approval.

Doug hesitated for maximum effect and said, "The one thing we wanted to make sure of when developing our plan was how we could constructively help our senior citizens to continue to lead happy and productive lives. I was talking to Bob Chester at the hardware store a couple of months ago and he suggested that we ought to consider a Senior Center where seniors could come to socialize and get involved in projects that interest them. I personally thought it was a great idea. When I presented the idea to the committee, Les Albright said we could get folks to carpool our seniors to the center if they need transportation. Jim Thorne followed that with having lunch served to them. Needless to say, the committee was a hundred percent behind the center." Everyone expressed their approval with the now spontaneous applause.

"Finally, and as they say, last but certainly not least, is a revitalization of our downtown area. You have only to walk downtown in the evening to see that our main street literally become a lonesome thoroughfare after dusk. We are losing a valuable source of revenue by not trying to energize that area. Let us know what you think of this idea. We presently have several hundred retail stores including a bank, a pharmacy and several small restaurants on the avenue. There are other stores and a gas station on the side streets but, like the avenue, many of these stores are not open for business at the present time. The retail outlets that are there service the needs of a very limited number of customers and in a very superficial way. Most of us take our business out-of-town to the malls with their wider selections and discounted prices - not to mention the wider selection of restaurants. We strongly believe that downtown can be made into an attractive showplace and a thriving source of income for retailers. Think of what a thriving downtown business community would do to the tax base of everyone living in our town. Simply, we'd be paying less taxes each and every one of us." The audience vocally approved that pleasant thought.

"There's more to it than just a tax savings, though. Think of the convenience of not having to play bumper cars every time we go to the mall. Those long walks from the parking lots will be a thing of the past."

The mayor signaled for a slide projector to be turned on. The lights were dimmed and a screen was lowered. Using a pointer he proceeded "Here is an architectural design of how we envision the new downtown area. The plan calls for 350 shops which include room for two large department stores on either side of town. Thirty five of the shops are designated to be restaurants which will undoubtedly serve as magnets for a wave of enthusiastic shoppers. The restaurants will feature a wide variety of dining choices to satisfy the most discriminate tastes. They'll be fast food for the real food lovers among us." He looked at the kids and winked. "We will insist upon conservative storefronts. No gaudy fast food signs will be permitted. We'll maintain a dignified decor - one that will invite shoppers to be comfortable when they spend their money - which, incidentally, we look forward to becoming *our money*." The obligatory laugh was heard.

Doug proceeded to explain, with the help of the slides, suggested store designs that were being reviewed. It was obvious that major construction would be necessary to achieve the kind of look that was depicted in the sketches. "We also plan on building a two story parking facility which will be more than adequate for the kind of traffic we're expecting. There will be no parking on Main Street. Vehicles will be able to drive down Main but they'll be no accommodations for parking on the avenue. And, let me not forget that we have talked to one of the major motion picture chains who are anxious to build a multi-theater complex to exhibit first run movies in the center of town where the old Palmer House used to be." It was obvious that everyone was impressed by the forward-looking Mayor standing in front of them with a plan for improving their town. The smiles on their faces confirmed their approval.

"Let's see if there are any questions before we proceed," Doug volunteered. Several of the present retailers held up their hands to be recognized.

"Mr. Mayor, I'm Jim Bassett. I own the little antique shop down on Main and Prospect. I have to tell you. I think this all sounds just great but, at the same time, it sounds awfully expensive. I mean we're talking about excavation work not to mention the actual cost of erecting new stores in those vacant areas. Mr. Mayor, where's the money coming from?"

Doug was ready for this question. "Yes, there will be costs involved for the town, Jim, but I think we have that pretty well covered. First of all, the incoming retailers will be responsible for the cost of designing the outside of their shops and, of course, equipping the inside. It would be unfair not to tell you that we have already talked to the folks at Macy's, Lord and Taylor, Nordstrom and Nieman Marcus who, after seeing and hearing of the plan, wanted to sign up immediately. To be fair, we'll set up an impartial screening process to determine which of those fine stores will be our neighbors."

"Bill Holtz, Mr. Mayor. Where is our share of the costs coming from? I know we don't have much of a reserve to handle costs of that magnitude. Aren't we putting ourselves in hock to get things going?"

Again, Doug was ready. "Very simply, Bill - no. We talked to Governor Fitzrandolph about our project and he thought it was a splendid idea. He has committed an amount from his Emergency Town Improvement Budget to cover our going-in costs. You might recall that the governor had a bill passed recently that gives him discretionary powers to award incentive funds to towns in the state who can justify a bona fide need for advancing their economy and quality of living in their towns. He felt we certainly qualified on both points."

Doug saw that he was on solid ground in saying, "We are all very confident that this plan can be made operational immediately. The Council and I have agreed that we would not pursue this program unless you, our neighbors, agree that we should go ahead. May I ask with a show of hands how you feel about the project? Please raise your hand if you're with us?" The entire auditorium rose with their hands raised and stormily agreed.

"Thank you, ladies and gentlemen. Thank you for giving us the confidence to proceed with your plan for the future. We're looking at a two year time frame to complete the four projects. Dave Christopher, our chief contractor, tells us that he can do better than that. With his track record, I'm sure we can."

Four color brochures and professionally scripted slide presentations were developed as ammunition for the Committee members to aggressively sell the program to enterprising retailers. One member was heard to say after making several presentations, "Now *that* was an easy sell. These guys had heard about us and were just waiting to sign on." Macy's and Nieman Marcus won the lottery among the four department store contenders and were rewarded with the two plum locations. Forty of the existing retailers remained and three hundred new entries were accepted. The Movieco chain began construction of their new luxury theatre facility immediately upon signing a contract for a long term lease.

The new Recreation Center became a popular meeting place for the young and the old alike. The Senior Center was a tour de force. Senior citizens became actively involved in a wide range of activities. Subjects of interest were taught in classes by eager volunteers. Two of the seniors met at one of the art classes and a year later exchanged "I do's" at the center.

Eighteen months later all four projects proposed by the Mayor's Committee were completed. The revitalization of the downtown area was a huge success.

CHAPTER 8

Two years after the ground breaking ceremony, Old Town's new downtown district was up and running and was described by the Special Projects Editor of the New York Times as socially friendly, aesthetically pleasing and economically vibrant. The Old Town Experience, as the media had romanticized it, attracted shoppers from as far off as New York City to experience something new in the way of suburban retailing. The weekends on the avenue took on a festive mood that attracted tourists who seemed to delight in being able to park their cars and stroll comfortably in an atmosphere of friendly conviviality. Weekend movie goers had to be sure to buy their tickets in advance to assure getting a seat for one of eight motion pictures being presented at the Cineco Luxury Theatre.

The Old Town Experience was a huge success. The tax payers of the town were rewarded when the downtown project succeeded beyond even the most optimistic expectations. Real estate taxes *were* reduced for the homeowners of the town. The savings were not overwhelming but as one long time resident said, "Well, at least the taxes haven't gone up like they've been doing for years."

Business Week magazine sent one of their top editors to do a cover story on the "evolution of a masterful experiment that was the brain child of America's Number One Mayor". The weekly publication was read by the nation's business community and was a favorite source of information for the political establishment across the country. Congratulatory messages inundated Mayor Cromwell's office and were forwarded to Pedro Cruz's office for immediate attention. It had been agreed that every letter was to be answered promptly. A mayor of a small Midwestern town had written a one-line vote of confidence with the comment - "Why the hell didn't I think of that."

Governor Hugh Fitzrandolph called a meeting with his chief political advisor to resolve a situation that, in his words, had gotten so completely out-of-control that it was unmanageable.

"That son-of-a-bitch John Russell is going to put a noose around my political career if we don't do something about him - and fast," said the exploding Governor. "I made him Lieutenant Governor thinking he was going to be of help to us. Help us? He's killing us."

Chandler Wright, his chief advisor, tried to calm him down. "Take it easy, Fitz. We can resolve this."

Fitzrandolph was not to be placated. "Look what he did yesterday. He hit a state senator. The son-of-a-bitch punched a New Jersey state senator in full view of the press corps who was covering that budget meeting. Christ, the media had a field day with that incident. You saw the network and local television coverage last night. They actually caught him on camera slugging that guy. And did you see the local news' headlines this morning. The *USA Today's* screamer was a beauty. *Guv slugs Senator*. They made it sound like I hit him."

Wright said, "I understand he hit Senator Bidwell because he felt slighted by something he said."

Fitzrandolph fumed, "He hit him because our boy was drunk. He was pissed out of his mind. That does it. He's embarrassed this administration for the last time. He's got to go. I won't have him screwing up my chances for reelection next time around."

"You might look on the positive side," Wright said, trying to get the governor out of his funk. "Bidwell *is* a Democrat. It's not as if he punched out a Republican." The governor did not find humor in the comment.

"Okay, Fitz, you're right. He has to be replaced. We'll have to be careful how we handle it, though. We don't want anybody saying we dropped a net over a man with mental problems or was sick and we abandoned him."

"I don't care how we handle it as long as he disappears," Fitzrandolph responded.

Wright was thoughtful, "We have to find someone we can throw in that slot right away. Any suggestions?"

Fitzrandolph took a deep breath and closed his eyes in an attempt to relax. When he opened his eyes and exhaled, he smiled for the first time that morning. "Matter of fact, I do," he said. "What we need is someone the people know and like - someone who will support what we're doing here and who will sit back and play the game. It would be nice, too, if that someone could get us some votes in the next election."

Wright responded, "And that is?"

The governor grinned and said, "Douglas Cromwell, Mayor-elect of Old Town up there in Bergen County. I was talking to the President the other day on the phone. He happened to mention Cromwell and told me he thought highly of the young man. Dewitt Marshall almost never volunteers saying anything complimentary about people unless he's convinced that person is highly capable and competent or is a guy who can get you some votes - or both. In Cromwell's case it's - *or both.*"

Wright was pensive for a moment, "That would be a good choice. Christ, the president has even gone on record before both houses of Congress as supporting him. Cromwell's a genuine hero who's been vaulted into the national consciousness with that stunt he pulled off at that school. He's also done wonders in giving that town a new identity. The media has been calling him *America's Number One Mayor*. Yeah, good choice, Fitz."

The Governor was now smiling broadly. "And guess what? He has Gino Cruz as his mentor. Not a bad guy to have on your team. Yes... yes, Cromwell's our man. Now, how do we approach him?"

Wright was very close to local politics throughout the state. "He has Lloyd Corrigan on his Town Council. He's retired now but he was a major player in the Republican Party when he was active. Let me talk to him. He'll know how to handle it."

Little did the governor's office know that Lloyd Corrigan was a friend of *The Group* and that he would certainly know how to handle this matter. Wright called Corrigan that afternoon. When Corrigan took the call and a voice said, "Mr. Corrigan, this is the Governor's office. Mr. Chandler Wright is calling." Corrigan smiled, knowingly. He was expecting the call. Hadn't he arranged for State Senator Pete Bidwell to deliberately make disparaging remarks about Lieutenant Governor John Russell's wife in full view of a press conference that was taking place? Russell, after his usual liquid lunch, was baited by Bidwell with the whispered comment, "Go ahead and hit me you drunk. Be a man and defend your wife. Take a swing at me."

Russell obliged and in an instant the press had an exclusive first hand story and the political career of a once favored Young Turk came to a screeching halt. Corrigan was also responsible for the President calling the Governor several days before and suggesting that it might be an appropriate time for Fitzrandolph to say some nice things about Cromwell without specifying the reason for the suggestion. The President was a political opportunist at all times with an eye on banking reciprocal favors. He was fondly referred to as the Barter King of Favors.

"Yes, Mr. Wright, this is Lloyd Corrigan. We've had the occasion to meet several times in the past. What can I do for you, sir?"

Wright said, "I remember you well, Lloyd. And, it's Chandler. Only my wife calls me Mr. Wright. Listen, Lloyd, I have to be up in your neck of the woods on Thursday. I was wondering if we can get together and discuss a matter that I think may interest you and the Mayor."

"Of course," Corrigan said. "Will you be available for lunch? We have some great new restaurants in town. We can meet at the Old Town Inn if you're available."

"Perfect. Suppose I meet you there at 12:30?"

"That would be fine. I'll see you then, Chandler."

Corrigan immediately called Douglas Cromwell and advised him of the conversation. "Doug, why don't you make yourself available on Thursday afternoon. Once I have my conversation with Wright, I'll call you and the three of us will get together and resolve what has to be resolved."

Corrigan and Wright met at The Old Town Inn on Thursday afternoon. Wright began, "What I'm going to tell you, Lloyd, must remain between the two of us. We don't want to embarrass the Governor with what I'm about to tell you."

"Of course, Chandler."

"The Governor finds it necessary to relieve the Lieutenant Governor of his duties. He has become somewhat of a political liability so he must be asked to step down. The Governor wants Doug Cromwell to take his place."

Corrigan looked dutifully astonished. "I had no idea that things had reached this stage. We've heard rumors, of course, about his strange behavior but never thought it was this serious."

"Let me call a spade a spade, Lloyd," said Wright. "The man is not doing the Governor any good in that office. He's creating problems that make his position untenable. We want Doug to take over. He'll be perfect for the job."

Corrigan thought for a moment, "I can't disagree with your assessment, Chandler. Doug would make a fine number two man. He's loyal, bright as hell and he's a solid party supporter. And, I might add, he wants to be in the winner's circle. He'd make a nice complement to the Governor. I, of course, can't speak for Doug, but I'll lend my endorsement if you want to discuss it with him."

"By all means," was Wright's immediate response.

"Tell you what. Doug's at home right now. Had some personal business to attend to today. Why don't I give him a call and get him over here. I think we can get his answer this afternoon."

Corrigan excused himself and went to one of the private phones in the manager's office. Doug picked up the phone on the first ring. "Doug, get over here right away. They've taken the bait. He's going to offer you the Lieutenant Governorship just as we planned. Right. See you shortly."

Fifteen minutes later, Doug made his appearance. Corrigan introduced Doug to Wright who could see immediately why this young man was receiving all the favorable attention. He was devilishly handsome, had a commanding presence and, by all accounts, handles himself like a seasoned professional. Wright had a fleeting thought - I hope he's not *too* good.

The three men bandied about small talk for five minutes and then got down to business. They talked for two hours. Wright did most of the talking while Cromwell and Corrigan interjected comments sparingly. Finally, Wright made the formal offer, "Doug, on behalf of the Governor, I would like to offer you the office of Lieutenant Governor of the State of New Jersey."

Doug's response was simply, "Chandler, I gratefully accept with humility and a promise that I will serve the Governor loyally and with dedication to his high office."

They all then shook hands. Wright took his leave and advised the Governor on his car phone that Cromwell had accepted. Cromwell and Corrigan couldn't help but notice that the present Lieutenant Governor's name was never mentioned in their conversation - a telling indication that his political career was at an end. Corrigan remarked, "You know, Doug, we could have found a spot for him somewhere in the administration given that we used him so callously, but his weakness for the booze could have hurt us one day." They both knew that there was a *take-no-prisoner* mentality sharply infused into every aspect of this important project.

Stage one of *The Group's* plan was complete. Douglas Cromwell was now the Lieutenant Governor of the State of New Jersey.

CHAPTER 9

Governor Fitzrandolph called President Dewitt Marshall just as soon as he got word that Doug Cromwell had accepted the Lieutenant Governorship. Fitzrandolph and Marshall had been close friends for many years. They met when Fitzrandolph was a junior senator from New Jersey and Marshall was a newly elected Congressman - also from the Garden State. They were helpmates in the Congress and continued to maintain a close relationship in their more eminent positions in the political arena.

"Dewitt, he's accepted. It worked out perfectly - just as we planned."

The President was pleased. "Ah, that's good news. Good job. Now we can get our ducks in a row for reinforcing your position with those fickle voters."

"I guess I'll never understand how one minute you're king of the hill with the voters and suddenly - because of a change in their mood on one issue - you're king of the dung heap. I honestly didn't expect them to react so badly to that tax bill. After all, the increase was marginal compared to the benefits that we were projecting. Those new filtering plants could have done wonders for the quality of water in the state."

Marshall laughed, "You know as well as I do that no matter what you do to improve the quality of life of your constituency, you're bound to have some negative reaction. It goes with the territory. I must say though Fitz, old boy, you really stepped into it - you got an entire state pissed off at you."

Fitzrandolph was now laughing, too. "Pissed off, big time. They not only rejected the proposal but they've held the damn thing against me to this day. I just hope that your boy can help get those voters back on line or I'll never win that second term election."

The President stifled his light hearted manner and became serious. "I think we can depend on him to get you back on the good side of your recalcitrant tax payers. It's truly amazing how this young man comports himself with people. It's not just that school thing. He has a natural ability to make people comfortable with him and believe what he tells them. They trust him for the simplest of reasons - he's trustworthy. I guess his magic is that *he* believes what he says. He's honest and straight forward. He's also damn smart. Look where he is with that company he works for. He's one of their top guys and he isn't forty yet."

"Reminds me of another fellow I know who actually became President of the United States," said Fitzrandolph.

Marshall thought for a moment then said, "You know, you're right. He does remind me of myself when I was young and trying to get my feet on the first rung of that slippery political ladder. Maybe that's why I like him."

Fitzrandolph smiled and added, "Your idea of letting him be my front man with the voters is a good one. We'll use his charisma to soften my image with them. First thing is to get their negative feelings about that tax increase out of their heads. Once that's done, we can concentrate on having him in the right place at the right time to do whatever is necessary to get me back in this office at election time."

"That's the idea, Fitz. Make him your "go-to" guy. He'll be a big help in a lot of other ways, too. And, you're going to like working with him. He's really a nice young man who, if my political instincts tell me anything, it's that he's going to go far in this crazy world of craziness we chose for ourselves."

"Well, Doug will be in to see me first thing in the morning. I'll keep you updated, Mr. President."

"Good luck, Mr. Governor. We'll talk."

Sharply at 9:00 a. m. the next morning, Doug Cromwell was sitting on a couch in Fitzrandolph's office having a cup of coffee. They immediately seemed to enjoy each other's company. After a suitable fifteen minutes of non-political talk, Fitzrandolph asked Doug to please call him Fitz and proceeded to be completely honest with him about his poor press with New Jersey taxpayers.

"I'll need your help on that score, Doug. We have to get the voters in a positive state of mind about what we're doing for them to make their home state an ideal place to live. I think the many programs we've initiated for our people are progressive and right on the mark for what's needed. If we can get that defunct tax proposal relegated to a zero level of interest in their minds, I think we can convince them that the current administration is doing a credible job. I want you to feel free to do whatever you think will achieve that end. Talk to people, make speeches, come up with ideas you think will work for the people and for us. I *want* to be reelected, Doug, and I'd like your help in achieving that end."

"Be assured, Governor, that I'll dedicate myself to the job." He smiled and added, "And, when you're reelected, I'd like to be at your side as your second term Lieutenant Governor." They both laughed and for the first time since *"that damn tax bill"* was rejected by the voters, Hugh Fitzrandolph had a feeling of calm and assurance that a bright future was again on the horizon.

The new Lieutenant Governor and Lloyd Corrigan were having dinner together to review where they now stood on Doug's climb to the top office in the country. The next several years would determine just how long that journey would take. Corrigan advised that he had talked to Gino Cruz who said that *The Group* was pleased with the way the first step of their plan had progressed. They hadn't anticipated the ease in which things fell into place but, as Gino said, "A little luck is always handy to have around. The Lieutenant Governor's drinking excesses were a blessing in disguise." Gino had no remorse for people who couldn't discipline themselves in the unforgiving world of bureaucratic uncertainty.

Corrigan reminded Doug of their agenda. "Okay, we're now positioned to make things happen. We don't want to rush into anything that will make the Governor suspicious of our motives. We'll go slowly. First thing is to get the voters to rekindle that same warm feeling they had for him as when they put him in office. That shouldn't be difficult. Fitz has been so wary of the backlash of that tax proposal that he never did satisfactorily explain to the electorate the absolute need for those water purification plants. Cruz and Cruz are now putting together a comprehensive report that will provide justification for the tax. It should convince even the most beleaguered of tax payers that the Governor did the right thing. They'll spin off a speech or two from the material and we'll arrange for the Governor to present the facts on one of those Sunday morning political forum television programs. We'll then arrange for you to appear on the same program before he speaks - that way, the television viewers will have a nice friendly feeling for what follows. That will be the first move in establishing your close relationship with the Governor."

Doug smiled at the prospect and said, "After that - and after suitable intervals of time, I'll arrange to make speeches in different parts of the state promoting a list of voter-friendly proposals. Always with the Governor's blessings, of course. I think that the speeches prepared by *The Group* are right on the mark. I'm particularly anxious to see how audiences will react to the complete elimination of tolls on the New Jersey Turnpike."

Corrigan allowed a suggestion of a smile to cross his lips. "That won't be anything compared to the outburst we'll hear from across the river when they find out we're going to press for elimination of those New York City taxes levied against Jersey residents working in the city. That'll be a fight - but win or lose - we'll make points with the Garden State voters for the effort."

"Always remember, Doug - Fitz and Marshall are joined at the hip in political matters - and we need the President. We don't want to do anything that suggests to the Governor that you're after his job. We don't need his office as a next step in getting you into that Washington Merry-Go-Round so let's bend-over-backwards to get him reelected. We're working on something now that should open up the Vice-Presidency in a couple of years. During that time, we have to make sure that the President and the Governor become your number one fans for making you the logical candidate for the job."

Cromwell spent over half of his time during the next year traveling around the state spreading the message that the Fitzrandolph administration was in the forefront of trying to better the lives of its constituency. He took it as a personal challenge to enlighten the voters about the sensitive Water Purification Act that voters rejected in a special election the year before. He knew it had been a pet project of the Governor to get the legislation passed so he was hoping to rekindle a broad scale interest in the bill. If he could get the voters enthused on the positive aspects of the bill, he felt the Governor could again feel good about having put his personal imprimatur on the project; particularly if it could get him back in the good graces of the electorate.

He also set the stage for issues that could be expected to be warmly received by the voters of the state. Once there was a strong indication that the voters were in favor of a particular course of action, the Governor would pick up the gauntlet and run with it. If the voters were lukewarm to an idea or rejected it completely, it was shelved and forgotten. Only voter-friendly measures were pursued. This strategy proved successful time and again.

After persistent lobbying and fence mending by Cromwell, the Water Purification Act was reintroduced and brought back to life in a second special election. This time it won approval by an overwhelming margin. The bill was submitted to the state legislature and passed enthusiastically. Governor Hugh Fitzrandolph was out-of-the-dog-house and back in the good graces of his New Jersey constituency. His poor public relations image became yesterday's news. He accepted the plaudits and reclaimed his image as a staunch champion for substantive public causes. He was not unmindful, though, that it was the aggressive diligence of his Lieutenant Governor that turned the tide for the bill's eventual success while turbo-charging his career at the same time. Cromwell's doggedness was rewarded. The media had discovered a new and attractive politician and *The Group* were provided with the kind of publicity that could not be bought.

Pam St. Pierre was casually chatting with Jim Wilson, head of the NBC-TV News Department, about the day's happenings when a news items about Douglas Cromwell appeared on his muted television screen. He turned up the volume. "He sure is an impressive guy, isn't he?" Wilson said, smiling.

Pam agreed, "He sure is. I covered the school incident that first put him in the limelight. I interviewed him at the hospital. He's certainly gotten some good press since then. We might just see a new headliner on the Washington scene if he continues the way he's been going."

They both stared at each other for several moments. It was St. Pierre who expressed their mutual thought. "What do you think about a follow-up story on him? He's gotten himself on a fast track over there in New Jersey. I've heard rumors that he's being primed for Governor after Fitzrandolph serves another term. Six years from now he could be sitting in Trenton as the number one man. And, let's not forget, he reputed to be the President's protégé."

Cantrell's eyes began blinking rapidly which was a sure sign that an idea had grabbed him. "Listen, I have an idea. We have the Vice-President slated to talk about the administration's plans for the economy in that two part interview we're doing on *Friday Night Wrap-up* in three weeks. Why don't you call Cromwell and see if he'd like to be the lead interview. He can set the stage for Cumming's appearance which, let's face it, isn't going to be the most exciting television fare we've ever put on our dear network. Cromwell will fit in nicely and provide a nice contrast in styles."

St. Pierre smiled at the humorous and apt comparison. "Absolutely. Good idea. I'll get on it first thing in the morning."

Cromwell eagerly agreed to the interview when she called the next morning. "Thank you for asking Ms. St. Pierre. It will be good to see you again."

"Please call me Pam," was her reply.

"Only if you call me Doug."

"Agreed," was her playful response. "The show will be aired in three-weeks so we'd like you to meet with our staff and set things in motion. I'll be doing the interview with you so we can get together at your convenience to discuss the particulars."

He quickly picked up on the offer, "My convenience is for dinner sometime this week if you're available?"

Pam was not expecting the suddenness of his response which brought a smile to her lips. "I'm available tomorrow evening if that's not too soon," was her light hearted response."

"No, that's perfect. May I suggest that we meet at Rudolph's at Park and 54th at 7:00 o'clock?" Rudolph's was the most sought after sophisticated eatery in a town famous for its culinary excellence.

"I'll be there," was her closing remark as she hung up the phone. She thought to herself, what a coincidence. He couldn't have known that Rudolph's is my favorite restaurant. Ah, well, I at least know something about him - he has excellent taste.

But Cromwell *did* know that Rudolph's was Pam St. Pierre's favorite dining spot. It wasn't entirely by chance that the two were brought together. *The Group* had done their homework in their investigation into the life of Pamela St. Pierre. Given her background and influential blood line, they had agreed that she could be useful to their plan.

She was a graduate of the very proper Kensington College where she spent four years sharpening her intellect and social skills before formally entering the ranks of her privileged world. She was also a maverick, a nonconformist, who wanted more from life than just a meaningless existence consisting of afternoon teas at the Plaza and a socially prominent but loveless marriage. Upon graduation, she enrolled in the University of Missouri School of Journalism, reputed to be among the elite of the journalist schools in the country. Her friends considered her actions to be very bourgeois - a middle class act that had no place in their stately world of selectiveness. Pam had no interest in the frivolous life that her friends had chosen. She wanted to be intellectually active and close to what was happening in the world.

Her first priority was to get an entry level job as a cub reporter with *The New York Times.* She felt that getting a junior position with the premier newspaper in the country would allow her to thoroughly learn the basics of the business at her own pace and thus prepare her for her ultimate goal of reporting news at the international level. She talked to her father, a former Congressman, about her plans and he suggested that, if she had her sights on the international desk of the *Times,* she might want to seriously think about spending a couple of years with the Office of the Secretary of State in Washington where she could receive a solid education in foreign affairs.

"The Department of State is the lead U. S. foreign affairs agency in the government and the Secretary is the President's principal foreign policy advisor. Spending a couple of years with State could give you a solid background and valuable insights into the workings of not only our government but others as well." Her father went on to explain that he and the Secretary were old friends. "I know he'd be pleased to bring you into the Department and get you placed in the right spot for maximum exposure to what goes on there."

Two weeks later, Pam began at State as a staff assistant. She learned quickly and advanced to Executive Assistant where she was responsible for the Secretary's official trips both domestic and international. She became an indispensable asset to the President's key cabinet member by keeping his schedule on track during these trips. The contacts she made around the world were to serve her well in the years ahead. Later assignments at State in the Office of Protocol, the Bureau of Intelligence and Research as an analyst to Department policy makers were invaluable to the education she had hoped for. There was a time during her stint at the State Department that she fostered the persistent dream of one day shouldering an important political responsibility.

However, after spending three years at the State Department, Pam decided it was time to take the next step in her career goal. Her credentials with the State Department and her father calling in a favor owed by an indebted former associate got Pam the position with *The New York Times* that she had originally wanted. She had worked hard as a junior reporter until one day, several years later, she saw her opportunity to shed her junior status when the Times' Social Editor dropped dead while leaving the Waldorf Astoria after a Saks Fifth Avenue fashion show luncheon.

The Managing Editor of the paper, Max Kauffman, was beside himself, "I never figured that old battle ax would drop dead on me. She was always too mean to die. We have no backup. Is there anybody around who can fill in for her until we find a replacement?"

Pam had heard the comment and spoke up, "I've done some work with Miss Pearson. I can do that job." She quickly presented her resume to the Managing Editor with particular attention to the fact that her family was a conspicuous member among the wealthiest and socially prominent families of New York's Social Register.

"Sounds good to me," Kauffman said, welcoming his not having to take on a problem involving a department of the paper that had nothing to do with real reporting. "You've got the job. Ah, what's your name?"

"Pamela St. Pierre," she answered, vowing that no one at *The New York Times* would ever again have to ask that question. I'll make sure they know who I am, she promised herself.

Pam was born for success. She had been made Society Editor almost immediately after taking the temporary assignment but soon came to see this type of reporting as a mindless task for mindless readers. She knew that the only way to be thought of seriously in this business was with serious reportorial assignments. It took another five years to establish herself as a dedicated and professional reporter. She was not averse to self-serving divisiveness in making career moves.

Max Kauffman learned to respect her but, when she asked to be assigned to the International Desk, he balked. Kauffman was a bachelor but not one by choice. He was physically unattractive and careless about his personal habits. Matching clothing was a problem for him. He was often seen wearing a black and brown sock at the same time. Some less charitable associates were heard to refer to him as *uncouth and just plain damn ugly*. He was, however, the consummate professional in his responsibilities at the *Times*. Pam saw him as an opportunity.

She invited him to her penthouse apartment on Fifth Avenue for cocktails and supper one evening. He was surprised and flattered by the sudden attention and readily accepted. She plied him with more martinis than he was capable of handling. Pam was careful not to get him too inebriated as she was planning on convincing him to make a decision important to her career that evening. Her wiles proved to be too irresistible for the hapless executive. When he woke up the next morning he realized that he was not in his own bed and he was naked. It looked as if there had been a terrible ruckus in the bed during the night. The sheets were all askew and the blanket was strewn halfway across the bedroom floor. When he turned, he saw the half-clad form of Pamela St. Pierre smiling back at him. She said softly, "That was wonderful, Max. And you won't be sorry that you assigned me to the International Desk. I'll make you proud."

Pam never married – not because of lack of offers – but setting aside the time for a proper courtship was too restrictive to a promising career. Sex was not a stranger to the sophisticated and beautiful Pamela. She enjoyed sex. More than that, it was something she pursued but never on a casual basis. Sex for sex sake was not productive, she reasoned. I want favors in exchange for any favors I provide. That way, there will be pleasure and something tangible to show for my efforts. *The Group* found Ms. St. Pierre's moral standards to be repugnant, but at the same time, they viewed her as a potentially useful pawn in Douglas Cromwell's future.

St. Pierre was not to be denied her success. After several years of news reporting from around the world, she returned to the United States as Chief White House Correspondent. Her reputation abroad followed her and her coverage of the national picture only enhanced that reputation. She enjoyed interviewing people who held commanding powers. As a correspondent who explained international and domestic politics to Americans, she had no equal. Her journalism won her many awards. A unique style and integrity for the facts gave her a reputation as the doyenne of the *New York Times* press corps.

Pam had always missed the vitality of the New York scene. She asked to be reassigned when she felt a sense of completion for the repetitious monotony of reading reports to a television camera on the steps of the Capital. Her wish was granted. Max Kauffman had longed for her return. He had sharpened his ability to handle martinis during the years she was away. He was ready for some interesting action although he was never really sure if he had, in fact, seen action on that memorable night in her apartment. She returned to New York and went back to the *beat reporting* that she had thrived on in her earlier years. It was during that time that the paths of Pamela St. Pierre and Douglas Cromwell had crossed. She was now ready to renew that old acquaintance.

And *The Group* was interested in seeing how the relationship between the two would develop. After all, they reasoned, Douglas Cromwell will need a wife in his quest for the White House.

CHAPTER 10

Friday evening couldn't come soon enough for Pam. What's wrong with me, she wondered. Why am I feeling like a school girl going on her first date? I've got to get hold of myself.

Doug arrived at the restaurant fifteen minutes before the agreed-upon time. He slipped a fifty dollar bill to the maitre'd to make sure that their table was in a non-conspicuous corner of the exclusive Barbizon Room. Pam came directly from her office so she was dressed in a conservative business suit tailored to showcase her ample proportions. Doug tried not to stare at her low cut blouse when they sat down. A tastefully chosen Hermes' scarf provided cover for the swells of her generously-sized breasts which Doug knew would be a distraction for him all evening. Pam saw his momentary glance and felt reassured that they might be talking about more than the interview on this special evening.

Doug opened the conversation as they sipped their cocktails. "I never did thank you for that really nice story you wrote about the Old Town incident. You made me look better than I deserved."

She countered, "I don't think I did you justice. Your selfless act of compassion for other human beings sent a message to all Americans that they should be caring for each other. You set an example for everyone that day, Doug. It was heroism in its purest form."

Doug quickly changed the direction of the conversation, "Thanks, Pam, but let's not talk about me. Tell me about yourself."

Doug listened carefully as Pam related her background. He actually knew more about her than she probably knew or remembered about herself, but he sat spellbound as she told of her childhood years growing up in New York City, as the youngest child of a prominent family. He was further fascinated by her tales as a correspondent for *The New York Times.*

"You've really had a remarkable career, Pam, and it's not over yet. You have an exciting future before you." He would like to have added - and I'd like to share it with you.

"I have no regrets in my life, Doug - except one, maybe."

"And that is?"

She continued, "That I've never met anyone with whom I could share both my exciting moments and the quiet ones. I'd like to settle down one day and stop jumping all over the world. I'd like to share my life with someone for whom I have deep feelings. But... that hasn't happened yet."

Doug's eyes found hers, "It will happen, Pam."

The maitre 'd, as if on cue, politely interrupted and recited Chef Henri's specials in French indicating to Pam that Doug was either a regular patron or someone who was just naturally comfortable with the language. He responded in a relaxed, unstudied manner. Dinner proceeded with a delightful give and take of small talk with moments of both seriousness and humor. When they had finished their meals, Doug suggested an after dinner drink.

Pam said, "I'd love one but, you being the gallant gentleman you are will undoubtedly see me home so let's have it at my place." Doug's face flushed. He readily agreed.

They decided to walk to Pam's apartment as the evening air was brisk and invigorating. They joked and laughed most of the way. It was obvious to other evening strollers that these were two young lovers enjoying each other's company.

The doorman at her Fifth Avenue condo gave them a courteous greeting. He obligingly pressed the *up button* of the penthouse elevator and then went back to his duties. When they were comfortably settled in her apartment, Pam announced, after fixing them both a drink, "I'm going to get comfortable. Here, let me have your jacket. We both look too formal and too unfriendly." Doug had noticed that the living room had automatically become bathed in a sea of soft light when they opened the front door. Low instrumental music simultaneously enveloped the room. Doug wondered if this was a normal occurrence when entering the room or, perhaps, someone had planned the mood-induced greeting.

Doug was enjoying his drink when Pam returned. She *had* made herself comfortable - and then some. She was now wearing a long flowing red satin gown bunched with a gold lame belt that accentuated her slim waist line. The contrast between the red gown and her golden white skin was electrifying. Because of the clinging gown, Doug didn't have to wonder what she was wearing under the gown. What he did see was a tempting glimpse of a long shapely leg that peeked from behind the folds of the gown whenever she moved. He was rewarded with an even more tempting view of her milky white breasts.

Pam was carrying a small photo album when she sat down next to Doug on the oversized couch. Doug asked, "What do we have here family pictures?"

She smiled coyly and said, "What I have here are some photographs of you that were taken at various times after the school incident."

Doug thumbed through the book and recalled seeing these candid shots repeatedly over the last six months. The last photo was one of Pam in a very skimpy two piece bathing suit that left little to the imagination. "I don't remember having worn that outfit in any of my pictures," he said somewhat anxiously.

"Oh, how did that get in there?" Pam laughingly protested.

Doug saw his opening, "What I'd like to see is the original of that picture."

Pam dropped any pretense of coyness and said with a determination he hadn't seen all evening, "That's easy. Follow me." She stood up and proceeded to the stairs leading to her bedroom on the second floor. Her robe dropped to the floor. Following her up the thickly carpeted stairs afforded him with an erotic view of her entire body. She was more beautiful than even his highly stimulated imagination could envision. She turned towards him when they reached the top of the stairs. Her golden skin gleamed. His eyes followed her flat belly up to her taut breasts. As he bent down to kiss her neck, his lips brushed over her hard protruding nipples. He felt himself throbbing with desire. His lust became overwhelming. They were both primed for the encounter that they knew was inevitable. They never reached the bed. They fell to the floor in a passionate frenzy. He kissed her body from her head to the tip of her toes. She kept repeating the words, "Yes, yes - now, now!"

As she arched her back, he knew he was experiencing the most exhilarating feelings a man could feel for a woman. When they had exhausted each other, they both knew that, in that moment, they had fallen inescapably in love. They were quiet for a long time - just staring at each other tenderly with a complete sense of fulfillment. Pam finally broke the silence, "I'm in love with you Doug."

Doug responded, "I've been in love with you since the first time we met."

"We should do something about it, don't you think?" she said.

Low warm words answered. "We will, sweetheart."

Doug then took her for the second time that evening - this time with greater intensity. Pam told him that she had never experienced such complete sensual satisfaction. Her moans and cries of joy left no doubt in Doug's mind that they were meant to be together for the rest of their lives.

That evening was the beginning of a relationship that was to endure and be tested many times during the years they were together. Doug had no doubts that the political uncertainties of his quest for the nation's highest office were to be a challenge for both of them.

They were married on a somewhat dismal spring day after an intense six month relationship at St. Bartholomew Church on Park Avenue in midtown Manhattan. The ceremony and the reception that followed were attended by members of the Social Register and political luminaries from around the country. The President of the United States and his wife made an unprecedented appearance to give the couple a memorable sendoff.

Doug had been living in a comfortable four-bedroom home in Princeton, N. J. after his appointment as Lieutenant Governor. Pam and he enjoyed their suburban lifestyle in the upscale community of one of America's most prestigious universities. Their social life now revolved around their newfound political contacts, old friends and new acquaintances that were becoming legion.

Pam maintained her Fifth Avenue penthouse which provided solitude from the everyday political associations and a base for the many New York social and entertainment diversions they enjoyed. He still maintained his condominium apartment in Old Town as he had a special affection for the town of his political birth. The couple was assured financial security during their lifetime together. Pam and Doug came to the marriage with plenty of money – she from an obscenely large trust fund and he from an aggressively successful investment portfolio that included high performing Sierra Industry stock options awarded to privileged executives of the firm.

They both attacked their separate careers with a renewed vigor and their love for one another was recharged as time went on. Pam introduced Doug to many of her friends and associates in the media world who delighted in being on a first name basis with someone being touted for higher political office by no less than the President of the United States. He made sure that the media had easy access to the Governor particularly if a flattering news story was in the offing for his boss.

Many of the more important and influential were invariably left with Doug's signature offering, "You should meet the President the next time he's in town. Let's see if we can work that out." And it was not just an empty offer. Whenever the President *did* visit the New York area, Doug made sure - always with the President's and Governor's approvals - to invite a select group of media functionaries to an informal cocktail party or social event for personal introductions and warm conversations. Pam's penthouse served as the setting for many of these occasions and her role as hostess added a note of style and sophistication to any occasion.

She was a willing and extremely capable *gal Friday* in helping to frame the political destiny of her husband. These informal occasions also served another purpose. It was Pam's idea that these instances could be used to encourage subtle fund raising appeals among both sympathetic and borderline supporters of the Republican Party line. She started the ball rolling by inviting her well-heeled Social Register friends to meet the President and his wife in more intimate surroundings. The President was delighted with this suggestion and the support of this young and influential couple. He made it a point to nurture their friendship from which a genuine fondness developed between the Marshalls and the Cromwells.

All of the publicity projects developed by *The Group* began to show results almost immediately. With Pam's influential connections, *Time Magazine* and U. *S. News and World Report* spotlighted Doug's picture on their front covers along with supporting story features. *Time* referred to him as "the President's boy" while *U. S. News* concluded their article with the hackneyed line - "keep an eye on this rising star in the political spectrum".

Sunday morning political television shows provided politicians of every ilk with invaluable exposure to voters around the country. *The Group* targeted NBC's Kevin Blessington as their number one choice for Doug Cromwell's initial appearance on network television. Blessington's no-nonsense insightful style of inquiry complemented

Doug's easy going, straight-from the-shoulder responses. Doug made sure to speak glowingly of the Governor and the President on every occasion that presented itself. *The Group* was always cognizant of the need for their support in bringing closure to Douglas Cromwell's journey to the White House.

After serving three years of his first four-year term, Richard Palmer, the Vice-President of the United States suddenly began to show the strains of his daily bouts with the responsibilities of his office. His responses seemed to be less decisive even when dealing with the more mundane issues that presented themselves. It appeared that his every move was a calculated effort. The President viewed his physical deterioration with some alarm at first and with greater concern as his mental attitude began showing signs of aberrant behavior.

The Vice-President was scheduled to chair a meeting in Paris to discuss the use of nuclear weapons as a deterrent to the ever-increasing threat of terrorism around the world. Representatives of the United States' principal allies were to be present. The President had a hard decision to make. He knew that the Vice-President was not up to the demanding tasks that were expected of him. He didn't want to embarrass Palmer, but the country could not be placed in a compromised position by poor representation at so important an international meeting. It was decided that Secretary of State Robert Kildare would replace him at the meeting.

From that day on, Richard Palmer's responsibilities were gradually diminished. After a thorough physical examination, the President's personal physician was frank to say that the Vice-President's condition bewildered him. He reported to the President, "I've never seen such a dramatic change in so robust a person in so short a time. I gave him a complete physical just three months ago that certified his being in excellent health. He's taking no medication that could be suspected of causing such a sharp decline in his health. His blood chemistry was normal and there were no signs of any abnormalities present. I ordered further tests just the other day and nothing - absolutely nothing - could be found that speaks to his problematic behavior.

The President nodded grimly as he weighed his options. "Bob, I have to make a very painful decision. As you know, Richard and his wife have been my personal friends for many years. He's been my right arm through the good and the bad times. Tell me honestly, do you think that his condition will become progressively worse and, if so, will he be able to effectively carry on with his duties during what could become a critical time in the country's history?"

Long was reflective about what he was about to say, "His mood swings are very erratic. I hate to say it but I believe he has become borderline psychotic. I would suggest a complete review of his mental capacities. And to answer your question - no, in his present condition, I am of the opinion that the Vice-President will not be able to effectively perform the duties that will be expected of him in the future; particularly, if something should happen to you."

The President looked at Long with his lips tightened in a thin line. It was a full minute before he spoke, "Let me get back to you, Bob. I have to give this some serious thought."

The President knew the decision before he left his office that evening. Richard Palmer would have to be replaced. The logical replacement would be Bob Kildare, but hell, he told himself, I can't pull him away from his current duties. He's doing an extremely capable job where he is and I don't have anyone to replace him. Besides, American public consensus would be that I'm a complete fool in changing that valuable a horse in midstream. No, he's not the man - too valuable right where he is.

Then a voice within him whispered, Douglas Cromwell, and reverberated in a demanding and uncompromising voice - DOUGLAS CROMWELL.

The President had been fooling himself in considering anybody else for his Vice-President. Of course, it would be Douglas Cromwell. Hadn't he been subconsciously priming young Cromwell for the job ever since Hugh Fitzrandolph had selected him as his Lieutenant Governor? Yes, of course. Three years as Vice President and another four when I'm reelected will fine tune his skills for my job when the time comes. He'll be a young president in the mold of John F. Kennedy. He smiled and added - but this one will be a Republican president. I'll be ready for that Ambassador assignment to the Court of St. James in three years. Julia's an Anglophile. She always liked the English and their country. Or maybe I'll run for one of those senatorial seats? The voters might like to see a former president with a fine record of accomplishment as their junior senator from New Jersey. I could be a powerful force for the party in that job.

All of a sudden, there were no doubts in his mind about Douglas Cromwell becoming his Vice-President. His final thought was for devising a dignified and comfortable way for his old friend Richard Palmer to leave office.

A week later, the President called a press conference at the White House and proudly announced that the Vice-President was stepping down to take on a new cabinet position - Secretary of Administration Communications. His job would be to act as arbiter and coordinator of all communications between the White House, the Congress and the American people.

A smiling Richard Palmer and his wife joined the President and Mrs. Marshall to officially congratulate and thank the Vice President for his years of devoted and loyal service. At the same time, the President announced that, in counsel with his new Secretary, a successor has been chosen and would be announced at a special session of Congress in two weeks when he was due to address both houses on fiscal matters. Vice President Palmer will carry on until his successor is named. In his state of uncertainty, the Vice-President was grateful to his longtime friend for allowing him to gracefully exit the office that he knew he could no longer handle.

No one was surprised to hear that Douglas Cromwell would be the next Vice-President of the United States. Both houses stood and applauded the appointment when it was announced.

The Group met in Washington on the day of the appointment and vowed to provide the former Vice-President with continuous support in his new assignment. As Gino Cruz said to his associates, "That's the least we can do for a man who unwittingly relinquished his office to accommodate our plans. You'll be happy to hear that the mind altering drug he was given will not have any permanent effect on his well-being. Once the drug has run its course, he will be as good as new and with our support, I might add, he will become a key player in the present administration."

Dr. Bob Long, the President's physician, was also rewarded for his help in diagnosing and declaring the Vice-President incapable of carrying on as the President's number two man. A short time later, he was named as a permanent consultant to the prestigious International

Medical Academy. Periodic conferences around the world provided him and his wife with the travel opportunities they weren't able to enjoy being anchored to an office in the White House.

CHAPTER 11

Andrew Davis Stuart was a 56-year old four term U. S. Senator from the state of Alabama who enjoyed the distinction of being the Democratic Party's Minority Leader. He had evolved, after many years of paying his dues, as the official spokesman for his party. His six-foot three-inch broad shouldered frame and his corpulent pouch made him an imposing figure on the floor of the U. S. Senate. His expansive good old boy twang gave him a kindly grandfather demeanor that suggested a man who could be trusted and relied upon to do the right thing even when contending with bipartisan matters.

Outward appearances belied the true measure of the man. In truth, Senator Stuart was, in the words of many Washington insiders, "a snake looking for an opportunity to strike". Thus, among his associates in the Senate, he was lovingly referred to as *The Serpent* and always with a derisive chuckle that spoke to the reality of the man's true character. He had a three chin creased smile which was unbecoming to the dignified mien he tried to project. His solution to this unflattering fault of nature - and an excessive appetite - was not to smile too often. He seemed always to have a malevolent look about him. Some thought this sometimes lack of cordiality to be a sign of a man of serious intentions towards his Senatorial duties. He was an old hand at turning negative impressions into positive appearances.

Senator Stuart was determined to become the Democratic candidate for President of the United States in the next national election. He continually demonstrated a flawless knack for seizing the limelight in the competitive war of political oneupmanship. He was confident that in the next four years he would be able to whittle away at Dewitt Marshall's solid standing with the American public. There were many vulnerable issues on Marshall's plate that were ripe for political assault. He was convinced that Marshall could be brought down with a strong unified party resolve backed by a reasonable amount of political guile and strong financial backing. He hadn't calculated that Douglas Cromwell would be Marshall's Vice-Presidential choice. His advisors felt that Richard Palmer would have been an easier target for the kind of attack dog campaign that they saw would be necessary to unseat Marshall.

Stuart had developed the habit of referring to Cromwell as "that kid" until his supporters reminded him that the new Vice-President represented a formidable vote-getter who must not be underestimated. Given the cavalier attitude of Stuart towards Cromwell, his most senior advisors suggested that the Minority Leader needed an indoctrination as to the past accomplishments and future potential of the young Vice-President.

At first, Stuart dismissed the suggestion with a disdainful wave of his hand, but he thought better of the idea when he heard that Gino Cruz had been working behind the scenes to secure the Vice-Presidency for this relatively unknown national politician. When the facts about Cromwell were revealed, Stuart realized that he hadn't been kept informed of the Republican talent coming up from the ranks. He openly berated his advisors for this oversight. What he now saw was a potentially dangerous adversary who would be likely to repeat as Marshall's running mate four years from now and a likely Presidential candidate in eight years. What he didn't see was *The Group's* timetable for Doug Cromwell becoming President of the U.S. in much less than eight years. His move into the White House was scheduled to happen within the present term of office.

Stuart's admonition to his staff was a challenge expressed with an edge to his voice, "Okay, I've heard the press agent version of the life and times of Douglas Cromwell. Now, let's get down to the nitty gritty.

Royce Bell, one of Stuart's old-time staffers who had earned the right to express his views freely with his boss, said pointedly, "Andy, we don't want to get down and dirty with this guy. We need more than gossip and innuendo to bring him down. He's got a lot going for him. Nobody seems to ever have seen him step over the line or do anything improper, illegal or unethical. He's a national hero who has the confidence of the President and being referred to as his successor. And he's a friend and protégé of Gino Cruz. Christ, let's not forget Cruz's influence here. And let's not forget that he's married to a very influential former *New York Times* correspondent and now one of NBC-TV's top on-camera political personalities. He's got a lot of heavyweights on his side not to mention the Governor of New Jersey who has been kicking the Democratic Party's ass for years. No sir, Andy, this V. P. has to be handled with kid gloves."

Stuart surveyed the mountain of evidence attesting to the righteous character of Cromwell. "Okay, so he's Jesus Christ incarnate. But, no one's perfect. Get me something on the dark side of this character's life. He can't be *all* Mr. goody-too-shoes, can he? Come on, boys. You know what we're looking for. Who's been paying him off for whatever reason? Who's he screwing behind his wife's back? Get me something I can use against this bird. Let's delve into his past and see what we can dredge up. There's got to be something there we can use."

Bell said, rubbing his hands together nervously, "I tell you, Andy. The guy looks clean. Between us, I have to tell you – he appears to be one hell of a guy."

Stuart said, angrily, "Bullshit. Don't give me that nice guy stuff. If a group of good-old-boys can't outsmart a bunch of Yankees, then you ought to be ashamed of yourselves. Get out there and get me something juicy."

The die was cast. Douglas Cromwell's life was in for close scrutiny by a group of experienced muckrakers. Paul Levine, a legal counsel on Chairman Stuart's important Subversive Activities Committee was unofficially assigned the task of finding anything compromising in Cromwell's past to discredit the Vice-President. Levine was also advised that creative ways of maligning the Vice-President's character and credibility would be looked upon favorably by the senior Senator from Alabama. Levine employed the services of two professional private detectives who immediately put out feelers to get the ball rolling. Gino Cruz became aware of the undercover activity instantly and put in motion an order to discourage this counter productive exercise.

Two days later, Levine reported to Senator Stuart that his two undercover agents were seriously hurt in an automobile accident on I-95 the night before. He said they were blind sided getting off the highway from a ramp exit and that witnesses reported that it looked like a deliberate attempt to drive them off the road. Stuart's antenna went up. He instinctively knew that Douglas Cromwell had a past that someone wanted kept secret. The Senator also intuitively assigned the name Gino Cruz to his file of likely suspects.

Well, well, well, he thought. So those boys want to play hardball. Mr. Cruz best watch his ass if he thinks I'm going to lie down for him. He knows well enough not to think that. Unfortunately, Stuart's thoughts were simply bravado on his part. Whenever he came head to head with Cruz, he came out second best - repeatedly.

Cruz saw that Senator Stuart's bid for the Presidency was nothing more than a side show. But, he reasoned, it could be a time-consuming nuisance. Cruz said with a hint of venom, "Let's catch this fool before he gets any grandiose ideas about damaging Cromwell's reputation with his amateur attempts at character assassination. Here's what we'll do." He then went on to explain how they would diffuse the Senator's superficial crusade to derail their plans.

Stuart had put the machinery in motion to investigate the life of Douglas Cromwell in anticipation that something incriminating would turn up. The initial report was conspicuously lacking in anything suggesting a misspent way of life or even the hint of a moral stumble along the way. The language of the report was factual and laudable when speaking of his character and lifestyle. It seemed that he had dedicated himself early in his life to simply being a caring human being. He was ambitious and sometimes self-serving but who the hell wasn't, Stuart said to Paul Levine.

Stuart was about to dismiss the report as being useless when something in the report caught his eye.

> *Mother - Maria Cromwell nee Sierra. Born Havana, Cuba, February 2, 1939. Daughter of Alberto Sierra - 1899-1959 - Chief Executive Officer, Sierra Holding Co., (diversified corporate holdings). Fidel Castro nationalized several Sierra businesses in 1959 after allegedly murdering Sierra shortly after the takeover.*

Senator Stuart prided himself on having a photographic memory. When he saw the name Sierra, it immediately sparked a responsive association. He thought for a minute and then said to Bell, "Cromwell Advertising. Didn't they handle the advertising for many of the Sierra businesses?"

Bell smiled at the rhetorical question, "Beats me, but we must have that information somewhere in the building. Let me make a call. Bell made his call, asked the question and waited. A minute later, he hung up the phone and smiled at his boss. "Right, Cromwell Advertising handles *all* of Sierra's business.

Facts began clicking off in Stuart's mind. "And if memory serves me correctly, the Sierras are pretty tight with Gino Cruz." Stuart's recall started working on overdrive. "Matter of fact, Cruz was Sierra's legal counsel, wasn't he?"

Bell looked confused, "So what's that got to do with what we're after?"

Stuart found himself becoming energized, "I don't know but let's look at what we have. Sierra Industries. Gino Cruz. Cromwell Advertising. Douglas Cromwell. We can't seem to pin anything on the kid so maybe there's something in this cast of characters that will lead us to something that can be damaging to our young friend."

Bell interjected, "I wish you'd stop calling him 'the kid'. It makes it seem like you're not taking him seriously."

Stuart ignored the rebuke. "Let's face it," he said, "the Sierras haven't always been on the up-and-up building that empire of theirs. And, need I say that bad things start happening when Gino Cruz is in the neighborhood. David Cromwell's relationship with the Sierras and possibly Cruz is something worth thinking about, too."

Bell looked doubtful, "My gut feeling is that we'll hit a dead end trying to tie all these characters together. It's a long shot but, I've been wrong before."

Stuart was persistent, "A long shot? Maybe, but let's take a harder look."

Bell had Levine do a comprehensive search into the Sierra-Cruz-Cromwell connection and what was discovered was revealing on several levels. Cruz's law firm still represented the family's large business conglomerate Sierra Industries. Juan Sierra was now Chief Operating Officer of the company and his contact at the law firm was Gino's son Pedro. Pedro was David Cromwell's best friend going back to their days in Cuba. Bell said that there was nothing strange about that as Cromwell Advertising is the agency of record for all Sierra's advertising and promotion; however, when a check was made of Cromwell's airline travel records, they showed a regular schedule of trips from Chicago to Washington which were arranged through

Cruz's office. Hotel reservations were also handled and paid for by Cruz.

Stuart said, "They're not just talking advertising. Cruz has no interest or involvement in the company's marketing operation. Might be interesting to see what they're talking about."

Cruz had friendly ears all over Washington. He was advised by an informant in Stuart's office that the Senator had someone prying into his business and that of the Sierras and Cromwells. Cruz said, "I don't know what he's up to but no more pussyfooting around. Tell Carmine Cato I want to see him - the usual place."

Cato was a contract enforcer who specialized in killing people for money. He was a sullen, dangerous-looking man with hardened features and a penchant for hurting people. He enjoyed delivering pain. The following day the two men met at a secret location in Georgetown. Each left separately fifteen minutes apart when their business was done.

Several evenings later, a stranger came to the Stuart residence on the evening that Mrs. Stuart regularly played bridge at their country club. Their servant had the night off which the stranger knew to be the case. The man slipped on a black hooded mask just before he rang the bell. A revolver with a silencer attachment was firmly position in his right hand. When the Senator opened the door, the man - without saying a word - punched him and let him fall backwards to the floor. The stranger reached down and grabbed him by the neck while at the same time kicking the door shut.

He then said calmly but menacingly, "Senator, you listen and you listen good. This investigation you're conducting with Levine... it stops right now. Do not continue this witch hunt or I'll kill you." He then gave Stuart a sharp slap in the face to emphasize his threat. "Make no mistake. I will kill you and your wife if you don't take this seriously."

Stuart was paralyzed with fear. He could only stammer, "I... I...I understand. Please don't hurt us."

"I want to hear you say you understand what I have just said," the man said.

Stuart raised his arms protectively, "I do. I do understand. We'll stop. I promise."

The man's final words were said with a menacing finality, "Don't make me kill you. Just stop what you're doing and you and your wife will be safe." The masked stranger then gave Stuart a sharp kick in the leg leaving a bruise the color of midnight. He then disappeared into the night.

Stuart stayed on the floor for the next ten minutes. His head moved slowly from side to side trying to understand why this was happening to him. He had been frightened into a state of numbness. When he lifted himself from the floor, he knew that he had to talk to Royce Bell who was sitting in Stuart's den a half hour after receiving the Senator's panicked telephone call. Stuart nervously described the unwelcome visit.

"Christ, Andy, we've got to back off this Cromwell thing right now. If Cruz is involved - and you can bet your ass he is - he'll have it done. He *will* have you killed."

Stuart was outraged, "What kind of society is it we're living in when some psycho can come to your door and threaten your life - and you can't do anything about it. I'm as United States Senator, for chrissakes."

Bell looked at his friend and said, "It's a society that we created for ourselves. It's imperfect, for sure, but, in this case, we have to be realists. That crazy son-of-a-bitch will do it. Let's drop this hot potato right now."

Stuart was a man who was defined by the Vietnam War. He had seen his share of killing and wanted no more of it - particularly since this one would be of a personal nature. He swallowed his pride along with a clot of dried blood that had accumulated on the inside of his mouth from the blow. He shook his head and said, "You're right, of course. But what's this incident tell us? It tells us that Cruz is up to something involving Sierra and Cromwell and they don't want the world to know what that is."

"Whatever it is, it's not worth getting you killed for. Let me think about this and see if we can't come up with some way of getting answers without getting ourselves directly involved."

Stuart had the last word, "For chrissakes, I'm a United States Senator."

CHAPTER 12

Senator Stuart called off his prying wolves but he was not about to forget the threat to his life even though he was beginning to think the warning was just a bluff. On the other hand, that shot in the mouth was not a bluff and it gave him cause to be wary of reacting in too cavalier a way towards the situation. For now, discretion would have to be the better part of valor. He wasn't about to get himself killed by acting foolishly when he knew he could achieve what he wanted by more reasonable means. *Subterfuge* and *deceit* were honored words in the political lexicon and were faithful companions to the wily Stuart. For now though, the Cruz message was loud and clear. Hands off.

An excited Royce Bell barged into Stuart's office a week after the Senator was attacked in his home. He looked around before speaking, "Andy, I woke up at 3:00 o'clock this morning with a great idea as to how we can get Cruz out of our face. If we're going to try and get something on Cromwell - or at least Cruz and the Sierras - we're going to have to get somebody other than our people to unlock what needs unlocking. Right?"

"Right," said Stuart, not sure of what he was agreeing to.

"Okay, so what we need is to get somebody close to Cromwell to do the leg work for us." Stuart was listening intently. Bell continued, "Suppose, just suppose we were able to get someone very close to Cromwell to look into his past. Let's say that *that* someone was asked to do a story on the life and times of Douglas Cromwell for one of the leading television networks. You know, for one of their news magazine programs. It would be a very comprehensive series that would let the American public get to know him on both a professional and personal level. In the bargain, we would get to know our friend a lot better and, importantly, his connection with Cruz and company. Everything above board, mind you. Just a subtle way of getting any hidden information that might be lurking in the Vice-President's past."

Stuart immediately picked up on where Bell was going with his tale. "You mean his wife."

"Right. She's one of NBC's top investigative reporters with a reputation for doing everything by the book? No yellow journalism - just the straight unadulterated facts when reporting a story."

"She's all of that but how do you plan on getting her involved?" asked Stuart.

"You might remember that Bob Cantrell is my brother-in-law. He's been the head guy of the NBC Television News Bureau here in Washington for a number of years. Bob owes me a couple of favors not the least of which is that I bankrolled his mortgage when he bought that big house in Georgetown. My sister never lets him forget that little favor. We can get him to talk Pam into doing the story. She trusts his judgment. He's given her story assignments in the past that have worked out well for her."

"What's to prevent Pam from suppressing anything that she feels will be damaging to him? After all, they *are* married and she's not about to report anything that will compromise him."

"All we're trying to do is find whether there is any association between Cromwell and anyone who might have dealt from the bottom of the deck in their careers. We're not asking her to do an in-depth investigation of these characters - just a straight forward and seemingly innocent reporting of the facts. As for her discussing her assignment with her husband, Cantrell will simply tell her not to do that as NBC doesn't want any bias affecting her objectivity. Like I say, she trusts him implicitly. She's been around long enough to know that truth about impersonal journalism."

Stuart was cautious, "Sounds risky. We don't want anything to come back and bite us on the ass."

"He'll be very discreet. We can confide in him. We can start off by telling him that there just might be a major story in it for him. He'd sell his soul for a political scoop."

"Even if you can work it out, what happens if she discovers something that could be a liability to her guy? What then? She'll just walk away from that part of the story."

"If that happens, we'll at least get to know what it is they don't want us to know. She'll confide in Cantrell with whatever she finds. That's the way they work. But, again, all we're looking for are associations or connections between Cromwell and anyone else. She doesn't know what we're looking for. She'll be reporting the facts as she sees them. Once we uncover anything, we'll let someone from out-of-the-Washington circle do the digging for the specifics. And when we do uncover anything, we'll break the story in one of the New York newspapers and let them take the heat for disrupting the President's plans."

"We'd better be right about this death threat being a bluff. It's my ass that'll be on-the-line. Chrissakes, I'm a U. S..."

"I know," Bell chuckled, "you're a U. S. Senator. I guess this is what they mean when they say that politics is a dirty business."

Bob Cantrell asked Pam to join him for lunch to discuss an idea that he was sure would interest her. They met at the Watergate Hotel for lunch and he broached the subject after a short interval of small talk. "You know, that husband of yours is really starting to make a name for himself in his new job."

Pam agreed, "I'll tell you, Bob, I think he has the horsepower to go all the way to the top. Three years as the number two guy and another four when the president is reelected, will put him in the running for Marshall's job at the end of the two terms."

Cantrell was encouraging, "At the end of that time, he'll know more about the office of the presidency than any vice-president before him. And, I might add, Pamela St. Pierre Cromwell is quite a queenly name for a First Lady."

Pam dismissed the remark with a wave of her hand, "Are you trying to get rid of me?"

"That would be impossible," he said with a grin. "But, you know, we could be a big help to him down the road with appearances on some of our public service shows. We could start him off with a fifteen minute interview with Gail James on her Wednesday evening show. We'd then follow up with *This Week in Washington.* I'll tell you, we really hit the jackpot when we brought Winfield Cody in from the field to host the show. He's taken it right to the top of the rating charts opposite the other network political programming. Doug's session with Cody could be discussions of the President's programs - you know - make the American public aware of everything Marshall is doing to move his agenda forward. Let's face it; politicians have a way of targeting issues without really making much sense of them to the electorate. I'm not talking about Doug, of course. He could be the voice of reason in making us all understand that political mumbo jumbo we're bombarded with."

"Hey, that's not bad. Douglas Cromwell - *America's Voice of Reason.* We can use that," was Pam's quick take on the catch phrase.

"Let's face it, Doug would be the ideal spokesman for the administration. It could be a great opportunity for him. I have to believe that Marshall would be eager for his vice-president to take such an important leadership role"

"Of course, he would - they both would," Pam answered. "They'll do whatever is necessary to further the president's programs. And frankly, Doug and I have never really talked about what will happen eight years from now but sometimes I catch him staring into space and I just know where his thoughts are."

"And where are they?"

"Sharply focused on the warmth of the Oval Office."

"Okay," said Cantrell, let me put a tentative schedule together and talk to Doug. What we'll need from you is a background study of him. It'll have to be objective as we don't want anybody coming back and telling us something about Doug that is damaging to his image. Won't happen but you know those NBC Continuity guys. They're sticklers for making sure of the facts about anyone appearing on their network."

"That'll be no problem. Doug's life is an open book."

"Of course. And seeing that our network's need-to-know policies are so exacting, let's be sure of our footing before we drop it in their laps. Why not make a list of the people that you know Doug has had dealings with over the years. It'll be helpful to our moderators and show hosts in framing discussion points. I don't mean the butcher or the baker. Mostly people who are in the political news like fellow politicians, lobbyists, state and local types - you know - anybody who can shed some light on Doug's views on things important to the country. And, oh yeah, if he knows the New York Yankees' Derek Jeter, maybe he can introduce me to him."

"Matter of fact, he does know Jeter. He hates him. Doug's a White Sox fan." They both laughed and Pam said, "I get the picture. I can get that list together rather quickly. I won't bother to tell Doug. We don't want him to think he's up against a new Gestapo."

Cantrell agreed, "That makes sense." They concluded their meeting with Cantrell wondering why one of the brightest talents in television never thought to question a policy that obviously had no basis in fact. Even if one of their subjects did have something unfavorable lurking in their background, the network would welcome such a flawed guest. After all, controversy and exposing dark moments in a person's life are their stock in trade. Pam probably never thought of the inappropriateness of the request as she undoubtedly feels that her husband has an untarnished past.

Pam said, "I'll get things moving before I leave for Miami on Monday morning. I'm just finishing up that feature *Cubans in Miami* for next Tuesday's *Week in Review Show.* I want to get an interview with Mayor Cadilla whose been kicking up a storm again on his favorite hate subject - Fidel Castro. I'll be back as soon as I get the interview."

"Poor Fidel," said Cantrell, "nobody seems to love him. Okay, see you during the week."

Cantrell met with Cromwell and explained the plan to have him represent the administration on the NBC-Television Network. Cantrell made sure to cover himself by saying that they were putting together a resume of his background for the network's clearance group. Cromwell responded, "Let me get back to you, Bob. Being new at this, I'll want to check it out to make sure I'm not stepping on anybody's toes."

Cromwell brought the proposal to the attention of *The Group* before he spoke to the President. The President's approval would be mandatory, but Gino Cruz and the others would have to first agree. Gino's response was to the point, "A capital idea. Let's do it."

CHAPTER 13

Pam Cromwell knew that gathering background information on her husband was just a formality necessary only to satisfy the network's need-to-know policies. These procedural rules were always a mystery and a gigantic waste of time to staff members of the News Department. Their attitude was that the *suits* want it so let's just do it and get it out of the way. Such was the mindset of Pam when she began her research into Douglas Cromwell's past.

For three of the years that Pam was a student at the University of Missouri, she took on assignments as a freelance researcher and analyst for a private research firm. She knew that the career she had mapped out for herself as a reporter would require an understanding of the fact-finding techniques necessary to develop and present credible stories. She worked at honing these skills and after several years of due diligence, became recognized as a gifted researcher.

Later in life, she gained a reputation of someone whose commentaries were never doubted as she made sure that her facts were always well-grounded. She attributed this flattering comment to her early research experience while at college and later at the State Department. She was particularly skillful at unearthing carefully hidden facts that were thought to be beyond recovery. She had the uncanny knack of being able to draw people out into revealing conversations.

Pam allowed herself a week to research Doug's past and to write a report which she submitted to Bob Cantrell who glanced at it then tossed it on his cluttered desk. His disinterested manner suggested to Pam that, indeed, this was just something for the network files. Once she left his office, Cantrell retrieved the file and began reading it.

Cantrell could find nothing of interest in the parochial language of the report. He handed the document over to Royce Bell at Senator Stuart's office and forgot about it. Bell had a sensitive nose for flushing out any inconsistencies that appeared to be meaningless by themselves but could take on a significance when linked with other relevant facts.

The report provided the demographic history of the forty-five year old Vice-President including a detailed medical record of his health which was confirmed in one word - excellent. His educational background was concisely laid out to include his undergraduate and post-graduate degrees from the University of Chicago. His career progression at Lucas Industries showed a chronology of well-deserved promotions and highly positive performance reports. The highlight of the report was the heroic deed that he performed in Old Town, N. J. that first brought him into the public eye.

Bell read each and every point in the report looking for anything that suggested any inconsistencies in the young man's life. One of the entries disturbed Bell's orderly mind only because it appeared to be a misplaced listing. He wondered why the listing *imm. inoculation - 97751002* was listed separately when to his mind *immunization inoculation* should have been reported in the medical section of the report. Bell mentioned the discrepancy to Frank Fleming, the aide overseeing that the report was polished before sending it on to Senator Stuart.

"Boss, you're not reading that listing correctly. *Imm. inoculation* isn't a medical designation - it's *immigration inoculation.* We were thrown off too when we saw that listing sitting alone without an explanation of any kind. When we discovered that the word was *immigration,* we checked his birth certificate to see where he was born, and found that he was born in Chicago on January 10, 1952. That inoculation was given to him two days before that date in Havana, Cuba. Just doesn't make sense, does it?"

"No, it doesn't," said a confused Bell who added facetiously, "What in the world was he doing in Cuba two days before he was born in Chicago? That Cuba thing could be some kind of a mistake." Bell thought for a moment and said, "Tell you what, let's do this. Get in touch with Pat Moran over at Immigration Services. He's one of our friends. Just tell him who you are and ask him to check out that serial number in the listing. If there's anything, that number should tell us who received that inoculation. And, tell Pat that we need that information in a hurry."

Less than a half hour later, Moran called Fleming and announced, "That inoculation was given to an anonymous baby boy on the date in question. Not much more information in the inoculation report. Oh, yeah, there's a guardian signature on the form - Alberto Sierra."

Unknown to Senator Stuart, his conversations in his four room office suite were being unofficially monitored when *the Group* learned that he was a potential threat to their operation. His phones were *bugged*, too. It was through this constant surveillance that they learned that Stuart was privy to the potentially damaging information about Sierra. Gino Cruz couldn't understand why his friend Alberto had allowed his name to be associated with that immigration report. Sierra had taken great care to assure that he was not identified as being the father of the boy. He had made arrangements for his infant son to be raised in the U. S. by a close associate and friend. He even had the boy's birth certificate falsified and recorded as a legitimate birth in the state of Illinois. Certainly, the boy had to be inoculated before leaving Cuba and entering the U. S., but why did Alberto allow his name to be recorded?

Pedro Cruz came to Alberto's defense. "You must remember, Gino, we hadn't at that time made any commitments to each other regarding Douglas' future. It was an understandable oversight."

Gino merely grunted his acquiescence, "What's done is done. It's time for damage control. According to Bell, three people know of this situation - Stuart, Bell and their man Fleming. They must be neutralized immediately. There's too much at stake to ignore their delving any deeper into our business.

Pedro said, "This could derail our entire plans if..."

Gino interrupted, "Nothing is going to interfere with our plans. Here's what we're going to do." Pedro listened carefully without saying a word.

That evening, Senator Peter Harris of New York personally called Frank Fleming at his home. "Frank, this is Pete Harris. How are you?"

Fleming was not only surprised that Harris called him directly but that he called him at his home. "I'm fine, Senator, thank you."

"Tell you why I'm calling, Frank. I've heard some good things about you and I've got an important position to fill here in my office. I was wondering if you might be interested in talking to me."

Fleming was rendered speechless for a moment. He knew Harris to be a ranking member of the Republican party and very influential in the halls of Congress. He was also a close personal friend of the President. Fleming's immediate thought was that he had always been a lukewarm Democrat so it wouldn't be a major compromise for him to rethink his party loyalties. He responded enthusiastically, "Why, I'd be delighted to meet with you, Senator."

"Good, Frank. Suppose I have my car pick you up in front of the Lincoln Memorial at 11:00 tomorrow morning. No sense letting anybody know we're talking in case you decide not to join us."

"No worry about anyone learning of our meeting, Senator. Senator Stuart and Royce Bell are scheduled to leave by private jet for a conference in Kansas City this evening. They'll be gone for five days."

"That *will* be convenient, Frank. See you tomorrow."

"Until tomorrow, Senator."

When the two men met the following morning, Senator Harris outlined the position he had in mind for Fleming. "Frank, we had you checked out carefully before deciding to ask you to join us. You came up with high marks. We found that you're a dedicated associate whose loyalty is unquestionable. That's important to us, Frank. All of our people know that maintaining a trust in one another is the reason that this administration has been the fine-tuned working unit it is. We must have your assurance that you could work within that framework. Confidentiality is important to all of us. Incidentally, the starting salary is $200,000 a year, a generous expense account and all of the usual government perks.

Fleming didn't need a stone wall to fall on him to understand the implications of Harris's words, "Absolutely, Senator. I assure you that at no time will you ever have reason to question my dedication or my loyalty to yourself or the President."

"That's what I wanted to hear. I see grand things ahead for you, my boy. Welcome aboard."

They parted after lunch and Fleming was driven back to his office near the Capital Building. Senator Harris speed dialed a number in Washington. "It's done," was all he said and hung up.

Frank Fleming had been neutralized.

Senator Stuart and Royce Bell flew out of Dulles Airport in a private jet the following morning. Both men were encouraged by the news that there appeared to be something in Douglas Cromwell's background that could disrupt the Vice-President's seemingly tranquil life. They discussed their participation in the forthcoming meeting they'd be attending in Kansas City during the next several days in which the Senator was to be the keynote speaker at the conference-ending banquet. They were enjoying an early morning drink about two hours into the flight when the captain excitedly requested that they buckle their seat belts. The plane began lurching from side to side. Suddenly, the left engine sputtered and stopped completely. Moments later the right engine stopped and flames appeared around the mounting. The pilot tried desperately to put the plane in a glide position but the nose of the plane refused to stay level and the aircraft plunged in an uncontrollable dive straight into a wheat field just north of St. Louis, Missouri.

The Senator's last utterance on earth was not the words he would have chosen for inscription on his tombstone. "We're screwed."

Washington was shocked to learn that the Democratic Party's presidential torchbearer had died in a Midwest plane disaster along with his chief of staff. No one survived the ill-fated tragedy. A ceremony honoring the memory of Andrew Davis Stuart was held at the Washington National Cathedral several days after the crash. The service was attended by every political luminary of consequence in the nation's capital.

President Marshall had never been more insincere about a statement of condolence as when he said in tribute to the adversarial Senator, "Senator Stuart was a leader who helped shaped the U. S. in becoming a world leader. Let's remember him as our inspiration and friend. His efforts will live on and will serve as our compass in the years ahead."

The truth was that the President thought of him as a pompous, self-serving dinosaur who had no business being part of the American ruling class. Marshall was completely unaware as to the actual circumstances of the Senator's demise.

Gino Cruz's only comment on hearing of the Senator's death was, "It looks like our Democrat friends will need another candidate."

While he had only a marginal chance of ousting Dewitt Marshall in the next election, Democrats were depending on Stuart's candidacy to at least influence votes for a number of Democratic senatorial and congressional candidates in important swing states. Now the party had no one to compete against the Marshall-Cromwell ticket that was a cinch to win the next national election.

CHAPTER 14

Pam Marshall was having breakfast alone at her home in Washington when a special messenger delivered a letter. When she opened it she found a message that cryptically stated in bold letters - *IMM. INOCULATION #97751002 - Immigration Service at (203)-473-9000 can provide details.* Pam was confused as the letter was unsigned and the messenger was unable to provide the name of the sender. She had no way of knowing that the note came from Bob Cantrell's office. It was his way of telling her that there was something in her husband's past.

She recognized the inoculation number as being the same notation that had appeared in the background report she had prepared for NBC. Pam had a contact at Immigration whom she could rely on for information of a confidential nature. A phone call found him at his desk and fifteen minutes later, Pam had the information she was looking for.

How could Doug have received an inoculation in Cuba two days before he was reportedly born in Chicago, she wondered. His birthday was etched in her mind so she was thoroughly confused by the inconsistency. What in the world was he doing in Cuba in the first place - if he was there at all, she reflected. She would ask Doug about it when she saw him later that evening; however, the troublesome thought persisted. Why wouldn't he have mentioned Cuba to me before? It's probably just some silly mistake. But then again, she thought, let me do a little more checking before I talk to him about it.

Pam's trip to Miami was planned for the next day. She landed at Miami International Airport and was met by Deputy Mayor Maria Sanchez. "Welcome Mrs. Marshall," she said as she introduced herself. Maria Sanchez was an attractive forty-two year old of medium height and dressed stylishly to complement a trim figure that suggested a regimented life style including regular visits to a local fitness center. She and Pam enjoyed a casual chat while they were being chauffeured to the Mayor's downtown office where the local NBC-TV crew had already set up their recording equipment. They had a short meeting with the Mayor to discuss the logistics of the taping session after which Pam and the Mayor prepared for the interview. Pam knew that Cadilla was an outspoken critic of the Castro regime so she directed her attention to that issue.

The Mayor said that he had left Cuba when he was still an infant. "My father never had a chance to leave his beloved Cuba. He was murdered by Fidel Castro and his cutthroats before he could leave the island. His childhood schoolmate Alberto Sierra was also murdered by Castro. Fortunately, our fathers made sure that their families left Cuba safely before all the butchery occurred." Pam momentarily took her eyes from her notes when the Mayor mentioned the name Sierra. That was the name she uncovered on the immigration report. She made a mental note to ask him about the Sierras when the interview was completed.

Pam changed the subject and encouraged Cadilla to talk about the life that his fellow displaced Cubans had made for themselves since coming to Miami. The Mayor spoke eloquently about the determination and sacrifices that families had made in the past forty years in finding a new life for themselves in America. He added that many Cuban-Americans still dreamt of the day when they could return to their native land after the oppressive Communist regime was overthrown and freedom was introduced to their country. He was confident that this change would occur in his lifetime.

When the interview was completed, Pam asked him about his family and particularly their time in Cuba. She learned that both the senior Cadilla and Sierra were, at one time, very important and influential men in Cuba. Both had their business and personal property nationalized when the new government came into power. Another of their close associates and friend Gino Cruz had wisely left Cuba a year before the revolution. The three were so close socially and in their business dealings that they were referred to in very respectable terms as *The Group.*

"They were something to behold, I'm told," Cadilla offered. "They not only controlled much of the commerce in Cuba but they exerted political influence that served to place their indelible mark of power on every major piece of legislation of that era."

Pam said, "You mentioned Gino Cruz. From what I know of him, he is still a very formidable political lobbyist in Washington."

"He and his son Pedro maintain a highly successful law firm in Washington," said the Mayor not wanting to volunteer information for which he might be criticized later on. "I know nothing of them being lobbyists. I have met Pedro several times and he is cut from the same bolt of cloth as the senior Cruz. They are both very bright and knowledgeable and very - what shall I say - committed when they get their teeth into a project. It is said that they can be quite aggressive at times with those who take an adversarial position in testing the resolve of those commitments. He's consumed with a hatred for Castro and what he did to my father, Sierra and his fellow countrymen."

When they parted, the Mayor asked Pam to give his regards to the Vice-President. "I look forward to meeting him one day soon."

"I'm sure you'll both enjoy that meeting," Pam said.

Pam and Maria Sanchez had a late lunch as Pam's flight was not scheduled to leave until 7:00 p. m. Pam used the time to ask the Mayor's aide about the Cadilla and Sierra families. She was particularly interested in the Sierras but didn't want to appear too obvious by focusing the discussion entirely on them.

Maria said, "They were both close families. There were a number of offspring in both families which both Alberto and the Mayor's father took great pains to raise in a way befitting such prominent families." Maria's first martini put her in a warm and chatty mood which prompted her to unintentionally reveal something that caught Pam by surprise. "Yes, they were very close families. The children were treated almost like royalty by their parents. It's rumored that Alberto had fathered an illegitimate son a year or so before he was murdered and went to great pains to assure that the child was adopted and raised by a close friend in the United States. They say that he could have put the child in an orphanage, but Alberto wanted him to be brought up by someone whom he knew would give the boy the kind of life he would have wanted for one of his own children. But, that of course, was impossible. Alberto could never bring an illegitimate child into his family.

Pam asked off handily, "Oh, where was he brought up?"

Maria thought for a moment, "I don't know but I think it was somewhere in the Midwestern part of the United States.

Pam's heart sank, "And whatever happened to that child?"

"Nobody seems to know anything more about the boy. At least I've never heard anything. He just left the island and I guess is living comfortably somewhere in America." Maria suddenly appeared as if she had revealed something she really never meant to reveal. She smiled self-consciously and added, "Truth of the matter is that I don't even know if the rumor is true."

After her second martini, Maria said something that further piqued Pam's curiosity. "Fidel probably knows the truth of the young man's whereabouts. I should ask him about it." She then quickly added, "That is, if I should ever meet him again."

Pam asked, "Oh, you've met him before?"

Maria became very uncomfortable. She ended the conversation abruptly, "Oh, everybody seems to have met Fidel Castro at one time or another. He is a very visible presence with the people of Cuba."

After lunch, Pam was driven back to the airport for a flight back to New York. Her parting thought when she was comfortably settled in her first class accommodations was, could it be? could that boy be...? She found it difficult to even mouth the name she was thinking. And what was that vodka-induced conversation all about? Maria Sanchez met Castro. I wonder what the circumstances were.

Maria Sanchez was normally highly suspicious of anyone from outside of the Cuban-American community showing too great an interest in her native Cuba. The fact that the Sierra name came up in her conversation with Mrs. Marshall made her especially apprehensive. She realized that the two martinis she had for lunch betrayed her usual cautiousness on the subject. She recognized that her remarks regarding Castro were totally inappropriate. It was particularly regretful that her comments were made to the wife of the Vice-President of the United States.

The city of Miami had always been recognized as one of the nation's premier tourist destinations. American and foreign tourists found the city to be a welcoming host during the cold winter months of the year. It was a lucrative revenue source for the municipal coffers of the city. The responsibility of keeping the administration's tourism business energized was in the very capable hands of Deputy Mayor Sanchez. It was an important job and one in which she excelled.

Her strong promotional and public relations skills were never more in evidence as when each year she addressed the Annual Meeting of Domestic and International Travel Agents at the Miami Convention Hall. Her factual and professionally delivered presentation was always enthusiastically greeted by this veteran group of worldwide travel consultants. Her attendance at this important annual meeting would invariably result in sizeable booking commitments by large convention groups. These committals along with her other talents for bringing tourists to Miami were major contributors to the growing economy of the city. She became deluged with job offers from other cities in the Sunbelt section of the country seeking her expertise in developing their winter tourist business. Her answer to the offers was always the same, "Thank you, but Miami is my home."

A fact about Maria Sanchez, known only to Cadilla, was that she was a confidante of Fidel Castro. The Cuban dictator was obsessed with the need to know "the deviate and subversive thinking festering in those traitorous former Cubans hiding in Florida". He relied on Sanchez to secretly provide him with any such information. She was well-paid for her services. In addition to the business association, Sanchez had enjoyed a social relationship with the bearded leader for a number of years. She had been his mistress when she lived in Cuba and later when she emigrated to the U. S. She kept in touch with him through reliable intermediaries and covert trips to Cuba when the occasion demanded her *special* attention. They became good friends even though his libido in recent years was beginning to betray him.

Cadilla became aware of Sanchez's veiled relationship quite accidentally through an informant who had once been a close associate of Castro during the early days of the revolution. The Mayor was not hesitant in using this information to further his own political career and he knew just the person who could accommodate him.

Gino Cruz was always looking for incriminating facts that could be safely tucked away into a person's confidential file and used for political advantage at an appropriate time. Cruz's advice to Cadilla, when learning of this liaison between his Deputy Mayor and Castro, was for Cadilla to appoint Sanchez as one of his deputies and to use her relationship with Castro to gather information that could be passed on to the dissident groups in Florida. Cruz told the mayor that he would not only be reinforcing his position with the Cuban-American community by agreeing to this double agent role by Sanchez but that she could be used to provide Castro with bogus information regarding the dissidents. Cadilla also knew from experience that Cruz knew how to return a favor - so he agreed wholeheartedly. After all, didn't he have his sights on one day being addressed as *Governor* Vincent Cadilla?

The one important fact that Cruz had not told Cadilla was that he had recruited Sanchez to play a major role in *The Group's* plans for Douglas Cromwell. An attractive financial inducement and promises of an accelerated political career convinced her that her future would be well-served by playing along with Cruz. She was told to make herself available for an important assignment in the near future. He assured her that the task she would be asked to perform would be in keeping with her professional specialties. Sanchez was a patient opportunist.

When Pam returned to her office at Rockefeller Center on Monday morning, she was about to call Bob Cantrell and tell him what she had discovered; however, she decided to wait until she had something more substantive to report. Besides, she told herself, suppose I find something about Doug that we don't want to share with NBC or anyone else, for that matter. No, I'll keep everything to myself until I know that there's nothing out there to hurt him."

Pam's reasoning was sharpened by the thought that there might actually be something lurking in Doug's past that could impact negatively on his presidential aspirations. If that baby boy received an inoculation on January 8, 1952 and his birth certificate was issued in Chicago two days later, chances are the child was brought to this country on the eighth or ninth of January. There must be a record somewhere of the flights from Havana to Chicago on those two dates. She decided to contact a close college sorority sister and former roommate Janet Patrick who was now in a high level position with the Central Intelligence Agency. Pam was confident that Jan would know where that information was if it existed at all after forty-five years. Her years as a correspondent would not let her reject any possibility - no matter how vague - when chasing down a story.

A call to Janet revealed that all passenger flights and passenger listings for all domestic and international flights in and out of the United States were maintained by the Federal Aviation Administration in Washington, D. C. These records, she was amazed to find out, went back to 1946. When Patrick heard that Pam was interested in a Havana to Chicago flight, she said, reflectively,

"Flights in and out of Cuba at that time were very active. I don't see a problem in getting the information."

"What's the best way to get that information, Jan?" Pam asked.

"That's easy. Ask me to get it."

Pam laughed and asked, "Jan, can you get me that info?"

"Why I'd be happy to, Mrs. Vice-President. Would this afternoon be too soon?"

"I knew I could depend on you, Jan girl." She suddenly became cautious, "Jan, this is personal and confidential. Okay?"

Patrick replied, "My lips are sealed."

When Jan got back to her later that afternoon, she reported that there were six flights from Havana to Chicago on the days in question. "Let me know what name you're looking for and I'll check the passenger lists. I have copies of them here."

Pam wasn't sure of what she was looking for so she asked if Jan could fax copies of the lists to her home. Again, Pam was being cautious as she didn't want anyone in the office seeing the faxed copies and start wondering what they were.

"Sure. They're on their way."

"Thanks, roomy. I'll talk to you soon."

Pam hung up, grabbed her purse and left the building. She hailed a cab and was at her apartment fifteen minutes later. True to form, Jan had sent the six fax copies to her. Pam scanned the first list and found no familiar names. The second list turned up nothing. The third list was a different story.

Names of three first class passengers on Flight 586 leaving Havana at 11:00 a. m. on January 9, 1952 and arriving in Chicago at 3:30 p. m. stopped her cold. Mr. and Mrs. David Cromwell and a nameless child. Pam stared at the names for several minutes not knowing what to think or say. When she regained her composure, she knew what she must do next. She went into Doug's home office and opened his personal file draw and withdrew his birth certificate from a sealed envelop safely tucked away in the fireproof drawer. The date of birth was confirmed - January 10, 1952 - and the place of birth was the Chicago Memorial Hospital. Mother and father were David and Maria Cromwell. Maria's maiden name was listed as Sierra.

She quickly went into her room and booted up her computer. She opened her internet connection, clicked on her favorite websites and then clicked on *Biographies*. She typed in Alberto Sierra which provided her with several links to other informational connections. Within minutes, she had the complete history of the Sierra family and learned that Maria Cromwell was indeed the daughter of the powerful Alberto Sierra. The business activities of Sierra were chronicled in great detail. Further, Cromwell Advertising of Chicago was recognized as a major contributor to the success of Sierra Industries through their forceful advertising campaigns created for a broad range of consumer products that were household names in the United States.

Pam summarized in writing what she had discovered at this point. She enumerated her facts or suspicions.

* Alberto Sierra is suspected of having an illegitimate son. The child was inoculated on 1/8/52 as reported by Immigration Services for a trip from Havana to Chicago. FAA records show that Mr. and Mrs. David Cromwell and the child traveled together on a flight that left Havana for Chicago one day later. Chicago Memorial Hospital recorded a birth of Douglas Cromwell on 1/10/52.
* David Cromwell's wife Maria is the daughter of Alberto Sierra and Cromwell has strong business and social connections with the Sierra family.
* Gino Cruz was also a close friend and business associate of Alberto Sierra. She also made note that Deputy Mayor Maria Sanchez seems to have known or knows Fidel Castro.
Also, Mayor Cadilla's father was a close friend of both Alberto Sierra and Gino Cruz. They were referred to as *The Group* in their business dealings.

Pam mentally summarized her facts and suspicions that led her to the conclusion that Doug Cromwell was in fact the illegitimate son of Alberto Sierra who arranged for David and Maria Cromwell to adopt the boy several days after they left Cuba for the United States. She understood why they might want to keep the adoption a secret but why hadn't Doug told me about it.

Pam's suspicions were now confirmed by the conflicting timing of the two dates. If I could only get a DNA sample of Alberto Sierra and match it to a blood or hair sampling of Doug's. I wonder if that's at all possible given that Alberto has been dead and buried over forty years ago. She typed DNA in the keyword box of her internet connection and was immediately wallowing in more information about the subject than she had hoped for. She reviewed the background section of the text and found the information she wanted. DNA testing *had* been done on bodies that had been entombed for long periods of time. While this information was encouraging, it brought with it its own set of problems. How do you get a DNA sampling from a body that has been entombed for forty years. She answered her own questions. You dig it up and takes samples. But how, she wondered.

Janet Patrick's duties at the CIA were never openly defined for public consumption and would never be found in any of the job description manuals of the agency. Pam used to quip that she was a master at intrigue which meant she dealt in anything that needed doing that couldn't be classified as official business. Pam called her again and told her the problem.

"How do I get a DNA test? she asked.

"Ask me," was Janet's now familiar response.

"A couple of problems. One of the subjects has been dead for forty years and his body is entombed in Cuba. It's Alberto Sierra," was Pam's cryptic answer.

"And can you tell me who the *match* is?" asked Janet.

Pam felt she could be candid with her friend. "It's Doug. My Doug."

Janet was business-like in her reaction to Pam's revelation that Douglas Cromwell was the subject. "I'll need a sample of his blood, saliva or even his sperm for a valid test."

"I think I'd like to try for the sperm sample, Jan. The other two aren't very interesting options. I can have it for you tomorrow morning."

"Lucky you," was Janet's appreciative reply. There was a hesitation on the phone. "I'll have something for you in two weeks if not sooner. And, oh yes, Mrs. Vice-President – have a fun evening." A conspiratorial laugh was their closing comment.

Doug Cromwell was greeted by muted lighting and soft music when he arrived home that evening. Pam was sitting in the living room in a seductive satin gown that immediately signaled to him that maybe he had better take a quick shower and shave before dinner. A sudden rush of lustfulness told him that they might be having a late dinner – if they had dinner at all.

The following morning, a special delivered package was delivered to Janet Patrick at her office. A week later, Pam received a phone call on her private line, “It’s a perfect match.”

“No doubts?”

“None.”

Now Pamela Marshall knew for certain that Alberto Sierra and her husband were blood-related. She also knew that he was not a naturalized American citizen. She was reminded from a course in government at the University that “no person except a natural born citizen – or a citizen of the United States – shall be eligible for the Office of the President”. In truth, Douglas was not a naturalized citizen of the United States nor was he ever a citizen. His birth certificate was a forgery.

CHAPTER 15

The President had decided even before he had chosen Douglas Cromwell as his Vice-President that his protégé would not be a figurehead as so many before him had been. Marshall wanted him to be an important contributor to policy decisions and he wanted him to be his Vice-President for the next six years. He was convinced that Cromwell was the man who could enhance his reelection prospects and emerge as his heir.

Cromwell's popularity with Americans and his emerging strength within the Republican Party made him the ideal spokesperson for future state and congressional races throughout the country. The President made it quite clear that "when Doug travels around the country, he is speaking for the President of the United States". He became a charismatic campaigner for the party and the administration's point of view. Doug was sure to always leave the impression that he had no agenda except the President's. He was careful to leave the impression that he had no plans of running for anything other than the vice-presidency in the next election. He took a deferential position to the President at cabinet meetings and ceremonial occasions. They talked several times a day either in person or by phone.

The President began relying on him more and more as time went on. A high level of trust between the two men grew over time. They both became confident that they could depend on each other no matter what the circumstances. This mutual trust was obvious to those within and outside of the administration. The Vice-President's candid opinions and assessments of situations were well-respected by Marshall. He had an open-mind to other people's opinions but was steadfast in his personal beliefs.

One of the best kept secrets in Washington was the health of President Marshall. At fifty-nine, he had had a heart attack, quadruple bypass heart surgery and wore a surgically installed pacemaker. The only thing that the American public knew about his heart problems was that, two years before, he had an emergency operation to repair a damaged artery in his heart. That incident was played down by a sympathetic press as a harmless procedural necessity. The miracle of modern medical technology and the advantages of a short recuperative period allowed the severity of the President's heart attack and attending procedures to be hidden from America.

The artfulness of Gino Cruz was never more in evidence than during the aftermath of the President's heart attack. The President's personal physician, who was a friend of Cruz, made sure that the Marshall was *vacationing* in an isolated location during his recovery. Those closest to the Chief Executive agreed that secrecy in the matter was in the best national interest. They all also recognized that gossiping about the President's recovery could be detrimental to the health of their job security. His absence from Washington was jokingly referred to as a second honeymoon.

The press seemed to enjoy the humor of the occasion. Such were the advantages of a President who had developed a warm and cooperative attitude towards the media over the years. Besides, during his short recuperation, the duties of the Chief Executive were ably handled by his young Vice-President. Business as usual seemed to be the accepted norm during this difficult time.

Democrats were not unmindful of the President's health status; however, they wisely decided that making an issue of it could be counterproductive. An unsympathetic attack on a President, who enjoyed national poll ratings higher than any past chief executive, was viewed upon as a risky strategy.

Dewitt Marshall was advised that his most recent heart problem would not hinder his ability to finish his present term of office. He was also assured that he would be able to manage a run for reelection. His advisors had warned him that, while he would undoubtedly be reelected - particularly since Senator Stuart was no longer on the scene - the chances of him finishing his second term-of-office were, at best, slim to non-existent. Their advice was summed up succinctly with a statement to him from his campaign manager, Bob Thornton. "Dewitt, win the reelection, settle back in the Oval Office for a year and then let your Vice-President take over". Bob Thornton's sage advice was tempered by his having been the beneficiary of many favors from Gino Cruz during his long career in Washington.

Marshall was a pragmatic politician. He had long been accustomed to adapting to changing circumstances. He knew that Thornton was right. The pressures of his office and his failing health were against him finishing a second term. He decided that Douglas Cromwell would be President of the United States in just four years. He reflected on what had to be done to prepare Doug for this eventuality. They would need a blueprint for success. There was much for the young man to learn in that time. He would have to give him greater responsibilities so that he'll be ready for the move.

He particularly knew that he would have to develop a profound grounding in America's role on the world stage. Mastering foreign policy in the short time he had would require professional guidance. Marshall recalled that Pam Cromwell's background was heavily steeped in foreign policy and the international scene given her experience at the State Department and as a journalist for *The New York Times* and the *NBC-Television Network.* He'd remember to point this out when he met with Gino Cruz in three days.

Marshall had wisely decided to tell Gino Cruz of the plan for Cromwell's future. After all, hadn't Gino been the guiding force in his own political career. His help had been invaluable. When they did meet, Cruz listened attentively without saying a word. "I'm going to need your help, Gino. We'll have to rally as much help as we can in the short time we have to make sure he is prepared for the job he'll be taking on. I know you've been helpful to him in his career since that day in Old Town. He's now going to need that help more than ever. Your political influence can smooth the road ahead for him as it did for me. Can we depend on you for that, Gino?"

Cruz silently congratulated himself for what he had just heard. All of *The Group's* efforts on Cromwell's behalf were coming to fruition as planned. He smiled sympathetically and said, "Of course, Mr. President, of course. You have been a good friend for the many years we've known each other. I treasure that friendship. I will do whatever you feel is best for you and whatever is necessary to see that Doug follows comfortably in your able footsteps."

Cruz also knew that one of Marshall's ambitions after his Presidency was to become a United States Senator from the state of New Jersey when he retired. Whether his health would allow him to seek that office was a choice for the President. Cruz tested the waters. "Mr. President, you're too young a man to simply retire when you leave office. Might I suggest that your home state of New Jersey would be proud to have you represent them in the U. S. Senate were you to be of mind to seek that office. The pressures on your health would be much less as a Senator and I think I can assure you that your election would be a certainty."

Cruz eyed Marshall with a knowing look that provoked an immediate response from the President. "When the time comes and given a healthy mind and body, I would be honored to stand for nomination for that distinguished office by my home state friends. In the meantime, I will be happy to share whatever wisdom I've accumulated over the years so that our friend Douglas can reach the heights of his destiny."

"I know that your friendship and counseling will always be important to Vice-President Cromwell, Mr. President," Cruz assured him.

Cruz knew that Marshall's chances of winning a Senatorial seat were not a practical alternative given his medical history. At the same time, he was satisfied that Douglas Cromwell's bid for the Oval Office was now inevitable. The backing of the President of the U. S. made that a certainty. Before they parted, Marshall suggested his idea of using Pam Cromwell to sharpen Doug's foreign policy skills. Gino smiled knowingly. He had planned on doing just that when the time was right. "What a good idea, Mr. President. Let me look into that."

Cromwell's journey to the Oval Office was quickly put on a fast track once Marshall had made the decision to cut short his term in office following his reelection. *The Group* immediately directed their total attention to the task of establishing young Cromwell as a presidential talent. Never was there to be any overt suggestions that he would be replacing Marshall during their time in office. Never was there to be any implication that the President was going to step down and let his Vice-President takeover.

Rather, the media spotlight was to be focused on the visible missions of Cromwell's Vice-Presidency. He would immediately begin developing strong opinions and positions on popular issues and begin speaking with more authority on substantive policy questions. His positions would always be carefully thought out and analyzed for glitches that could be interpreted as being detrimental to his forward progress. He would begin being more visible with the American electorate than any other modern vice-president.

As time went on, he began contributing to policy decisions – always with the encouragement of the President. Marshall was confident that the difference between the counsel he received from Cromwell and everyone else was that his Vice-President's advice had no personal agenda. He was a charismatic campaigner. As his national popularity developed, Republican Party strategists planned for him to campaign in fifty congressional races that were in play in a cross-country tour from New York to California in support of the forthcoming elections.

The Group had positioned Cromwell as a conservative and a staunch opponent of abortion and racial preferences and an advocate of rigid anti-crime choices. Supporting his conservative point of view, he was recognized as a strong proponent of more individual tax cuts, more pro-business tax breaks, less environmental regulation and more energy development on public land. His views on high tech weapons both for tactical use and for strategic purposes were highly accepted by the majority of Americans. While he was steadfast in his beliefs, he was always willing to entertain other opinions if there was a chance that his views contradicted those of a majority of the electorate. He became adept at side-stepping unpopular issues. His eyes were always focused on the mission – the overthrow of Castro and his government – and any compromises to that objective became non-issues to him.

It was always uncanny that Gino Cruz knew what was happening in the world around him without his leaving the confines of his relatively secluded existence within the Beltway of Washington, D. C. He knew of Pam Marshall's conversation with Maria Sanchez and the momentary lapse of prudence on the part of the Deputy Mayor in revealing that she knew Fidel Castro. It would have meant nothing to him if he hadn't known that the Vice-President's wife was a determined journalist who looked upon every celebrity association as a newsworthy item. An unlikely connection but Cruz's mind was cunning and inquisitive and receptive to the most unlikely possibilities.

He wondered. Pam Marshall and Maria Sanchez seem to have hit it off which she might not have done under more sobering circumstances – but, still, she saw fit to unwittingly mention knowing Castro to the Vice-President's wife. I just wonder if Pam Marshall could be useful to our plans for her husband. The situation would have to be handled carefully. After all, she might not be amenable to being part of something as divisive as what we have planned for our bearded friend. She could be helpful, though. I'll have to discuss this with *The Group* to make sure we're on solid footing before bringing her into our confidence. Yes, she could be a significant asset to our plans.

The Group spent the next several months finalizing their plan for having the American people view Douglas Cromwell as the next logical contender for the nation's top office. Once he reached that high office, they were confident that their dream for the overthrow of Castro would begin in earnest. They would have to be sure of that the offensive weapons they marshaled to achieve their goal were in order.

High on the list of *unknowns* was the Vice-President's wife and how she would react to the daring plan they had organized. The lingering question was whether she should be told of the plan of action and given the opportunity of participating in the duplicity that would be necessary once Doug became President. And once she was told of the plan and she rejected the offer to join them - what then – would her uncompromising journalistic principles become a roadblock to their program? Would she become a relentless hindrance to Doug in his everyday activities when she discovered that some of his policy decisions were distasteful to her? And worse, would she feel compelled to report her feelings in her reportorial assignments? Gino Cruz summed up *The Group's* sentiments on the matter, "There was too much at stake not to treat this issue with the utmost urgency."

Pam Marshall was dealing with doubts of her own regarding her husband. Now that she knew that Doug was actually a Cuban by birth, she felt that Doug had been less than forthright with her in not revealing this rather basic truth about himself. There was no point in putting off discussing the issue with him. There's undoubtedly a good reason why he didn't want it known that he was a Cuban by birth and later adopted by an American couple, she reasoned. I just don't want him to think that I was deliberately looking into his past without his knowledge. She would have to come up with a logical rationale for having found the truth as to where he was born and then casually ask him about it at dinner one evening.

Two days later, Pam and Doug were having a candlelit dinner at the Vice-President's residency when she played her hand.

CHAPTER 16

"What a delightful dinner that was," Doug remarked while coffee was being served. Pam pretended she hadn't noticed that he had unhitched his belt one notch which she accepted as a silent compliment to her meal selection. She no longer cooked meals – she just planned them. Doug was telling a story of the rather pretentious senator from one of the southern states who had imbibed too freely at lunch that afternoon and who promptly fell asleep at the podium while addressing his colleagues.

Pam smiled at such a humorous incident taking place in the august halls of Congress. "I can just picture his expression when he woke up. I'll bet no one even noticed it. They were all probably asleep, too."

Doug chuckled. "The poor fellow was led to his seat and immediately fell asleep again." They both laughed at such an unlikely image of the very pompous senator.

Doug was in a jovial mood all evening. Pam thought this would be an ideal time to bring up the subject of his birth. She had planned how she was going to approach the matter without sounding like she had been prying into his past.

"Oh, by the way, my secretary handed me a cryptic handwritten note just before I left the office today that said – *the Vice-President was born in Cuba and adopted by an American couple. Lucas Industries is owned by the Sierra family.* "I have no idea who sent it or why it was sent in the first place. Any ideas?"

Doug didn't respond immediately. He at once became suspicious of his wife's less-than-creative attempt to validate the truth about his birth. He smiled inwardly and thought to himself – this is so unlike Pam pussyfooting around something she obviously knows more about than she's saying. He also knew that she would be persistent until she had what she was after. Her tenacity for getting to the bottom of things was one of her journalistic strong points. Besides, he reasoned, it's apparent that she just trying to confirm something she already knows or suspects. The one thing he did not want was to lose her confidence in him by lying or hiding anything especially since it looked like the cat was already out-of-the bag. When he spoke it was with the ease of someone who was used to responding to unexpected surprises. "Sounds like a political maneuver of some kind to me, he said."

Pam was not to be put off so easily. She tried a little humor. "You know, I always thought you had a Latin look to you. I think that's what attracted me to you in the first place." Her coy remark gave him the added confidence to tell her the truth.

"The truth of the matter is that I do have some Latin blood flowing through these political veins. Those two references actually apply to me. I *was* born in Cuba and my father was actually Alberto Sierra who *did* own Lucas Industries. It's a family ownership now."

"Really? We never talked about that, did we?"

"No, we never did. Not only was it politically expedient not to make an issue of my having been born in Cuba but I didn't want you to be burdened with any negative associations that our political friends might find – or create - to feed their insatiable propaganda machine. You have enough to think about with your NBC responsibilities."

"You know my feelings for you, Doug. My goodness, I'm in love with you. Nothing can change that."

"You're right, darling. I was wrong. I should have told you. There's really no reason that you shouldn't have known." Doug suddenly looked at his watch and interrupted himself. "Pam dear, you'll have to excuse me for just one minute. I promised to call Senator Ford at 9:00 o'clock on a matter that is quite urgent. Let's continue our conversation when I return. It'll take just a minute."

Doug proceeded to his study and dialed Gino Cruz's confidential phone number. No one but Gino ever answered his private phone. The familiar voice answered, "Yes?"

"Gino, its Doug, something just came up and I think we should discuss it right away." Doug proceeded to explain the anonymous note that Pam said she had received. He added that he thought the note was actually a ploy – just Pam's way of sparking a conversation on the subject. He then explained that, given her curiosity about his birth, this would be a good time to bring Pam into our confidence. "It's something we've discussed a number of times before, so let's do it before she begins to become suspicious of things she might hear down the line when things begin heating up."

Gino didn't respond. Doug knew that Gino was a master of the *pregnant pause*. It always seemed to give him confidence that he had put the other party on the defensive in their conversation. Doug diffused this childish tactic by quickly continuing.

"Gino, I know it's a risk but I have a strong feeling that she'll not only go along with what we've planned but will want to join us. I know where her loyalties lie and they're not on the side of Castro. We've discussed the pros and cons of the situation often. I know she'd be sympathetic with what we're doing – at least, the move to enter into a free trade agreement with Cuba. That's all I would tell her. Not the subsequent scenario if a free trade agreement and a more relaxed travel restriction policy between the two countries became a reality."

There was a prolonged silence on the other end of the phone. Gino finally responded. "She *could* be a big help given her influential position with NBC. It would also make your life easier if she were one of us." Gino seemed to have a second thought and said, "On a limited and selective basis, of course."

"Absolutely, Gino. She'd be on a need-to-know basis at all times."

Gino was again momentarily quiet. Finally, he said, "She's a very bright lady who could ask many distracting questions given that sensitive nose that all news journalists seem to have been born with. If she were made aware of the broad strokes of our plan, maybe she wouldn't be so inquisitive about some of the things she might hear later. I must say though, I shudder to think of the consequences should she decide not to join us after our having disclosed classified information to her. I ask myself, would her journalistic curiosity for getting a choice news story take precedence over our demand for absolute secrecy in all matters pertaining to the project?"

Gino let that thought sink in and then reinforced his doubts, "You're right, Doug, it could be a risky move particularly if what we're doing is leaked. Revealing our plans to the American public could destroy all that we've worked for. We can't have that, can we?"

"Of course not, Gino. As we agreed, the plan is paramount."

"Then having said that, you realize the consequences should she be informed of our plans and then decide not to join us. Or, maybe, have a change of mind once she is with us for a time. Saying she would keep quiet about what she learned would not be enough. She would have to join us and stay the course to assure that confidential ties were honored."

The prolonged silence was now on Doug's end of the phone. He finally said, "I don't think she'd ever say anything were she….."

Gino interrupted with a decided edge in his voice, "As I said, Doug – being quiet would not be enough." The implication of the threat was all too obvious.

Doug reacted. "I'm convinced that she'll choose to join us and I wouldn't even suggest it if I didn't think she could make important contributions to our agenda." Doug knew that if he were wrong, life could become problematical for his wife.

Gino's voice was dry and precise as he responded, "Go ahead, Doug, but precede with caution, my friend. Be very careful what you tell her."

"I shall, Gino. I shall." Doug then hung up and joined Pam.

"Sorry, dear. I had to get something out of the way before tomorrow morning. They fell into an uncomfortable silence before Doug smiled and resumed their conversation. He explained that he was the illegitimate son of Alberto Sierra and that he was adopted by Maria and David Cromwell shortly after his birth and brought to America to live.

"My real mother was a correspondent for Time Magazine. My father had an affair with her over a number of years. She died giving birth to me. My adopted mother is the daughter of Alberto. She and David met while he was serving a tour of duty in the Navy in Cuba before Castro came into power. It was during this time that he met and became close with the Sierra family. As for Lucas Industries, you know that story; I went to work for them after graduating from Columbia Graduate School. I advanced comfortably through the corporate system in a number of different jobs. I became involved in every operational facet of the company and was eventually appointed a senior vice-president after I had been with them for a number of years. I was actually being groomed for the presidency of the company until it was decided that something more important was to take precedent over my business career.

"You did very well at Lucas in a very short time," Pam said.

"Yes, I did. I became very close with Juan Sierra who was running the Lucas operation along with directing their other family businesses. He was my benefactor from the beginning. He knew I was his father's illegitimate son but that didn't matter to him. He treated me like a brother from the start. The care and love along with the education and training that I was given by Maria and David Cromwell were responsible for my being so successful in the business world. David, who is an absolute genius in the world of marketing and advertising, taught me well the lessons of being the best at whatever I attempted in life. I was a very lucky fellow to have that kind of support."

"Luck's always there, Doug. What you had was intelligence and a willingness to make sacrifices to achieve your objectives in life."

"Well, being related to a Sierra gave my career a jump start, that's for certain. I shall always be grateful to my parents and the Sierra family. I'm truly indebted to them." Doug stared into his wife's eyes trying to determine just how much he should tell her. All he saw was an inquisitive look that he knew could only be satisfied by him being as honest with her as practicality would allow. That practicality did *not* include admitting that his heroism at the school in his hometown of Old Town, N. J. was planned for the purpose of starting him on a carefully orchestrated political career. He was sure that her feelings for him would be severely tested if she knew his part in that deception. Nor did it include revealing the phase of their plan that was a closely guarded secret known only to the members of *The Group.* That part of the project could not be disclosed to her under any circumstances – at least, at this time.

Doug began hesitantly, "Pam, what you must remember is that everything I have done and will do in the future is because of a pledge - a covenant of honor is the way we all think of it - made between people whose families had been cruelly and brutally murdered by a ruthless dictator in control of a country just 90-miles from our shores. Our group has vowed to honor a sworn commitment to rid Cuba of Fidel Castro and the government he brought to the island almost fifty years ago. Alberto Sierra and many of his friends were cruelly and unjustly murdered by the Revolutionists. Castro knew that they would be a continual thorn in his side if they were allowed to continue their outspoken views championing a free Cuba. He had others do the killings but, make no mistake, it was Castro who gave the order to eliminate these fine men."

"And look at all the others his tribunals condemned and executed as being traitors to the country," Pam said, sympathizing with Doug's commentary.

Doug nodded his agreement and continued, "Alberto's boyhood friend and later business associate, Gino Cruz, avoided being a victim of the *Death Squads* only because he left Cuba a year before Castro came to power to practice law in the states. He has since nurtured a hatred for Castro and vowed to avenge the death of his former friends. Gino Cruz was a patient avenger. He formed a group who harbored the same dedicated commitment to rid Cuba of Castro. The others in the group were Alberto's oldest son Juan, Gino's son Pedro, my adopted parent David Cromwell and me. For purpose of anonymity, we called ourselves *The Group.* Nothing – absolutely nothing – could divert our attention from this dedication and, over the years, not one of us has lost the burning commitment for fulfilling our covenant with one another"

Pam was becoming anxious to learn about the plan Doug kept referring to. "I can understand how committed you all could become to the idea of exacting vengeance on Castro and that corrupt government of his. The plan you speak of – what is that?"

Doug hesitated at this point knowing that what he was about to say was disingenuous. He regretted having to limit what he was about to tell her. He was sure she'd be sympathetic to the free trade issue but could have grave doubts about the ultimate resolution that *The Group* had on its agenda. "Pam, this will undoubtedly sound bizarre and unlikely to you but years ago – twenty five to be exact – *The Group* devised a plan to educate and train me for one job and one job alone – to become President of the United States. Once I became President, it was felt that a concerted effort could be made to unseat Castro's government with the complete support of the United States."

Pam was overwhelmed, "You mean there was a planned effort from the beginning to make you President for the sole purpose of *getting even* with Castro?" Pam didn't expect an answer and she received none. She said, "I'm sorry, please carry on."

Doug continued, "Contrary to the United States' present policy regarding a free trade agreement with Cuba, the administration would do a complete three hundred and sixty degree turn and support such a treaty. The President of the United States would lead the charge in convincing America that such a policy would be beneficial to the United States and to making Cuba more receptive to a free and democratic government. We're convinced that to make the free enterprise system work within the bounds of a Communist government, we must first give the country a standard of living that will awaken them to the advantages of a free-wheeling society."

Pam reacted immediately, "It's about time someone took a realistic view towards our relationship with Cuba. All we've been doing so far with our quarantine is to drive them deeper and deeper into the Communist orbit."

She then took a deep breath and said, "That seems like a very ambitious program considering Castro could very well be dead by the time you're able to carry out your program. He *is* getting on in years."

"Castro is no longer important. We want to rid Cuba of the government he brought to our country." Pam was taken aback to hear Doug refer to Cuba as *our country.* Doug continued, "If he's alive at the time, a legal punishment will be exacted for what he did. We expect the people of Cuba will be only too happy to oblige him on that score; particularly if they suddenly saw that they might lose their newfound life style. So you see, in the end, our revenge will be that one day soon Cuba will become a democratic government. No more Communism and no more Castro. And then – and only then – will we feel that we have fulfilled our obligation to those who died needlessly."

Pam was moved by Doug's words, "Free trade with Cuba is exactly what I have been preaching in my editorial commentaries. I'm convinced that it's the only way the Cuban people will understand what we've been advocating for the past fifty years. I've had to downplay those commentaries only because the top boys at NBC felt it was too controversial and would most certainly create problems with the ratings and some of our super-conservative advertising clients. I'd love to be more outspoken on the issue."

Doug had suspected correctly what her reaction would be but he had to be absolutely sure of her position in the matter before she was given the opportunity of joining *The Group.* What he told her was all the information that would be made available to her – at least for the time being and until they were totally assured that she would be amenable - if at all - to the more daring phase of the plan. In the meantime, she would function as a quasi-participant.

When Doug asked her if she'd be interested in participating as a member of *The Group,* she agreed wholeheartedly. The only reservation she had – and which she kept to herself – was that too much of their plan was being left to chance. Helping Cuba improve their standard of living was all well and good but, why should the Cuban people rebel against Castro if he's providing them with an economically sound way of life. Either the group is being very naïve – which I don't believe for one minute – or I'm not being told the full story of what they have in mind.

Before going to bed that evening, Doug called Cruz and explained what had transpired with Pam emphasizing that she was just told about the *free trade* proposition and the plan to lift travel restrictions between the U. S. and Cuba – and nothing else. Cruz seemed pleased but Doug was always somewhat wary when Gino *seemed* pleased.

CHAPTER 17

A week later, *The Group* convened at 8:00 a. m. at Pedro Cruz's twenty-acre estate in McLean, Virginia where both he and Gino lived in separate homes. Each member was picked up at their home by a limousine provided by Cruz and Cruz. The drivers were carefully selected for their ability to keep their mouths shut about the passengers they shuttled about and the conversations they might hear in transit. David Cromwell had flown in from Chicago for the meeting. Pam and Doug Cromwell arrived together. It was to be her first exposure to *The Group.*

The purpose of the meeting was to introduce Pam to everyone and to familiarize her with the Cuban project. *The Group* had dinner together the night before to make sure that everyone understood what would and would not be revealed to their newest member. Doug was still somewhat confused as to why Gino had been so easily swayed to allow Pam to join them. He knew there had to be a reason other than Gino's reasoning that she could become too inquisitive about some of the things she might hear if she were left out-of-the-loop entirely.

A leisurely breakfast was served before they got down to business. As was the custom, Juan acted as host. He welcomed everyone and was especially gracious in recapping Pam's resume of accomplishments; particularly her strong suit in foreign policy. Juan encouraged her not to be reticent about speaking up on any occasion as they were interested in hearing her point-of-view on things she'd be hearing for the first time.

Juan began, "Pam, we know that Doug has filled you in on our commitment to rebuild Cuba into a democratic nation. Our agreed-upon strategy for accomplishing this rather mammoth undertaking is really quite simple and will, of course, be put on hold until Doug becomes President. It's no secret that President Marshall's health will probably not survive another four years after his recent reelection. He has graciously agreed to let Doug take over two years into his second four-year term."

Pam was truly surprised. She knew, of course, that her husband was being groomed for the Presidency, but she was unaware that the timetable for that happening was only several years away.

Juan noted her silent reaction to the news and pressed on, "I would start by saying that it is vital that anything we discuss at this and any subsequent meetings must remain confidential. I'll emphasize this point by stating the obvious. America must never know that President Marshall is even contemplating not completing his second term. A leak of any kind could impact negatively on our plans and Doug being able to make a smooth transition to the Oval Office."

Pam said, quietly, "You would never have to worry about me having a loose tongue. I know how important this is to all of you and, believe me; I'm completely sympathetic to what you're trying to do." They all nodded and looked to Juan to continue.

Juan smiled and proceeded, "We all want to see Cuba become a democratic nation during Doug's first term of office. We believe we can convince the Cuban people that our form of government is in their best interests by demonstrating to them the advantages of a free market society. To do this, we'll obviously have to negotiate a free trade agreement with our septuagenarian friend. We must remember that in spite of an improved economic picture since the early 90's, life still remains hard for the average Cuban who is becoming more and more dissatisfied with their habitually empty existence and for the leaders responsible for their flawed lifestyle. We want to feed on that discontent which we'll begin doing with passage of the trade agreement."

Pedro interrupted on cue. "The initial thrust will be for the President to develop a working relationship with Fidel Castro. To do this, Doug will have to swallow a major serving of crow given the strong stand America has taken in the past against any kind of a free market economy for Cuba. He'll contact Fidel through diplomatic channels and request that he be permitted to travel to Cuba to discuss the possibility of a trade agreement between their two countries. He'll voluntarily and categorically state that America is not interested in changing their present form of government. He will emphasize that his administration's only interest in joining with Cuba is to develop a meaningful commercial association that could be economically beneficial to both countries. President Cromwell will convince the Cubans that this relationship will dramatically change how the world views them both as an international ally and as a trading partner. Their leadership will be made aware of how an improved standard of living will not only benefit all Cubans but will earn them the respect and appreciative support of their fellow countrymen. They'll also be assured that passage of free trade legislation by both Houses of the U.S. Congress will be quickly approved once the specifics of the accord are agreed upon. We have taken an unofficial poll of our friends in the Congress and received assurances that passage of the bill will indeed be enthusiastically supported."

Gino had taken a personal hand in making sure that passage of the bill would be a *fait accompli* once it was submitted. He had debited the political payback side of his ledger to get these assurances.

Gino spoke up. "Any economic strength Cuba has today is strongly dependent upon their tourist business which has been growing at a healthy nineteen percent a year. Certainly, sugar, nickel and tobacco are Cuba's biggest export industries but it's tourism that has the potential to make a difference in their becoming major players in the world market. Prior to the Revolution, Cuba was the leading tourist destination in the Caribbean, but lost that standing after the U.S. embargo was imposed in 1961. Today, the Bahamas and Puerto Rico receive four times as many visitors as Cuba. The Bahamas get fourteen tourists a year for every local resident while Cuba gets one tourist a year for every six Cubans. So you can see there is still a gigantic upside to the business they could be doing."

Pedro interrupted and expanded on Gino's words, "And while Cuba's tourism is now the fastest growing in the world and it's the country's largest single source of foreign exchange earning almost $2.0 billion a year, only thirty cents of every U. S. dollar spent by a tourist actually stays in Cuba because imports needed to support this industry are so high. They need funds to build new hotels and renovate the older ones. Improving their beaches to accommodate the pampering needs of sun-worshipping tourists will become high on their list of required priorities. Low interest loans by the U. S. will be made available at the proper time to accommodate judicious spending programs designed to help attack these needs. Foreign investments will be encouraged to share in the rich potential of Cuba's new economic turnabout. The ban on Americans traveling to Cuba will, of course, have to be lifted."

Gino continued, "Tourism in Cuba is a corrupt enterprise. The government runs international tourism as a state monopoly; private competition is either strictly controlled and heavily taxed or banned entirely. About 150,000 Cubans have jobs related to tourism and these prized positions are used to reward government supporters. Blacklisted persons – people with a history of 'antisocial' activities - are banned from participation in the industry. Limiting employment to political cronies is just one of the ills preventing Cuba from becoming an economically vibrant economy. So, tourism will be our target of opportunity to help Cuba reach its potential.

Juan jumped in, "We have even arranged for one of the foremost tourist specialists in the United States to lend a hand in providing the Cuban government with the necessary expertise that will be needed to revitalize their existing tourist resources. Doug mentioned the other day, Pam, that you had the occasion of meeting with Deputy Mayor Maria Sanchez on your recent trip to Miami. I don't know if you're aware of her preeminence within the travel industry. She's in great demand as an advisor in helping many of the cities in the Sunbelt states build their local tourist business. She's that good, we're told."

Again, Gino nodded his approval. He had been confident that the arrangement he had made with Sanchez a year before would begin paying handsome dividends once their plan started unfolding.

"Yes, I did meet Sanchez," Pam said. We had lunch together and, after a couple of martinis, she mentioned that she had met Castro. I got the distinct impression that their relationship was anything but casual."

Gino smiled, knowingly. "No, not casual at all. She is his mistress. She and Mayor Cadilla of Miami work in unison in feeding Castro with bogus propaganda and he in turn provides her with equally spurious information which is passed on to the Mayor's compatriots in South Florida. It's all very unproductive because nothing of meaningful value is ever passed along by either party. Both Castro and Cadilla know they're being scammed but they both have their reasons for letting the charade go on. It allows Cadilla to maintain credibility with the Castro opposition in South Florida. As for Castro, let's just say that it would be unfortunate for Sanchez if the Premier's libido suddenly took a turn for the worse. I don't think he would tolerate playing the fool if his sexual treats were no longer available to him."

Pedro laughed and said, "It goes without saying that the health of Cuba's economic life will undergo an instantaneous awakening once the free trade agreement is in place and the ban on Americans traveling to the island is lifted. We expect Cuba and the United States to forge a bond that will be viewed by the world as an unselfish attempt by the United States to mend relations that were thought to be unsalvageable. Once the economy becomes vitalized, we fully expect the Cuban people to recognize that it was America's free trade program that was responsible for their turn of fortune. It will be at that point that a propaganda campaign extolling the virtues of a democratic form of government will begin."

"It will be subtle at first as we'll have to be careful not to show our hand early in the game. The trade agreement and putting an end to traveling restrictions will provide the Cuban people with a visible sign of just how the free enterprise system works. The propaganda campaign will cautiously remind them that their improved lifestyle is the result of the American capitalist system working for the people. We'll have to tread lightly here and rely heavily on the anti-Castro factions on the island and in Miami to carry the message. By the same token, we don't want innocent people spending the next twenty years in a military prison for promoting subversion. These folks will be warned that they have to monitor themselves carefully to make sure they don't become too visibly aggressive in their propaganda efforts."

Pam asked, "Are conditions that bad? Can they put you in jail for speaking out against the government?"

"They absolutely can and will," Pedro responded.

"How do we get to the people then?" Pam asked.

"Pedro continued, "As we all know, it's virtually impossible to use the Cuban-based media to communicate messages that promote subversion. All media is operated by the government and is tightly controlled to prevent anti-government messages from being broadcast or printed. For example, the government has put in place appropriate legislation intended to intimidate and severely punish independent journalists and dissidents in Cuba who telephone stories to Miami-based media who then broadcast the messages back to Cuba. They don't play games when it comes to preserving the Communist line. However, there are groups of dedicated dissenters who are willing to risk harsh government penalties in their quest to change the political landscape of the country. These dissidents are wise in the ways of frustrating the government's attempts at blocking political rhetoric from reaching the people. We fully expect to take advantage of that boldness."

"Won't Castro come down pretty hard on these dissidents when he discovers that they're responsible for his troubles – and won't he be expected to punish them in some way?" Pam asked.

Doug, who had been noticeably quiet during the meeting said, "Yes, he will, but we expect them to do enough damage to have a significant effect on the mindset of the Cuban people before that happens."

Pam was flustered. "You mean you're expecting that these people will be punished when they're discovered?"

Gino responded, "There are casualties in every war, Pam."

Pedro quickly continued his presentation as he didn't want Pam's questioning reaction to stalemate the discussion.

"But, while propaganda will always have its place in influencing the minds of the people, the important action will be in the form of a series of major roadblocks that will prevent the government from enjoying the fruits of the free trade agreement. Their tourism program in particular will come under severe fire. These mishaps will have the appearance of being the work of anti-government groups or, better still, the work of committed Cuban Communists who feel that Castro is prostituting their principles by doing business with America. The United States will be sympathetic and offer its full cooperation in trying to combat these subversive activities. The impression left with the Cuban government will be that the U. S. is not only completely blameless for these unfriendly acts, but that it is has rallied around its neighbor in a selfless way."

Three hours later, having exhausted the meeting's agenda after a morning of healthy dialogue, Gino suggested that they adjourn knowing that the Vice-President had a meeting of his own back in Washington that required his presence.

Pam was energized by the dialogue of the morning. "I want you all to know that I look forward to being part of this project. I recognize that your motivation hinges on an element of revenge in what we'll be doing, but giving eleven million people the opportunity to enjoy a democratic way of life will, I believe, more than justify our actions."

While Pam was sincere in her laudable comments, she still had a questioning feeling that she wasn't being told the whole story. How can such a poorly conceived propaganda concept change a nation's philosophical direction and why are they so confident that the people of Cuba will credit the democratic process for any success that a free trade agreement would provide. After all, any success that is achieved will have been accomplished under their present government's leadership. Won't we just be reinforcing Castro's position with his people, she wondered.

She and Doug left right after lunch.

It was Gino's meeting that afternoon. He felt that he had to clear the air as to why Doug and Pam were not being included in the afternoon session. He directed his comments to David Cromwell as he didn't want his friend to think that his son and daughter-in-law were not going to be taken into their complete confidence.

"David, as you know, we purposely left Pam out of our meeting this afternoon as, quite frankly, we're still not sure how she would react to some of the harsh measures we've built into the plan. She'll, of course, be told later on. And, I think it would be wise to hold off bringing Doug completely into the picture at this time as we want him to concentrate on his duties as Vice-President. Preparing himself to be President will be a fulltime job in the months ahead. Naturally, as with Pam, he'll be told of the complete details at a later date but, for now, let's not create distractions that might affect his judgment."

David agreed completely. "Yes, by all means. They'll both have to know the specifics eventually, but let's wait until they're both completely settled into their new roles.

"Good," Gino said, pleasantly. He looked at the others and his lips tightened into a thin line of determination to let them know he was now ready to discuss the graver phase of the plan. "I am convinced that President Cromwell will be successful in bringing Castro to the bargaining table to negotiate a free trade agreement. The terms of the deal will be too enormously attractive for his government to reject. Pedro and his people have assured us that the mechanism for Congress' acceptance of the treaty is now firmly in place and that the ban on Americans traveling to Cuba will be jettisoned with the mutual acceptance of the agreement.

Gino hesitated for effect and said, "Now, let's review just how we expect to use the pact to leverage the economic collapse of Cuba.

CHAPTER 18

Pedro began the discussion. They were all familiar with the overall planning and all of its ramifications. Nothing had been more important to them than the covenant they had entered into with each other many years before. Gino had insisted that the basics of their plan be reviewed periodically so that everyone understood and maintained the commitment necessary to assure its success. Pedro knew the scenario by heart as he had spoken the words many times before.

"Fidel has adopted a more conciliatory approach towards a free trade agreement with the U. S. ever since the Soviets abandoned him. Okay, we'll give Cuba their trade agreement and use it as the carrot for relaxing tensions between our two countries. It will be the springboard for moving towards a more open relationship with them – or so they will think."

Juan added, "A trade agreement between the two countries is bound to happen sooner or later, anyhow. Most Americans and the Congress seem to be in agreement that the old policy of isolating the island never did work."

Pedro shook his head in agreement and continued. "As we discussed this morning, their economy is in bad shape. The only industry they can depend on to help them get back on their feet is tourism. Tourism is doing relatively well in Cuba even though the increases they've been seeing have had virtually no impact on the lives of most Cubans trying to make ends meet. Fidel recognizes that he has become dependent on the revenues generated by the influx of foreign travelers; particularly since the Soviets are no longer contributing $6.0 billion a year to his economy. They were supporting Cuba economically, politically and militarily and, when that aid was withdrawn, Cuba suffered an economic loss that has been devastating to them. Tourism is their one hope right now of putting some balance back into their economy."

Juan quickly added, "Their problem is that they really don't have the expertise to make tourism work for them effectively. They need American tourists and an intelligent plan to make it happen. That's where we come in. Once Cuba accepts the very generous terms of a

U. S. trade agreement, we'll be in a position to convince them that an *intelligent* tourism program, coupled with an aggressive gaming strategy, will breathe new life into his failing economy. We've seen several independent studies indicating that Cuba will receive several million U. S. tourists annually when the sanctions are lifted which will be worth billions of dollars to them. And let's not forget all the other international business they'll be enjoying."

David added, "Cromwell Advertising, in the interest of international harmony, will volunteer its services to develop a marketing program that will address the growth opportunities available to the country. The plan will include structuring a Tourist Board that will control every aspect of the marketing of tourism in Cuba. I will personally take charge of this consulting assignment. As mentioned this morning, Maria Sanchez, Miami's Deputy Mayor, will be joining us. She'll be asked to head up the Board and spearhead the drive to make it the most sought after tourist attraction in the Caribbean. Her expertise in the world of travel is legendary. Cuba will welcome her with open arms."

Gino smiled and thought to himself that Castro would certainly welcome her with open arms – at the very least – as he had on all of her previous visits to his reportedly lavish bedroom suite.

Mayor Cadilla was to be the intermediary between Sanchez and *The Group.* Gino saw no reason for her to think of her assignment as anything but helping to build a friendly relationship between the two countries. Her closeness to Castro presented too great a security risk for her knowing anything but the bare essentials of her assignment. Sanchez was a political animal. Her trust was bought with the promise of a responsible job within the current administration in Washington once she completed her assignment.

Gino recognized early that they would need professional help in bringing gambling to Cuba. He understood completely that to the international traveler, leisure traveling and gambling were like conjoined twins – each one being dependent on the other. Gambling was the frosting on the cake for any successful tourism program.

He had contacted an old acquaintance who was known to be the godfather of American casino gambling. Joseph "Buddy" DeLuca was now a respected member of the Atlantic City community who had acted as an advisor to all of the major casinos that had opened for business in the U. S. and the Caribbean during the past forty years. He was a shrewd and highly successful Las Vegas businessman prior to his move to New Jersey. Atlantic City was in his debt for the special expertise he brought with him. While DeLuca's reputation had been subjected to severe criticism by gaming regulators in the past, he was respectfully recognized by *the right people* as the last word in the ways of casino management. He was a true friend to Gino Cruz as was Gino to him. They enjoyed each other's confidences in the most sensitive of matters. Gino also relied on him to handle assignments of a highly private nature. A handshake was all that was required to bind a verbal agreement between them.

As Maria Sanchez was to be the tourism advisor, DeLuca would be the untitled consultant of gaming development in Cuba. In addition to his uncanny knowledge of the people and operational complexities associated with the gaming industry, he had at his disposal a group of associates whom he referred to privately as *Buddy's Boys.* These carefully selected individuals had the reputation of being convincing negotiators in their special field of endeavor which DeLuca defined as *diplomatic persuasion.* One of these colleagues was Carmine Cato whose last assignment for Gino was the neutralization of Senator Andrew Davis Stuart.

Gino continued, "We project that once the trade agreement is in place, it will take between two and three years for Cuba to become the independent economic force that will set it apart from their neighbors in the Caribbean. Importantly, the only condition that the U. S. will demand – perhaps, request is a more friendly word – is that the Cuban people be allowed to participate in this newfound economic boom. Jobs cannot be restricted to party loyalists only."

"The new construction and all of the other capital improvements will create widespread employment for the very people who have been excluded from making a living wage since the Revolution. Not only will they enjoy a rewarding standard of living, but they will gain a self respect for themselves that will preclude Castro from ever attempting to revert back to his former fiscal mismanagement ways."

"It will be at that point, when prosperity becomes a reality and a way of life in Cuba, that the U. S. will undertake - and there is no other word for it - a *sabotage* program to completely destroy the rejuvenated economy of Cuba. We'll simply refer to it amongst ourselves as the *Disruption Agenda.* Sabotage is an ugly word."

Gino sat back with a look of satisfaction that defined the pleasure he experienced every time they reached this point in the story. He decided to continue the narration himself. He enjoyed articulating the darker side of the plan."

"At the right time, we will introduce measures that will discourage international travelers from ever again considering Cuba as a vacation destination. And, we'll create a firestorm among Cubans as their economy ceases to provide their government with the financial independence that they had been enjoying ever since entering into the free trade agreement with the United States."

"The country's newly acquired standard of living will collapse under the weight of a rapidly declining economy. They'll be wholesale unemployment starting with the tourism sector and escalating to all areas of the national economy. We'll arrange for the workers to actively protest against the government's handling of the falling economy. We'll instigate widespread unrest within the country. The free fall from economic independence will be so sudden that the government will be unable to control its rapid descent."

A conspiratorial smile crossed Gino's lips when he said, "And even if Castro realizes that he's been deceived – it won't matter. We expect conditions in the country to be in such a sorry state of disrepair by that time that no matter what he says or does will have any meaningful effect on the inevitable collapse of his government."

Pedro took over, "All right, that's the broad picture. Now, let's talk about how we're going to create this disharmony. We all agree that the economy of Cuba will spring to life once tourists begin discovering the lure of the island. The Cuban government will be required to make major financial commitments to satisfy the capital expenditures necessary to support the free trade business that will have been created. It will be necessary for them to spend a greater share of their national budget on these capital improvements than they had at any time in the past. This investment necessity should weaken their Treasury considerably and also overburden their credit obligations."

Gino stopped for a sip of water and then continued. "Causing disruptive political situations in Cuba through covert methods have been done before, of course. Declassified documents revealed that President John F. Kennedy sought to expand sabotage against the new radical Cuban government shortly after taking office in 1960. An Executive Order in 1961 directed a review of intelligence work, including 'highly sensitive covert operations relating to political action, propaganda, economic warfare and sabotage'."

"Declassified documents also revealed that President Kennedy sought to expand sabotage against Cuba in the days leading up to the Cuban missile crisis. The ongoing work of the government-sponsored *Operation Mongoose*, a once secret plan to breach the early government of Fidel Castro, was an ongoing project in 1962 that included the penetration of U. S. intelligence infiltrators into the Cuban community, assassination plots, sabotage raids, economic sanctions and even plans for a U. S. military invasion."

"Be that as it may, we will not go to the extremes of the ill-conceived and poorly executed programs initiated during the Kennedy administration. Our program will be precise and orderly. Our covert operations will be conducted in such a manner that, if uncovered, the U. S. government can plausibly disclaim responsibility for them. In addition to the dissident groups in Cuba, Mayor Cadilla of Miami will be instrumental in inciting the anti-Castro groups in South Florida once the *Disruption Agenda* is up and running."

Gino nodded to Juan who carried on, "The tourist business that we created will then fall on hard times thanks to carefully planned and destructive incidences that will leave lasting impressions on foreign visitors. Cuba will no longer be considered a suitable vacation destination. The de-escalation will begin slowly with tourists being abused in the local restaurants and the streets of Havana. Thefts of personal belongings at the resorts will escalate. Shoppers and sightseers will be treated rudely and cheated in their purchases. Suggestive remarks to women will most certainly spark threatening and physical responses from their escorts. This disruptive behavior will be staged at highly visible resorts with the intent of undermining return visits to the island and to encourage negative word-of-mouth disparagement of the Cuban travel experience."

Pedro couldn't hold back his enthusiasm, "Once this low-level of dissatisfaction is felt, a stepped-up and more serious level of anti-tourist activity will be initiated. Many of the conveniences that tourists are accustomed to receiving at the posh resorts will suddenly lose their polish. A series of unexplained minor explosions at the hotels and tourist attractions will echo throughout Cuba and the world. These planned detonations will be monitored and every precaution will be observed to assure that no one is within range of the blasts."

They all knew that such assurances were never bulletproof or even reasonable. It did however mollify *The Group's* conscience that their intent was not to put people's lives at risk in their personal vendetta.

Gino dismissed the thought and resumed, "These ear-shattering explosions will occur simultaneously to assure that they are viewed as part of organized plots rather than coincidental accidents. The objective will be to frighten people into believing that their stay in Cuba is fraught with dangers that the government is unable to control. These missions will be carried out by people who will have been trained in the art of destabilization."

"And to protect the U. S. from claims that they are involved in a conspiracy to create dissension throughout the island, we have enlisted the help of Brigadier General Thomas P. Cullen, Commandant of the U. S. Marine Detachment at the Guantanamo Bay Naval Base. He has been an ardent foe of Communism all of his military career and would delight in seeing Cuba become a free nation under a democratic rule – *and*, I might add, he's not particularly partial to that happening in a peaceful and non-violent way."

"General Cullen will see to it that homemade bombs are detonated near the mine fields that fringe the perimeter of the American compound to give the world the impression that America is being singled out because of their partnership with Castro's Cuba. The fault for these unfriendly acts will be laid at the doorstep of right wing groups on the island."

"One of these incidences will take place on an evening when representatives of the Cuban, American and international media will be attending a banquet hosted by General Cullen honoring Fidel Castro and members of his government. Castro will be invited to be the featured speaker of the evening which will give credence to the belief that America is trying to build a lasting relationship with the Castro regime in spite of their political differences. Nothing will be further from the truth, of course."

Pedro added, "The U. S. delegation on hand for this special occasion will be 'outraged at the lengths that certain special interest groups will go to create disunity between Cuba and the U. S.' These unfriendly incidences will give the U. S. justification for the buildup of a stronger military force at Guantanamo."

There was a satisfied smile on everyone's face when Pedro had concluded. Gino stood up, nodded his approval and continued, "And as Fidel is agonizing over his crumbling tourist business and an economy that is again becoming a serious problem for him, we'll throw another monkey wrench into his already unsettled world."

Gino grinned slightly, maintaining his cool exterior, "Losing tourist dollars will not be the end of his troubles. Fortunate is the country that is able to produce vast supplies of oil to meet their own demands. Fortunate, too, is that nation who can create an export market around the world for their product. Cuba is not one of the favored nations who enjoy either one of those distinctions. Cuba must import most of their oil to satisfy their domestic needs. They currently import 53,000 barrels of oil a day from Venezuela – and that's about half of Cuba's daily oil consumption. They receive this oil on preferential terms including long term, low-interest loan payments. Were that oil supply cutoff or suppressed in any way, Cuba would be victimized by shortages that would be difficult to replace."

Pedro took his cue, "It might be argued that they do have domestic oil production to fall back on but the truth of the matter is that their production capabilities are quite limited. It does present them with a challenging dilemma. They see off-shore drilling as being essential to the island's economic recovery and its independence from high oil prices - but that option presents its own problems. They control about 44,000 square miles of waters in the Gulf of Mexico off its northwest coast, although only 4,000 square miles are set for oil exploration. They more than understand that deep-sea oil exploration is risky at best so they proceed cautiously."

"To add to their predicament, environmentalists and Florida's tourism promoters argue that drilling off Florida shores would hurt the sensitive coastline and could endanger Florida's multibillion-dollar tourism industry. Any spills are very difficult to contain. They can move quickly by currents that pass in front of the Florida Keys and the Florida coast. The last thing Fidel wants is a bad American press just when he thinks his economy is about to go into overdrive. So, while Cuban officials say they are launching their first deep sea oil exploration, we believe they will undoubtedly take a wait-and-see attitude so as not to upset their Florida neighbors and the rest of America."

"And, we'll most certainly keep that issue in the forefront of the American press," Juan added.

"So, to sum up," Pedro concluded, "We build up their tourist business and then, when it appears that Cuba is out of the woods economically, we destroy it as decisively as we built it so that the economic fallout impacts the credibility of the sitting government. The country's newly acquired standard of living will collapse under the weight of a rapidly declining economy. The demise of their tourist business should achieve this end, but if not, we will take extreme measures to see that Venezuela does not sufficiently service the oil needs of their Caribbean ally. That course of action should do the trick but, if not, their domestic oil production program will then become our quarry."

Gino ended the meeting with his standard closing, "Any questions?"

David asked the only question. "I realize that these plans have to be tentative at this time given that nothing is going to happen until Doug becomes President, but what can we do now to soften Fidel's attitude towards the U. S. and particularly this administration? I think we should begin developing some kind of immediate relationship with Castro so that we can gradually ease our way into his confidence."

Gino replied, "Yes, that's an excellent suggestion, David. Why don't we all think about it and regroup at a later date when we have some concrete thoughts." The meeting was then adjourned.

David Cromwell walked away from the meeting with the haunting feeling that Cruz was not being forthcoming with certain facts about the plan. Like Pam, he thought that Gino was taking too cavalier an attitude towards Pam joining *The Group* with little or no resistance on his part. He didn't buy Gino's acquiescence to Pam joining them on the grounds that she could be a potential liability if she accidentally learned something about the project that was distasteful to her. No, he thought, her addition to *The Group* was for a specific purpose which Gino doesn't feel should be shared with the others – at least, at this time.

He satisfied himself with the naïve thought that Gino would tell them when he was ready.

CHAPTER 19

Pam Marshall was about to learn why Gino Cruz was so agreeable to having her join *The Group* without as much as a mild rebuff. It really didn't make sense to her that she was invited to join them in the first place. They really don't need me, she reasoned. There must be something going on here that I'm either not getting or am not being told. And, why hasn't Doug said anything to me unless, of course, he isn't being told either.

Cruz knew that Pam joined a group of NBC associates on Tuesday evenings to catch up on the week's happenings and to enjoy a friendly evening of carefree conversation. Doug never expected her to be home until quite late so Gino took the opportunity to talk to Pam about an important matter without Doug knowing that they had met. Gino called her at the office at about 4:00 p. m. that afternoon.

"Pam, its Gino Cruz. How are you this fine afternoon?"

Pam was somewhat startled by the call as she knew that the mysterious Cruz didn't make it a practice to call anyone; particularly, at this late hour of the working day – unless it was a matter of utmost importance. "Hello, Gino. This is a surprise. I was just about to leave the office for a weekly get-together with the staff but what a pleasant surprise."

Gino's responded cordially, "Pam, I was wondering if you might have a few minutes this evening to meet with me and discuss something that could be important to all of us?"

Pam was stunned by the abruptness of the suggestion. She thought she would try some humor to allow herself to see where this conversation was going. "Gino, are you hitting on me?"

The silence on the other end of the connection was followed by an outburst of laughter that was completely out-of-character for the somewhat reserved Cruz. "Pam, my dear, I would be most happy to hit on you if I had the capability and fervor to act upon my lascivious inclinations. You flatter me by even putting that thought in my head."

"Gino, you're underestimating yourself. You have but to ask," she said testing the limits of continuing this innocent banter which made him seem less intimidating.

Cruz was genuinely pleased with the tenor of the conversation knowing that it was Pam's way of showing that she was not overawed by the powerful persona of Washington's foremost political guru.

"Pam, as much as I'd like to see where this very flattering conversation might go, I would like to have dinner with you this evening to discuss something that could be politically important to both of us."

Politically important was the kind of language that commanded Pam's immediate attention. She did not hesitate. "What did you have in mind, Gino?"

"If you can free yourself up this evening, why don't we have dinner at Aquarelle? It's right across from the Kennedy Center – five minutes from Georgetown. I can have my car pick you up at 7:30 p.m. I can promise you a fine dinner and some interesting conversation."

Pam's didn't hesitate, "A lovely restaurant. I'll meet you there at about eight."

Pam arrived at 7:45 p. m. and Gino arrived fifteen minutes later. They poked fun at the conversation they had that afternoon and settled down to a carefree cocktail and idle chit chat. Halfway through the meal, Gino edged his way into the reason for their meeting.

"Have you ever thought of eventually having a political career, Pam? Your background at the State Department, the *New York Times* and *NBC* certainly gives you a leg up on most of these fledgling political wannabes coming along today. Why in the short time as the Vice-President's wife, you've developed a reputation as being a very politically astute person. You've also developed a good measure of respect and friendship with some very important people on Capital Hill. I've mentioned your name to many of them and asked how they thought you'd fare in the political arena. They were unanimous in stating that they thought you'd make a great candidate and, more importantly, a winning candidate. One of them actually said that one day there was going to be a woman in the White House and that gal should be Pam Marshall."

"I'm holding out for first woman pope," Pam replied with a staged dismissive wave of her hand. At the same time, she remembered the recurring dream she had for most of her adult life of holding down an important political office.

Gino was not a man to mince words, "What would you think of stepping into the vice-presidency when Doug becomes president in a couple of years?"

She gave the question the respect of one asked by someone who never joked or was flippant about anything that dealt with political matters. She looked at him hard before answering. "What makes you think I'm vice-presidential material? I'm a journalist not a politician. As a matter of fact, I've always avoided strong party affiliations as I never wanted personal considerations influencing my coverage of a story." She again stared at Gino with an inquisitive look and asked, "What prompts you to even ask that question, Gino?"

"I have my reasons," Gino said. "But before you answer me, let me rephrase the question, "How would you like to be the first woman President of the United States?"

Pam laughed and played along with the running humor they were enjoying. "Yes, I'd like that, but I have to warn you, I have a dinner date tomorrow with Doug so I won't be able to take the Oath of Office until Thursday morning."

Gino was learning quickly that he liked Pam Marshall; mainly because she wasn't intimidated by him. He liked that in a woman; particularly, a beautiful one, but he wasn't about to be put off by her casualness of a subject that he had given long hours of thought. He became serious with his next comment.

"Are you aware that since the late 1960's, the number of voters who say they are willing to vote for a woman president has increased from 45 percent to 75 percent. Three out of every four voters now feel comfortable with a woman leading the nation. Look at the number of women holding political office in the country."

Gino had one of his people research the numbers so he knew he was on solid footing when he stated, "Would you have believed ten years ago there would be eighty seven women serving in Congress and seven as governors – or that today there are sixteen women who are their state's lieutenant governors. By last official count there were over two thousand women holding down statewide offices. Women are widely accepted as having expertise in areas such as foreign policy, health care, education, economic issues, concern for the elderly.... well, the list is endless. Believe me Pam, America *is* ready for a woman to be President of the United States and it's going to happen in the not-to-distant future."

"But why me?" Pam asked, genuinely mystified. "Here are these talented people, having worked for many years to hone their political skills, and along comes Miss Television Personality, without any office-holding experience saying, for starters, that she wants to be the Vice-President and maybe later on the President of the United States. Don't you think, Gino, that she would be laughed right off her soapbox? And how about the party leaders? I have to believe they would unquestionably be looking for someone who had held a responsible public office and who could provide the experience and leadership to qualify for the offices you're talking about."

"I honestly think that if you were to decide here and now that you would at least consider the possibility that the vice-presidency would be within your reach – and would be willing to spend the next four years preparing yourself for the office – I have no misgivings in saying to you that it can be made to happen."

Pam saw the seriousness in Gino's comment and momentarily became light-headed. "But, how, Gino? How does one prepare herself for an office that has no apparent definable responsibilities other than to sit in on Cabinet Meetings and not act bored?"

Gino laughed, "Well, that's about the best definition I've ever heard of a vice-president's role. But that stereotype has changed. The national media has brought the office into the limelight so it has forced the second-in-command to take a more commanding position in administration matters. Further, because the vice-presidency is perceived to be a ready access to the presidency, better qualified individuals have accepted the role of vice-president. The office has become a spawning ground for the Oval Office."

"Gino, I don't want you to get the wrong impression that I wouldn't like to take on the challenge, but is it legal or even proper for the President's wife to become his Vice-President? Do you really think that Americans would accept such a notion?"

"I absolutely think they would not only accept the idea but with the proper presentation of your credentials, I think they would unanimously accept Pamela St. Pierre Cromwell as their Vice-President. They've already accepted you into their homes night after night with very convincing approval ratings. The latest Gallop poll on that score has confirmed that you have one of the highest ratings of anyone included in their survey," Gino said with conviction.

Pam saw that Gino had done his homework and what at first had appeared to her to be a frivolous conversational diversion, had become a serious test of intent. She thought for a moment and said tentatively, "Yes, but how would Doug feel about having his wife on his coattails day and night and even second guessing him on occasion? We do have our contentious moments, you know."

A slight smile crossed Gino's lips, "I don't think that would be a problem. Remember, Doug is a very committed public official who is very generous in accepting advice that will promote his agenda. No, you would be an invaluable asset to him. You know yourself that he has the highest respect for your intelligence and judgment."

"Yes, but I….."

"Believe me, Pam, that should not be a concern of yours in making a decision." Pam's thoughts again suddenly focused on her recurring dream of someday becoming a political somebody. Now, that *would be* a somebody, she quipped to herself.

Gino brought out his heavy artillery of persuasion. "As I see it Pam, we could immediately place you in a visible and titled position in the State Department. I have often spoken of you with Secretary Lansing. He spoke glowingly of your time with them at State and said that you would be a welcomed addition to his staff should you ever decide to become involved in government service again. Your time at State would allow the American people and party leaders to see the strength of your mettle. Your father-in-law would get behind you with a public relations campaign that would showcase your professionalism and devotion to your country. Doug would spend two terms as President with you as his Vice-President. When he completed his final term of office, you would very naturally become the Republican Party's nominee for the Oval Office in the next election." Gino paused long enough to add import to his next statement.

"Believe me, Pam, I've been involved in politics all of my adult life and I have never seen a more perfect fit for a person becoming this nation's first woman chief executive." With those words, Gino knew he had only to ask her again the question he had asked her when they began their conversation. "Pam, would you like to be the first woman President of the United States?"

Without hesitation, she said, "Yes, Gino, I would."

Gino had a satisfied smile on his face when he said, "I was confident you'd say that. I was so sure that I confided in Tom Beckwell that we were going to discuss the matter. He was quite pleased about it even though he knew you'd have to relinquish your duties at the network." Beckwell was the President and Chief Operating Officer at the NBC-Television Network.

"Tom and I go back a long way. He'll keep our secret until the time is right for an announcement. I took the opportunity of suggesting to him that he think about a one-hour formatted Sunday evening show with you as the hostess discussing and analyzing the national and international news of the week. I didn't presume to elaborate on any more than that, but he thought the format could work well for a 7:00 p.m. time slot. He said it would be a rating grabber for their prime time shows later that evening. He was confident that with you fronting the show he could line up some very important newsmakers."

"I am simply amazed the influence you exert, Gino. You seem to know everyone who needs knowing and you're constantly in the forefront of what's happening in this country. How in the world do you manage such a complex world of political intrigue?"

He sidestepped the question very deftly, "I do my best, Pam. I do my best." Oh, and by the way, I have told no one of what we've discussed here – not even Doug. I was pretty sure of what your answer would be, but to play it safe, I kept it quiet. Let's keep it that way until I've had a chance to finalize some of the details which should take a couple of days. You can tell Doug then – if that's satisfactory with you?"

Pam agreed. They finished their dinner after which Gino dropped Pam off at her home. He reflected on their conversation as he was driven home. His initial impression was that she might become a problem when certain elements of the plan were revealed to her which, he discovered, was totally unfounded. Two weeks prior to the conversation they had that evening; he had his special investigators conduct a meticulous background check on Pam. There were gray moments in her career to be sure, but nothing that could prove damaging to her seeking high political office. While her misdeeds were mostly frivolous affairs, there were several incidences that could prove personally embarrassing to someone held in such high esteem by a public that enjoyed destroying people they put on their pedestal in the first place.

One of Pam's omissions of judgment involved her personal stock portfolio. She had held a substantial position in Universal Global Communications for a number of years and she had more than tripled her investment during that time. The chief financial officer of the company and a personal friend of the family, advised her that the government was investigating several of the company's accounting procedures and that they had raised serious questions about the true profitability of the company over their most recent five year reporting period. He further advised her to sell her holdings immediately.

She took his advice along with a considerable profit as had he and three other company officials. A week later the value of the stock dropped precipitously when the government findings were revealed. The stockholders who took the major loss were employees of the company whose company-managed retirement funds were seriously compromised. The federal government filed *insider trading* charges against the officials who were prosecuted and sentenced to short *country club* jail terms. Pam avoided being included in the charge when her father interceded on her behalf. Her involvement never became public.

The upside of this incident to Gino was that he now had incriminating information about Pam Marshall that could be used as bargaining leverage should it be needed in the future.

Gino spent the morning and most of the afternoon of the next day on the telephone with congressional leaders and friendly lawmakers who had proven many times in the past to be sympathetic towards a man who controlled a rich arsenal of persuasive weapons. Reciprocation was always the bargaining chip. It was the rare politician who wasn't looking to be the recipient of a political advantage that would best serve their constituency at home and, more importantly, the growth potential of their own pocketbooks.

He advised them that the Vice-President's wife was leaving her regular and highly respected television assignment with the NBC-Television Network and trading it in for an important position with the State Department. Her specific responsibilities would be revealed when the Secretary of State made the official announcement. Gino confided in these *special friends* that he would also need their support in the future as Pamela Marshall had aspirations for high political office and she was not one to forget her loyal friends. That strong a statement by Gino Cruz, and the fact that he was taking a personal interest in her career, was enough to convince this group of important legislators that a cooperative attitude on their part would be politically well-advised.

Satisfied that a solid base of support was in place, Gino called Pam at her office and suggested that this evening would be a good time for her to tell Doug of their conversation. "You might want to cushion the fact that we talked before consulting him by saying that I wasn't sure if there was any interest on your part to begin with. Tell Doug that I didn't want to get his hopes up before getting a preliminary go ahead from you. He has enough distractions to contend with right now without adding to them. Tell him that I'll call him tomorrow and we'll talk about it."

Pedro and Juan were aware of the meeting between Gino and Pam. Gino had filled them in earlier on Pam's decision. He picked up the phone and called David Cromwell at the Watergate Hotel where he was staying to tell him the news. Upon hearing the disclosure, David again got the uneasy feeling that Gino was not always forthcoming with certain members of *The Group* – including himself.

CHAPTER 20

Doug and Pam had talked often about her dream of one day entering into politics so he wasn't completely surprised when she told him of her plan for returning to the State Department as a first step in a turnabout career move. Actually, he thought the idea had great merit. He had always encouraged her to do what she felt in her heart was the right thing. What did surprise him though was that she hadn't told him of her private meeting with Gino. Doug thought that it would have been nice to have gotten a call to say where she would be that evening. However, he placed no significance on her oversight. After all, he reminded himself, she's always been her own person.

Doug often thought that she'd make a strong political candidate once she finally decided where she was going in her career. As for her becoming his vice-president when he was president would be an interesting turn of events. She has all the natural ability for the job and she's one of the smartest people on the Washington scene right now. And, that was not just my opinion. She was certainly thought to be one of the brightest among her circle of media colleagues. She'll be perfect for the job. She'll have been on the fast track at State before she's asked to step into the vice-presidency. As far as I'm concerned, she's ready now to take on some major responsibilities. Think of how ready she'll be in a couple of years. And, if a man with Gino's political savvy and influence championed the notion in the first place, then that only reinforces the wisdom of such a move. And when I step down, the presidency could very well be in her future with Gino Cruz and *The Group* behind her.

Gino did call Doug the following morning and they had a friendly chat about Pam's political future. No mention was made of Doug not having been included in the initial discussion.

A week later, Secretary of State Robert P. Lansing made the announcement at his regular weekly press conference that "the Vice-President's wife has graciously agreed that she would be joining his staff as Director of Policy Planning which will have the rank equivalent to Assistant Secretary." He characterized her as extremely intelligent with a mature and encyclopedic knowledge and understanding of world politics and America's place of prominence in it. His flattering remarks told America that he held Pamela St. Pierre Cromwell in great esteem and that she would play a primary role in all foreign affairs activities. Left unsaid was the rotation plan for her to spend a period of time in the various bureaus and offices of the Department of State to ensure that she will have mastered a thorough understanding of U. S. foreign policy and be recognized as one of Secretary Lansing's trusted advisors. And that would only be a short step away from being appointed Foreign Relations Advisor to President Dewitt Marshall.

Two days later, the President of the NBC-Television Network announced that Ms. Pamela St. Pierre Cromwell would headline a news-information half-hour program on Monday evenings at 7:30 p.m. He was careful to mention that her new weekly show had the complete approval of the State Department. It was felt that this unprecedented move to feature a highly placed administration insider as the moderator on a public service formatted show would provide the American public with a fresh and authoritative perspective of the fast-changing international and national scenes.

The Democratic Party had their own problems to worry about after the untimely death of Senator Andrew Davis Stuart and his chief advisor in an airplane crash several months before. The Democrat's Minority Leader had been the party's choice to unseat Dewitt Marshall in the next presidential election. He was considered the one candidate who was capable of giving the popular President a competitive run for the Oval Office. They now needed a candidate to fill Stuart's shoes.

Senator Mark A. Thornberry was the party's choice. He was young, boyishly handsome and an articulate spokesman for the party's agenda. To give him national recognition, party leaders had arranged for him to lock horns with the President over a Republican senior health care bill that Marshall wanted passed. The bill was important to senior citizen voters in Florida and California with whom the Republicans were trying to curry favor. Senator Thornberry took an aggressive position against the bill and won the day when the bill was voted down by both Houses of Congress. This small victory was followed up by a series of television lectures by Thornberry entitled "Issues in Doubt" which lambasted many of the Administration's programs.

While having lunch with Gino Cruz at the White House one afternoon, the President asked Cruz what he thought should be done about the divisive tactics that Thornberry was using to embarrass the administration. "Do nothing, Mr. President," was Cruz's immediate response. He then explained his reluctance to recommend doing anything which sparked a humorous reaction and an immediate change of attitude by the President. They then enjoyed their lunch after which Cruz returned to his office. He was met by Pedro and Juan Sierra who also seemed anxious about the "Issues in Doubt" campaign that seemed to be getting some attention.

Pedro was the first to speak, "Gino, I think we should take some action to diffuse what they're saying. It would almost seem that they're deliberately misrepresenting the issues in the hopes of giving Thornberry some quick publicity."

Gino understood their concern but only smiled and said, "Let's let him ramble on for awhile if it will help him get his party's nomination. We want him to be their candidate. We want nothing to interfere with his continuing as the Democratic hopeful up until close to Election Day."

Pedro and Juan then smiled knowingly. "Gino, what do you have up your sleeve?" Juan asked.

Gino explained, "An extremely well hidden fact is that the good Senator has a robust and unnatural appetite for young men. At times, his debauchery goes well beyond the limits of acceptable behavioral standards for a high ranking elected official of the U. S. Senate - or anyone else, for that matter."

Gino was made aware of Stuart's fixation for same-sex liaisons by one of his private investigators who discovered the information quite accidentally while gathering background information on the Senator in his hometown. It seemed that Thornberry videotaped and photographed many of his youthful indiscretions which the investigator found in a sealed trunk in his parent's home on an evening when the Senator's parents were out-of-town. Included were compromising letters identifying many of the Senator's friends and several prominent congressional associates.

Gino facetiously said that he had too much respect for the Congress of the U. S. to even think of making the American public aware of the homoerotic behavior of one of its leading members. "But", he said with a menacing glow, "we'll surely use this information to convince the good Senator that he's riding the wrong horse in the forthcoming election. Incidentally, I've talked to the President about this situation and he concurs with our assessment and that we should do nothing right away. Let's just let our friend go through the motions. If necessary, we'll make his misdeeds public, but I don't think it will come to that. Let me say this – that man will never be President – a fact that should encourage us not to become distracted from our main task of supplanting Castro and his gang with unproductive issues. Don't worry, we'll have them sitting on the sidelines before this is over."

Gino would never use the word *blackmail* when referring to his ability to negotiate a favorable political position with documented facts.

Senator Thornberry was not aware that his past indiscretions were on the brink of destroying his once promising career. He realized that he would be the underdog in the next national election so he knew that he would have to begin early making realistic plans for his White House bid. He was aware of Douglas Cromwell's puritanical reputation and decided that trying to besmirch his *good guy* image with the American public could hurt him.

Sherman Cotswold was a close associate of the Senator from the days when they were both undergraduates at Dartmouth College and later the Yale Law School in New Haven. Degrees in hand, they both joined a prestigious law firm specializing in corporate law with an aside in servicing political lobbying groups. They became intrigued with the role of the lobbyists and developed a political awareness that prompted them to become active members of the local Democratic Party.

After a time, they became mesmerized with the idea of running for political office. They knew that they would have to combine their talents to make any kind of a mark in the mercurial world of politics. They decided that one would be the candidate and the other the behind-the-scene planner and mastermind. Sherman suggested that Mark be the candidate as he had the personality and was certainly the more charismatic of the two and thus best suited for that role. He chose for himself to be the behind-the-scene chief-of-staff. After all, he told himself, I'm a hell of a lot smarter than Mark and my dark side will allow me to make decisions that would repulse him. He recognized early that there were certain unpleasant things that one had to do in this career they were choosing for themselves. He knew that Mark was not strong enough to run roughshod over people or in making unpopular decisions when the chips were down. They agreed on the arrangement and became an unbeatable combination which, years later, resulted in Mark Thornberry becoming the youngest Senator ever to be elected to the U. S. Congress.

One evening, Thornberry and Cotswold were having a serious discussion about the Senator's chances of actually winning an election against Cromwell. Cotswold said, "Right now, I give us little or no chance of that happening. The guy is going to be tough and if we don't think of something to make him look like the bad guy – well, we lose before we begin."

"What the hell can we do?" asked Thornberry. "Cromwell's path to the White House is being directed by Gino Cruz and, as we well know, he has never ridden a loser. Without Cruz controlling the strings, we could compete against Cromwell and maybe even beat him. But – and this is a big *but* - Cruz would have to disappear."

"So, we make him disappear," was Cotswold's easy reply. "We eliminate him."

Thornberry made a face and snickered, "You've been seeing too many bad movies. You don't eliminate somebody like that. Who's going to do it? Not you, that's for sure."

"Of course not," we'd get a professional to do it."

Thornberry stared at his friend for several moments and laughed, "You know a professional who does things like that?"

"No, but I know somebody who does."

"Listen, Sherm, don't you go getting yourself into something you know nothing about. I don't want to lose you. You're the mastermind in this partnership. I'd be lost without you and not just professionally." Thornberry stared into space for a moment and finally said, "It's a hell of an idea, though. Cruz gone would solve a big problem for us."

"Tell you what, I'll look into it. Don't worry, I'll be careful," was Cotswold's final remark.

Gino Cruz had learned of the Thornberry-Cotswold plot to find someone to eliminate him through surveillance devices that he had placed in Thornberry's home. Cruz made it a standard practice to have "hidden bugs" placed in the homes and offices of people of consequence whose conversations could be useful to him at a future date.

That evening, Cotswold received a telephone call at his home from a voice he didn't recognize. The caller actually had many different names. This evening he was Rob Roy. "A friend told me that you were looking for someone to handle a sensitive matter for you."

Cotswold was expecting the call so he didn't hesitate in answering, "Yes, can we meet and discuss what I have in mind?"

"Of course, will you be at home this evening?"

"Yes, I'm home now and will be here all evening," was Cotswold's answer.

"Okay, I'll call you at eight o'clock and tell you where we'll meet," the stranger said and then cut the connection.

A half hour later at 6:00 p. m. the stranger, dressed in a jogging suit, rang Cotswold's door bell. "Good evening, Mr. Cotswold, my name is Rob Roy. You're expecting me."

Cotswold was taken aback. "I was expecting your call later on, but come in. We can talk in the library."

Cotswold had never had this type of conversation before so he was hesitant as how to begin. The stranger saw his dilemma and said, "You're interested in having someone eliminated, is that right?"

"Yes, yes," Cotswold stammered. He had been assured by his contact that this man could be trusted implicitly so tell him exactly what you want and why you want it done which is what Cotswold did. The stranger listened carefully. When he had finished, the man nodded his head and said that he understood what was needed. "The fee will be $20,000," he said, "and the job could be done within the week. You can pay me when the job is completed."

Cotswold breathed a sigh of relief when he realized that the conversation had taken no more than twenty minutes. He said to himself, this guy really *is* a professional. Cotswold saw the man to the door and concluded by saying, "You don't have to tell me how you're going to do it. I'm sure the media will be quick to pick up on the story."

The stranger jogged the three blocks away where he had left his car. The short ride to McLean, Virginia brought him to Gino Cruz's home. Cruz was expecting him. "I got the whole conversation on tape Mr. Cruz. I guess he didn't think to check me out more thoroughly before asking me to kill you," said the stranger - known to Cruz as Carmine Cato.

"These fellows aren't familiar with our way of doing business, Carmine. Here, let me have that tape." Cruz put the tape into his tape recorder and listened to the conversation between Cotswold and Cato. Satisfied, he said, "Okay, here's that way we'll handle the *hit*." While Cato was completely familiar with the scenario of how they would make it appear that Cruz was the victim of an attempted assassination, Cruz wanted to make sure that there were no slip ups. Cato was a very capable professional, but his brain sometimes shifted into neutral gear at the wrong time so he had to be constantly reminded of what it was he was supposed to do.

"Tell me again, Carmine, what are you going to do?" asked Cruz.

Cato responded, "When you leave your office, I'll fire three shots at you. I'll make sure they hit the wall behind where you'll be standing."

Cruz's cold staring eyes felt that a final cautionary comment was in order, "Remember and this is important, Carmine. Don't let any of those three shots hit me. I don't want to........"

Carmine interrupted with a hurt expression, "Hey, boss, what'd you think I'm stupid. I would never shoot you. Don't worry I'll miss with all three shots." Cruz heard the words but was still somewhat wary of Cato being able to differentiate between real targets and a simulated victim when he pulled the trigger.

"As soon as it's done, you are to call Cotswold and arrange to meet him that same evening at his home to confirm that you killed me. It's important that you remember to tape that conversation – just like you did the first one you had with him. We'll have Thornberry and Cotswold right where we want them once we have those tapes. No slip ups, Carmine. Let's make this a clean job. Okay?"

"Okay, boss."

Cruz was now confident that Senator's predilection for same sex relationships and his complicity in a premeditated murder scheme, would unquestionably seal the fate of Mark A. Thornberry.

At four o'clock the following Thursday, Gino Cruz was leaving his office on Pennsylvania Avenue when a slow-moving Mercedes Benz automobile came driving by the main entrance of the building. Simultaneously, three shots rang out. Cruz fell to the ground when the three shots came dangerously close to hitting him. The car then sprang to life and was gone before any eyewitnesses could identify the license plate of the vehicle. Cruz looked around to make sure that a friendly free-lancing reporter from the Washington Post had seen the incident as planned. The story of the attempted assassination of Washington's foremost political guru would be the newspaper's headline in the morning edition.

Cato called Cotswold immediately after the incident and told him that he would see him at his home in about an hour. Cotswold agreed. When they met, Cato boastfully said, "Well, the son-of-a-bitch is dead. I'll take my money and be off."

Cotswold smiled and said, "You got him? You actually killed him?"

"That was the deal, wasn't it?" said Cato. He saw that Cotswold was completely overjoyed by the news which encouraged him to try a scam that had worked for him in the past. He said as he took a silencer equipped revolver from his shoulder holster, "You know I've been hired to kill *you*, too."

"Cotswold was confused. He said nervously, "What? Why do you want to kill me?"

"Because someone paid me to do it."

"Who? Who would want to kill me?"

"It's not important."

"You'd kill me just for money?"

"That's what I do. And, it's a lot of money."

"What's a lot of money?"

"I'm getting twenty grand for the job."

Cotswold looked somewhat more at ease knowing that he was being put in a negotiating position, "Twenty thousand dollars is not a lot of money. I'll give you seventy thousand not to kill me. In cash. Right now."

"Where's the money?"

"In the wall safe behind that picture."

"Deal. Open the safe but be careful what you take out."

Cotswold opened the safe and extracted a large metal box. He cautiously opened it. Cato saw that the box contained a large number of packets each containing a considerable number of one hundred dollar bills. Cotswold removed seven of the packets and handed them to Cato saying, "Seventy big ones. Okay?"

Cato took the money, lifted the silencer and shot Cotswold between the eyes. He then emptied the box and the safe and left. His parting remark was, "Okay."

Cruz was furious when he heard what Cato had done. He openly berated him for having needlessly killed Cotswold.

"Why did you do it, Carmine? We were out of the woods with Thornberry and Cotswold. We had the taped evidence to neutralize both of them and you go and jeopardize our plans with an unnecessary killing. Not a smart move, Carmine." Cato did not even try to justify his actions.

When Cruz was alone he called Bud DeLuca on his safe telephone. Cato worked for DeLuca so it was only professional courtesy that he be advised of the mishap. DeLuca took the news quietly and said, "He's always been one of my most dependable people. What could have caused him to act so irresponsibly?"

Cruz said, "Cotswold's safe was wide open when they found him. I suspect that Cato robbed the man and then decided to kill him to avoid detection. The trouble is that he's a high profile Washington insider. His murder will have to be investigated. Granted, Cato is always careful about not leaving fingerprints so there's no way the trail can lead back to us, but still, Cato has become a dangerous liability."

There was moment of silence on the phone. DeLuca then said decisively, "I'll send him on a special assignment to Detroit tomorrow morning. That'll keep him out of the way for the next several weeks." Nothing more had to be said.

The next morning Cato caught an early morning flight out of LaGuardia Airport for Detroit.

Carmine Cato was never heard from again.

CHAPTER 21

Pam and Doug Cromwell had a great deal of work to do to prepare themselves for the roles they were expected to fulfill in the coming years. The duties of Vice President were simple. The U. S. Constitution only empowered him to preside over the United States Senate and cast tie breaking votes. One of the founding fathers had said jokingly that he was only assigned that responsibility so he'd at least have something to do. Other than that, the Vice President's responsibilities were loosely defined and totally flexible. Executing assignments at the request of the President was the closest to a job description that was available to describe the second-in-command's official duties.

When discussing the role that Doug would be playing in the Marshall administration, the President's instructions were explicit, "Hogwash, Doug, I don't want you to be limited by requests from me. I don't know who made up those rules, but, as of right now, we're going to shelve anything that curtails your freedom from doing what you think is best for this administration. As I mentioned to you, I want you to begin speaking with more authority than any other modern vice-president. I don't think Franklin D. Roosevelt's Vice-President John Nance Gardner was far from wrong when he said, 'The vice-presidency isn't worth a pitcher of warm spit.' Well, we'll give the office a little more respect than that. I want you contributing as an important insider to policy decisions. Take on visible missions. Let the people know that you're not being manipulated – that you have a mind of your own. Speak for me. I trust your judgment."

Doug always reacted well to one of Marshall's pep talks. "I'll be there for you, Mr. President. Both Pam and I are looking forward to the next four years. We see great things happening for you as we go into the new millennium and we're proud to be a part of it."

"You've been doing a terrific job so far, Doug. Just remember that you're going to be a key force in politics for years to come – as will Pam. When my time is up, we'll make sure that you get the party's nomination for my job. Just think of it, one of the country's youngest presidents and the first female vice-president in the nation's history.

You'll make a fine team. And I want both of you to start carving out a conspicuous place for yourselves in the media spotlight."

Doug grinned and said, "Pam was telling me last night that she is taking on greater responsibilities over there at State. They now have her in the Office of Protocol as Deputy Chief under Bob Chester. She'll be directly assisting you and me and the Secretary of State on official matters of national and international protocol. It will give her a great learning experience in planning, hosting and officiating at ceremonial events and activities for visiting heads of state. She'll also act as coordinator for all protocol matters for your travel abroad. It's an ideal assignment for her. She got a taste of it when she worked for the State Department before. She'll do a good job and the experience will serve her well for what's coming up for her in the future."

The President said, "Well, she's a clever woman. I have a strong feeling that she'll leave an indelible impression when the history of my administration is written. She'll also be a key player in your administration in the not-to-distance future." Marshall reflected and added, "And let's not forget her administration when you and I share that room at the retirement home."

"We both have a long way to go before that happens, Mr. President."

Marshall smiled and continued. "I was discussing with Secretary Lansing how best we can get Americans to begin viewing the two of you as a team. He suggested that an international tour would be an ideal way for the future President to begin developing foreign policy contacts and who better to be your go-between than Pam. So, if you agree, here's what we'll do."

Marshall went on to explain that Doug's recent twenty-four state tour of the country was a huge success in not only getting several important administration messages across to millions of Americans on a personal level, but gave them a chance to see America's number one political pinup boy firsthand.

"You made a lasting impression on America with that trip, Doug. You're beginning to stockpile some impressive voter confidence that will be useful in the days ahead. Now, let's see what you can do with a European audience. First and foremost, the purpose of a European trip will be for you to reassure our friends and allies that America is steadfast in their support of them. It will also provide you with the opportunity to explain American policies in several of those countries that are neutral towards us. It'll be good for you to get a first hand look at some of the birds you'll be dealing with when you're in the Oval Office. Eyeball to eyeball relationships are always more productive than those transatlantic telephone calls. Most importantly, the trip is intended for Europeans to get to know Vice-President and Mrs. Douglas Cromwell. It'll also begin giving Pam an ongoing working knowledge of the Vice-President's office."

"We'll both look forward to the trip, Mr. President."

"And one more thing, Doug, please stop calling me Mr. President when we're alone. Dewitt or *your highness* will suffice nicely."

Three months later the Cromwells left on a month long tour of six European nations for what was referred to by the Democratic press in America as a diplomatic boondoggle. However, public opinion polls told a different story. Americans viewed the event as a romantic journey for America's *Royal Couple.* They thought it was a great opportunity for the young Vice-President to become involved in international affairs. Besides, rumor hungry Americans were looking forward to the news and gossip of the social life they would be enjoying abroad. The Cromwells seemed to command media attention wherever they went.

The first stop in their itinerary was England which was judged to be America's strongest ally in the European community. The British people greeted them enthusiastically when they arrived which spoke volumes for the esteem the two countries held for each other. The British Prime Minister and his wife led the official greeting party. The couples became fast friends during the Cromwell's short visit.

Pam had always enjoyed visiting England and thoroughly enjoyed Doug's discovery of traditional London under the veneer of its modern ways. The British capital had appeared to her less English and more international since her first visit there many years before. The gent with the bowler hat and the stolidly British attitude was less in vogue. One was more likely to see someone with a turban and speaking in a mysterious dialect than the proverbial Englishman with his impeccable diction. The city had become increasingly multicultural but still, she noted, continued to abound with the same culture and charm of days gone by.

The British ways and historical sites were familiar to Pam but Doug just couldn't get enough of the city's historic sights and the surrounding countryside. The couple genuinely liked the English – a feeling that was heartily reciprocated. The well-known British reserve was no where to be found in its attitude towards the American couple.

The Vice-President was invited to address the British House of Commons. His speech reviewed the strong bond that the two countries enjoyed during times of peace and conflict and reinforced America's continued commitment to "a nation of strength and dedicated to safeguarding the ideals that allow both our countries to live in a free and democratic society." The speech was warmly received by the British people and applauded in the press.

The next stop was Paris, who like their neighbor across the English Channel, were just as giving of themselves in their greetings in welcoming the Vice-President and his wife.

An official sightseeing tour of Continental Europe's premier city left Doug with a nostalgic feeling that he had been to many of the historic places he was seeing for the first time. Pam told him that it was an emotional response that everybody felt when seeing these magnificent cities for the first time. We've all grown up with Buckingham Palace, Notre-Dame and the Eiffel Tower so it's a *déjà vu* experience when seeing them firsthand.

The reception by the French was friendly. Pam decided to take a page from Jackie Kennedy's *tour de force* when she and President Kennedy visited Paris in 1961. Jack's humor and Jackie speaking to them fluently in their own language won the Kennedy's immediate acceptance with a people who become indignant with Americans who attempted to speak their language and did it badly. Pam's command of the language was no less than flawless. Doug introduced her one evening before a banquet in which she told a humorous anecdote in French regarding their trip. The audience was delightfully surprised and generously applauded their approval. The press treated her kindly which seemed to take the edge off any initial misgivings the delegation had about the reception they would receive in France. Marshall had warned them, "The French are a peculiar lot. They don't like anyone suggesting to them what they should be doing – particularly Americans."

The Vice-President was invited to address a group of leading French government officials and other dignitaries on the evening before their day of departure. While Doug always felt comfortable about ordering a meal in French in stateside restaurants, he opted to deliver his speech in English on these official occasions. He jokingly told Pam that he didn't want to jeopardize our relationship with France with his schoolboy French.

The receptions the Vice-President's party received in the other European nations on the schedule were equally as satisfying. Germany, Spain, Italy and Russia came under the spell of the youthful and outgoing American couple. The Soviet head of state Vladimirovich Ouspenkaya was surprisingly informal with the Cromwells. His casual manner and cordiality belied the hard line he had taken with the U. S. in the past even on social occasions. This behavioral change gave the delegation hope that future dealings would be more resilient particularly when the two political leaders began calling each other Doug and Vladi.

The last country on the schedule was Italy – and deliberately so. Pam had always harbored a desire to return to this wonderfully romantic country which she had visited many times in her capacity as a news journalist and State Department aide. Her secret desire was to return to southern Italy and share the wonders of the beautiful Amalfitan Coast with someone very special. Doug had told her that they would only be going to Rome on this trip but Pam convinced him otherwise with her romantic descriptions of the picturesque small towns and their intoxicating beauty. She further goaded him with promises of seductive evenings out of view of the ever present Secret Service.

Six months after their successful European tour, the Cromwells said farewell to a cheering crowd at Dulles International Airport for a month long trip to Asia and the Far East. The trip was judged to be of a more sensitive nature than the previous one simply because American policy in this part of the world was viewed quite differently than their European allies. Japan and China were the focal points of this diplomatic mission. India, Korea, Vietnam, the Philippines and a homeward bound stop in Saudi Arabia were included.

In reflecting on his worldwide tour, Doug had to agree with President Marshall's assessment that eyeball-to-eyeball diplomacy was important to his developing a practical point of view and working relationship with other world leaders. The Vice-President came home with a resounding victory for the administration and a personal satisfaction of accomplishment.

Over the next several years, Doug Cromwell created a new image for the office of Vice-President of the United States. President Marshall smoothed the way for his becoming an important insider contributing to policy decisions. The President invited him to be present at every cabinet meeting and made sure that he had a meaningful contribution to make at each of these sessions. He quickly earned the respect of the heads of the sixteen major executive departments of the government.

His intuitive executive style soon made him principle spokesman for administrative policy. His high profile speeches which centered on building President Marshall's domestic agenda were favorably regarded and chiefly responsible for Americans understanding and accepting the administration's programs. He and the President met at least once a day and had lunch once a week in the Oval Office that quickly became a common meeting ground for them.

The Vice-President's appearances were always a welcoming sight at state and local political functions as he invariably drew large crowds wherever he went. He developed a talent for departing from prepared texts and speaking off-the-cuff. He came across as friendly, forthright and even funny on occasions.

He and Pam made it a practice to host at their residency non-partisan dinner parties and conferences of specialists and newsmakers from various sectors of government, industry and the arts to present and discuss new ideas and developments on a wide variety of subjects.

Douglas Cromwell's burgeoning popularity within the Republican Party made him a political target outside of it. The opposition party forged a negative campaign against him that fell on deaf ears across the country. Americans simply refused to believe anything that suggested that the Vice-President was anything but a heroic figure.

Pam Cromwell's career was also on course and flourishing. After spending a year as Deputy Chief in the Office of Protocol at the State Department, her next assignment was at the Bureau of Legislative Affairs. As chief liaison between the State Department and the Congress, she performed a critical role in advancing the President's and the Department's legislative agenda in the area of foreign policy.

The assignment lasted only eight months as the President decided he wanted her at his side to keep him informed on foreign policy matters. She moved into an office in the White House with the title of Foreign Relations Advisor to the President and became an important addition to the chief executive's administrative family.

The Group now had their presidential hopeful in place to be the Republican Party's nominee for the top office at the next election which was eighteen months away. They had prepared well for this eventuality. Early national polls indicated that Doug's bid for the presidency would be a cakewalk. The consensus among Washington insiders was that the next election would confirm that Douglas Cromwell would be the next President of the United States.

But that was not to be the case. Circumstances decided that he would not have to wait until the next election for that honor.

CHAPTER 22

Dewitt Marshall was a highly accomplished equestrian most of his adult life. While attending college he had qualified for the U. S. Equestrian team that for years was a leader in national and international competition. Marshall never lost interest in the sport. He continued to perform competitively during the years he was fighting his way into political prominence. And he didn't let the presidency interfere with his passion for the sport although, befitting his maturing years, he now rode competitively only on special occasions. Whenever possible, he made it a Saturday morning ritual to join friends at the Colonial Riding Academy in Culpeper County, Virginia to nurture his consuming hobby.

One beautiful Saturday morning in May, wearing his usual protective helmet and vest and riding his trained thoroughbred horse *Trusted Friend*; he was thrown from his mount after executing three flawless jumps. The horse had gone over the fourth jump when it suddenly stopped and catapulted the president over his head. Marshall broke his neck at the first and second vertebrae when he hit the ground. He was rushed unconscious to the local hospital and wasn't revived until an hour later. He was placed on a respirator to control his dangerously labored breathing and it was only after a long painful rehabilitation that he was he able to breathe on his own. But the damage had been done. Marshall would never be the same.

A group of medical specialists, including the President's personal physician, agreed that the President Marshall would be unable to fulfill the responsibilities of his office due to his physical disability.

Article II of the Constitution of the United States was very clear on the vice-president's role when a sitting president was unable to continue in office. It provided that *"the vice-president became president whenever the president dies, resigns, is removed from office or cannot fulfill the duties of the presidency"*.

Nine vice-presidents became president by filling such a vacancy. Gerald Ford was in the unique position of being the only President of the United States never to have been elected to either the presidential or vice-presidential office. He was appointed to the vice-presidency by President Richard Nixon when Spiro Agnew had resigned his office in 1973 under faultfinding circumstances. Ford was then elevated to the presidency when Nixon resigned in 1974. Douglas Cromwell was about to break that precedent when President Dewitt Marshall became incapacitated.

The Vice-President took the oath of office on the same day that the President was judged unable to continue in office. It was a solemn group that crowded into the Oval Office that day. Gino Cruz was the only one who seemed to be enjoying the occasion although he tried to hide his pleasure behind a pair of darkly tinted glasses. Pam looked on proudly as the Chief Justice of the Supreme Court spoke the solemn words of the Oath of Office that the new President repeated in his rich baritone. "I do solemnly swear that I will faithfully execute the Office of the President of the United States, and will, to the best of my ability, preserve, protect and defend the Constitution of the United States."

With those words, Vice-President Douglas Cromwell became President of the United States.

When the ceremony was completed, everyone convened to the State Dining Room which was referred to as the best smelling room in the White House because of the preponderance of meals that were served in the room on special occasions. It was both a sad and happy day of non-partisan cordiality. Congratulatory messages tinged with sympathy for the outgoing president flooded the White House.

When Pam and Doug were alone that evening, Doug fell into a pensive mood. "What are you thinking about, dear," she asked with a note of concern.

"Oh, I was just thinking how fate seems to dictate who we are and how we live our lives. Here we are sitting in the White House sooner than we had planned because of an accidental turn of events. I guess it was inevitable that we'd be here, but I wish Dewitt could have served out his term of office. It would have been fitting. He's a good man."

"Yes, he is," Pam said sympathetically. She chose her next words carefully. "Doug, I have all the confidence in the world that you're going to make a truly great president. The only concern I have is that there are so many issues and challenges that you're going to have to deal with that I'm just afraid your commitment to the Cuban project will prevent you from doing your best for *all* of the people - not just *The Group.*"

"But that's the reason we're here in the first place, he replied. Cuba must be high on our list of priorities but, I can assure you, I fully expect to live up to all of my responsibilities as president. There's much to be done and I'm going to need your help more than ever. Together, sweetheart, we can do the job that is expected of us. We're going to make history before this is over. And, speaking of making history, isn't it about time we turned in."

Hearing those words made Pam feel better about the doubts that had been festering within her. She smiled and said, "I'll meet you on the field of honor in a few minutes."

Again, the Constitution was explicit regarding a president's appointment of his vice-president. "*.....the President shall nominate a Vice President who shall take office upon confirmation by a majority vote of both Houses of Congress*."

At a press conference two days later, President Cromwell announced that he was nominating Mrs. Pamela St. Pierre Cromwell as his Vice-President as mandated by Amendment Twenty Five, Article 2 of the Constitution. It was a foregone conclusion that the Congress would approve the nomination. He wanted to work a smile or two into his speech so he added, "Well, actually, the Constitution didn't mandate that Mrs. Cromwell be my Vice-President. That was my choice." Predictably, the guests laughed. He then went on to chronicle her credentials and some of the responsibilities she would be taking on. He concluded by saying, "And, by the way, Vice President Cromwell is my wife.

The next day, the President received a telephone call in his office from Gino Cruz. "Again, congratulations, Doug. Yesterday was a wonderful day for you and Pam and the country." He then became businesslike and said, not wanting to reveal anything that might suggest to anyone listening that there was more to their relationship than just a political endorsement, "May I suggest Mr. President that the conversation we had regarding the selection of your cabinet is of immediate concern to you. I would be very happy to act as a sounding board if you would like to discuss your selections."

Doug had never had a conversation nor was there ever any mention of Gino becoming involved in his cabinet choices. He saw it as Cruz's way of insinuating himself into the cabinet selection process. Doug hadn't even considered this possibility. Doug thought quickly, "By all means, Gino. Thanks for the offer. My schedule is quite overloaded for the next week as you can well imagine, but by all means, let's talk during the middle of the week and set something up for the following week." Gino agreed and disconnected.

All of a sudden, Doug had a strange feeling in the pit of his stomach. He had never considered that Gino would be involved in any aspect of the presidency other than the Cuban Project. Gino and Cuba – that was to be his only involvement. Or was it, Doug wondered. He assumed that was the only reason he was brought into the picture in the first place. I guess I shouldn't be surprised though. He's been tight lipped with members of *The Group* about several things. The emptiness he was feeling quickly turned into the realization that Gino had probably planned on being a principal player in his presidency all along. He was most likely planning on gradually establishing a position of influence over the Oval Office but, because things have happened so quickly over the last couple of weeks, he undoubtedly feels he has to make his move now. After all, he was looking at a window of a year and a half before Doug became president. He probably thought that time was on his side and there was no hurry to show his hand.

Doug started wondering whether he was just imagining that Gino had an ulterior motive. He's been fair with me and he certainly seems to have Pam's welfare on his mind. I'll have to talk it over with Pam and dad and keep my eyes open.

David Cromwell had been having thoughts of his own about whether Cruz was being upfront with *The Group* about his management of the Cuban Project. It was only after Doug told him about Cruz's design for having Pam becoming Doug's vice-president, and eventually president, did he develop grave doubts about the man's intentions.

Cromwell Advertising had done a superb job of initiating a public relations campaign that helped to establish Doug as every American's favorite politician. As he had already enjoyed a high rating in the national popularity polls, the job of enhancing his image had begun on an already broad level of national acceptance.

David Cromwell took a special delight in preparing his son for the presidency. He was always sensitive to *The Group's* long-term plans for Doug getting the top job and, in turn, exacting revenge on Castro's government; however, lately he began viewing the Cuban proviso as being a complicating factor in what could otherwise be a smooth sailing opportunity for his son. From the beginning, he had always thought that *The Group's* point of view towards Doug's presidency was too restrictive and perhaps even too self-serving.

He had often voiced the opinion at their meetings that he felt that the American people would never understand a foreign policy that was heavily postured towards the rebirth of Cuba as a democratic country. Americans were interested in issues concerning a myriad of problems right here in their own country. Certainly, he believed, how could they be expected to get excited about a country of over eleven million people who chose a way of life so completely at odds with their own? Were Americans actually interested in whether Cuba was a communist country? Cruz's response to that question was always, "We'll make them interested."

Maria Sanchez took off at night once a month in her privately owned Cessna from an isolated airfield just west of Miami and, once she was out of the airport's radar surveillance, headed due south. Airport log records indicated that she was flying to a rarely used airstrip outside of Red Bay, a small town northwest of Panama City on the Florida panhandle. The airstrip logs always indicated that she landed approximately forty-five minutes after leaving Miami and returned to Miami three days later. The airport manager received a cash payment for his under the table certifications. She was careful to tell her office and friends that she was visiting her ailing mother who lived in Red Bay. The truth was that Maria's mother did live in this western Florida community, but she hadn't seen her daughter in several years. They didn't get along.

The reason for the subterfuge was that, on these occasions, Maria made a secret visit to Cuba to see her lover Fidel Castro who arranged for a close associate to meet her at an unidentified landing site close to Havana. Radar detection officials would dutifully ignore the aircraft's familiar identification markings. She and Fidel would then enjoy an evening and daylong session of intimate conversation and aggressive love making – which was not always successful due to the biological limitations placed on a man of his years. On these unsuccessful occasions he would become resolved and say that tomorrow will be better. It never got any better or, if the truth be known, was never that satisfying for Maria. She had been using the dictator's lustful fantasies for years to benefit her own agenda. Her special feelings for the aging dictator were real, but she now had an even stronger reason for continuing the relationship.

Gino Cruz had made her an offer of a top level governmental position in Washington, D. C. for her cooperation in a sensitive and highly secret project. Simply, she was to help forge a working relationship between the Cuban dictator and the President of the U. S. that would pave the way for a trade agreement between the two countries. She was to begin by telling Castro that she heard a high ranking government official at the White House discussing with Mayor Cadilla of Miami the question of a free trade agreement with Cuba. Further, she was to tell Castro that this official said that it was reported that President Cromwell had reacted positively to the suggestion and remarked that he would like to discuss the possibility of a treaty with Castro directly.

Fidel Castro spoke Spanish in his everyday life in Cuba and made it a practice to speak only in his native tongue when dealing with *outsiders*; particularly in political dialogues. He also spoke and understood English quite fluently but this was not common knowledge and he took great pains to keep it a secret. He insisted on using a translator when speaking to anyone who could not converse with him in Spanish. He liked the interim between the time he spoke and the translation as it gave him more time to think of his response. He always spoke to Maria in English.

"You mean that the President Cromwell would be agreeable to such an arrangement?" was his response on hearing her news. "Do you really think that was a serious conversation that you overheard?" Castro was getting excited.

Maria didn't want to overplay her hand. "I don't know. The conversation that Cadilla was having sounded sincere, but I have no way of knowing just how serious President Cromwell was when he said that."

"My sweet Maria," he said, "I would most certainly like to see a trade agreement with the United States. As you know, we have been having severe economic problems since the Soviets deserted us. Our economy is … what is that quaint American expression - in the crapper? A trade understanding with the U. S. could help us become a serious nation again."

Maria knew what his next words would be. “I would be indebted to you for life, dear Maria, if you could get more information for me on this matter. If you think it appropriate, I would personally see that your Mayor Cadilla was royally rewarded for such information. And, need I say that my lovely Maria would also find it monetarily satisfying were she able to provide me with assurances that Cromwell was sincere in his comment.”

Maria said, “Mi querido, Fidelito. You don’t have to offer me anything for something that would make me happy. If Cuba and the United States were able to negotiate a trade agreement then maybe I wouldn’t have to sneak into your bed every time I desired to see you.”

Castro took Maria in his arms and kissed her passionately and gently eased her on to his bed. Five minutes later he had struck out again but, being the eternal optimist, he convinced himself that tomorrow would be different.

CHAPTER 23

On a moonlit evening in May, a short stocky figure and a slightly taller one boarded a Citation X Jet just prior to midnight at a private airfield outside of Washington, D. C. Once they were comfortably seated, the aircraft became airborne and climbed to 22,000 feet. It then settled on a 550-mile-per-hour cruising speed traveling in a southerly direction.

Two hours later, the plane landed at the same airstrip outside of Havana that Maria Sanchez had arrived at several weeks before. The limousine that had brought her to Fidel Castro's home greeted the two men.

Castro was at the door welcoming his two guests. "Gino, my dear friend, how good it is to see you. And Pedro, you're as handsome as ever. You remind me of your father when he was your age. Come in, come in and make yourselves comfortable. We have a light supper waiting for you." Cruz could not help but notice that the home was well-guarded.

It had been several years since Castro and Cruz had seen each other but they had been in constant contact since the days when Castro was organizing and training his forces in the Sierra Maestra Mountains in southern Cuba. It was Cruz who had inculcated Castro with the need for a reformed socialist government in Cuba while they were in their senior year at the Jesuit Belen School in Havana. They both entered law school at the University of Havana in October 1945.

By 1947, both Cruz and Castro had become prominent figures in Havana politics where active student participation in the political process had become an unofficial part of the curriculum and a sometimes violent sport. He and Castro became outspoken advocates for government reform and were constantly in the forefront of student demonstrations. Their speeches were characterized by government and school officials as being inflammatory and dangerous to the welfare of an orderly government. They and their cohorts committed political acts of violence against opposition groups that went far beyond the usually harmless rhetoric tolerated at a learned university.

Castro was soon exhibiting a zealot's uncompromising passion for the movement. He and Cruz became known as dedicated revolutionists who could be seen leading street mobs against police lines in protestation marches and terrorizing opposition groups. They were accused of being involved in the murder of several opposing student leaders but those charges were never legally upheld. They had learned well the lessons of political confrontation.

It was during these years, and subsequent years, that Cruz and Castro formed a bond to bring a new form of socialism to Cuba – one not founded on the Marxist model of class struggle. The historical obedience to Moscow which had characterized most Latin American Communist parties since their creations in the twenties and thirties was the main cause for the discordant relationship between the "old" Cuban Communist party and the new breed of communists that were making their presence known in very aggressive terms. The old party's philosophy found it almost impossible to attract the new generation of rebels who no longer sympathized with the official and outmoded Moscow line. It was mainly through their leadership that the new movement began to take center stage. It was advanced and looked upon as an enlightened government that the people could understand and support.

The two men constantly discussed the political structure of this new government. They had a meeting of the minds that Cruz would eventually be the one to lead the new party but Castro's highly inflated ego eventually convinced him that his destiny, and that of the party, would be better served if the reins of government were placed in his hands. He less-than-modestly recognized that he had become a leader of political brilliance and charisma – qualities that would serve him well when the choice had to be made as to who would lead the new government. He had also carefully developed and nurtured strong personal relationships within the party. These liaisons were to become negotiable assets for him when personal loyalties and choices were put to the test.

Castro became a scheming opportunist and began to view Cruz as an obstacle to his own ambitions. He knew exactly what had to be done for him to be acknowledged as leader of the movement. Importantly, Cruz would have to be out of the country when he made his move. Castro had a concerned look when he broached the subject with Cruz, "Gino, the one thing that worries me is the reaction of our friends in Central and South America and the United States to our taking control of the government. Their exports are important to our economy and we certainly cannot afford to lose their manpower and financial support. We must have their continued friendship if we are to succeed."

Cruz agreed, "Of course, I've always assumed they would continue to be sympathetic to our cause. What makes you doubt that they would not be supportive?"

Castro continued, "All I'm saying is that it would be prudent to make certain we can rely on them. We should think about sending one of our people to visit each and every one of them to ensure ourselves of their friendship."

Cruz had been taken in. "Yes, I agree, that should be a priority." He thought for a moment and added, "But it cannot be just anyone – it would have to be either you or me."

"Yes, you're right and I think you'll agree that it should be you. I have no talent for diplomatic jousting. You have always been the one to bring sanity to the conference table. And who better than you when it comes to recruitment and getting into the pockets of sympathetic contributors? If you agree, Gino, I think it should be you to make that journey." Gino knew Castro was right. So, instead of joining Castro in the mountains of the Sierra Maestra Mountains to help organize and train the revolutionary force, Cruz made the trip abroad. Castro now had several months on his side to consolidate his position as leader of the movement.

Gino never suspected the duplicity of Castro's actions. It was only when he returned to Cuba after an arduous but successful trip did he learn of the underhanded methods that Castro brought to bear to ensure his leadership position in the new government. The underground movement that he and Cruz had so carefully built proved to be the spawning ground of the true warriors and martyrs of the Cuban revolution. They endured great hardships while in the mountains preparing for the inevitable confrontation with the Batista forces. During this time, Castro's brother Raul was at his side as was the shadowy Marxist figure of Che Guevara who was to become a romanticized legend of the Revolution.

Cruz's efforts abroad resulted in a steady flow of aid in the form of weapons, men, food and medical supplies that began arriving at the Sierra Maestra with great regularity. Cruz's hard driving efforts were recognized by the Fidelistas as being responsible for Castro's ability to move as quickly as he did towards his victorious march into Havana on January 8, 1959. Cruz was applauded for his selfless efforts on behalf of the Revolution, but he had lost the preeminence he once enjoyed as the movement's founding leader. Fidel Castro had soundly outmaneuvered him.

Gino Cruz was outraged when he learned that Castro had betrayed him. Cruz had been the guiding force in establishing the movement and was now being left out in the cold. He knew that he could never usurp Castro's leadership at this late date. He had become much too strong with his supporters. He berated himself for not realizing what Castro was doing from the start. He acknowledged that it was his own fault for being stupid and unsuspecting of his *friend.* The humiliation of that experience would haunt Cruz for the rest of his life.

Another incident of a personal nature gave him further reason to characterize Castro as a double-dealing backstabber. While Castro and Cruz were law students at the University, Cruz became infatuated with an undergraduate student named Angel Lorenz. She was the strikingly beautiful daughter of a well-to-do Cuban surgeon who had fought in the underground against Batista. Angel was also politically active. She became intrigued with the outspoken stand that Castro and Cruz were taking against the present government and became an active member of their protest group.

Angel admired both men for their unrelenting dedication to the cause they were championing. Castro's fiery manner and charismatic image were particularly impressive to her, but it was Gino Cruz's sensitive and caring manner that reached her heart. Romantic infatuation turned into a genuinely caring love affair. They vowed they would marry once Cruz has established himself as an attorney in Havana.

While Cruz was traveling abroad visiting friends of the movement, Castro became fascinated with Angel. He convinced her to join him in the damp jungles of the Sierra where he was to carry on his crusade for Cuba's independence. Castro had an uncanny talent for leadership and a decided lack of aptitude and patience for administrative responsibilities. Angel was efficient and painstakingly focused on the details of the movement's daily activities. She became indispensable to him in organizing the "business" of the Revolution. She protected him from well-meaning but time-consuming confederates who were constantly trying to engage him in conversation. Castro developed a confidence in her that included her counseling him in both organizational and personal matters. She took on the mammoth job of handling his correspondence that had become voluminous. Maintaining administrative and personnel records became her responsibility. And, when the sun went down, when the pressures of the day became sometimes overwhelming, she was there to comfort him.

When Cruz returned from his trip abroad, Angel confessed that she no longer had the same feelings for him. She said that she had become so committed to the work of the movement that everything else had become meaningless to her. Cruz knew that to be a lie. He also knew that Castro had again deceived him.

He resolved to find a way of taking revenge. His immediate reaction was a raging need to get even – to strike back. Then he calmed down and his practical side took over. He decided not to act rashly. He thought about the consequences of killing Castro but decided that his actions would be considered by Castro's followers as a traitorous act that could backfire on him. It would undoubtedly get me killed, he wisely reasoned. No, I will have to be patient and find a way to crush him even if I have to destroy the movement we've worked so hard to create.

Such was the extreme bitterness he felt for the situation in which he found himself. His seething anger was further compounded when Castro had Alberto Sierra murdered. Sierra was the patriarch of the powerful Sierra family and a dear friend of Cruz. While their political sympathies often clashed, they were able to remain close up until Alberto's death. Castro had never admitted to Cruz that he ordered the killing; however, it was obvious to Cruz and everyone else that Castro was responsible for the cowardly act.

Cruz never revealed his true feelings for Castro's acts of betrayal. He wanted nothing to stand in the way of their relationship until he had time to formulate a plan for deposing him. It was during these dark days that Gino Cruz developed his sharp instincts for mistrusting anyone and everyone; particularly those professing allegiance to him. It became a cautionary counsel that was to serve him well over the years.

Eventually, the Revolutionary forces marched from the mountains to Havana and took complete control of the country. At the same time, Cruz had decided his course of action for exacting the revenge that had become an obsession with him. He knew that he could no longer stay in Cuba as he would need the freedom of movement to build associations and friendships that could be used to his advantage against his enemy. He also knew that the U. S. would never befriend a Communist country so close to its shores so there would eventually be a major confrontation of wills between the two countries. He saw this disharmony being used to his advantage. He was always cautious not to let his emotions reveal his hatred for Castro. Ironically, he would need Castro's friendship and trust as weapons against him.

Cruz confided in Castro of his plan of coming to the U. S. and establishing a law office in the nation's capital for the purpose of championing their cause with the rich and powerful Americans. Cruz assured him that he would proceed to develop contacts with influential lawmakers who could be convinced to do his bidding - for a price – and that bidding would be highly focused on the future welfare of the new Cuban government.

He felt no compunction whatsoever for having lied to Castro about his mission. Castro understood the need for a sympathetic America if only to leave him alone to run his country. Cruz said that he would be up front in letting the Americans believe that he was sorry for his having aided the new Communist government and would do everything within his power to see that Cuba eventually became a democratic force in the hemisphere. Castro saw no harm in this ploy but rather saw it as an opportunity to rid himself of Cruz's presence in Cuba. He agreed wholeheartedly. They shook hands and two weeks later, Cruz was on his way to America. He eventually became a U. S. citizen.

After several years in America, Cruz became an active player in the tooth-and-claw world of American politics. Ably supported by his son Pedro, the law firm of Cruz and Cruz became an influential and effective political force in Washington. When the two put their collective minds together to solve a particularly troublesome problem – it got solved.

Cruz was still not sure what course of action he would take to exact his vengeance. He was a patient avenger. He had been prepared to wait years, if necessary. He acted decisively only after his son Pedro came to him with an ingenious idea involving a President of the United States. The plan that was finally put in place was daring and fraught with risks. It demanded stealth and patience. Juan Sierra, the son of his old friend Alberto and a good friend of Pedro, was brought into their confidence. Juan also lived with thoughts of revenge for the man who had murdered his father.

CHAPTER 24

Juan Sierra, Pedro and Gino Cruz gathered in the elder Cruz's office to discuss the status of their plans in light of Doug Cromwell's sudden change of residence to the country's most famous address at 1600 Pennsylvania Avenue. David and Doug had not been invited to this gathering as the discussion was meant only for the ears of the threesome.

Gino began, "Actually, our plans haven't changed in any way. Timing has been affected but that just means we have to be more diligent in our efforts to make sure everything is on a sound footing. Maria Sanchez met with Fidel last week to tease him with the suggestion that she had heard that President Cromwell would welcome a meeting with him. She offhandedly said that she thought it had something to do with the President trying to find a common ground for a trade agreement between the United States and Cuba. Of course, Fidel played along letting her know that he was receptive to such a meeting. She in no way knows that we had advised Fidel earlier to expect this kind of dialogue with her."

Juan said, "Fidel is a good actor. He can handle her."

Pedro responded, "Why we even needed her is beyond me. It was Fidel who suggested that she be involved so that he could be assured that she would make that boudoir flight to Cuba every month. He wasn't interested when I suggested that there were many ladies in Cuba who would welcome his attention. I actually think the old reprobate is in love with her. I guess he has a heart after all."

Gino said, "You'll remember that we need her not only because she has a relationship with Fidel but she's also the expert who will make our life easier with her knowledge of the tourism business. As for Castro having a heart, the evil son-of-a-bitch has a heart only when it serves his purpose." He suddenly became momentarily angered, "I should be the one sitting in that seat of power – not him. He's mismanaged things from the beginning. Look at what the Soviets did to Cuba when they couldn't govern their own country. Sure, the Soviets came along and pulled his chestnuts out of the fire for a time but, as we saw, they weren't able to sustain a permanency in Cuba. Cuba's trade with the Soviet bloc accounted for almost ninety percent of Cuba's total imports when the Ruskies moved on. Fidel found that this heavy degree of dependency cost his country dearly. He's treading water at this point and we're going to be the ones to throw him a life preserver. Mind you, it'll be a very untrustworthy lifeline but it will keep him afloat for as long as we need him."

Gino's face was now beet red. He noticed that Pedro and Juan exchanged looks that clearly indicated that they had heard this tirade before. Gino smiled knowingly and said, "Well, that's the past. Let's now talk about the future."

Pedro moved on, "Doug's people have firmed up the details of the trade agreement. They're ready for some serious dialogue with the Cubans once the groundwork is laid here at home. We have to remember that, once the President begins promoting the idea with the American public, we can expect some heavy resistance from some very vocal quarters from around the country. Not the least will be the hard-line elements in the Cuban-American community in Florida who want no engagement whatsoever – or even dialogue – with the Castro government. You know, it has always amazed me how that small special interest group has been able to influence decisions affecting such an important international issue."

"Let's face it," Juan added, "Americans just don't take much of an interest in Cuba. It's a classic case of the vocal minority intimidating the silent majority and the politicians listening to the ones making the most noise."

"That's true," said Gino, "but that do-nothing attitude seems to be changing ever since the hard-liners in Miami began defying U. S. laws in several high profile incidences that have made Americans begin questioning where their sympathies lie. A case in point was the incident involving the young Cuban boy Elian Gonzalez who was found clinging to an inner tube floating off the Florida coast after his escape from Cuba and brought to Miami by his rescuers."

"That really became a high profile case," Pedro continued. "The U. S. Cuban community demanded that the boy remain in the United States with relatives rather than returned to his father in Cuba. It became a highly contested incident and the subject of an international dispute. The boy was finally sent back to Cuba but, by many accounts, the Cuban-Americans lost public sympathy for their stand by putting political ideology above what was best for the boy. Our dissident friends lost a considerable measure of support over that incident."

Juan said, "We can, of course, expect some opposition from our Democrat friends on the other side of the aisle; however, I don't expect them to resist too strongly. After all, they've been screaming for a free trade agreement for some time. So we'll give it to them. I think the only reason they expressed an interest in it was because the GOP has been dead set against the idea ever since Marshall first came into office. Actually, the Democrat support should prove to be a blessing in disguise. We'll let them be in the forefront of proposing the pact so that when it's eventually recognized as being a dismal failure, they can suffer the consequences of having proposed a shipwreck in the first place."

Gino said, "The next step is for the President to contact Castro through proper channels. It would be nice if he could just pick up the phone and call him but, in our sophisticated world of diplomacy, that would be out of order. Doug is going to have to go through proper channels. Let's have Doug and Pam get the boys over at State working on the details right away. And, in the meantime, we can begin our campaign of letting America know of the administration's intentions of pursuing a pact with the Cubans."

Pedro had a final comment, "I have something I've been meaning to mention that I hope it's just my imagination. Has anyone else noticed that Doug has been a little testy lately when we try to discuss matters unrelated to the Cuban project? I don't know what it is but it almost appears that he sometimes looks upon us as not being part of the total picture. I hope he's not losing his commitment as to why he's in the Oval Office in the first place."

Juan agreed, "Yes, I have noticed somewhat of a distant attitude lately."

Gino nodded his agreement, "I've been aware of a change also. It may just be a disorientation brought about by the sudden change in his becoming President. I'm glad that you both noticed it. Let's all keep our eyes open and be on the watch for any missteps along the way. We're very close now to a final solution to what we've all worked so hard to achieve. We don't need any problems at this late date."

David Cromwell decided to stay in Washington for a few more days as he wanted to have a serious conversation with Doug about the unsettling thoughts that he had about Gino Cruz's part in his presidency. He called Doug at the Oval Office and suggested that they have dinner together if he were free this evening.

"As a mater of fact, Pam and I were going to have a quiet supper at home this evening. Why don't you join us? We haven't had a long talk about things in some time."

"Good. Then I'll see you at about seven," David said. "Shall I bring the wine?" Doug laughed and said, "No, just you."

When the two of them got together that evening before Pam joined them, it was as if a heavy weight had been lifted from their shoulders. They both had somebody they could talk with comfortably about *"the Gino situation"*. Doug said that he and Pam had spoken about the matter several times since his telephone conversation with Gino. He said they both were mystified by Gino's attitude towards how he apparently perceived his part in the administration.

They talked for about a half hour before Pam joined them. "Pam thinks we might just be overreacting to Gino's take-charge attitude, but, quite honestly, I think it's a situation that can't be ignored," Doug said. "We don't want this to build up a head of steam so that it becomes difficult to manage. I don't have to tell you that he can be very persuasive and even threatening when he's of mind to take control of a situation."

David was firm, "We can't let that happen. We'll continue to make sure that the "Cuban" proceeds as planned but we're going to have to draw a line on the question of presidential priorities and responsibilities – and particularly, Gino's unwelcome meddling."

Doug said, "We have to make sure that we all understand that the President's first priority is the responsibility to his office."

Pam was noticeably quiet as the two men discussed the situation. While she loved Doug very much and would be completely supportive of him in his presidency, she did have her own ambitious expectations for the future. And, she was confident that her future was closely allied to Cruz's continued support for her. He had convinced her that the presidency was hers for the taking once Doug had completed his two terms of office. There was no doubt that Cruz could guarantee that journey so she was being cautious about making any comments that might jeopardize her present position with him.

She also knew that any strong opposition to the role Gino might have conceived for himself regarding Doug's presidency would be met with a strong resistance from Doug and David. She did not want to get caught in the middle. Gino was not a man to compromise his ambitions.

She played it defensively, "Gino is a take-charge guy but maybe we can have that work to our advantage rather than trying to cut him out completely. After all, his political connections are a potent weapon. Doug, your presidency can only benefit from his magic touch."

Doug responded, "I think we all agree that he has the political muscle to get things done. Welcoming his help is not the problem. His being too much of a take-charge guy *is* the problem. He has a controlling personality that shifts into high gear once he gets his foot in the door. He'll want to rule the roost and, believe me, he's a past master at taking charge."

David said evenly, "We all knew of Gino's iron handed ways when we began this project. It's only lately that he's shown a side of himself that goes beyond the original Cuba commitment." David thought for a moment and said, "Let me have a talk with Juan. He'll know what to do about this situation."

Two days later the President began a low key campaign that would let the world know that the United States was interested in developing talks with the present Cuban government on the subject of a mutual trade agreement. Subtle remarks were interjected into the President's weekly nationally televised press conference suggesting that this course of action was being seriously considered. No specifics were given as it was the administration's intent to gauge the public's reaction to the suggestion before moving ahead.

As it was an important news-breaking story, the attending press representatives questioned the President extensively after he had completed his prepared speech. It created a media sensation for about two weeks after which time it was relegated to a somewhat secondary role to other more important current news items.

The President then made a stronger statement during his press conference the following week that tentative plans were being made to begin talks with Fidel Castro. The press did not appear to take an adversarial position with the announcement indicating to the administration that interest in the subject was waning quickly. A national poll was quietly conducted to determine the initial reaction of Americans to the trade pact. Eighty three percent of the respondents voted in favor of a free trade agreement with Cuba. Given that strong a vote of confidence, the president decided it was time to contact the Cubans.

CHAPTER 25

The highest category in the Saffir-Simpson Hurricane Intensity scale is described as a Category-5 hurricane that has a wind speed that reaches up to 155 miles-per-hour. In an average year, the Atlantic Ocean and Caribbean Sea areas can be expected to have twelve named tropical storms. Nine of these storms will develop into hurricanes with six of them becoming *strong* hurricanes. There are no more dangerous hurricanes than a Category-5.

The National Hurricane Center in Miami reported that a Category-5 hurricane was headed for Cuba – and it was coming with a vengeance. Several years before, a Category-5 killed at least 9,000 people and made 2,000,000 homeless in Honduras, Nicaragua, El Salvador and Guatemala. The Caribbean was a breeding ground for deadly hurricanes.

President Cromwell was advised of the alert as it was anticipated that a storm of this magnitude would, in all likelihood, travel north and hit the Florida Keys once it had devastated western Cuba. When he heard the news he immediately knew how he could ingratiate himself with the Cuban dictator.

Without hesitating, he buzzed for his secretary. "Get me Fidel Castro on the phone, Mrs. Abrams."

She responded routinely, "Yes, sir." She turned to leave but suddenly stopped and asked, "Who, Mr. President?"

"Castro. I have to talk to him right away."

She assumed he was joking so she responded in kind, "I assume you will want one of their new convertibles. I understand they're the most comfortable sleepers there are."

He laughed and said, "No, Mrs. Abrams, I really want to talk to President Castro. You know, the Cuban fellow. The State Department will know how to reach him. Ask someone to get me his number."

An hour later, she returned with a senior official of the State Department in tow. "Mr. President, this is Mr. James Houghton, an official of the State Department. He insisted on speaking with you before you made that call to President Castro."

Houghton nervously suggested to the President that there was an official policy for contacting the head of a foreign government. He further submitted that the President might want to rethink the advisability of contacting the dictator of a country whom the United States did not officially recognize.

Cromwell smiled and asked Mrs. Abrams to get Secretary of State Bob Lansing on the phone. "Bob, we have a little problem here which I wonder if you could resolve." He then explained to Lansing what he was trying to accomplish by speaking directly to the Cuban president. "Okay, Bob, yes, we're still on for Friday evening. Pam is looking forward to it." He then handed the phone to Houghton who listened without saying a word.

Houghton's response was, "Yes sir, I understand. We just thought that….." The connection was broken. The shamefaced official then handed Pam a three by five index card with the name and private telephone number of Castro's administrative assistant printed in block letters. Pam thanked Houghton and escorted him from the President's office.

Mrs. Abrams then dialed the private number of Castro's assistant who, when told who the caller was, thought someone was playing a not-too-humorous joke on her. Mrs. Abrams motioned for the President to pick up the phone and identify himself.

"Hello, Miss Mendez. I know this is not usual procedure but I must talk to President Castro. I wonder if you would see if he's available to speak with me."

She was immediately suspicious that this was a prank call but, then again, she told herself, suppose it really is President Cromwell. If it was and she hung up, Fidel would verbally abuse her for a week when he found out the truth. No, she thought, I'd rather have him think of me as being careless rather than inept. "Yes, Mr. President, let me see if he is in his office."

Normally, Castro would have hung up on his assistant for delivering such an unlikely message, but Maria Sanchez had told him several weeks before that President Cromwell was interested in talking to him. He took the call and answered cautiously, "Yes." He motioned for his translator to pick up the extension.

"Hello, President Castro. Thank you for taking my call. I have looked forward to meeting you for sometime and hope that we can meet in person in the not to distance future."

Castro recognized Cromwell's voice. "I am flattered that you have taken the time to call me, Mr. President. Yes, I would very much like to meet you," he said in his native tongue which was immediately translated.

"We will meet soon, Mr. President. Let me tell you why I'm calling. I just received word that there is a Category-5 hurricane building up in the Caribbean. My people at the Hurricane Center in Miami tell me it should be hitting western Cuba in two days."

"Yes, the news reached me several days ago, but nothing was said that it would be a Category-5 hurricane. That is serious. I will contact my Institute of Meteorology as soon as we have completed our conversation."

Cromwell pursued, "I won't keep you long, Mr. President. I just wanted you to know that the United States is fully prepared to lend whatever assistance you feel is necessary to ease the hardship that the Cuban people will undoubtedly feel when the hurricane reaches its full strength. I have taken the liberty of contacting the U. S. National Oceanic and Atmosphere Administration and directed them to put a "Hurricane Hunter" aircraft at your disposal to mark the exact center of the storm. They tell me that it's the only reliable way to make predictions of the storm's intensity and direction. They, of course, would man the aircraft and report directly to your people at the Institute of Meteorology. They did confirm that it will undoubtedly be a Category-5 when it reaches your western borders. They also suggested that it will probably be necessary to evacuate your people from that area before the storm hits."

Castro responded after the translation was completed. He said with a choke in his voice, "Mr. President, I don't know what to say. You are being more than generous with such a kind offer."

Cromwell concluded by saying, "We can have large numbers of veteran rescue workers flown down on a moment's notice should you feel they could be of service. I have already talked to our Secretary of Commerce who, as we speak, is arranging for foodstuffs and medical supplies to be airlifted to you. I have been through one of these hurricanes myself," he lied, "so I know how serious the devastation can be."

Castro was overwhelmed, "I am beyond words. I have heard that you are a very caring man, Mr. President. Now I know why that is said of you."

"Let me not keep you on the phone, Mr. President. I know you have much to do in the next couple of days. Please call me on my secure line if we can do anything – anything – to help." He gave Castro his protected telephone number.

Castro closed with a sincere, "Thank you, Mr. President.

In replaying his conversation with Pam, Doug laughingly said that when they finally do get together, they're going to have to get on a first name basis. "We both overdid that *Mr. President* formality to death." He then called his father and relayed to him the conversation he had with the Cuban dictator. David was delighted that Doug had taken it upon himself to make the initial contact.

"The process would have become bogged down in red tape had the State Department become involved. I'll call Gino right now and fill him in. He might be miffed because you didn't first discuss the matter with him, but that's all right. He's going to have to get used to the fact that you're the one who will be leading this charge. The sooner he understands that, the better off we'll all be."

Gino was piqued when he heard the news from David. His response was predictable. "That's good news, David, but I think, in the future, it would be best if *The Group* becomes involved in major decisions like that before any of us act alone. We could be walking into a minefield if we're not completely sure of the ramifications of what we're up against. That being said, I think we can safely say that we're now ready to turn up the heat on our friend Fidel.

Hurricane Donna hit western Cuba with 140 mph winds on a Friday morning and continued into Saturday evening. As predicted by the American "Hurricane Hunter" aircraft that was monitoring the situation carefully, the storm began as a Category-2 hurricane and, as it made its way to the coast of Cuba, it developed into a Category-4 with winds of 130 mph. The wind speed escalated to 142 mph and the storm was classified as a Category-5 by the time it made landfall. Residents braced themselves for what was expected to be the most devastating hurricane ever to hit the island

Hurricane Donna traveled from the east. It was a Category-2 level when it brushed the island of Jamaica and was far enough south to have avoided the southern shores of Cuba. It surged north when it reached Isla de Juventud and continued north where Cuba's most western region Pinar Del Rio received the brunt of the hurricane's most destructive force.

Waves, twenty feet above normal, pounded the vulnerable beaches. Coastal properties were attacked unmercifully. Boarding up and battening things down proved to be a useless protection against the hammering persistence of the wind and water that quickly enveloped the entire area. Major property damage was evident everywhere. Many towns were completely flooded. Massive evacuation of residential areas located on the low ground proved to be a precaution that saved a great number of lives. There were casualties but less than the number that might have been expected were it not for the early warning alert by the American President. Castro credited President Cromwell for his quick and compassionate action in saving the lives of many Cubans that day.

The full force of the storm began ebbing once it left the region. It finally traveled north missing the southern coast of Florida and was reduced to a heavy rainstorm when it reached the Bahamas. By international agreement, Atlantic and Caribbean tropical storms are given names that can be used again in later seasons unless the initial storm has caused a significant number of casualties. In these cases, the storm's name is retired; never to be used again. Hurricane Donna's name stood high on the list of names that were retired.

As President Castro later said, "We are accustomed to hurricanes on our tiny island so we were prepared to protect ourselves. But you can never be fully prepared for the kind of storm that hit Cuba this week. We console ourselves in the thought that conditions would have been much worse if we hadn't received help from the United States. President Cromwell provided us with an early warning of the hurricane's awesome intensity that enabled us to be better prepared for it when it did arrive. He rushed volunteer doctors, nurses and other medical professionals to their naval station at Guantanamo even before the hurricane struck our land. He had anticipated that they would be needed. Food and medical supplies were also gifted to us. The people of Cuba will be eternally grateful to this compassionate leader for his help in our time of need. Thank you, Mr. President, from the people of Cuba."

When Gino Cruz heard Castro's heartfelt expression of gratitude, he responded in typical fashion. "Good, now we have the son-of-a-bitch right where we want him. He owes us."

CHAPTER 26

David Cromwell and Juan Sierra had always been honest with each other. Their friendship went back to their youthful days in Cuba before the Revolution. They often reminisced about "the good old days" when the only thing on their minds seem to be trivial things that had nothing to do with the likes of a Fidel Castro. David never minced words with Juan and the conversation they were about to have would be no different.

David began, "That hurricane seems to have been a fortuitous happening. I have to say I was both delighted and somewhat surprised that Doug took the bull by the horns and contacted Castro. That was a very presidential thing for him to do although I suspect that Gino would have preferred that Doug had talked to *The Group* before putting himself on record like that."

Juan smiled and said, "Well, you know Gino. He likes being in the forefront of any decision involving our little Cuban expedition. But, he certainly can't fault Doug for what turned out to be a major coup for our side?"

"True, but as you well know, Gino can get a little testy when things aren't done to his liking. Has he said anything to you about the incident?"

"Yes, he said something to Pedro and me about it. You have to discount some of what he says at times, but he did appear upset about Doug going it alone with Castro. He's taken it upon himself to be the mastermind behind giving Castro his comeuppance so something like that is naturally going to rub him the wrong way."

David shook his head understandingly, "I do sympathize with him on that score. Doug should have warned us about what he was going to do, but it seems that we're going to have to play by a new set of rules since Doug has moved into the Oval Office. He can't have people thinking that he's taking orders from Gino or anyone else for that matter. After all, he *is* now the Chief Executive Officer of the country. He's has to be his own man or, let's face it, he won't be respected."

"Yes, I guess what you say is true," Pedro said, "but Gino's a little long in the tooth to change his ways overnight."

"Granted," David agreed, "But we can't have Gino trying to influence the President with his own personal agenda. Let's face it, Juan; Gino carries a lot of weight here in Washington. I think the power of the presidency will be too great a temptation for him not to try and build on that power base. Don't misunderstand me. We all know Gino's thirst for power and that's all right. We've all benefited from his sometimes questionable ways of doing things. But we can't let his ambition for political control jeopardize Doug's credibility with the people who put him in office. We must keep him focused on the Cuban project and not issues that have nothing to do with that commitment."

Juan looked sadly at his old friend and said, "David, this has been a concern of mine ever since we dreamed up this presidential scenario. Everything seemed so clear cut when we started. You're right. Gino's lust for power and Doug actually becoming President before we expected it to happen, has turned out to be a complicating factor to the covenant to which we've all committed ourselves."

"How does Pedro feel about this situation or haven't you and he talked about it?" asked David.

Juan smiled, "Oh, we've talked about it. Nobody knows Gino like Pedro. He recognized early in the game that Gino was after more than just revenge against Castro. That's paramount in his mind, but more than just revenge, he wants to embarrass him in the eyes of the world. He wants Castro's legacy to be that he's nothing but a foolish old man who achieved nothing more than to condemn his country to second-rate status among the world powers. Pedro has come to realize that, after all is said and done; his father is a bitter and dangerous person who will go to extreme measures to satisfy that end. And, he knows that to achieve that goal, he must be able to control Oval Office decisions that might impact on that obsession."

David peered at Juan with an unsettling look, "Juan, I must ask you to talk to Pedro about my concerns regarding Gino becoming involved in other than Cuban matters. Were it to get out-of-hand, we could lose everything we've all worked so hard to achieve. We must control his unreasonable fixation for power."

"I understand, David, I will talk with Pedro," Juan replied.

The President thought that Gino should be given the courtesy of knowing his plans for beginning a dialogue with Castro. Doug's strategy was simply to pick up the phone and call him and suggest that they meet to discuss a mutual trade agreement that would be beneficial to their two countries; simple and to the point. Doug anticipated some opposition from Gino when he told him, but Gino actually reacted favorably to the idea knowing that the hurricane scenario had created a rapport between the two leaders that would have taken at least six months to duplicate.

The telephone call was taken enthusiastically by Castro. He readily agreed to a meeting in a neutral location which, it was decided, would be Mexico City. Castro had friendly ties to the country and the United States was a consistent supporter of the government of Mexico. Pam handled the official details with the State Department who made all of the arrangements for a meeting between the two heads of state. When the President heard that they were planning on scheduling the two day meeting in four months, he balked and said, "That doesn't make sense. Let me call Fidel and see if he'll be available in two or three weeks."

After severe objections from the State Department that three weeks would not allow time to prepare adequate security for the President, the meeting was set after a hurried call to Bob Lansing who told his people to "back off and do what your President asks".

President Cromwell again personally called President Castro and confirmed the date for a meeting. Security measures were hastily coordinated with the Mexican Security Division and the meeting was scheduled three weeks from the day the two presidents talked. Given the short lead time available and her past experience with the State Department, the Vice-President was asked to supervise and coordinate the seemingly endless details of the trip. At the same time, she helped author and put the finishing touches on the formal trade agreement that was being recommended. It was agreed that Lansing would be the lead administration official on the trip. He would personally make the presentation to the Cubans.

The selected group of security personnel who would accompany the President's party to Mexico were actually Army Special Forces Rangers dressed in civilian clothes but armed sufficiently to provide protection and decisive fire power should the occasion arise. The President's personal Secret Service unit would also be present.

As expected, the roar of protest around the country was lively when the news became public that Cromwell was meeting with Castro to discuss a free trade pact. No greater protest was heard than from the volatile Cuban-American dissidents in south Florida. Cromwell was castigated by the outraged community for his recognition of a Communist government that committed unspeakable crimes against the people of Cuba. The prospect of Castro's government actually managing to survive and eventually renewing economic relations with the United States filled the embittered Miami exiles and their right-wing political sympathizers with horror.

The President purposely asked that Air Force One be scheduled to arrive in Mexico City one full hour before Castro was scheduled to arrive so that he could welcome the Cuban dictator along with the President of Mexico Camilo Montalban. Cromwell wanted to conspicuously demonstrate to Castro and the world that he was perfectly willing to play second banana to the Cuban dictator's role in this worldly event.

When the two leaders met at the airport, the greeting was warm and cordial but necessarily formal. Castro insisted on maintaining the charade that he needed an interpreter with him at all times even though President Cromwell knew that "the rascal speaks and understands the English language as well as I do". A motorcade from the airport to the Residential Palace of the Government was a spirited spectacle for the two presidents who rode side by side in the back seat of a limousine that was heavily protected by bulletproof construction and a phalanx of mounted and armed Mexican army officers. The nervous Montalban rode in a second limousine directly behind the two visiting leaders. His eyes were in constant motion looking for any signs of likely disturbances by his unpredictable countrymen. When the motorcade finally arrived at its destination, the president was heard to exhale an audible sigh of relief.

Cromwell and Castro were staying at the Palace for the two nights they'd be in Mexico City. A banquet was held in the evening of the first night. Cromwell made sure that he would have a private conversation with the Cuban president as soon as they were comfortably settled in. He wanted Castro to be in the right frame of mind when they met officially the next day. It became a challenge to see if he could charm this enigma in khaki.

When they met privately, Cromwell saw that his lungs were in for a difficult two days given the Cuban dictators propensity for a seemingly continuous need to puff on his favorite Cohiba Esplendidos cigars. Cromwell had been warned that, while Castro had given up the smoking habit in 1989, he very recently decided to reacquaint himself with a habit that had quickly become an addiction. That nuisance aside, he found Castro to be sociable and naturally friendly. He was a big man, quite handsome and while he supposedly had a morbid preoccupation with his health, appeared to be in good physical condition. Rumors suggested he had a heart attack, colon cancer, lung cancer and many other maladies that convinced his enemies that he was not longed for this world. But, his appearance gave no credence to those wishful thoughts. Cromwell's immediate impression was that he looked like he was ready for another seventy-five years of active leadership.

Secretary of State Lansing wanted to rehearse his presentation with his associates while Cromwell had a private chat with Castro. He wanted to get to know Castro better and to encourage his thinking about the benefits to Cuba of a carefully planned tourism program. Cromwell had purposely selected Mexico City as the site for their meeting as Maria Sanchez had told Cruz that Castro envied what tourism had done for Mexico's economy. He knew that if Cuba could have that same kind of success, its road to economic prosperity would be assured. Cromwell was hoping to reinforce Castro's ambition of following in Mexico's footsteps. After all, he told himself, we expect that tourism will be the cornerstone for Cuba's emergence from a purgatorial existence to one of complete and utter failure.

As soon as the two men sat down to have a leisurely talk, Castro smiled and said, "Mr. President, my calling you Mr. President and you calling me Mr. President gets to be tiring, don't you think. I would like you to call me Fidel and may I call you Douglas? I think we would both be more comfortable with each other without such formality."

Cromwell laughed and said, "By all means, Fidel. And my friends call me Doug."

"That's much better, Doug. And between us, I hate to tell you what my friends call me," the Cuban leader said, lightly.

Cromwell slipped comfortably into asking Castro about conditions in Cuba since he disassociated himself from the Soviets. Castro answered frankly, "It is no secret, Doug, that conditions in Cuba have not been good since their departure. I have been encouraged that things could change for the better when I received your very gracious telephone call warning us of the hurricane. We are all very grateful to you for your concern."

Cromwell said, "There should be no political differences when a nation is threatened by a hurricane or any natural disaster like that. It is important that we forget conflicting politics and cooperate with each other. We were very pleased that our people and their counterparts at your Institute of Meteorology worked so well together. It proved to many people in America that our two nations can work together amiably when we put our minds to the task."

Castro nodded his agreement. "I had always hoped that we could come to the conference table and negotiate a program of coexistence. Perhaps our meetings during the next two days will be the beginning of a new era of cooperation and friendship between us. Your predecessor President Marshall has said repeatedly, and in the harshest terms, that the United States could never consider improving relations with Cuba until we had free elections, released all political prisoners and exhibited other fundamental changes toward a fully democratic society."

"Yes, that was his position," Cromwell conceded.

You understand, Doug, that we are a socialist country and that our two forms of government are diametrically opposed to one another. We will not change. As much as it would pain me to see a trade pact between us fail because of these differences, please be aware that I would have to walk away from any talks that would be conditioned on a reform to our socialistic system. We simply cannot be……"

Doug held up his hands defensively, "I'm glad you brought that up, Fidel. Let me say this - should we come to an understanding as to a mutually acceptable trade agreement this week, it will be with the understanding that we, the United States, will in no way in the future put any restrictive requirements on your government for changing its political focus. Likewise, we would ask that Cuba honor that same understanding insofar as trying to influence our democratic principles."

Castro's eyes told the American President that he had said exactly the right thing in calming any waters of distrust that might have existed between the two leaders. He responded, "Mr. President – Doug – I think we understand each other perfectly and I welcome your friendship." Both men shook hands and ordered another drink.

Cromwell then directed the conversation to a seemingly innocent observation that was made simply to casually infuse the word *tourism* into their chat, "Mexico is truly a breathtaking country, Fidel. I understand that those towering mountains and high rolling plains cover more than two-thirds of the country. It's simply breathtaking." He hesitated before saying, "President Montalban and I were discussing the economy of his country before your plane landed. Manufacturing, agriculture, mining and tourism are all important contributors to their success, he was saying. He was particularly expansive about the millions of tourists visiting Mexico each year. The money they spend brings in substantial income to their national treasury."

Fidel looked wistfully, "Yes, I know of their situation. Cuba once enjoyed a very lucrative tourist business. It still brings in $2.0 billion a year, but we know that it could be much more. Forgive me for saying, but if there was no ban on Americans traveling to Cuba… well, that could solve many of Cuba's economic problems. Perhaps one day that will become a reality."

Cromwell smiled inwardly and said to himself, Gottcha. He ended the conversation saying, "Maybe we can discuss that tomorrow, Fidel"

Doug had one haunting reservation which he related to Secretary Lansing later that evening. "I wish that conversation hadn't been so cordial. I'm beginning to like the son-of-a-bitch."

CHAPTER 27

The following morning, representatives of the United States and Cuba gathered in the Palacio Nacional for the meeting that would release Cuba from the trade embargo that they were forced to live with since October 1960. The restraint was originally conceived as a way of pressuring the Castro regime to democratize their newly formed government but it failed to achieve that objective and remained a failure for over forty years.

Business interests in the United States resented the embargo as it denied them access to significant business opportunities on the island. They were persistently lobbying to trade with and invest in Cuba. They argued that the Cold War was over and that Cuba was in no way a threat to U. S. security. The powerful American farm lobby was particularly vocal in advocating the right to sell agricultural products to Cuba.

Castro himself had developed a conciliatory approach as evidenced by his positive response to the White House's proposal to meet and discuss the opportunities available to both nations. President Dewitt Marshall was conspicuous in successfully preserving the anti-Castro status quo when he was in office. The administration direction took a sudden turn for the more friendly approach to the subject when Douglas Cromwell became Chief Executive Officer.

Cromwell had invited a number of state governors to join the American delegation but many of them found excuses not to attend as they didn't want to be associated with something that might turn out badly and antagonize their voting constituency. Three cabinet members – Secretaries of State, Commerce and the Treasury - joined their President along with a number of State Department associates and legal counsels. Procedural control of the meeting was maintained by Secretary Robert Lansing. He was designated as chief spokesman for the United States.

Castro saw the meeting as the perfect occasion to further his leadership position within the world community. He also knew that the agreement would give his reputation a meaningful boost with his countrymen. His standing with them could use a healthy lift, he told himself, as his popularity was showing signs of faltering.

Castro's Council of Ministers was well represented. Seven of Cuba's twenty-seven Council ministers made their entrance into the Palacio Nacional led by First Vice President and Minister of the Revolutionary Armed Forces General Raul Castro Ruz, the brother of the Cuban leader. Fidel Castro was the President of the Council of State. Intelligence sources had advised the American delegation that only three of the ministers of those in attendance had any relevancy to the trade agreement; Roberto Martinez, Minister of Agriculture, Ibrahim Morales, Minister of Domestic Trade and Ricardo Perez, Minister of Tourism. The other ministers present were there for moral support and a show of unity.

When everyone was settled, President Cromwell stood before the group and made a short welcoming speech. His remarks were directed to Castro who smiled amiably when his interpreter had finished the translation. Castro returned Cromwell's comments with a fifteen minute discourse on how good it was to be in Mexico City with "our American friends". Knowing Castro's penchant for oratory, Secretary Lansing nodded his head to an associate across the table who immediately developed an uncontrollable coughing spell that caught everyone's attention. After a moment, the Secretary said, "John, you had best have a glass of water," and immediately proceeded with introductory remarks as to the purpose of the meeting. Cromwell smiled as he and Lansing hadn't discussed this strategy for derailing the Premier's marathon expressiveness.

"President Castro, Ministers of the Council of State and members of the Cuban delegation, on behalf of the President and the people of the United States, let my say that this is truly a distinct pleasure for all of us to be able to sit in conference with you to discuss a trade agreement between our two countries." On cue, several members of the American delegation echoed an enthusiastic agreement, "Here, here."

The secretary continued, "Let me say that we in the United States are fortunate in having laws that permit us to negotiate trade agreements and present them to our Congress in Washington, D. C. for approval or rejection." Lansing went on to explain that the Congress has granted this authority to every president since 1974. This authority - formerly named the Trade Promotion Authority – allowed President Cromwell's administration to actively negotiate a

Free Trade Agreement between the United States and the countries of Central America. We are pleased to say that agreements have been signed with Costa Rica, El Salvador, Guatemala, Honduras and Nicaragua. Last year, these Caribbean Basin countries combined represented the seventh largest export market for U. S. firms, purchasing more U. S. exports than China, India and Russia combined. U. S. imports from Central America totaled $11.8 billion last year. These free trade agreements have been highly successful for everyone concerned and have sent important signals to other Latin and South American nations that the United States has the political will to negotiate in good faith with any of our neighbors that embrace free-market reforms and the new business opportunities they offer."

President Cromwell said, adding fuel to the fire, "We have moved quickly to build free trade relationships with individual nations. Chile is now the first of our partners in South America. We have finalized a bilateral trade agreement with them several years ago. Today, the United States is Chile's most important trading partner, with U. S. goods and services accounting for about twenty percent of Chile's total imports while U. S. consumers buy sixteen percent of all Chilean exports. Chile alone ranks ahead of Russia and South Africa as a market for U. S. exports."

Secretary Lansing saw that the Cuban delegation was reacting well to what they were hearing. He stoked their interest further, "You're undoubtedly aware of our Chambers of Commerce in America. These are independent, non-profit, business organizations who promote trade and investment within the United States and with countries beyond our borders. There are actually twenty one countries in Latin America and the Caribbean who enjoy American Chamber of Commerce representation. One of the oldest is the Chamber of Commerce in Argentina which was founded in 1918. They now have more than six hundred corporate members. These members represent the U. S. business presence in the country and account for the majority of the $8 billion-plus in bilateral trade and $47 billion-plus in investment in the last ten years."

Cromwell again added a comment, "I was talking to the President of Brazil just the other day who was telling me how pleased they have been for the many years they have had an association with their American Chamber of Commerce dating back to 1916. They have a group in Rio de Janeiro that is comprised of over 500 Brazilian and foreign companies and 2,000 corporate executives. Their member's exports total $5.0 billion per year, and in the domestic market, members generate $20 billion in sales annually. The Chamber of Commerce in Sao Paulo has similar results.

Cromwell and Lansing were deliberately throwing out large factual numbers knowing they had to be impressive to the delegates. He saw from their sideward glances that the figures had impressed them so he decided to close his introductory remarks on a high note. "I know that you are aware of these facts. I think you'll agree that they do illustrate just how successful trading with each other can be," he said looking at Minister of Domestic Trade Morales.

Lansing then turned his attention to Minister of Tourism Perez. "I think that President Cromwell has a message for the delegation on that subject that will particularly please you, Mr. Perez."

Cromwell stood, "I know that prior administrations have strongly opposed any effort to loosen sanctions against the Cuban embargo until it undertook meaningful political, economic and labor reforms and respect its citizen's human rights." Cromwell hesitated and stared into the eyes of Castro. After a momentary pause, he continued, "As of this moment, the United States will no longer pursue that initiative. We have come to you today to ask you to join with us in a Free Trade Agreement. We ask nothing of a political nature from Cuba. The United States has no designs on your country's sovereignty. We will not interfere with the way you run your government. That is your business. And, regardless of your accepting or rejecting our offer, I am announcing officially that the ban on Americans traveling to Cuba is being lifted. Americans will be free to travel to Cuba as they are free to travel to other countries around the world."

The Cuban delegation looked at each other in surprise and rose in unison to applaud the announcement. Castro joined them and gave Cromwell a bear hug. "Gracias, gracias, El Presidente," he enthused.

Lansing took control of the meeting by holding up his hands and saying, "We don't have to tell you gentlemen what the lifting of the travel ban will do for Cuba's tourist business. Based on reasonable expectations, we believe that you can expect one million American tourists to be visiting Cuba in the next twelve months and spending $2.0 billion. We had some very knowledgeable people develop a plan for handling a tourism program of those proportions. Just suggestions, mind you. We certainly don't mean to interfere with Minister Perez and his obviously talented associates but we'd like to submit the proposal to you simply as a suggestion for dealing with this unexpected bounty."

The Minister of Tourism was so overjoyed at the thought of his office of responsibility being propelled to an influential position of dominance within the government that he quickly said, "Of course not, Mr. Secretary. We are honored to have your input." For the remainder of the meeting, Perez had visions of American tourists throwing money at him.

Castro stared at his hands deep in thought. He was trying to think of something appropriate to say that would immediately express his true feelings and at the same time be brief. He noticed earlier that the Americans were not favorably disposed to long oratory. He finally looked up and said, sheepishly through his interpreter, "Where do I sign?"

CHAPTER 28

The Mexico City Conference was acclaimed a huge success. Even the Communist bloc countries that had lost political interest in their former ally, expressed admiration for a world leader who had championed an enlightened view of international cooperation in the interest of doing what was morally right even though it wasn't necessarily politically correct.

A formal Trade Agreement was approved by both the United States and Cuba which was ceremoniously signed by Secretary of Commerce Harold L. Hopkins and Cuba's Minister of Domestic Trade Ibrahim Morales in the presence of the International Trade Committee at United Nation's headquarters in New York City. President Cromwell's initiative in spearheading this landmark and highly controversial decision made him the odds-on favorite within the international community of receiving the Nobel Peace Prize in the coming year. It would be only the sixteenth time since 1902 that an American would have received this honor. Only two other American Presidents, Theodore Roosevelt (1906) and Woodrow Wilson (1919) were among this distinguished group.

Louis Karmazin was a retired internationally prominent business entrepreneur who had for many years been an active executive member of the U. S. Chamber of Commerce. He was responsible for training the leadership of many of the foreign American Chambers of Commerce around the world in the techniques of dealing with U. S. business interests. He was fluent in six languages including Spanish.

Karmazin was a close friend of the Secretary of Commerce who asked him, as a personal favor, to come out of retirement and serve for a one-year term as the interim Director of Cuba's American Chamber of Commerce. During that time, the Secretary said that it would give his trusted friend ample time to establish the office and train his Cuban replacement. Karmazin agreed wholeheartedly. He then immediately called his friend Gino Cruz and told him that he had accepted the assignment. Cruz had told Karmazin a month earlier that the Secretary would be offering him the appointment. Cruz was never more in command or more manipulative than when any detail of the Cuban Project was at issue.

Cruz allowed himself a smile of contentment. Everything was going according to plan. He picked up the phone and dialed Bud De Luca's number in Atlantic City. "Bud, Gino here. Lou Karmazin is in place. I'd like to get together and review your plans for the casino part of the operation. Suppose we meet in Miami next Wednesday. I could use some sun and I want you to meet Maria Sanchez. She's the tourist gal I talked to you about the last time we talked. She can be a big help. She's close to Castro and she really has the smarts when it comes to tourism. Lou is going to offer her a job as tourist consultant to Cuba. Okay, I'll see you at the usual place for breakfast on Wednesday morning.

De Luca was prepared when he met Cruz in his suite at the Fontainebleau Hotel in Miami. He had spent the last eight months with a team of Las Vegas and Atlantic City casino specialists developing a plan that mirrored the success developed for these two models of gaming sophistication. Given the amount of gambler traffic that could be expected by the Cubans following the lifting of the travel ban, it was obvious that the present facilities on the island were totally inadequate to satisfy the needs of large numbers of tourists. Only about 80,000 U. S. citizens visited Cuba each year, but lifting the travel ban would result in millions of Americans indulging themselves in the somewhat uncharted pleasures of the island; particularly when tourist flights were made available from major American cities.

It would be necessary, they agreed, that the first order of business would be to enlarge the Jose Marti International Airport to accommodate the hordes of deep-pocketed visitors expected. Another pressing and immediate need would be to upgrade all of the existing major tourist hotels. Cuban tourist hotels were now classified from one to five stars, though it was often necessary to subtract one or two stars from the published category to arrive at something approximating international standards. Customer service at a Cuban-run hotel was often referred to as a *foreign concept*. Converting some of these tourist hotels to state of the art casinos and modernizing the rooms would be essential to satisfying the initial wave of tourists descending on the island. These casino specialists were also unanimous in their opinion that a vigorous and hard-hitting advertising campaign was another top priority.

De Luca handed Cruz an impressive-looking leather bound presentation portfolio saying, "If Cuba expects to get their hands on those American tourist dollars, they'll have to understand that it's critical that they invest in the construction of a number of large and luxurious resort hotels on their beaches. Renovating Cuba's present hotels will be okay as openers but you only have to look at Vegas and Atlantic City to see that their drawing cards are the big lavish resort hotels with all their tourist-friendly amenities. That has been the future for gambling casinos in America and it will be no different in Cuba."

Cruz agreed, "I don't think anybody will give you an argument on that score."

DeLuca nodded and continued, "I have a complete proposal prepared for the Cubans that will outline exactly what their major needs will be in terms of things like number of resort hotels, casinos, types and number of restaurants, personnel that will be required to service these various venues - and much more. Our guys really went the full nine yards on this one. The Cubans are also going to have to do some major overhauling of several of their cities – particularly, Havana." De Luca explained that Havana was the key to attracting tourism to the island. It was the largest city in the Caribbean with 2.2 million inhabitants and is Cuba's political, cultural and economic hub. It's the logical destination for the tourist looking for a week or two in the sun.

"The trouble with Havana of today is that it looks like a used car lot with pre-1960 American automobiles in various stages of disrepair scattered all over the place. They're an irritating eyesore to any newcomer to the city and a sign of a visible regressive society. The buildings and streets are in need of long overdue baths and some extensive plastic surgery. Havana suffers from deteriorating sewage and waste disposal systems and their water supply is in bad shape due to antiquated and leaky plumbing. The housing in the city isn't in very good shape either. Nearly half the housing is in bad repair and thousands of city residents have had to be evacuated for their own safety. Each year about 300 Havana buildings collapse and it's estimated that 88,000 dwellings will have to be demolished."

Gino said, "Do you have anything good to say about the city?"

"Well, there's not a helluva lot to say about that. There are the usual historic tourist sights, beautiful beaches and the people are unreservedly friendly. The bottom line though is that while Cuba has great potential, it needs a lot of work. That's all in the proposal. Importantly, the Cubans will have to examine carefully their fire and police protection capabilities, their public transportation facilities and bringing their sewage standards up to snuff. And let's not forget their recreational and tourist facilities. Well, you get the picture. Like I say, it's all in the proposal which you can examine at your convenience."

Gino complimented his friend, "I have no doubts that the recommendations reflect your usual competency, Bud. Cuba truly is a beautiful country but we mustn't lose sight of the basic reasons that tourists come there. Warm sun, good food and gambling are what they'll be looking for." Gino thumbed through the proposal until he found the section *Newly Planned Resorts*. He read quickly a summary of the three major resort hotels that were planned for new construction and then turned to the one that was described as 'the world's largest and most opulent five-star resort". He smiled at the suggested alternate names given to it by the planners – *The Castro Pavilion, Fidel's Palace, La Casa de Fidel* and even *The Brothers Castro.* De Luca's comment to the planners was, "This is serious business. Let's not be wise-asses about it." Gino thought that even if Castro were amused by the planner's flight of fancy, he would never allow his name to be associated with a gambling establishment. And who said that Castro had a sense of humor in the first place? The names were excised from the proposal.

Cruz was impressed by the description of the resort. It was to have 5,010 deluxe guest rooms which were suites providing a minimum of 650 square feet of living space. The room amenities included marble European-style bathrooms, marble foyer entrances, two large televisions, a mini bar, and the outside rooms had balconies overlooking a panoramic view of Havana and the ocean. More elaborate suites included luxurious beds, private dining rooms, wet bars, in-room saunas, steam rooms and sophisticated audiovisual systems.

The casino offered 125 table games and 4,000 gaming machines, slots, video poker, keno, craps, blackjack and a poker room in a setting of 110,000 square feet including a large sports bar. The Race and Sports Book featured two separate choices for gaming action.

There were eight restaurants in the hotel with offerings from elegant fine dining to less formal and casual dining. A variety of dining options ranging from gourmet French and Northern Italian to Asian fare and other carefully selected ethnic choices were to be found throughout the resort. The 60,000 square foot live-performance entertainment complex with seating for 1,500 would showcase top performers and special events. The many sporting activities that would be available at the resort included scuba diving, snorkeling, deep sea fishing, tennis, windsurfing, volley ball, catamaran sailing and kayaking.

The *Pool's Eye View* featured three large pools and a spa with more than thirty treatment rooms, saunas, steam rooms and whirlpools. Shoppers would be able to stroll along *Via Fidel*, a promenade with a collection of upscale boutiques featuring famous designer clothing names. Exotic plants and flowers decorated The Greenhouse and Botanical Gardens in the lush gardens surrounding three sides of the resort.

Gino reviewed the other two resorts in the proposal and saw that they closely resembled each other in their content but differed in their thematic treatment which set them apart from each other. There was *Paris of the Caribbean* with an Eiffel Tower replica in the center of the gardens surrounding the entrance to the hotel. Plans called for displaying paintings of Monet, Renoir and other famous French artists in *The Louvre Room.* There was *The House of Faberge, The Louis XIV Room in The House of Kings* and *The Forum Room in the House of Caesar.*

The Roman Coliseum Resort Hotel told visitors that they were entering a land of seductive beauty and romantic charm. The Italian influence was evident throughout the hotel including the guest rooms.

De Luca had included carefully sketched layouts of the three luxury hotels prepared by architectural designers who had drawn up the plans for several of the major resort hotels in Las Vegas and Atlantic City. These art renderings were impressively illustrated in four-color glossy reproductions.

The construction time for completing each of the hotels was estimated to be eighteen months from the date of approval. The names of several North American and South American construction contractors were included in the proposal. Each of these builders was experienced in resort planning and construction. Gino could see that the planners had wisely followed their stateside successes.

Also included in the planning proposal was a marketing recommendation prepared by Cromwell Advertising spelling out in detail a program for advertising and promoting the benefits of vacationing in Cuba to the adventurous eye of the American tourist. David Cromwell had personally created a highly imaginative advertising campaign that clearly established Cuba as one of the world's premier tourist destinations. There were never any charges that David received this plum assignment because of his relationship with Douglas. David Cromwell was recognized by the Cubans as the best man for the job. Besides, nepotism was not an ugly word to them. It was an intelligent way to assure a friendly base of cooperative associates.

De Luca, Karmazin and the senior member of the American planning committee met with the Ministers of Tourism, Domestic Trade, Finances and Prices and Construction along with the Cubans who would be responsible for the actual construction management of the resort hotels. De Luca saw, from his experience with similar situations, that there was a complete understanding among the Cubans of the intricate details that were being presented to them. They were duly impressed with the American effort. A thorough discussion of the plan resulted in minor revisions being made and a commitment by the Minister of Construction to incorporate the American plan in a proposal of their own which would include their financial assessment and funding of this capital project. He announced that the final plan would be presented to Fidel Castro for his approval in one month.

The Americans were not present when the final presentation was made to Castro who was anxious to begin changing Cuba's fortunes so he approved everything that was recommended. He voiced his one serious concern in clear and simple language, "How are we going to pay for all of this? All of this work must be done within the next year and a half. We will have to begin paying out tremendous sums of money almost immediately. Our new trade program should be functioning in short order but we will not have the needed cash in our treasury or sufficient collateral to honor our immediate commitments."

The Minister of Finance and Prices said, "That's true, Mr. President. We will have to establish credit with the United States and some of our friends in South America. Venezuela, Mexico and Chile have always been friendly to our credit solicitations."

"No, we will not borrow money from the United States," Castro bellowed. "It is enough that we are in their debt for the trade agreement. I do not want to be beholden to them for financial aid." Castro continued to feel that President Cromwell may not, after all, be the honorable man he professes to be. I have no choice at this time but I shall monitor our relationship very carefully, he told himself.

When the Minister of Finance put out feelers to several Central and South American allies, he found that extending Cuba the credit that would be required for this gigantic enterprise was beyond their risk acceptance. Yes, they said, they would help Cuba but you must recognize that you now have the richest country in the world as your ally. The United States will be only too happy to extend you the credit you require. Castro had no choice. He had his Minister contact the Secretary of Commerce who was expecting a call of this nature.

"Why, of course, Mr. Minister. I know the President is sympathetic to such a request and I'm sure the Congress would be amenable. I will get back to you rather quickly on the matter."

The loan for the full amount requested by the Cuban government was approved. Cuba prepared for the adventure that would change their destiny – short term, for sure – and the United States held the trump card in the relationship.

CHAPTER 29

Within a year and a half, Cuba's reciprocal trade program with the United States resulted in a dramatic turnaround in the island's economic stability. They were now enjoying a thriving export and import business that was viewed by other trading partners in the region with respect and an element of envy. The partnership was being heralded as a testament to "the good that can be achieved by nations of goodwill and possessing a strong determination to live in international harmony".

Gino Cruz's response when he heard that comment made by the Secretary General of the United Nations was, "Wait until they see the measure of goodwill and harmony we give that son-of-a-bitch Castro in the not too distant future."

The United States Congress was quick to approve a large loan to the one-time American antagonist which enabled the Cuban Ministry of Construction to proceed with the mammoth task of revitalizing the physical appearance of several of their tourist cities. Planners concentrated their major effort on the city of Havana as it was felt that this once beautiful city offered the greatest potential for satisfying large numbers of American tourists.

There actually had been relatively very little new construction in Havana since 1959. One boastful achievement of the revolutionaries was that they had rid the city of the miserable slums that once encircled Havana which were replaced by modern apartment buildings. Non-descriptive prefabricated apartment blocks were also built providing much needed housing at affordable prices.

A large number of Cuban families acquired title to their homes because of The Urban Reform Law of 1960. A proviso of the law enabled Cubans to convert their rent payments into mortgage payments on a five to twenty year basis making owners out of renters. Cubans paid no property taxes which explained in part how they were able to survive on the meager salaries they were paid. The law was the difference between starvation and living a somewhat comfortable but meager existence for the vast majority of Cubans.

The historic centers of cities like Havana were fortuitously saved from being demolished by greedy land grabbing developers who were simply told by the revolutionary government to "keep their hands off our glorious heritage". Rather than becoming part of the dark side of that heritage, the developers wisely backed off.

Renovation of the existing hotels proceeded rapidly to assure that tourists would have a place to stay and gamble while construction was being completed on the three new resort hotels. The Hotel Nacional built in 1930 and the twenty-five story Hotel Habana Libre, once called the Havana Hilton, were the first to be renovated. The plan called for The Hotel Nacional to be leveled to the ground once it had served its purpose as a temporary sanctuary for American tourists. In its place would arise *The Roman Coliseum Resort Hotel.* The other two resort hotels were expected to be completed shortly after.

David Cromwell and his team of advertising professionals had made a trip to Cuba shortly after the trade agreement was resolved to present the advertising campaign to the entire staff of ministers and a select group of responsible government officials. Castro showed up at the meeting unannounced to satisfy himself that his interests and those of Cuba were being presented to America in the most sympathetic of terms. He was not disappointed. He was particularly impressed by the depiction of himself as a benevolent leader. He began imagining that maybe now Americans would begin viewing him with greater respect once the campaign was launched. He would make sure that the Cuban people were told what he was doing to bring American dollars and prosperity to them. I can use some respect from that quarter, too, he told himself. That was for sure.

While Cuban guide books advised tourists not to offer money to officials to gain preferential treatment, the truth was that corruption was quite rampant on the tiny island. One irrefutable fact was that everything in Havana had a price tag and a person's wallet was the entry fee for participation. There was a legion of elected officials who were constantly being *wined, dined and pocket-lined*, as a popular New York radio host had phrased it. An unidentified Switzerland banking source had let it be known that Fidel himself had an active Swiss bank account that reportedly contained over a billion American dollars. Deposits to the account were made on a regular basis through a clever and shrouded banking channel, according to the tipster. Hearsay, perhaps, but nobody seemed to doubt its validity.

As soon as American business interests became aware that a trade agreement was being discussed in Washington and Havana, manufacturers of industrial and consumer products in the United States began evaluating how best to take advantage of this potentially dynamic trading environment. Corporate America's resourcefulness was at its professional best when there was a buck to be made. Those companies with friends at the Department of Commerce were rewarded with encouraging confirmation that a trade treaty was imminent. They were reminded that the names of contacts at the Ministry of Commerce in Cuba could be made available to *special friends* within the Washington Beltway - and just about everywhere else in the country provided they realized that the *quid pro quo* "you scratch my back and I'll scratch yours" was a condition of the offer. Friendly information was judged to be both a valuable business asset and a justifiable business expense.

The signing of the treaty was anticlimactic. Discussions and negotiations for the sale of goods and services were agreed upon well before the official announcement. American businessmen could be found in Havana during this time looking for investment opportunities. A sign of the hard driving commercial vitality that was created became apparent when cargo ships began flooding Cuban ports with food, clothing and medical supplies. The unloading of industrial farm equipment and other heavy manufacturing machinery were a further sign of future business prosperity.

Cuba's export business was also given a boost when its local resources became American investment targets. The main agricultural product in Cuba had always been sugar. Until the early 1990's, Cuba produced about 7 million metric tons annually; a level that was surpassed only by Brazil. Fuel shortages led to a partial return to manual harvesting and, by the late 90's, production had fallen to just 3.2 million tons – the lowest level in fifty years. Cuba had lost its preeminence in the world sugar market.

That all changed with the advent of the trade agreement and the credit availability for modernizing Cuba's more than one hundred and fifty dilapidated sugar mills while at the same time closing down those that were uneconomical. Once the mills were brought up-to-date, production and sugar prices soared enabling Cuba to once again take its place among the world's leading sugar producers. Increased production brought many Cuban workers back into the labor market and the island could again boast that seventy percent of its export revenue came from sugar. The United States and China became the major importers of Cuban crude and refined sugar.

Other crops including tobacco, coffee, rice, corn, sweet potatoes, beans and tropical fruits conjointly enjoyed increased crop production and all eventually became lucrative export candidates. Fuel shortages in the early 90's also restricted the movement of the Cuban fishing fleet but that too changed with the influx of working capital into the market. A variety of fresh fish was shipped daily to eagerly awaiting markets in the north.

Cuba was rich in mineral ores, especially nickel. The mines when infused with needed manpower and the latest technological equipment, proved to be once again the country's third-largest revenue producer after sugar and tourism.

But it was tourism that was primarily responsible for Cuba's turn of fortune. American tourists came to the island slowly at first but, once they returned home and spoke glowingly of their vacation, others followed. Press junkets were organized by Maria Sanchez, the newly appointed Travel Consultant to Cuba, which turned into positive endorsements of the *new* Cuba by some of America's most critical travel reviewers.

Cromwell Advertising's campaign was launched with a television, radio, magazine and newspaper campaign that gently scolded travelers that, "It's not a vacation if it's not Cuba". Personal endorsements by popular television and movie stars were used to convince impressionable Americans that a good time was to be had in the *new* Cuba. The hotels promoted prepaid tour packages which in the tourism business was a safe way to assure easy profits. It was estimated that a million American tourists visited Cuba during the first year since the travel ban was lifted. Second year predictions were for that figure to double. Forecasts for the future of travel to Cuba were indisputably optimistic.

Gambling was the driving force behind the success of Cuba's travel program. American dollars flooded the market once the three resort hotels and the renovated hotels with their state of the art casinos were operating at full capacity. The Cuban government historically ran all international tourism as a state monopoly which assured a rich source of income for their Treasury. Private competition was either closely controlled and heavily taxed or banned completely at the convenience of the government.

Around 140,000 Cubans had positions directly related to tourism and those jobs were filled by party loyalists as a reward for their service to Fidel Castro. A family's political background was always the determining factor in selective employment and other social and economic benefits in Cuba. Never was a blacklisted person allowed to profit from participation in the travel industry; however, because of the preponderance of workers needed to service the revitalized gaming industry, workers were not scrutinized as carefully for their political affiliation as they were before the industry's resurgence.

It was because of this employment laxity that Gino Cruz's agents in Cuba were able to slip quietly into the employ of many of the resort hotels and heavily-populated tourist attractions. These hidden assets would bide their time until they were asked to perform acts of sabotage that would create an unsettling tourist climate in Cuba.

The general mood of Havana changed when the tourists came in droves. Cubans, who could barely keep their heads above water before the tourists came, were now living a more tolerable lifestyle and could afford some of the American products that they saw in the bodegas and pharmacies throughout Havana. The designer clothing that was displayed at the malls were still out of reach for most Cubans but other less expensive American clothing items were to be found for the consumer with a limited budget.

Fidel Castro received high marks from Cubans for his management of the economy. Life appeared to be considerably better for the average Cuban family. No one could know that the country's warm feelings about its financial security were in for a rude awakening.

CHAPTER 30

Over the next two years, President Cromwell was a patient observer of Cuba's successful journey from economic uncertainty to a respected trading partner within the international community. He and Castro were being praised by world leaders as the architects of Cuba's new era of economic prosperity. Cubans began viewing their president more favorably coincident with their improved standard of living. They also developed warm feelings for the President of the United States whom, they felt, was most certainly their benefactor and a great humanitarian.

The Group agreed that Cuba would be allowed to enjoy their state of euphoria for another six months before undermining their rejuvenated economy. "Six months should do the trick," Cruz had said. "They'll be in even better shape than they are now. Their fall into economic hell will be all the more dramatic if their economy is operating at peak performance when we pull the rug out from under them. "There's no rush to rush the inevitable. We've waited this long so let's stay resolute a little longer. Cuba will be brought to her knees in good time."

Doug Cromwell could now devote a majority of his time to the domestic problems of the country. The nation's economic barometers were beginning to show early signs of faltering. He had to take charge and show the American electorate that he was on top of things. He could not afford to lose their confidence. And he did have an election to think about down the road.

But he need not have worried. The ever-present opinion polls continued to give him high marks. The political editor of *The New York Times* confidently predicted, "Were there to be a presidential election today, incumbent President Douglas Cromwell would be a shoo-in for reelection." The latest survey indicated that a very small percentage of Americans felt that he should be spending more time solving domestic problems rather than concerning himself with Cuban affairs. This perception was however considered insignificant and therefore a non-political issue, but Doug did agree that he should be spending more time on domestic issues. White House aides had convinced him that Americans really didn't care if Cuba continued as a communist state. Secretary of Commerce Hopkins said, tongue in cheek, "What they did seem to care about was making reservations for a Cuban vacation now that the way was made clear for them to travel to the island."

Tourist business by Americans to Cuba *was* thriving. The latest forecast was that 2.5 million Americans would be traveling to Cuba in the current year. The Minister of Construction was happily making arrangements for two more state owned resorts to be built on the pristine beaches outside of Havana. He convinced Castro that the tourist traffic from America justified these investments. Cuba's financial commitments to the United States and other nations were growing exponentially, but Castro remained confident.

While Doug was busy with his other presidential responsibilities, Gino Cruz was actively reassuring himself that the dismantling of the Cuban economy was on track. One hundred carefully selected *mischief makers* had been assembled and trained over the past year for the express purpose of creating both physical and psychological disruptions on the island.

Bud De Luca was responsible for coordinating the placement of associates in key roles that enabled them to recruit anti-Castro sympathizers for the underhanded work that had been carefully planned. These dissidents were made to believe that their involvement was to create political disharmony on the island which they heartily welcomed. Cruz was confident that the planned disruptions would be in good hands under De Luca's direction.

Presidents Cromwell and Castro spoke many times a month by telephone during this time. Their conversations were always cordial. Cromwell stuck to his bargain with the Cuban dictator that the United States would not interfere in any way with Cuba's political identity. In a moment of frankness, Castro confided that his people had warned him to be very careful in his dealings with the Americans; all they want is to change our style of government and they will do whatever is necessary to achieve that end.

"I told them in no uncertain terms that they need not worry. President Cromwell is an honorable man who gave me his word that he is not interested in changing how we run our country and he has given us a free hand in managing our part in the trade agreement." He laughingly added, “I also told them that I would have them shot if they interfered in any way with our relationship with President Cromwell.” When Castro detected a lack of understanding for his revolutionary humor, he added, “I was only joking, of course.”

The one person closest to Fidel Castro was his brother Raul. Raul had been a friend of Gino Cruz during their younger days in Cuba. The truth was that they were still friends. They would meet on occasions in Cuba when Cruz made clandestine trips to visit Fidel. Cruz was careful to maintain his friendly relationship with both of the brothers. Having a suspicious nature, Fidel always wondered what Raul and Cruz talked about when he was not present.

Raul was constantly warning his brother that he must be on his guard when dealing with the Americans. “I know you think that President Cromwell is a high-minded man, Fidel, but there is something unsettling in the air that tells me his intentions are not as noble as you believe them to be. I am very uneasy about this relationship.”

Fidel smiled and chided his younger brother, “You have always been a suspicious person, Raul, even as a boy.” He reflected for a moment and continued, “Do you think me so naïve that I wouldn’t have thought carefully about the motives of the Americans. I must admit, in the beginning, I believed Cromwell acted so generously because he thought it was simply the right thing to do. I still believe him to be an honorable man in many ways, but I no longer believe that his intentions towards Cuba are as innocent as they appear.”

Raul sat up in his chair, “Why do you say that? You talk to him sometimes several times a month, at least, and you always say that he has never given you cause to suspect his motives. So, why do you think that now?”

Fidel nodded and said, “That is true. What makes me think that something is underfoot is that everything is running too smoothly. It’s as if there was some mysterious puppeteer controlling the strings to make sure that there are no bothersome trivial matters that could be distractions to something bigger and more important to American interests.”

Raul laughed and said, “Now who is the suspicious one, brother?”

Fidel responded, “Yes, I have become suspicious of their motives. “Here’s what I think, Raul. I am of the opinion that the Americans expect that one day; all of the economic success we are experiencing will tell Cubans that it was not us but the Americans who are the reason for our good fortune. And I foresee that our people will convince themselves that the only way to continue that prosperity is to support a democratic government just like the United States. I believe that is the impression the Americans are deliberately trying to create with our people. And, do you know, my dear Raul, there will be nothing we can do about it. We will be so committed to a trading relationship with the United States that we will be unable to walk away from them."

Raul said, "We knew all along that the Americans would never retreat from their position of wanting our government to simply disappear. But, why are they waiting? This is the ideal time for them to act when they are in a position of absolute strength."

Castro answered, "I can only believe that Gino Cruz is the reason for Cromwell not taking a more aggressive stand against us. When Gino left Cuba many years ago, it was to build his influence abroad so he could help assure our success with the revolution. He has become a powerful influence in Washington, and has maintained a loyalty to our cause over the years. He has been the voice of moderation with every United States President since Kennedy. There have been several major efforts over the years by unfriendly people in America to invade Cuba under the pretense that we were committing terrorist acts in their country. There were even accusations that we were again bringing atomic warheads into Cuba for a surprise attack on them."

"Yes, I know, but there has never been a shred of evidence to suggest that Cuba would be a threat to the strongest nation in the world," Raul said. "I really don't believe Americans think we would entertain the notion of attacking them with atomic weapons. I have always looked upon those charges as being ridiculous and not worthy of serious consideration."

Fidel frowned and said, "There will always be charges that Cuba will remain a threat to the safety of Americans if Fidel Castro remains as its leader and it has always been Gino who, through his contacts in the American Congress, has diverted any aggressive acts against us."

Raul reinforced his brother's assessment of Cruz's contribution to Cuba. "Gino is a true patriot to our cause. He has always been able to protect us against our silent enemies in America. And when Gino is gone, I believe he has trained his son Pedro to carry on for him. It's odd but I always thought he was jealous of you becoming leader of our movement and not him."

"You're wrong, Raul, Gino knew from the beginning that he could never lead the movement. He is brilliant in many ways but he could never inspire men to do his bidding. He always had a real passion for the revolution, but he could never instill that fervor into the minds of young revolutionaries."

Raul knew that Fidel's characterization of Cruz was a rationalization to assuage a guilty conscience. The simple truth was that Fidel had downplayed Cruz's talents quietly among his associates to enhance his own position of leadership. Fidel had always misjudged Cruz's motives and, in this case, it was a serious miscalculation. It was unfortunate that such an intelligent and crafty man such as Fidel would not have seen the road signs along the way that would have told him that he was dealing with a formidable enemy and not the compliant friend he pretended to be. Never did he suspect that Cruz was his sworn enemy because he had murdered his best friend Alberto Sierra when he took control of Cuba. Or that Castro was responsible for having tricked Cruz into leaving Cuba so he could take control of the movement. And finally, that Cruz nurtured a hatred for Castro for having deceived him a second time by turning his one true love against him.

Had he been more aware of Cruz's feelings and ambitions he would have known – or at least suspected - that Cruz was committed to relieving his former friend of his most valuable possession – his life.

CHAPTER 31

The Group waited the agreed-upon six months before giving Bud De Luca the go ahead to put in motion the plan to discredit the Cuban economy. It was to be a gradual program of seemingly innocent mishaps designed to set the stage for more extreme misadventures later on.

Audrey and Geoffrey Wickersham of Ottumwa, Iowa were one of the first American couples to visit Cuba after the travel ban was lifted. They decided to return a second time as their first visit was "without a doubt, the most *splendific* vacation we ever had". They made a two-week reservation at *The Roman Coliseum Resort Hotel.* They were into their second week of their "*marvelific*" vacation and having the time of their lives. Mrs. Wickersham liked creating attention-getting adjectives to express her traveling moods.

They were scheduled to meet friends for dinner one evening when a somewhat inebriated driver cancelled out the rest of their vacation. As they were waiting for a limousine to pick them up, a cab driver lost control of his vehicle and careened into the valet parking booth at the entrance to the hotel. Mrs. Wickersham was busy telling a hotel guest that she and her husband were having a perfectly *awesomific* time when the rear fender brushed Mrs. Wickersham in passing which sent her crashing into a guard rail. She lay on the ground in excruciating pain until a house physician came and pronounced that she had a broken leg. As she was taken away in an ambulance, she was heard to say, "The worst, the absolute worst vacation of my life." Three days later the Wickershams were heading home to Ottumwa on a privately chartered flight.

De Luca had hired a string of observers whose job was to report any and all misfortunes experienced by American tourists. These accounts were to be carefully summarized and forwarded to De Luca who would send them to a *special friend* at the Associated Press office in New York. This information was routed to AP clients around the country for inclusion in their local editions.

When De Luca received the report of the Wickersham's accident he was furious. He had told his *mischief makers* that they were to go slow at first. "We don't want any blood or anybody being carried away in a body bag at the start," was his command. "We'll start with annoying inconveniences that tourists will gripe about among themselves and when they get back home. We'll step up the action once we see how things are going. We don't want people getting hurt." He thought for a moment and finished his sentence, "unless it becomes absolutely necessary."

When De Luca was told that his people had nothing to do with the Wickersham mishap; that it was simply an accident, he smiled and said to himself that, no matter who was responsible, it was actually a pretty good kickoff for what was to come.

Maria Sanchez was taking her job as tourist consultant very seriously. One of the first things she did when she had accepted the assignment was to set up a damage control tourist center on her computer. She knew from experience that tourism had many sensitive pressure points that, if not monitored continuously, could result in some untidy if not disastrous situations. She had learned the hard way that a negative word-of-mouth campaign started by disgruntled tourists was something that was to be avoided. She had seen inconsequential incidences take on a life of their own and cause irreparable damage to thriving tourist businesses.

She still knew nothing about *The Group's* scheme to sabotage Cuba's tourist program so she too was cataloguing anything that smacked of tourist dissatisfaction. She had warned Castro earlier of the potential dangers of ignoring tourist complaints and he was in agreement that each matter should be handled on an individual case basis. She told him of the Wickersham incident as an example of the kind of mishap that could create ill feelings towards his program. Castro said that he would not tolerate any incidences that could cause Americans to think poorly of Cuba. He asked Maria to write a letter to the Wickershams in Iowa inviting them to return to Cuba for a two-week stay at the expense of the Cuban government.

"I obviously cannot become involved in each and every incident of that nature in the future," he said. "We cannot avoid unpredictable accidents from happening but we can set a procedure for handling such matters." Normally, Castro would have very little patience for becoming involved in anything that a lowly public official could handle. His wanting to become involved spoke to his obsessive need to keep his tourist economy on track.

Maria said, “I have already arranged for you to receive a report once a week that outlines any problems involving tourism. We will respond to each one as they happen to avoid undue publicity.”

Castro was satisfied that Maria had the situation under control. He suddenly had a feeling of lustful good humor. He was looking at her well-shaped legs with a salacious leer when he said, “My darling Maria, I feel like an Olympian today. I think I would like to try for the gold medal this evening.”

Maria smiled coyly and said, “I always look forward to your athletic accomplishments, sweet Fidelito.” Her thoughts ran counter to what she had said. He’ll be lucky if he can win a silver medal – or even qualify - the way he’s been performing lately, she told herself.

The Cromwell administration was running like the finely tuned Patek Phillipe watch that was presented to him by the President of France on his last visit abroad. He became totally focused on domestic issues and let his Secretary of State be the administration’s front man and spokesman on day to day international affairs. The Vice-President was visibly a helpmate to her husband in her duties as second-in-command. She was proving herself to be a formidable member of the President’s staff of advisors.

The Cromwells developed a reputation for being a hands on managerial team with a willingness to bend over backwards to be fair in their dealings with administration associates as well as leaders of the opposition party. Cruz was less interference on matters that were not really his concern now that the Cuban Project was building up steam for a final showdown. There was always less stress within *The Group* when Gino was preoccupied with what was happening in Cuba.

Mr. and Mrs. Robert McKissick were leaving El Centro Habana Restaurant late one evening after enjoying a traditional Cuban meal. They decided to walk back to their hotel as it was the type of evening that called for a leisurely stroll before having their usual after dinner drink at the hotel bar. As they walked along the Avenue de Maceo, two men stepped from the shadows of a side street and, brandishing small revolvers, relieved them of their valuables. The two men were gone as quickly as they appeared once they had taken the jewelry and cash the McKissicks had with them. They reported the incident to the police when they returned to their hotel and were told that the theft would be investigated. The case became a closed issue when the police reported that neither the thieves nor the jewelry could be located.

A hotel employee made a note of the complaint and added it to a list he had been compiling which he passed on at the end of each day to an anonymous stranger who paid him for the information.

The following day, two young secretaries vacationing from their jobs with a New York advertising agency were accosted while jogging in a quiet section of a street adjacent to their hotel. They were carrying nothing of value except inexpensive costume jewelry. Three young youths darted out from a hidden doorway and began hassling and fondling the two defenseless women who began screaming hysterically for help. They were rescued only when a police car came along to intercede. The youths ran off laughing. When the two policemen saw that no physical harm had been done to the women they immediately dismissed the incident as "just some kids looking for a feel". They said they would report the incident and that the women should not be jogging alone like that as some shady characters hang out along these streets.

The two women reported the incident when they returned to their hotel. An employee of the hotel was quick to record the information on an index card which, later that day, she would add to the list she was assembling and which she would exchange for cash at days end.

Management at the newly constructed Hotel Internationale began receiving complaints from guests that they weren't receiving clean bed linens. Their beds were made up in the morning but the linens were not fresh and in some cases downright messy. The hotel investigated these complaints and found them to be justified. The cleaning personnel swore that they always change the linens in every room and would never think not to do so. Hotel security investigated and could only confirm that the linens had not been changed. The maid service personnel were warned and special monitoring groups made certain that any such incidences were not repeated.

The assigned *mischief makers* had made their point so the troublesome linen enigma at the Internationale was transferred to other hotels.

Charlie "Beefy" McCarthy was Vice-President in charge of Special Corporate and Municipal Sales for the General Motors Company in Detroit. He was in Cuba to meet with the Minister of Transportation Juan Cardoza and his staff to discuss the sale of a fleet of Chevrolet trucks and passenger cars for use by government officials, municipal work projects and special unnamed sources. The Russian-made vehicles currently being used were becoming a major problem; they could no longer be adequately maintained due to the lack of replacement parts from their former ally. McCarthy's wife Catherine had joined him as they planned on enjoying themselves at one of the resort hotels once he concluded his business with the Cubans.

Part of the deal Cardoza was negotiating involved a Cadillac Sedan de Ville for each member of the Council of State and the Council of Ministers. It was important therefore that nothing interfered with the negotiations and that the McCarthys were afforded first-class treatment while in Cuba. They were guests of the government at *The Roman Coliseum Resort Hotel.*

When Cruz heard that a key executive of one of the major corporations in the world was to be discussing a business arrangement with the Cubans, he immediately saw it as an opportunity for furthering unrest with the unwitting help of a high profile American business executive.

McCarthy gained his nickname "Beefy" at a relatively young age when he discovered the pleasures of food and drink. He presently tipped the scales at 265-pounds which on a frame of 5 foot 8 inches gave him the appearance of a heart attack waiting to happen. Charlie loved to eat. It was his passion in life. The *mischief maker* assigned to the hotel saw him as the perfect mark for what Gino had in mind.

The evening that he closed the deal with Cardoza, he and his wife celebrated with a very special evening at *The Venetian Room* at the hotel. Charlie was normally a meat and potatoes man but he also had an affinity for swordfish. The waiter had assured him that the hotel's swordfish catch would be the best tasting that he had ever experienced so Charlie ordered the swordfish. His wife ordered the filet mignon. He was so intent on enjoying himself that he failed to notice a strange odor when the swordfish was served to him. Nor did he detect the sour taste when he swallowed a large bite of the serving; however, his digestive tract told him immediately that he had eaten something offensive and angrily rejected it. Charlie was only slightly relieved when he burped loudly and then regurgitated the offensive morsel all over Mrs. McCarthy's new Dior gown which she was wearing for the first time.

"Charlie, you son-of-a-bitch, look what you did," she screamed hysterically. It was then that Charlie gave her a second helping of his erupting rogue swordfish. She was now not only beside herself with anger, but she too became physically ill. Her afternoon lunch quickly married Charlie's swordfish on the front of her gown. Waiters rushed to their rescue with large napkins to smother the offensive sight. One of the waiters in his zeal to control the lava-like flow on Mrs. McCarthy's gown gently brushed her bosom which invoked an outcry of further rage, "Charlie, this guy's feeling my tits, get him off of me."

Most of the repulsed diners in the surrounding area left the restaurant immediately. The maitre'd was beside himself trying to apologize for the unfortunate situation. When Charlie regained his composure, he berated the hotel for serving contaminated food letting everyone within earshot know of his unhappiness. When the Minister of Transportation heard of the incident, he too, was profusely apologetic. He knew that the unfortunate situation would get back to Castro and the other Ministers which did not bode well for his future comfort at Ministerial sessions. Castro did hear of the incident. His angered comment was, "This better not effect my getting that Cadillac."

The contaminated swordfish had served its purpose. The McCarthy incident became the talk of the resort the next day. It was given a humorous spin when Mrs. McCarthy's reactions and verbal improprieties were repeated. The Associated Press contact in New York thought it would make a humorous sidebar for a feature they were preparing for their clients titled, "Problems in Paradise". The number of incidents they had received from De Luca justified a revealing editorial. And the widespread dissemination of an Associated Press position piece in the United States would certainly stimulate word-of-mouth discussion.

CHAPTER 32

Gino Cruz had a chuckle and a growing sense of satisfaction that things were working out exactly as planned. He was pleased when he read the account of the McCarthy's experience with the deliberately tainted swordfish. He was particularly gratified to see that the Associated Press had editorialized the collection of tourist adversities into a humorous but damning statement that characterized Cuba as being "a beautiful but troublesome island that better get its act together if Fidel expects to survive in the competitive world of tourism".

Sitting in his office gloating, he suddenly had a brainstorm. He asked himself, what did Maria Sanchez say about having been invited on several occasions to address a convention of international tourist agents? As I understand it, these people like to go to interesting and out-of-the-ordinary places for their meetings. The new Cuba fills that bill perfectly. Most of them have probably never been there given the long standing travel ban restriction. Cuba being the hot spot it is right now, they'll undoubtedly welcome the opportunity to see the island firsthand.

When he told Sanchez of his idea, she thought it an excellent suggestion but wondered why Gino would make a special call to promote something that was completely out of his realm of interest. She questioned him with a note of humor. "Gino, are you planning on buying stock in the Cuban government or have you suddenly developed a love affair for travel agents?"

Cruz returned the light remark, "I just wish I could buy stock in the new Cuba. From what I hear their economy has been running wild ever since that trade agreement." He paused and said, as if something had just occurred to him, "By the way, Maria, I was talking to Louis Karmazin the other day about you. Lou is retired but he still keeps his hand in. He's a very influential fellow who, coincidentally, is involved in setting up an American Chamber of Commerce office down there in Havana. I told him of your background and he thinks he has something you'd be interested in. I want you to call him the next time you're in Havana. Remember, I promised you that something interesting would come along for you. This could be it."

"You do keep your promises, Gino. Thank you."

"Lou is the reason I thought to call you, Maria. He was very interested when I told him of the tourist agent idea. Could be a big boost for Cuba. Why don't you look into it and get back to me."

Maria got back to Gino a week later. "I contacted the President of the International Association of Travel Agents who just got back to me. She thinks it's a great idea but their AITA convention is already booked for this year in Los Angeles. She did say though, as you suggested, that she's certain she can round up a hundred of the top agents in the United States to travel there as a private group and she's pretty sure she can do it with a four month lead time."

"Let's do it then, Maria. This will make you a hero with our Cuban friends. And, it'll be your idea. Don't even mention my name when you finalize things.

"That's very generous of you, Gino," she said.

Gino debited another favor due to his payback account. "We're friends, aren't we, Maria?"

Maria did contact Karmazin the next time she was in Cuba. He offered her the position of Cuba's Director of the American Chamber of Commerce. She readily accepted. Castro was instrumental in endorsing her appointment. A month later she was comfortably settled in a luxury apartment close to the Presidential Palace.

A hundred and twenty five female travel agents descended on *The Roman Coliseum Resort Hotel* and were greeted by a spirited welcoming committee headed by the Minister of Tourism Ricardo Perez. He advised them that they were to be guests of President Castro during their visit. The agents were delighted as they had anticipated paying their own expenses while in Cuba. Minister Perez added, "The President would also like you all to be his guests tomorrow for a very special evening of dining and entertainment at the Palace." Castro was pulling out all of the stops to ensure that these guardians of the tourist dollar felt like very special people while they were in Cuba. Little did his guests know that the entertainment mentioned would be at least an hour of uninterrupted oratory by the President. The occasion was too fertile an occasion for him not to take advantage of this captive audience.

Gino had prepared well for the surprises that were in store for the band of tourist agents who had come to Cuba to be better prepared to sell their clients on the allure of the island. If things worked out as Gino had planned, by the end of their visit, there would be very little enthusiasm for their recommending Cuba to their free-wheeling clientele – or anyone else, for that matter. His plan called for them to leave Cuba with strong misgivings for having come to the island in the first place.

When they arrived at their hotel tired and in need of a warm bath or an invigorating shower, they found that the resort's hot water heaters had sustained a mysterious shutdown. The reserve heaters were immediately brought into play but they could not generate the heat necessary to reinforce the main system. The problem was fixed two hours later which proved to be a terrible inconvenience for a group of pampered agents used to first class treatment wherever they traveled. At a cocktail hour later that evening, they joked about the unlikelihood of something like that happening at *The Roman Collie,* a resort with its professed reputation for excellence. They enjoyed creating their own nicknames for the exclusive hotels they frequented.

About a fourth of the group wasn't as tolerant when they returned to their rooms after dinner. The *Mischief Makers* had been busy again reorganizing the linen. It seemed to work the first time so used linens were retrieved from the laundry room and substituted for the fresh bedding. And again the complaints reigned on the night manager who had been subjected to the same problem several weeks before. He acted quickly. He fired the maids in that section of the hotel and arranged for new personnel to be available the next day. He would not tolerate a black mark on his record because of lazy shiftless people. Dirty linens and poor service were the heated topics of conversation among the travel agents the next morning at breakfast.

Fidel was livid when he got word of the two new incidents at the hotel. He fumed, "This could have serious effects on the economy of Cuba if it continues. I want those people at the hotel to know that they are committing treasonous acts by their neglect to do their duty. People have been known to be put against a wall and executed for acts of betrayal to the government. I want that deceit to stop or I will put a stop to it." The threat could not have been more intimidating.

He blamed his preoccupation with "those treacherous workers and their dirty linen" for his unsuccessful amorous performance with Maria that evening. Instead of his standard rationalization that "tomorrow will be better", he was now saying to himself, "I *hope* tomorrow will be better".

The following morning the group took a guided tour of Havana in three luxury buses. Castro wanted the tour to proceed safely and without incident so he provided an armed guard to precede the buses as they traveled through the streets and outskirts of Havana. Similar protection followed the buses during the trip. There were no incidents but the visiting agents wondered why it was necessary to have armed soldiers escorting them throughout the day. It gave them an uncomfortable feeling that something ominous was about to happen. De Luca's observers made copious notes of the comments made by the visitors when they stopped to sightsee and have lunch.

Castro was at his charming best when he hosted the dinner for the Americans that evening. He was told by an aide that they were beginning to get edgy about the little inconveniences that seemed to be plaguing the group. The nervous aide had the temerity to suggest that a short speech might be appropriate this evening. Castro said, annoyed, "I am always brief." He then spoke for forty five minutes in welcoming his guests.

A frumpy looking lady said to her companion, "Mavis, I thought you were king of the bullshitters. This guy beats you hands down." The evening was uneventful. The guests seemed to have forgotten the incidences of the previous day and settled down to enjoy themselves. Castro was the picture-perfect host.

The balance of the week was not without incidence though. There were no major disruptive occurrences but there were many annoying slights arranged to test the patience of a group of ladies accustomed to near-perfection in their travel accommodations. Cold meals that were meant to be served warm, untimely delivery of room service orders, long waits at the restaurants for meal service, rudeness from employees of the hotel when asked simple service-related questions, wake-up calls that never materialized and other annoying nuisances were shading the ladies' feelings towards the new Cuba.

A very special surprise was arranged for them on their final day. The ladies were not in a happy camper mood when they boarded the buses to take them to the airport. The group was uncharacteristically quiet during their trip from the hotel to catch an early afternoon flight to Miami. Their expectations for a relaxing and informative week were summed up succinctly by one of the disillusioned guests, "Now that's what I call a week straight out of hell."

Half way to their destination, one of the women in the lead bus let out a horrifying scream, "My God, it's a snake. There's a snake on the bus." Her cry of anguish was so alarming that another woman began shrieking, "Stop the bus – stop this goddamn bus and let us off." The driver instinctively jammed on the brakes causing the bus to careen from one side of the highway to the other. The bus finally came to a stop after causing many of the passengers to be thrown roughly about as they were all standing in the aisles trying to avoid contact with the still unidentified snake. Fortunately, there were no serious injuries. There was a mass exodus once the driver had opened the door. The other buses had also stopped.

Once everyone was off the bus, the driver picked up a stick from the side of the road and went to find the snake. He found it coiled up in a warm spot near the rear wheel mounting. When he coaxed the multicolored reptile out of the bus, several of the women became physically ill while others simply burst into tears and hugged themselves for comfort. One woman, not knowing how to vent her anger, took the discarded stick and started hitting the driver. In the meantime, the snake slithered away unmindful of the disturbance it has caused. The women boarded the bus to finish their journey once the driver convinced them that there were no more snakes on the bus.

When the ladies finally arrived at the airport, they checked in and then made a hasty dash for the bar and ordered alcoholic comforts to calm their nerves. Penelope Adams was responsible for publishing the AITA monthly newsletter sent to the 3,500 membership around the world. Hers was a strong organizational voice that resonated with authority on matters relating to the selection of choice vacation destinations. She said vindictively after her second double Dewars on the rocks, "I'm going to have a field day writing about this sorry trip."

And write it she did. Penelope indicated to the membership in no uncertain terms that Cuba's ability to service the tourist trade was going through an identity crisis. "It is the recommendation of the Association that we take a wait and see attitude with regards to recommending Cuba to our clients. They have a way to go yet before we can be assured that our clients will be serviced satisfactorily. We should be particularly cautious about recommending Cuba to long-standing clients. We feel strongly that client confidence could be diminished were Cuba to be recommended." This strong language was taken to heart by the membership. Their influence proved a death knell for Cuba bookings by travel agents throughout the United States.

When Fidel Castro heard of this disastrous turn of events, he challenged his Minister of Tourism Perez to explain the reason that tourism had fallen off during the previous quarter. "You are not doing your job, Minister. Perhaps someone else can do what you have failed to do."

Perez sensed that Castro was going to replace him. He rallied quickly. He had to talk fast even if he had to fabricate a reason. His prestigious position was at stake. "President Castro, Fidel, I believe it is the work of the dissident groups here and in South Florida who are sabotaging our program. I have it on good authority that the right wing *Back to Cuba Movement* has been spreading rumors among the press in the United States that American tourists are being maligned and abused in Havana."

Castro was skeptical of Perez's motives but thought that it was not unlikely that they could be to blame. He too had heard that rumor. "If someone is sabotaging our tourist efforts then it must be stopped immediately. We must have a full investigation." When Perez left, Castro called his Minister of Justice Marco Iglesias who was in his office a half hour later sweating profusely. "Find out Marco whether there is an organized effort to sabotage tourism in Cuba and if so, I must know who is responsible for such a traitorous act."

Iglesias was ill-suited for the responsibilities that Castro had bestowed on him many years before. He had never held a position other than within the Castro administration. He was Castro's cousin. His best friend was the Minister of Tourism. He called Ricardo Perez as soon as he left Castro's office. He told his friend of his conversation with Castro. "Do you think the Americans could be doing this to us?" he asked.

"Of course not. Why would they want to cripple an economy that they were responsible for creating in the first place? I think that would be a very dangerous path for you to take to even suggest such a possibility. Questioning the motives of the United States would not be a smart thing for you to do. Fidel has great confidence in President Cromwell and does not want to insult him in any way. No, I think you should put all of your resources into investigating the dissident groups here in Cuba. Our spy network in South Florida should be able to unearth any Cuban American involvement if there is any."

"Yes, I think you are right."

Perez looked around before continuing, "And, a word to the wise, old friend. These dissidents at home have been responsible in the past for many of Cuba's anti-government incidences. They are traitors to the core. I would suggest that, even if you can't find anything to incriminate them, you provide Fidel with evidence that they *are* the ones responsible for sabotaging the tourist business along with their allies in America."

"Are you telling me to falsify evidence to implicate the dissidents regardless of what I find to be the truth?"

"I am suggesting that you give Fidel what he's looking for. He doesn't want the Americans to be the responsible ones. It would be admitting that the trade agreement with the United States was a sham. At risk right now is the tourist business but, if we accuse the Americans of underhandedness, you can be sure that the trade agreement will disappear. That agreement is based upon a mutual faith in one another. Destroy that faith and you destroy any hope of continuing any kind of relationship with the Americans."

"I am in a very difficult position, Jose."

"Yes, you are my friend, so go out and find yourself some dissidents to blame for the difficult position you have inherited."

Iglesias knew that was exactly what he had to do.

CHAPTER 33

Castro had told Cruz on a secure telephone call from Cuba that his tourist business had fallen thirty five percent since "those meddlesome American tourist people visited Cuba". He meticulously recited the number of unfriendly incidents that had occurred since the travel ban was lifted. He had very concise statistics and details of the occurrences which varied from petty housekeeping complaints to serious assault and robbery charges. Cruz noticed that Castro sounded overwrought and in need of some serious handholding less he do something that would interfere with *The Group's* plans.

"Fidel, I think we should talk about this in person. Let me grab a flight tomorrow evening. I can be there in time for supper."

"That would be very helpful, Gino. I'll have my car meet you at the usual place. And, thank you, Gino. I miss not having you here." The connection was broken as Cruz muttered to himself, lying son-of-a-bitch.

Castro again bemoaned the situation he was facing when he and Cruz sat down to dinner the follow evening. Gino was sympathetic, "It looks like a deliberate attempt on somebody's part to destroy your tourist business."

Castro agreed, "At first I thought it might be a plot by the United States to derail our program, but my Minister of Justice has just completed an extensive investigation which proved conclusively that it was the dissident groups in Cuba who are responsible; not the United States. Thinking it is the United States just doesn't make sense. Why would they try to destroy an important segment of our financial system when President Cromwell worked so hard to help us to rebuild our failing economy? No, I have always believed President Cromwell to be an honorable man and I still believe it to be the truth."

Cruz couldn't believe that Castro had been so neglectful in absolving the United States of any responsibility in the matter. Fidel is no fool, he told himself, and he must know that the Americans had a hand in organizing such a plot. He's certainly aware that the right wing dissidents are in it too, but he also knows that they don't have the organizational skills to pull this off alone. The various splinter groups – and there must be at least ten of them that are aggressively active – have never been able to work together. I think Fidel is trying to find a goat to take the heat off the United States. He can't afford a confrontation with America. It would be a no-win situation for him. Win the battle and lose the war. An open conflict with the United States would be tantamount to destroying the trade agreement. At the same time, he also knows that if this tourist collapse continues, he will lose much of the income that the country is now enjoying. Our friend has a problem. Let's see how we can help him *not* solve it.

Castro continued, "*The Democratic Cuba Movement* is the strongest of the dissident groups and they have strong support from the venomous Miami exiles and their right wing political allies. Our investigation points an accusatory finger at their leadership. I have given orders that these leaders be taught a severe lesson. As we speak, they are being arrested and will be tried for treason. Perhaps their followers will be less willing to follow the orders of a doomed leadership if they witness what will happen to them if they continue their traitorous ways."

Cruz was supportive, "I think you are doing the right thing, Fidel. I find it difficult to believe that there are people in Cuba who are that intent and dedicated to destroying something you and I have work so hard to build for our homeland."

Castro looked at his friend long and hard. "Gino, you have always been someone I could depend on. Thank you for your continued friendship." The Cuban dictator had long ago wondered just how loyal Cruz was to him. He concluded that he could be confident that there was never any reason for him to question Cruz's loyalty. Besides, how could his old friend benefit from such a scheme? No, he convinced himself, he was fortunate to have Gino Cruz as a friend.

"Tell me, what can I do now to help you, Fidel?" Gino found lying to a liar was easy for him.

Castro said in an anxious tone, "I would like you to speak to President Cromwell and tell him these words. Tell him that we know who has been undermining our country with their disloyalty. Tell him that I must act against them otherwise they will seriously affect our chances of building a sound financial economy. Tell him that he will hear that I am doing ruthless things to stop these criminals. I would ask him to understand that they must be punished severely so that others will know that they too will be subject to the same harsh punishment if they continue their illegal activities."

Cruz knew that Castro was perfectly willing to execute large numbers of innocent people if only to convince the American President that he didn't suspect the United States of these unfriendly acts. The Cuban President was capable of conducting a reign of terror to protect the trade agreement with the United States even if it meant the temporary loss of the tourist dollar. He believed he could always recapture that lucrative business once the Americans stopped their veiled attempts at political espionage. A week later, Castro moved to fulfill his pledge to punish those behind the plot to subvert his ambitions for Cuba.

Alfred Alvarez had become a persistent thorn in Castro's side ever since he became leader of *The Democratic Cuba Movement* in the earlier 1990's. The Soviets had deserted Cuba by 1991 so Castro no longer had the economic leverage to convince Cubans that times were good. The economy simply lost its vitality with the exodus of the Russian ruble. The dissident groups throughout Cuba began to do their utmost to characterize Castro as the cause of this sudden change of fortune. Leading this charge was Alvarez's cry for democratic reform.

Castro had allowed the group to continue unimpeded during the good times. He saw that they were unable to frame a strong effort when the market for dissent was a weak cry in the forest. There was another reason. Alvarez was no stranger to Castro. Twenty years before at a mammoth government rally in the Plaza de la Revolucion, a deranged gunman attempted to assassinate the Cuban dictator during one of his marathon speeches to a crowd that filled the gigantic square. Alvarez was standing close to the speaker's lectern when the gunman fired. He had seen the gunman taking aim and he knew that his group would be blamed if Castro was assassinated. Alvarez threw himself in the path of the bullet which struck him in the shoulder. The gunman was quickly apprehended and summarily shot.

While Castro knew Alvarez to be a political irritant, he was so taken with the young man's courage and willingness to sacrifice himself that he became beholden to him. Alvarez was given a small home for him and his family. He was not the uncompromising zealot he had become years later so he accepted the home without protest. Castro later protected him whenever his name came up as being an enemy of the state.

But times had changed. A scapegoat was needed. Alvarez was arrested along with twelve of his cohorts and charged with being a saboteur and a traitor. Castro added his own condemning charge, "He should be shot just for being an ingrate. Get that house back."

The thirteen men were tried for the charges as outlined and an additional charge of possessing a large cache of military style weapons and munitions. The trumped up charges and the ominous threat that the militant group was in possession of lethal weaponry was enough to get an immediate ruling from the judging tribunal. Guilty as charged. The Castro-controlled media was quick to dramatize the seriousness of the movement's militant behavior towards the government. All nine of the men and four women were sentenced to face a firing squad the following week.

Castro had an ulterior motive in delaying the executions for a week. He knew that the American people would never tolerate being associated with a partnership that smacked of legal murder. And he was right. No sooner had the sentence been publicized than Castro received a hurried call from President Cromwell who knew he had to be tactful in light of what was at stake. Castro motioned his interpreter to pick up the extension.

"Mr. President – Fidel – I am in complete agreement with your decision to punish those disloyal traitors who have committed a cowardly and evil act against their own country. My administration is clearly behind you in meting out swift justice. However, I must tell you that we have been receiving an unprecedented amount of mail from Americans around the country heatedly criticizing these people being executed. They agree that justice must be served, but they are calling the sentence barbaric and totally unnecessary."

Castro pushed his advantage. "It is an extreme measure, Doug, but I must rally my countrymen in this time of crisis. The penalty must be severe enough for the people to recognize the danger that these people and people like them have created for our nation."

"I stand by my commitment to you that the United States will never interfere with your internal affairs, Fidel. I am just worried that the mood of the American people on this matter could very well tip the scales as to our future relationship. Their outraged response could take the matter completely out of my hands." Cromwell hesitated as he had now put the ball in the Cuban dictator's court. "How can we appease these cries for a more reasonable sentence, Fidel? What can I do to help you make a more moderate decision?"

Castro smiled a silent tribute to his own cunningness. He, too, was momentarily silent letting Cromwell think that he was considering alternatives. "If I could just stop these tourist distractions, I think I could convince our tribunal that a more judicious sentence would be appropriate. I don't like interfering once the voice of justice has spoken but, because of your deep concern, I will personally plead their case."

"Fidel let me see what we can do to help with this problem. We have people here who are quite good at analyzing and recommending solutions to problems such as the one you have. Let me call them together and get working on a solution. May I suggest that you delay the sentences of the accused until we have had another chance to talk?"

"Again, Doug, you are being very generous with your wisdom and understanding. Yes, by all means, I shall arrange for that immediately. And, again, thank you for being so caring for Cuba."

Cromwell slowly put the phone back on its cradle and said audibly, "I think I've just been had." Without a second thought, he called Gino Cruz and suggested that he convene a meeting of *The Group* as present circumstances called for an immediate parley.

When the five members got together, Doug began, "There's no doubt in my mind that he's on to us. He's playing a cat and mouse game. Having said that though, I don't think he's lost confidence in you, Gino. He always speaks highly of your commitment to Cuba whenever your name comes up. He sounds sincere so I think we still have that strong card to play against him."

Gino responded, "Don't be deceived by appearances, Doug. He's a past master at hiding his true colors. As for him not suspecting me, I don't know and I don't much care. I can play this buddy game as long as it serves our purpose. He thinks he has us by the short hairs with his little blackmail scheme. I say let's call his bluff. You can let him know that it's really none of our concern how he treats those prisoners. Sure, he'll execute them but he'll know once and for all that he cannot blackmail the United States." Gino's vindictiveness for the Cuban leader was beginning to manifest itself in a bitterly aggressive way.

David Cromwell was disturbed by what he just heard, "Gino, you're talking about sacrificing the lives of thirteen human beings who, as we all know, had nothing to do with this tourism plot. We can't just sit quietly and let that madman murder those people. Their deaths would be on our conscience."

Pedro Cruz was equally distressed, "Gino, this is starting to get out-of-hand. We said at the beginning that there was to be no bloodshed. We can't let him kill those people."

Juan Sierra concurred, "I agree. Let's tell Castro that we'll let it be known through underground sources that the United States would look unfavorably upon anyone who commits any further acts of aggression against our Cuban allies. We can then back off of the disruption campaign until we're able to come up with an alternate plan."

The President looked at the members and said, decisively, "No, of course, we can't let those people die for something for which we're responsible. Juan's idea is a good one. We'll give Castro a comfort level that will not only save those prisoners, but will give us time to regroup and decide on an alternate plan."

They all eyed Cruz waiting for a response. He was looking directly at The President when he said, "I guess I was overreacting. No, it would be unconscionable for us not to try and save those people. Yes, let's do exactly as Juan suggests. Mr. President, why don't you contact Castro at your pleasure and tell him of your intentions of having the CIA Director getting the word out to potential groups who could be responsible for his problems. Tell Fidel that the Director has assured you that the matter will be handled. That temporary subterfuge will at least prevent him from going off half cocked before we've had a chance to react."

The President smiled and said, "That's how we'll handle it." They then discussed several other matters that needed resolution and adjourned. Cruz went directly back to his office and called Bud De Luca. "Bud, let's meet. The usual place at 4:30 this afternoon."

When they met, Cruz brought his enforcer up-to-date on the latest development. De Luca was astounded. "You mean to say that after all that planning and all that field work, we're going to abandon something that has been working so well."

"Who said anything about abandoning our original plan? There's no need to scrap it. It worked for us and it will continue to work for us. Those tourist people will be reminding their clients of their Cuban experience for a long time to come. What we need now though is one – just one – final and memorable act of sabotage that will unequivocally place Cuba on the top of the list of places *not* to visit.

"What will your friends say about you going against their unanimous decision not to continue with what we've been doing?"

Gino winked and said, "I won't tell if you don't tell."

"Any ideas as to what that final and glorious deed will be?"

"I have an idea, but let's take a day and give it our best thinking, Gino said. "Let's meet on Thursday. We'll make our decision then."

"I'll be ready," De Luca said, looking forward to the challenge. "By the way, can I have people getting hurt in my thinking?"

Gino said simply, "Use your own judgment."

CHAPTER 34

When the two conspirators met, Cruz could see immediately by the animated expression on De Luca's face that he had come up with an idea for placing the final nail in Castro's coffin. And, thought Cruz, I'll bet that somewhere in that scheme people will be physically hurt.

De Luca couldn't suppress his enthusiasm. "Gino, I've been thinking of what you said about putting a cap on this tourist project. I've done a little research, too. What we need is something like the travel agent spin that worked so well but this time it has to be something so outrageous that it will create worldwide attention. It has to be a front page headliner."

Cruz warmed to the subject, "And that is?"

"Okay, here's what I'm thinking. One of Castro's biggest problems has always been the right wing Cuban Americans. What better way for Fidel to show his willingness to mend his ways than to invite a delegation from that community to Cuba for a reasonable discussion of their differences."

"You must be joking. Castro wouldn't be caught dead in a room with those people," Cruz said.

"I know," said De Luca, "but this time it will be with Cuban Americans who aren't out to get his scalp. Did you know that thirty percent of the dissidents in South Florida were around in 1959 and that most of them were the first to leave Cuba when Castro took power? They are the ones who are perpetuating this hatred for him and they are the ones who must be placated to quiet the fifty years of poisonous attacks against Fidel. The younger Cuban Americans in the group are quite moderate about the whole thing. They could care less about whether Fidel stays in power or not. They're really quite neutral."

Cruz had a doubtful look on his face but let De Luca continue. "Did you know, Gino, that this minority faction has formed an advocacy group within *The Democratic Cuban Movement* which they call *Elders for a Free Cuba.* This splintered group was formed for the expressed purpose of countering the appeasement attitude of the younger moderates. The elders are committed to honoring the organization's original goal of bringing freedom to Cuba."

"And you expect Castro to deal with people dedicated to putting him in his grave?"

De Luca was not sidetracked, "Did you also know that virtually none of the members of this older group have been back to Cuba since leaving fifty years ago and they've fostered a strong desire to return if only for a visit? They know their days are numbered and they want to see their homeland before it is too late. It is a favorite topic of conversation when the group gets together and one that I believe can serve our need for serving up the *coup d' grace* to Fidel's tourism ambitions."

"Where are you getting this information from, Bud?"

"I discovered it firsthand from someone who is a member of the group," De Luca answered. "But, let me continue. Suppose we were to arrange for Maria Sanchez to appear on a Miami television talk show and mention that she had it on good authority that Fidel Castro was having second thoughts about allowing Cuban Americans to return to their country for a visit. She would reinforce this statement by saying that Castro also suggested that he would welcome being host to the Elders if they would like to come as a group. She could then say that she questioned Castro about the rumor and Castro replied in the affirmative."

"Let her say that Castro's exact words were, "I know how I feel when I am away from Cuba for any length of time, Maria. How must these seniors feel not to be able to breathe Cuban air for over fifty years? If there were some way I could make amends for having denied these good people access to their homeland, believe me, I would do it."

"Bud, come on. Do you actually think that anyone in the Cuban community would buy him saying something like that? And what would be the point?"

"He would say something like that because *you* would convince him it would be for his own good." De Luca was on a roll. "But, let me finish. You would tell him that with all the negative publicity he's been getting lately that it behooves him to let President Cromwell know that he is bending over backwards to make peace with the people who are at least partially responsible for his problems. Let's say that a group of several hundred elders were to accept the invitation, Castro would magnanimously offer to put them up at one of the resort hotels for a week at the expense of the Cuban government. Group sightseeing tours would be arranged as well as private trips for those wanting to travel about the island reminiscing about times and places of earlier times."

"And, how does this benevolent act of high-mindedness help us in bringing down our friend?" asked Cruz.

De Luca rubbed his hands together and proceeded to describe the plan he had in mind. Cruz interrupted De Luca's telling of the scheme with the comment, "Christ, Bud, a lot of people could get hurt."

"You said to use my judgment," was De Luca's response. When he finished telling his story, Cruz closed his eyes and reflected on De Luca's words. When he opened his eyes, he smiled and said, "I like it. Let me talk to Fidel."

Castro knew he was between a rock and a hard place in his relationship with the United States. If the tourist business from the United States dried up, his economy would fall into serious disrepair and, if that happened, the Americans would invariably look unfavorably towards trading relations with Cuba. Castro was a proud man, but he was also a realist. He told himself that he must stop this downfall before it consumes us. I will have to go along with what Gino is telling me. I must retain Cromwell's goodwill and his confidence in me.

Castro and Cruz agreed to go forward with the plan. Maria Sanchez returned to Florida and was welcomed as the President of the Chamber of Commerce of Cuba. Talk show hosts were pleased to have the former Deputy Mayor appearing on their programs. Before she was halfway into the interviews, she would casually mention Castro's change of heart and his invitations to have Cuban Americans visit Cuba. *The Elders for a Free Cuba* jumped at the opportunity. A spokesman for the group called Sanchez directly on a listener call-in line and declared that they would be interested in talking about organizing such a trip. Sanchez said that she was leaving for Cuba on an evening flight and would advise President Castro of their enthusiastic reply to his offer.

The Cuban dictator wanted nothing to go wrong with the *Elders*' visit to Cuba. He gathered together his brother Raul who was Minister of the Revolutionary Armed Forces, his Minister of Justice, the

Minister of Tourism and Colonel Fernando del Toro, the dreaded Chief of National Security who consistently reinforced his reputation as a ruthless and uncompromising sadist. Castro wanted del Toro to be a visible presence at all activities involving the visitors as his reputation could be intimidating to the bravest of dissenters.

Castro made it crystal clear that he would not tolerate any mishaps befalling the Cuban Americans who would be arriving in two weeks. The Minister of Culture Jesus Iberra was assigned the task of organizing a full week of activities to keep the visitors interested and happy. A very important part of the itineraries were carefully guarded trips to the familiar towns and villages on the island that the guests might want to revisit to reminisce about memories of times past.

The Cubans themselves loved to have a good time and the former inhabitants of the island were no exception. The choices of entertainment options were varied including cabaret shows, Afro-Cuban folk music and jazz clubs. There was also dramatic and comedic theater as well as the old standby movies. Free entertainment was always available especially on the weekends with rumba parties and salsa music in the streets and squares. Spectator sports were also widely available. Group activities of the Elders were encouraged as security was an easier task when they were in large groups.

Iberra agreed that a cruise around the island would be an ideal way for the visitors to spend their next to last day in Cuba. He arranged to lease a large luxury Cuban yacht that would comfortably accommodate the several hundred visitors. The cruise was actually a suggestion made to Castro by Gino Cruz. Castro thought it was a fine idea. "It will at least keep them safely out of the main stream of potential danger being together on the boat," he told Cruz.

The third evening of their visit was to be a special treat. They were to be special guests of Major General Thomas Patrick Cullen, Commandant of the Marine Detachment at the Guantanamo Naval Base which was more familiarly referred to by the military establishment as *Gtmo*. The occasion was to be a banquet honoring Fidel Castro with an award from the United States "for his unfailing efforts towards a peaceful coexistence between the two countries".

The naval base at Guantanamo had an interesting history. The general enjoyed telling the story of how the United States was able to retain its presence in Cuba in spite of the turmoil involved in the hostile relationship between the two countries since Castro came to power. In 1903, Cuba leased the Gtmo base to the United States for $2,000 a year. The two nations signed a treaty giving the United States the right to establish a naval base on Guantanamo Bay. The treaty was renewed in 1934 with the stipulation that it could be cancelled only by mutual agreement or by a voluntary withdrawal by the United States.

In 1962, Fidel Castro accused the United States of territorial interference. He demanded that they give up the base immediately. President John F. Kennedy refused and sent Marines to protect the base. The incident of the lease provided General Cullen with a humorous story which he liked to tell. "And since that day, Castro has not cashed any of the annual checks that we have sent for payment of the lease. Castro has continued to maintain that our presence at Gtmo is illegal. He got even with us though. We have been forced to carry those annual lease checks as open items on our books which have really fouled up our bookkeeping records for the past forty years."

A party of two hundred and four Elders arrived at the San Marti International Airport from Miami on a cloudless and typically beautiful Cuban morning. The anxious and nostalgic looks on their faces was a clear indication to everyone at the airport that these were the very special guests of President Castro. Their expected arrival had been publicized extensively throughout Cuba. There was a mob of enthusiastic greeters at the airport to welcome them. Castro had issued a personal written order to everyone who was expected to interface with the visitors to treat them with the utmost courtesy and respect. The order was cosigned by Chief of National Security del Torres to add a note of finality that the order was never to be ignored. Further, the order for compliance was tactfully communicated to all Cubans by the government controlled media.

The military presence at and around the airport kept the visitors secure against any unlikely incidences. The people allowed to crowd at the arrival gate were carefully selected and monitored to assure an orderly passage through the airport to the buses that would transport the Elders to *The Roman Coliseum Resort Hotel.* The transfer was made without incident.

Castro remembered the sleepless nights he had when the travel agents were guests at the hotel. He directed his comment to his

National Security Chief, "Colonel, I shall hold you personally responsible should there be any complaints that the hotel is not servicing these people properly." Del Torres then made his position very clear with the hotel management that he would hold them and their staff personally responsible for any problems arising.

"Tell each and every one of your employees that Chief of National Security Fernando del Torres has personally guaranteed President Castro that there will be no problems at the hotel. And tell them that I will be severely uncompromising with anyone who disregards this order."

There were no incidences all that week to test del Torres' resolve.

In spite of their philosophical differences with the Cuban dictator, the Elders felt privileged to have been invited to attend the banquet being given to honor Fidel Castro by the Commandant of the Marine detachment at Guantanamo. The main reception area at the base was turned into a formal banquet facility.

President Castro arrived with his usual entourage and was graciously greeted by General Cullen. After dinner was served, the General introduced the guest of honor and presented him with the award on behalf of the President of the United States and the American people. General Cullen bit his tongue while delivering the address as he knew that the evening was merely a public relations ploy holding no real significance of honor by his country for this odious dictator. The guests applauded politely but they too seem to share the General's silent opinion. American and Cuban media representatives were present to chronicle the occasion. Halfway through Castro's acceptance speech, a number of loud and bone-chilling explosions were heard throughout the compound. Several of Castro's personal bodyguards quickly threw themselves on top of their leader to protect him from any harm.

General Cullen directed an aide to provide him with a report immediately as to the cause of the explosions. The aide was back ten minutes later with the news that it appeared to be a mortar attack on the perimeter of the base. The General was astounded, "A mortar attack? How did anyone get that close to the base to drop mortars on us? What was the watch doing?"

"Don't know, sir. Colonel Jackson's group is investigating it right now. It seems that there was a group of civilians seen in the area just before the detonations."

"Tell the Colonel that I want a report as soon as he finds out what's going on," was the General's dismissive comment to his aide.

Castro lifted himself to his feet and looked at the General in askance. The senior officer responded, "It's all right, Mr. President. Nobody was hurt. My boys are looking into it." Castro's first thought was that it was dissident groups letting the Cuban Americans know that they were not welcome in Cuba. He was furious. Everything was going so well. Why did those fools have to create a scene and why did it have to happen on the American naval base. And, worst of all, there were American news people on hand to record the disgrace.

"Let me arrange for an escort to accompany you to your palace, Mr. President," the general suggested. "They might still be out there knowing that you'll be returning to your home this evening. We'll want to be careful of an ambush this late at night."

Castro was insulted and showed it, "That won't be necessary, General Cullen. Our people can take very good care of us." The Elders appeared to be disoriented by the incident. The general took charge, "It's all right, folks. The explosions were a military night exercise that got a little too noisy," he lied. "I apologize for having frightened everyone. Why don't we finish our dinner and then we'll escort you back to your hotel." Cullen looked at Castro and deliberately embarrassed him by asking, "If that's all right with you, Mr. President?" General Cullen knew that Castro would never allow United States military forces to enter Cuban protected areas. He answered, trying to be diplomatically correct, "That's very generous of you, General Cullen, but again, I believe our security people will be more than able to escort our visitors back to their hotel. And, by all means, let us finish our dinners before we say good night."

General Cullen smiled in the knowledge that he had just "put down" the Cuban dictator. Another good story for his bag of officer club anecdotes, he told himself. The senior officer was not normally a malicious person but he truly hated the Cuban dictator for what he represented.

When Castro and Company and the Elders left, Colonel Samuel Jackson reported back to the general. "Sir, we've investigated the incident and are pleased to report that everything went off as scheduled." He laughed and said, "There were casualties, sir. Three goats, six rabbits and a stray horse were found dead near the explosive charges. No prisoners, sir."

Jackson then erupted into a non-military laugh and was joined by the General.

"Good job, Sam, I think we convinced the man that he still has dissidents coming out of the woodwork. Send that report to President Cromwell that I have ordered that additional troops be garrisoned here at Guantanamo in case of further disturbances. And, tell Major Geary up there in the Pentagon to *leak* that bit of information to the press. That should help to convince folks that Cuba is not a safe place for Americans."

Colonel Jackson smiled and said, "Sir, I don't think President Castro is going to like that." General Cullen merely returned the smile but said nothing. Jackson knew that look. He also knew that the general never used four letter words to express his feelings towards another human being. He just thought them.

CHAPTER 35

President Cromwell had just finished reading General Cullen's report of the "mortar attack" on the naval base at Guantanamo Bay. He smiled at the precise military language that made it sound like World War III had begun. I wonder how Fidel is taking this latest display of right wing unrest, he asked himself. Almost on cue, the telephone rang.

"Doug, it is Fidel," his interpreter's voice echoed. "I wanted to be the first to tell you of an unfortunate occurrence that happened at the banquet at your naval base last evening."

Cromwell interrupted him, "Yes, I know, Fidel. It was the headline story in the Washington Post this morning. I daresay every newspaper in the country has used it as their morning edition's lead story. And the television boys are having a field day with it, too. It doesn't look like those dissidents are going to go away, does it? They are a persistent lot."

"I am concerned how our Cuban American visitors will react to what has happened. Here I am trying to make amends for not allowing them to return to Cuba and this unfortunate incident occurs," Castro moaned.

Cromwell was sympathetic. "Yes, that was unfortunate. It's made people in Washington question whether Americans will be safe in Cuba; particularly traveling about as they're likely to do." He knew that he was making Castro nervous with that kind of talk.

"Doug, my Minister of Security has assured me that what happened last night was an isolated case. And it wasn't a mortar attack as someone hastily concluded. They were merely explosive charges that were set off to create confusion. He's convinced me that it was a weak attempt on the part of a few right wing individuals to make our visitors think that this kind of disruption went on all the time. These saboteurs want your people to go back home and speak badly of conditions in Cuba."

"As you know, Fidel, the Elders, as they call themselves, are highly regarded in the Cuban American community here in South Florida. I hope nothing else happens in the next couple of days that might put them in harm's way. That could be disastrous for trying to build friendly ties with these folks."

"We know that your people will be safe for the rest of their visit, Doug. We have arranged a cruise that will keep them isolated and protected from any further mishaps in the day remaining of their visit. We want to make sure that they will return to the United States in several days with a renewed enthusiasm for Cuba. Maria Sanchez has been very helpful to us. She has arranged for a television crew to be on hand when the Elders land in Miami to interview them about their visit to Cuba. We have treated these fine people very nicely since they've been here so we expect some very positive comments of their visit. Maria will arrange for the filmed interviews to be produced as a series of television commercials which will be scheduled on major television stations around your country."

Cromwell was genuinely pleased, "What a great idea, Fidel. I think commercials like that will go a long way in diffusing the negative publicity that the travel agents have created. I think the day cruise is also a good idea. That incident last night was unfortunate so we should concentrate on getting them back to America safe and sound and without any further controversy."

When Cromwell hung up he was sure that all of the tourist-unfriendly happenings would most certainly destroy any hopes Castro had of breathing new life into his tourist business. While Castro marginalized the incident at Guantanamo, it would most assuredly have an impact on the attitudes and travel plans of Americans. He smiled when he wondered who came up with the idea of suggesting that the explosive devices that were planted around the perimeter of the naval base were the result of a mortar attack. It was an unlikely scenario, but General Cullen always had a flair for the dramatic.

The detonations were actually carefully planned and carried out by the general's ordinance unit to simulate a mortar attack by right wing forces. He was comforted by the fact that no one had been hurt by all this intrigue but the publicity fallout would have a telling effect on Cuba's future.

What Cromwell didn't know was that the *capper*, as Cruz like to call it, was still to be heard from. It was a devious act that De Luca had concocted and which Cruz had eagerly approved.

On the morning before the Elders were scheduled to leave for home, they gathered outside of their hotel and boarded buses to take them to an anchorage at Havana's Marina Hemingway. It was the main season for cruising. The weather was mild, the winds reliable and hurricanes were unknown. The water around the island of Cuba was described as the most desirable and unspoiled scenic vistas between Canada and the Antarctic South Pole.

There was a contagious sense of expectation as the Miamians boarded the luxury yacht *Fidelista* which was an uncharacteristic display of opulence for a nation facing serious economic issues. The average hard pressed Cuban referred to it as Fidel's *Buta* which never failed to invoke a contemptuous snicker. Fidel's whore was an appropriate description for some of the activities that went on aboard the vessel.

Laughter and frivolous chatter echoed throughout the oversized yacht as the Elders enjoyed refreshments and a buffet luncheon while cruising close to the shores of northern Cuba. Varadero, the largest and most highly developed beach resort complex in the Caribbean and its twenty kilometers of unbroken white sand beaches could be seen in the distance. The high spirited mood continued into the early afternoon after which many of the passengers fell into a dreamy state of nostalgia; many were remembering the land of their youth when they could call Cuba their home.

The captain of *Fidelista* had spent sleepless nights thinking about his responsibility of keeping his passengers safe while they were in his charge. President Castro had issued a stern warning to him to "bring those people back to Havana safe and sound". Castro had even arranged for a highly maneuverable and heavily armed naval ship to chaperon *Fidelista* at a conspicuous distance to ensure the passenger's safekeeping.

No one seemed to be aware of the large ebony colored speedboat that was running parallel to their vessel at a distance of three hundreds on their port side. Many of the passengers waved. The lone person on the speedboat appeared to be wearing a wet suit. He waved back. *Fidelista's* skipper noticed that the sleek speedboat was slowly changing its course so that he was gradually drawing nearer to his ship. When the strange craft was within a hundred yards, it executed a sharp turn and headed straight for the unsuspecting cruiser.

Castro's skipper knew that the speedboat had been put on automatic pilot when he saw the pilot of the boat climb out onto its fantail and jump into the water when he was thirty yards from him. He knew he had no chance of avoiding the pilotless craft as it was coming with deadly accuracy at him with its engines at full throttle. There was a sickening explosion when the two boats met. *Fidelista* was doomed. It sunk in three minutes. There were no survivors. Most of the passengers were killed by the explosion of the initial impact. The explosives stored in the bow of the speedboat had made sure of that.

A smaller speedboat that had been shadowing the larger one picked up the man in the water and quickly sped away. The escorting naval ship saw the fleeing boat but opted not to give chase as its first priority was to rescue any survivors of the crash. When they saw that there were no survivors, it was too late to pursue the fast moving speedboat.

A ship to shore call from the escort ship alerted the authorities that *Fidelista* had been sunk by a fast-moving speedboat. A description of the killer vehicle was quickly transmitted to the helicopter. Almost immediately a rocket equipped military helicopter was on the scene scanning the area for the renegade boat that was traveling at top speed towards the coast of Varadero. The helicopter swooped down within loudspeaker distance to order the boat to stop. The boat responded with a burst of gunfire. The heavily armed aircraft returned the unfriendly fire with a professionally aimed rocket that struck the boat with deadly accuracy. The craft never had a chance to sink. It was reduced to fragments as soon as the deadly rocket struck.

Fidel Castro paled noticeably when he received the news that all of the Cuban Americans had been killed. He went into an accusatory tirade that was more vitriolic than any of his most bitter harangues. He blamed everyone from his Minister of Justice to the pilot of the boat that was providing the surveillance cover for *Fidelista.* No one escaped his wrath. After twenty minutes of a physically exhaustive outpouring of venomous charges, he suddenly stopped and sat down breathless. It was as if he suddenly realized that he could be damaging himself with his behavior. He closed his eyes for a full fifteen minutes without saying a word. Those in the room stared at him and said nothing. They were waiting for him to break the tension by speaking.

Finally, he opened his eyes and said, "I must talk to Gino Cruz right away. Get me Gino on the phone."

Twenty minutes later, Gino Cruz was on the phone and was the first one to speak, "Fidel, what is going on down there? I can't believe that with all that has been happening in Cuba; you let two hundred high profile people be killed like that. Do you realize the consequences of that having happened?"

Castro was defensive, "Gino, there's no way we could have stopped that disaster from happening. We purposely kept those people isolated so that there wouldn't be any problems. Who could predict that those responsible would blow up a ship with all those people aboard? What kind of people are we dealing with?" Cruz smiled at Castro's hypocritical outrage. This incidence was child's play compared to some of the crimes he was guilty of committing.

Cruz appeared sympathetic, "I talked to President Cromwell this afternoon and he was naturally upset. He said that he understands your predicament and the circumstances behind all that's happening. He wants to support you but he realizes that he can't do it alone. He needs your help."

Castro grabbed the proffered straw, "What can I do? I'll do anything to protect our trade agreement. I realize that this latest incident will shut down our tourist business with the United States, at least for a time, but there is the larger consideration. Gino, we must retain our trading relationship with America to survive. I believe we'll eventually be able to bring American tourism back to Cuba but it will now take time – much time, I'm afraid – to rebuild America's confidence in us." Cruz smirked and said to himself, not if I have anything to say about it - then adding – and you can bet that Swiss bank account of yours that I *will* have something to say about it.

But it was important to keep up appearances, "President Cromwell believes that the entire situation can be salvaged," he said, stretching the truth. "He feels strongly that you must maintain a strong denial to show the American people that you are guiltless of killing American citizens." Again, Cruz was using intimidating language to make Castro increasingly uneasy.

"We are blameless," Castro maintained, "and we must convince the President and the American people of that."

Cruz agreed, "That's right, Fidel, and you must do it in a sincere and direct manner. You must meet with President Cromwell and discuss the situation openly. In doing so, you will be letting it be known that you are sincerely trying to find a solution to this impasse. If you agree, I'll be more than willing to talk to the President and arrange a convenient meeting for you. I'd suggest that it be in Washington. Your new embassy would be an ideal place to meet."

"Yes, by all means," Castro said, "and the sooner the better."

"I'll talk to him, Fidel. And let me suggest that you do nothing to punish whomever you think might be responsible for yesterday's tragedy. Let's not have arbitrary executions at a time when the support of the American people is so necessary. As we know, they don't take well to what they consider unorthodox capital punishment. And I don't know if the news has reached you yet but the Cuban American community in Miami is in an uproar. Mobs have been running uncontrollably through the streets of downtown Miami ever since they heard the news. They're destroying storefronts, overturning automobiles and setting them on fire in their rage. The police are unable to control them. And the authorities are concerned that this frustration will spread to other Cuban American communities in the United States."

Castro became concerned when he heard this news. He began to suspect that he might be in grave danger coming to America; however, he had to agree to the meeting as he needed the United States to fortify his tenuous position at home. He became possessed with the thought that someone was going to do him harm once he stepped on American shores.

He confided in Gino Cruz about his concerns. Gino comforted him with the assurance that President Cromwell had arranged for a specially trained team of security personnel to oversee every step of his way while in New York. He even assured Castro that he would personally see to it that a hand picked ground crew would service his aircraft at Kennedy Airport to assure that there was no risk of sabotage while he was in the city. "You will be protected the minute you arrive until you return home, Fidel," was Cruz's parting promise.

Castro trusted Cruz implicitly. Before hanging up, he said, "That is very reassuring, my friend. Please let me know what the President says. Goodbye, Gino and thank you."

The President and Vice-President were enjoying cocktails in the Oval Office before dinner. The President had been deeply affected by the news from Cuba. He knew that this latest misfortune would destroy any hopes that Castro had for bolstering his economy on the pocketbook of the peripatetic American tourist. His instincts told him that trade with America would eventually deescalate when Cuba was no longer considered a productive trading partner.

Pam saw that Doug had lapsed into deep thought. She broke the spell as the President took a sip from his drink. "I guess it's over now. That unfortunate accident will certainly destroy what was beginning to look like a healthy tourist business for Cuba. It looks like *The Group* is the winner. You've achieved what you set out to do. Now we can start concentrating on President Cromwell being *everybody's President.*"

Doug said, "I guess I have been spending a disproportionate amount of my time on the Cuban project. But, yes, I think we've been successful in creating a career-ending environment for Mr. Castro."

"What happens next?"

"Gino thinks we should meet with Castro one last time here in Washington to let him know we're still behind him. Gino believes Fidel will create an international scene if he thinks we're cutting him loose without as much as a *by your leave.*"

Pam was curious, "I don't see what another meeting can do to change anything. He's lost the battle. I can only see a downhill slide into political oblivion for him at this point. Let's face it; American industry will no longer want to do business with him given the mood of Americans towards him and his government. Having him come to America is just delaying the inevitable."

"That's exactly what I told Gino. But, you know Gino; he has to have the last word. Actually, I get the uneasy feeling that he somehow wants the satisfaction of telling Castro that he was the one responsible for the troubles Cuba has been having. Revenge has been his motivator from the start. It's a revenge that has been unreasonable and relentless. It has poisoned his mind to the point that it has made him do unspeakable things bordering on criminal acts."

"What do you mean by criminal acts? I know he's a manipulator. That's been his stock in trade for most of his career. He certainly uses people to do his bidding, but has he actually been involved in criminal activities?"

Doug stared at his drink for a long moment asking himself whether this was the time to tell Pam something he had meant to discuss with her for some time. He decided it was the right time. "I know that you are in Gino's debt for helping you advance your career. He was there to help you bridge your jump to a responsible position at the State Department followed by that giant step to the Office of Vice-President. Mind you, it was your skill and ability that got you where you are today, but, like me, it took Gino to encourage and goad us into being our best."

Pam was not unmindful of Gino's role in her fast ascendancy to the White House. She said, "He *has* been a mentor to me and, believe me, I appreciate it, but"

Doug completed her sentence, "But, you're not going to let him duly influence you in your duties as Vice-President."

Pam smiled, "Among your other qualities, you're a mind reader. Yes, that's exactly what I was going to say. And I have seen how he has inveigled himself into your Presidency at times. He has no business doing that."

"Yes and I have decided to face the lion in his lair by simply and unconditionally telling him that his interference in the Oval Office will not be tolerated any longer. I will not be a party to murder or …"

Pam stopped him in mid sentence, "Murder? What does that mean?"

Doug realized his passion for Gino's manipulative behavior had inadvertently caused him to say something he hadn't intended to reveal. He quickly tried to recover his words but decided that Pam should know the worst about her benefactor.

"What I have to tell you I tell you because one day you'll be sitting where I am and, on that day, you'll want the freedom to run your presidency without undue influence from scheming and harmful people." When Doug again hesitated not knowing exactly how to express the enormity of what he was about to say, Pam said simply, "What murder, Doug?"

"I just discovered this myself. I had my suspicions, but Pedro confirmed them yesterday. Gino was responsible for the death of the Elders in Cuba. Unbeknownst to the other members of *The Group*, he quietly arranged for the collision that killed all of those people. He did it because he wanted to bring Castro down immediately. Pedro said that Gino was tiring of the childish game we were playing with him. He wanted it ended now."

"Why now? What's so urgent that requires him to lose patience this late in the game? From where I sit, Castro is through. He'll never survive world opinion once the truth is known that his economy is beyond recovery."

Doug said, sadly, "The reason Pedro told me that Gino was responsible for the death of those people is that his father is dying. He has cancer. It's a fast moving cancer that is inoperable and one that cannot be successfully treated. The doctors have given him no more than six months to live."

Pam was stunned, "Oh, I'm sorry. I am so sorry,"

"Yes, it was a terrible shock to all of us. Given the finality of his condition, *The Group* met last week when you were in California, to decide how to go forward with our plans. Dad said he had given great thought to the situation and recommended that we shut things down right now. He spoke convincingly that our covenant will have been satisfied once Castro is deposed. He believes, and we all agreed with him, that his removal from office will be inevitable once Cuba's economy reverts back to its former status."

Pam was puzzled, "I don't understand why it is necessary to have a meeting with Castro if it's a closed issue that he will no longer be a factor in governing Cuba?"

"*The Group* feels that the meeting will discredit him further. The United States is ostensibly recommending measures to shore up their falling economy but nothing will be resolved. Steps to counter the sabotage being committed against their tourist trade are to be discussed but, again, no resolution will be accommodated. The Cubans will be told that the United States cannot become involved in their domestic affairs because of the premeditated massacre of over two hundred of its citizens while on a goodwill tour of Cuba. They would be made to understand that if that were allowed to happen, President Cromwell's administration would be at great risk of losing the confidence of the American people."

"And what about Gino?" Pam asked.

Doug replied not looking at his wife, "He will have no choice. He will simply die when his time is up."

CHAPTER 36

Fidel Castro arrived at Kennedy International Airport along with a large entourage of diplomatic aides and security personnel. Many were bearded and wearing olive green uniforms and exited the Russian-made aircraft with a condescending arrogance. They strutted about like pompous peacocks.

Raul Castro was a conspicuous member of the delegation. Fidel wanted to make sure that the Americans understood that his younger brother was next in line to succeed him as president when he decided to relinquish that post. Included was the President of the National Assembly's Council of States who was ostensibly the head of government and state in Cuba. In reality, the National Assembly was a rubber-stamp parliament that never questioned the policy or actions of Cuba's top leaders – who collectively was one man – Fidel Castro.

A list of the names of the foreign visitors had been submitted to the State Department two months prior to their trip to America to allow the Federal Bureau of Investigation to determine if there were any known or suspected terrorists in the group. Government policing agencies had become very sensitive to the potential presence of foreign terrorist activities which increasingly had become a menacing threat around the world. The 1995 bombing of the federal building in Oklahoma City brought home the serious threat that terrorism could be to the safety of a nation's civilian population. Israel's experience with cowardly terrorism continually reinforced that apprehension.

It was determined that at least a third of the Cuban aides had a history of terrorist training. Many were identified as having actually participated in terrorist activities in South America and Africa. As a precautionary measure, a Secret Service agent was assigned to each of the suspects to assure that their presence was known at all times. Their daily activities were carefully monitored and reviewed for questionable behavior at day's end. A cross-check was made of anyone with whom they came in contact.

Castro had made a specific request that he and his staff be quartered at the world renowned Waldorf Astoria Hotel located in midtown Manhattan on Park Avenue. He had remembered with distaste his first visit to the United States as the new revolutionary leader of Cuba when his disheveled band of merrymakers stayed at the Hotel Theresa in the Harlem section of the city.

The attending publicity he received from the New York press was not favorable. One of the major tabloids had pictured several of his group as having killed and cooked chickens in their rooms and eating them for dinner. It became obvious that Fidel had not instilled his associates with the social skills that favored a good press. An unsympathetic reporter had unkindly suggested that "a cursory knowledge of the benefits of room service would have protected the visitors from being labeled as *uncouth and even barbaric"*.

Nor were their leader's social graces at the time likely to be applauded anywhere but the jungles of his native Sierra Maestro Mountains. However; on this occasion of his major political coup, he wanted to elevate his image to a higher plane; fitting for someone who was to be a major player in the newly-formed U. S.-Cuban alliance. The Hotel Theresa was no longer a suitable venue for the more sophisticated and worldly Fidel Castro.

The two day meeting was scheduled for September 10th and September 11th. The meeting was originally scheduled to take place at the newly planned Cuban Embassy in Washington, D. C.; however, the contractor had advised the Cubans that the construction would not be completed on schedule. They estimated that it would take an additional three months to complete the project which required the Cubans to find temporary quarters for their embassy staff. An influential Cuban moderate Jose Conterras, now living in the United States, was asked by the State Department to find temporary offices for the Cuban delegation.

Castro had requested that the temporary offices be located in the conspicuous financial center of New York City as he wanted to make a statement that Cuba was now prepared to take its place as a business partner with their new American ally. Canterras had a strong association with a brokerage firm whose offices were at Number One World Trade Center at the foot of Manhattan Island. The firm was planning on transferring several of their support departments to a new location directly across the Hudson River in New Jersey which freed up sufficient space in their ninety-second floor quarters to accommodate the Cuban diplomatic corp.

Castro had to be back in Cuba on September 12th for a meeting with the Venezuelan Trade Commission to finalize delicate negotiations involving Cuba's oil agreement with their South American neighbor. The matter demanded Castro's personal attention so he was to fly back to Cuba the afternoon of September 11th. The final meeting of the two day session was therefore scheduled for the early morning of that day. President Cromwell would host the meeting which promised to command worldwide attention. Space limitations restricted the number of attendees to thirty. A news conference was scheduled immediately following the morning session of the final day which was to end just before noon.

Brent Cummings, the Director of the F. B. I., had been outspoken in his disapproval of this site for the forthcoming meeting. "It's much too public, Mr. President. Under normal circumstances we'd have no problem, but with Castro leading the pack, we have to expect that he'll draw the crazies like a magnet. Once everybody's inside the offices, we can give you maximum protection. It's getting in and out of that place that makes me nervous. It's just not worth the risk, Mr. President. Let us find you another location."

President Cromwell reflected on the director's advice. "No, Brent, let's keep the meeting where it is. Fidel has specifically asked for something in the Wall Street area. He seems to think that Americans and his people at home will think of him as being more sympathetic to our trade deal by holding forth in a visible symbol of the capitalistic system. We'll be all right. Let's proceed as planned."

When the two men met on the first day, Castro knew he was in a compromised position. He had to admit that he had come to this meeting at the invitation – or more correctly, at the command of President Cromwell. He knew he had come to New York with his hat in his hand, but he in no way wanted to appear deferential to the American leader so - defensively and quite in character – he became a blathering bore. After hearing him for a non-stop thirty minutes, it became obvious that everyone from both delegations wanted him to cease and desist from his rambling commentary that was nothing more than self-serving and gratuitous.

Finally, Cromwell had enough. He shook his head and, in an attempt to make his words sound good-natured and at the same time deliberately disparaging said, "Fidel, you are the most loquacious person I have ever met and I've met some really long-winded folks in my time. Is there any way we can ask you to cut it short? We do have a busy schedule this morning so it is important that we stick to the agreed-upon timetable."

The room went dead silent. Castro, still maintaining his pretext of not understanding English, smiled and looked to his interpreter for a translation. The interpreter was at odds as how to relay the deprecating remark so that his leader would not appear offended. He thought quickly and translated, "Presidente, President Cromwell said that he has met some outstanding orators in his time and could listen to you all day if it weren't important to abide by the restrictive timetable to discuss the many matters that are important to us." The Cuban delegation was unaware that Cromwell was quite fluent in Spanish. It was an innocent ploy that permitted him to know what was being fed back to Castro by his protective associates.

Castro smiled at Cromwell and responded graciously, "Gracias, gracias, Mr. President." Cromwell knew, of course, that Castro understood what he had said even though he always waited for a translation from his interpreter before responding. He also knew that Castro got the message that he was no longer being considered seriously by the American President.

Castro was silently staring at Cromwell for a long moment. He finally said something he had not planned on saying. His interpreter translated. "Mr. President, my advisors had warned me before we entered into our trade agreement that your efforts on behalf of Cuba were nothing but a scheme to eventually destroy our government. I didn't believe them. I took you for being an honorable man who was truly interested in developing a lasting bond between our two countries. I still believe that to be true. I must ask you, man to man, am I wrong in believing that you continue to be a friend of Cuba?"

Cromwell could only glare at the Cuban leader with a slight smile. "Of course, Mr. President, it is only natural for you to question the credibility of our motives. Cuba was beginning to pull itself up from a dismal economic slide when things again turned sour. Misfortunate and unexplained happenings have occurred in your country, to be sure, but I can assure you, the United States has been your friend all along and will continue to support your government through these bad times."

Even as Cromwell spoke, he wondered how the suspicious nature of Castro would allow him to believe that the United States had nothing to do with Cuba's present troubles. It was true that Castro had his back against the wall, but the man was a fighter and wouldn't let a betrayal go uncontested if he felt that were the case. No, Cromwell thought, he's still probably clinging to the outside hope that the United States will bail him out of his present predicament.

Gino Cruz, who had purposely remained silent during the discussion, felt energized seeing Castro squirming and unsure of himself. His mind wandered to the early days when he and Castro battled in the streets of Havana to change a world that was not to their liking. He thought of the movement they had championed and the struggle they had endured to ensure a better way of life for their fellow Cubans. And he could not forget the deceit and final betrayal of a man whom he loved as a brother – at least in the beginning. What a lie that all turned out to be, he recalled bitterly. He reflected sadly on what might have been had he been able to deal honestly with the man sitting across the table from him. His only consolation was the knowledge that Fidel Castro would not be a problem to anyone after tomorrow. He would not be returning to Cuba. He would *never* be returning to Cuba.

The meeting continued once Castro had assured everyone that he believed the relationship between the two countries would continue in a trusting fashion. President Cromwell then addressed the issue of getting the Cuban economy back on a sound footing. An emergency plan had been developed by the State Department that centered on the unforeseen tourism problems that Cuba was presently facing and the suggested measures that could be immediately initiated to eliminate them. Assistant Secretary of State Bud Folsom, a troubleshooting specialist, made the lengthy presentation that seemed to put a more relaxed expression back on the faces of Castro and the other members of the delegation.

After a lingering lunch in a room that had been set aside for the occasion, the afternoon meeting commenced in a more relaxed atmosphere and a more spirited give and take attitude among the two groups. Congeniality mixed with laughter and small talk was more in evidence than was the case during their introductory session that morning.

A banquet was held at the Waldorf Astoria main ballroom in the evening. President Cromwell and his wife Pamela hosted the affair. Several important cabinet members and their wives were there to welcome the visiting dignitaries as were members of Congress and local politicians. Loquacious speeches attested to the friendly feelings among the two camps. The Mayor of the New York City welcomed the Cubans in surprisingly fluent Spanish. Accompanied by his interpreter, Castro made a speech which he prefaced with the remark, "I will only take a few minutes of your time." He then spoke non-stop for the next hour and a half.

The meeting reconvened at 7:30 a. m. the next morning. Raul Castro was not in attendance. It was reported that he had awoken that morning with severe symptoms of the flu. The truth was that he had imbibed a little too generously in the alcoholic offerings served at the banquet the evening before. One of the American diplomats summed up his problem succinctly, "The bastard is hung over. Let him suffer."

The agenda called for a review of the plan to rejuvenate the tourist business on the island. The Cuban Minister of Domestic Affairs gave a lucid analysis of what the trade agreement had meant to their government. He emphasized that the economy of Cuba had shown a marked upswing once the United States had become an active trading partner. The American entry, he proudly stated, also encouraged other foreign powers to deal aggressively with Cuban business interests.

The Minister of Justice followed with a condemnation of the dissident groups whom they had determined were responsible for the reoccurring mishaps that were resulting in a dramatic downturn in their tourism business. "We had been showing encouraging progress prior to……"

The Minister was interrupted by a sudden comment by President Cromwell, "That fellow's flying a little low, isn't he?"

Everyone then became aware of the low flying aircraft at the same time. Eyes followed the large aircraft with fascination as it banked and made a sweeping turn which put it on a headlong collision course directly towards the building. Castro had just taken a long drag on his Cohiba when his eyes caught a glimpse of the airplane approaching the large window at the foot of the conference table. As the plane came closer, Castro was heard to utter his first English-spoken public comment since he arrived in America.

"Shit. Holy shit."

AFTERWARD

Tuesday, September 11, 2001, began as a beautiful and tranquil autumn morning in New York City. Then, without warning, the unimaginable happened. From out of the blue skies two commercial jets, transformed by hijackers into fuel-laden missiles, crashed the pirated planes into the Twin Towers of the World Trade Center in New York City. The center consisted of seven buildings, including the two doomed towers, which were among the world's tallest skyscrapers. On a typical day, 50,000 people worked in the Trade Center and as many as 100,000 visited America's "living symbol of man's ideal dedication to World Peace".

On this fateful day, American Airlines Flight 11 departed from Boston's Logan Airport at 8:00 a. m. for Los Angeles with 81 passengers and 11 crew members. Forty seven minutes later, the Boeing 767 carrying 20,000 gallons of jet fuel crashed into the north tower of One World Trade Center devastating floors 90 through 100 in a blazing inferno. The 110-story building crumbled and crashed to the ground at 10:28 a. m.

United Airlines Flight 175, also a Boeing 767, departed Logan Airport for Los Angeles fourteen minutes later at 8:14 a. m. with 56 passengers and 9 crew members. At 9:02 a. m. Flight 175 slammed into the south tower of Two World Trade Center turning floors 78-87 into a fiery holocaust. At 9:50 a. m. the 110-story south tower suddenly collapsed.

Within forty minutes of each other, the two towers had disappeared from the New York skyline. At 4:10 p. m. Building 7 of the World Trade Center was reported on fire. At 5:20 p. m. Building 7 collapsed.

Rubble from the collapse of the World Trade Center covered 16 acres and was estimated to weigh 1.2 million tons.

The same day at 9:45 a. m., a third hijacked plane, American Airlines 757 Flight 77 departed from Washington Dulles Airport for Los Angeles with 58 passengers and 6 crew members. The Boeing

757 sliced into the southwest face of the Pentagon Building, the nerve center of the U. S. military near Washington, D. C., and detonated into a fireball.

A fourth hijacked Boeing 757 left Newark for San Francisco with 38 passengers and 7 crew members. United Airlines Flight 93 never reached its destination as its suicidal mission was thwarted by a group of passengers who sacrificed their own lives in a brave attempt to overpower the terrorists. The plane crashed in a field in Shanksville, Pennsylvania, 80-miles southeast of Pittsburgh. There were no survivors.

The one day carnage was labeled the worst terrorist attack in United States history. The loss of human life was reported at 265 on the four hijacked planes including the nineteen hijackers, 125 Pentagon personnel and 5,080 at the World Trade Centers, for a total of 5,470. It was the largest loss of American life in a single day since Antietam, the worst day of the Civil War, when 23,000 were killed or wounded. The dead in the 1862 battle were soldiers and sailors. On September 11th, they were ordinary men and women sitting down to begin a day's work.

Two world leaders were listed as casualties. President Douglas Cromwell and President Fidel Castro were killed instantly when the plane hit the first tower. They were on one of the floors that received the full impact of the crash. Thirty other officials of both governments were also listed as casualties.

Hidden in the list of fatalities was the name Gino Cruz, advisor to the President of the United States.

On the evening of September 11th, the Cuban delegation boarded their plane at Kennedy International Airport to return to Cuba. Raul Castro, who had been fortuitously "hung over" and missed the ill-fated meeting, had insisted that there was nothing to be gained by spending one more evening in the United States. Fidel had made it eminently clear that he wanted his younger brother to take over the reins of government when he stepped down. Raul understood that there would be opposition to his becoming president so there was a pressing need that he return to Cuba immediately to consolidate his political position within the party.

Raul knew that the ground crew servicing the plane had been carefully selected by Gino Cruz to assure the delegation's safety so there was no reason to delay leaving once they were boarded. He felt both a sense of loss for his brother and, at the same time, a feeling of exhilaration knowing that he would become President of Cuba once he was home to claim his rightful heritage. He decided to relax with several sleep inducing sedatives. He wanted to be fresh and alert when they landed in Havana. There would undoubtedly be a grieving and, at the same time, a congratulatory welcoming committee on the other end.

Raul was fast asleep when the plane past over the Florida Keys as were most of the other surviving delegates who, because of space limitations at The Trade Center, were unable to attend the morning meeting. Ten minutes later there was a tumultuous explosion aboard the aircraft that lit up the night sky. The explosion was so abrupt and devastating that the flaming jet simply disappeared into the dark waters of the Caribbean. Raul Castro's ambitious political designs were cancelled out that evening as were the lives of the remaining members of the Cuban delegation.

The American ground crew members who had serviced the aircraft prior to takeoff received the news with a knowing calm. Bud De Luca, dressed in coveralls, was heard to say, "Fidel was supposed to be on that flight along with the rest of them. Well, no matter, he got his due reward this morning. Gino would have been pleased." De Luca and his accomplices then left the airport.

On the afternoon of September 11th, Vice President Pamela St. Pierre Cromwell was sworn in as President of the United States by the Chief Justice of the U. S. Supreme Court. The new president was visibly shaken at the ceremony in which she took the oath of office. She was heartbroken as was the nation. A heavy melancholy was felt around the world. As painful the loss, she knew she had to pull the nation together by carrying on as she knew Doug would have wanted. Secretary of State Robert P. Lansing was named Vice-President of the United States later that week.

The following day, a funeral train moved slowly from Pennsylvania Station in New York City to Washington, D. C. The simple coffin contained a symbolic sampling of the debris from the Trade Center. A mixed contingent from the armed forces escorted the flag-draped coffin through the streets of Washington while a huge crowd stood deferentially silent. Everywhere men and women wept openly and without shame.

There was a brief simple service in the East Room of the White House. The coffin was then moved to the Capital rotunda where endless lines of mourners came to pay their last respects. The following day the coffin was placed on the funeral train and retraced its route back into Manhattan. A transfer was immediately made to a hearse and an escort of limousines traveled across the George Washington Bridge to Old Town in northern New Jersey. Pam had chosen Old Town as the final resting place for her husband as he always considered this quaint and friendly village as his hometown even though he was born and raised in Chicago.

When the procession reached the center of town, the coffin was removed from the hearse and placed on a caisson drawn by six brown horses. Following the caisson was a lone hooded horse, stirrups reversed and a sword hanging from the left stirrup – symbolic of a lost warrior. Marching at a slow cadence, the honor guard escorted the caisson through the center of Old Town to the cemetery north of the Franklin Pierce Middle School where, years before, Douglas Cromwell had begun his carefully orchestrated journey to the top office of the nation. Family, friends, political leaders along with representatives from foreign countries were assembled at the grave sight to honor the beloved president.

A military band sounded the sad notes of its burial hymn. Muffled drums beat slowly and a bugler played the haunting notes of *Taps* as the coffin was slowly lowered into the grave. Douglas Cromwell had come home.

As Doug had once said to Pam in a moment of reflection - “fate seems to dictate who we are and how we live our lives”. The reality of those words was never more evident than in the aftermath of September 11th. “And how we die” would have been a fitting closure Pam told herself when remembering his words.

The years of planning and the constancy of carrying out the revengeful covenant of honor by *The Group* came to a sudden and decisive end. When David Cromwell, Pedro Cruz and Juan Sierra were together in Washington for the services of the President and Gino, they sadly reflected on what was actually accomplished in having dedicated themselves to this seemingly impossible task.

David was remorseful. "What was gained by this insanity? What started forty years ago as an almost playful challenge of trying to avenge the death of Alberto Sierra has turned into a death sentence for my son. The two bright spots are that Castro is no longer around to advance his own homespun communist ideology and we have avenged the death of Alberto. But what a waste this has been for Douglas Cromwell. He was basically a good man who had a rich and promising career ahead of him. We instilled in him a passionate desire to be President of the United States and that ambition was betrayed and misguided by our own selfish motives."

Pedro said, "As much as I hate to admit it even to myself, Gino turned this vendetta into something that became cruel and ill-spirited towards many innocent people. We all have to accept blame for what has happened, though. We all signed on to his private covenant. We're all responsible for the good and the bad that came out of our decisions during the past forty years.

David shook his head in agreement. "Yes, we are responsible, but as of now, it's over – done with. We can all go back to our lives as they were before. As for me, I shall be retiring. I have some very capable people back in Chicago and our satellite cities to run Cromwell Advertising. I had made them a promise that I would sell them my interest when I retired. That's what I'll do."

Juan spoke up, "Like you David, I have very qualified people responsible for the various companies within Sierra Industries. I won't be retiring but what I will do is to take a step back and take a harder look at where we are and where we have to go. I want to concentrate on our international business. There's still a great potential overseas and I intend to see that we capitalize on the opportunities."

And, what about you, Pedro?"

Pedro stared at his two friends and then smiled, "I've decided to put Gino out of business. You know he had secret files on just about every politician or anyone of political influence in the country. These files were his source of power. If someone stepped out of line, Gino could tap into his files and pull out some incriminating tidbit that would decide an issue or someone's fate. Ever since September 11th I have been collecting these files which have been hidden away in various safe locations in the Washington area. Yesterday morning I destroyed each and every one of them. They are nothing but ashes."

David said, "Bravo, Pedro. Now what will you do?"

Pedro calmly replied, "Do? That's easy. I'm going to practice law – the legal way."

About The Author

Bill Kennedy is a former advertising executive whose first novel was *Diamond of Greed.* His second novel is *Covenant of Honor*. Bill lives with his wife Pamela in Wyckoff, New Jersey and is currently working on his third novel.

Printed in the United States
1009300003B